PASSI

KILLER

Yvonne McEvaddy

Yvonne McEvaddy

Yvonne McEvaddy

ISBN: 1470097818
ISBN-13: 978-1470097813

DEDICATION

I dedicate this book to the memory of my father, Sean Gaughan, who always got a kick out of my school essays. I like to think he's looking down on me now with that light of laughter in his eyes.

Yvonne McEvaddy

ACKNOWLEDGMENTS

I would like to thank my husband, Matt, for all his technical support, for being my first reader and always supporting me and believing in me. My thanks go to my mother, Mary, sisters, Martina and Fiona, and brother Fergal for being among my first readers and giving me excellent feedback. I wish to thank Susan Millar DuMars for reading my manuscript and giving valuable feedback, also for the classes she facilitates which are so much more than writing classes. A big thank you goes out to RJ Samuel, whose advice and encouragement has been invaluable. My heartfelt thanks go to all in the Javawriters group for providing me with a bit of insanity in the face of reality, and a bit of sanity when the world is too insane. Thanks to all the members of the Mystic Poets society for all the mad times in college which provided much inspiration. I wish to thank Garda Peadar Brick for providing me with information on police procedures. Any mistakes made in that regard are my own. I also wish to thank solicitor Noel Rhatigan for giving me advice on matters of criminal law that I was otherwise unaware of. I owe a big thank you to optician Colm O'Mahony for reintroducing me to the joys of the written word when my eyes failed me. Finally, thank you to all who have encouraged my love of reading and writing over the years.

CHAPTER ONE

Tuesday the 16th of September

Alex took a seat in the interview room and looked around at his surroundings. The walls were a non-descript color, almost grey. The room was furnished only with a table and four chairs. He leaned forward and placed his forearms on the table and, as it wobbled, immediately sat upright in his chair, trying different positions in order to get comfortable. There was a camera in the corner of the room pointed to where he was seated opposite Detectives Barbara Molloy and Mick Naughton.

Detective Molloy informed him that the interview would be recorded and stated for the record the time, date and people present. She then asked, "Why don't you tell me about your relationship with Sylvia?"

"We've been friends for a long time, very good friends."

"There's more to your relationship than just friendship, am I right?"

"There has been, yes, but not for a while now. When I knew how serious she was about Rick I moved on. It was convenient before that. I was in love with her; I don't deny that. When neither of us had any ties it was convenient for us to be together, but when Rick came on the scene I knew it was the end of the line for a romantic relationship between Sylvia and I."

"How did that make you feel?"

"Not like murdering Rick if that's what you're getting at."

"That doesn't answer my question."

"I don't see the relevance of this line of questioning. If you want to question me on suspicion of murder I believe I have the right to have my solicitor present." Alex glanced over to where Detective Naughton sat taking notes, and wondered if he was going to intervene, but the other detective didn't even look up from his notebook.

"Of course you have the right to representation. However, if you have nothing to hide you have no need to have a solicitor present," Detective Molloy said.

"I have absolutely nothing to hide. I just don't want my feelings twisted and construed as a motive."

"For the moment this questioning is just a formality. If you insist on bringing a solicitor into it I may just have to arrest you on suspicion of murder."

Alex sat up straight in his chair and steepled his hands in front of him as he said, "I won't be bullied. As my friends and I are doing you a favor by co-operating, I don't think it's too much to ask that we not be treated as suspects."

"It's Sylvia you're doing the favor for, not us. Of course it benefits us, but it's in the interest of Sylvia, and Rick's family, that this investigation gets underway as soon as possible. I'm merely asking about your feelings towards Sylvia. You're the one implying that your feelings make you a murder suspect. Now why is that?" Detective Molloy sat back in her chair and said, "Alex, let me clear things up here. I am aware that you and Sylvia have feelings for one another. I want background information on all of Rick and Sylvia's friendships and relationships, including work related relationships. This is all just a formality to see if something someone says may lead to a clue. I don't have any suspects at present; therefore I don't see any reason for any hostility or any solicitor involvement. So will you please just answer my question? I repeat, how did you feel when Sylvia and Rick entered into a serious relationship, knowing there could no longer be a future for the two of you?"

Although Alex felt that he should involve his solicitor he had no wish to be arrested. He suspected that Detective Molloy was bluffing, but didn't want to take any chances and so thought that it would be best to just co-operate. He raked his hand through his dark blonde hair so that it stood on end. "I just decided it was time to move on. I was happy for Sylvia, a little disappointed for myself, but I knew that if we weren't meant to be then there was nothing I could do about it," he said.

Detective Molloy raised her eyebrow and asked, "Wasn't there?"

"I resent the implication."

"What implication is that? You disappoint me, Alex; surely Sylvia was worth putting up a fight for. No grand romantic gestures?" Her eyebrows leveled out once more.

"No, I knew the best thing to do was to just let her go."

"Any regrets about that?" Detective Molloy asked.

"Of course I've had plenty of ideas for getting her back and moments of regret about not following through, but she's seen plenty of my romantic side over the years so I know it wouldn't have made a difference. Once she made her decision I just had to accept it."

"Did you find that hard to do?"

"No, not really; it's not as if she was ever mine to lose so I just had to continue with life the way I always have when she was with another guy. My only regret is that she has to go through what she's going through now."

"Underneath it all you must feel some sense of satisfaction though. After all, she's free now to be with you when she gets over this."

"I haven't even been thinking about that," replied Alex. He glanced over at Detective Naughton again, but all he heard from him was the pen scribbling across the page of his notebook. "How could you suggest such a thing? How could I possibly be feeling any sort of satisfaction when a friend and work colleague is dead, not to mention that Sylvia is so miserable? I'd want to be a cold-hearted bastard to feel satisfaction over that."

Detective Molloy raised an eyebrow again. "It stands to reason that with Rick out of the way you can now get the girl. I don't for one minute believe that the thought never entered your head."

"Believe it or not, since I heard of Rick's death I haven't been thinking about myself, but about Sylvia and how awful this is for her."

"I find that hard to believe."

"I don't like the tone of this interview. I really would feel more comfortable having my solicitor present." Alex had already taken his mobile phone out and dialed his solicitor's number. He wasn't going to take no for an answer this time. Screw this bitch, he thought as he listened to the dial tone. He was furious with the way the detective's mind was working and hoped his solicitor would help to rein in her line of questioning.

"Could I speak to Jim O' Laughlin please?" While he was waiting for his solicitor to come to the phone, Alex said to the detectives, "I suppose some privacy is out of the question?"

"Of course not; we'll just go and get some coffee," Detective Molloy said.

When Jim came on the phone Alex explained the situation to him and asked him if he could come down to the Garda station at his earliest possible convenience. Jim consulted with his secretary, and after juggling around his schedule a bit said he'd be right there. Alex hung up the phone but couldn't quite feel any sense of relief that his solicitor would be joining him. When he thought of how much pain Sylvia was in he just wanted to hold her and protect her. Having to stay in here and be questioned like this was escalating his anger with every passing moment.

While waiting for his solicitor he cast his mind back to the party Sylvia and Rick had hosted the previous Friday.

Cries of "speech, speech," broke out around the table. In answer, Rick stood up and touched his spoon to his glass to call for silence. He looked down at Sylvia and brushed a few loose strands of her red hair back into place. He stood there looking into her smiling eyes for a moment, and when there was a cough and a meaningful "ahem" muttered in his direction he brought his attention back to the room full of people.

"The only thing I'm happier about than having Sylvia in my life is that we were lucky enough to find this house. We're both delighted to have you all here tonight to help christen it. Your house warming gift, Kim, of a book of cocktails and a set of shakers will help with that." This was accompanied by laughter from the dinner guests. When the laughter died down Rick continued, "Dave, I'm going to need your expertise in mixing up those lethal cocktails you're so famous for."

There was a chorus of cheers as Dave's large frame bent in a half bow from where he was seated. "I hope none of you are working tomorrow," he said with a gleam in his eyes.

Elaine smiled over at her husband, and Gina winced, pursing up her tiny features, obviously in memory of the time she had to go in to work and wait tables after one of their parties. She had told them afterwards that she'd nearly thrown up in someone's dinner when she couldn't stomach the smell of the curry she was delivering to their table.

Julie looked nervous, her large brown eyes widening so much that Alex thought they might swallow her petite face, as she looked over at Alex who was licking his lips in an exaggerated manner, in anticipation of the whiskey sours that would soon follow.

Rick smiled in apology at her as well as at Maeve and Noel as he said, "Sorry guys, I should have warned you. You don't know what you're in for with Dave. And if you think you can politely refuse to drink his cocktails, you can think again. This guy would charm a saint into an alcohol induced stupor." There was more laughter at this and Rick took his seat again.

Now, as Alex sat shivering in the interview room, he still found it hard to believe that less than twenty-four hours later Sylvia had found Rick lying dead in the sitting room of their new house. He drummed his fingers on the table and wished his solicitor would hurry up. He just wanted this over with so that he could get back to Sylvia.

CHAPTER TWO

Meanwhile Detective Molloy went to the waiting room where Alex's friends, Sylvia, Kim and Gina, were waiting for him. She informed them of what was going on.

"Why would he need a solicitor?" Kim asked.

"He didn't feel comfortable answering the questions without one. It's his right to have one; it doesn't make him guilty," the detective replied.

"What you mean is that he wasn't comfortable with your line of questioning," Sylvia said. "Am I right?"

"You may object to my interview technique, but you will see results; I guarantee you that. You all had the right to have a solicitor present."

"The underlying implication being that as Alex was the only one to call a solicitor he must have something to hide," responded Sylvia. "Well I, for one, don't believe it for a moment. Now that I think of it, we should all have brought solicitors with us this morning. Oh I believe all right that you'll get results and that you'll solve this crime eventually, but I don't like your tactics and you're barking up the wrong tree completely, not to mention wasting time."

That outburst started Detective Molloy thinking that maybe Sylvia and Alex were in it together. She pondered the fact that there must be a reason Sylvia and Alex had both gotten defensive when confronted about their relationship. Why though? Surely if it was simply a matter of them wanting to be together Sylvia would have just broken up with Rick, which leads to the question of Rick's insurance, the house and his money. Sylvia could go to Alex a very well off woman. So she was very upset about

Rick's death, what does that really matter? Perhaps she's just very good at acting. A possibility, she thought, and not one to be dismissed lightly. She remembered having noticed Alex holding Sylvia's hand and looking at her with an expression of love in his eyes as she called Gina in to be questioned. I mustn't jump to conclusions, she told herself.

"I just thought you should be aware of the situation. I'm sure Alex would understand if you decided not to wait for him," the detective said.

"I'd like to talk to him please, and as for not waiting for him, out of the question," Sylvia said.

"I'm afraid you'll have to wait until we're finished questioning him before you can talk to him. I just thought you should know that it could take a while."

"That's fine; we'll wait, won't we, girls?" Sylvia said.

"Yes, of course we will," replied Gina.

The detective left the waiting room and went to get some coffee while she waited for Alex's solicitor to join them.

"Which one of you two mentioned Alex's feelings for me?" Sylvia asked, as she straightened up in the chair.

"I'm afraid I did," Kim answered, slumping forward slightly. "I didn't see the relevance. She asked the questions so innocently, as if we were just having a chat. If I had thought she was going to use that information against him I'd have kept my mouth shut."

"It doesn't really matter," Sylvia sighed. "She'd have found out in the end anyway. She's good at getting information; I'll give her that. If she's as good when it comes to finding the real murderer, then I guess I can't complain."

She got up to walk around the room and started to read the posters that were scattered around the walls – road safety, neighborhood watch, victim support groups. She figured that by the time they left she'd have a path well worn between her chair and the coffee machine and would know every word of each of the posters off by heart.

Sylvia cast her mind back to the last night she had spent with Rick and the horror of discovering his body.

On Friday night, after they had seen the last of their guests into a taxi, Sylvia started gathering glasses and sweet wrappers.

"Leave that, love, I'll get it in the morning," Rick said as he came up behind her and encircled her in his arms.

Sylvia turned into his embrace and said, "Thanks. I'll give you a hand before I go into Galway."

"There's no need. You head off early so that you'll be back early."

Sylvia gave him a look of incredulity. "You do know that no matter how early I go I won't be home any earlier; I'll just spend more money."

Rick laughed and pulled her with him up the stairs. When they got to the bedroom he pulled her to him as he said, "Come here my lovely shopaholic. Have I told you lately how much I love you?"

"Yes, but I think I can stand to hear it again," Sylvia murmured against his lips as she wound her fingers through his thick wavy brown hair. She wondered, not for the first time, how she had gotten so lucky. She often thought that it must have been something she'd done in a previous existence that had drawn this sweet and loving man into her life.

The next evening, upon arriving home from shopping, Sylvia entered the sitting room and stopped short as she saw a pool of blood seeping out from under the armchair. Dropping her shopping bags where she stood, she rushed over to the armchair. Reaching it she stopped up, afraid of what sight would greet her. She went around to the front of it and screamed.

She dropped to her knees beside the corpse of her boyfriend and took his hand in hers. She lifted his fingers to her lips, her hands going cold as she touched him, her tears falling onto his hand as she looked into his face which was frozen grey in an expression of shock. She didn't want to think about how horrifying his last moments must have been, but the expression on his face told her that he hadn't seen the knife coming towards him before it was plunged into his chest. She hoped that death was instant, that he didn't have time to feel any pain. Later, realization would come to her that he must have felt some pain as the knife tore through skin, flesh, tissue and bone to pierce his heart before it stopped beating, before he stopped feeling.

Sylvia didn't know how long she knelt at Rick's side before getting up to ring the guards, but when she did so darkness had fallen. She gave an account of what she had come home to find, but it didn't sound to her own ears as if it was her voice. It sounded as if she was hearing someone else speaking from a distance, someone broken-hearted whose voice sounded muffled and disjointed. Hanging up the phone, she went to the window, unable to make herself go to Rick's side again.

Rain pummeled down against the window while Sylvia listened for the Garda car. As the sirens wailed closer to the house she leaned in to the pane of glass, looking into the distance, trying not to see the reflection of the scene in the sitting room behind her, seeing instead the lights of the town a few miles away. As their house was on a hill it afforded them a spectacular view of the town on one side, the lake on the other.

Her gaze moved to the flashing lights of the sirens as she followed their progress up the winding road to the house. When the car came to a stop two guards and what looked like two detectives dressed in suits, emerged from the car, bending their heads against the rain, and she found herself at the door without being sure how she got there.

The introductions were lost on Sylvia. All she could do when asked what had happened was to stammer the response that she didn't know. She pointed to the sitting room as she collapsed onto the bottom steps of the stairs where she stared into space, not seeing or hearing anything going on around her. She shut herself off from her surroundings so that the hushed conversations of the guards, the arrival of the forensics team, and the hustle and bustle of the crime scene investigations all seemed like they were happening elsewhere.

After some time the female detective joined her and said, "Sylvia, I'm sorry to have to inform you that the man in your sitting room is dead. Did you know him?"

Sylvia stared into the woman's face with eyes that were glazed over. Of course she knew he was dead, but hearing it confirmed by an official somehow made it real. It gave her a jump back into reality, made the sounds coming from the sitting room closer, made the face in front of her own come into focus.

She stared into the broad, sincere face of the detective, and wished she could borrow the strength etched there, from the square jaw line to the solemn grey eyes. She replied, "Yes. Rick, he's my... was my boyfriend. We were going to spend the rest of our lives together." Then in between sobs, "How can I live without him?"

The detective who, Sylvia vaguely recalled, had introduced herself as Barbara Molloy asked, "Do you have somewhere to stay while your house is closed off for investigation?"

Sylvia nodded, as she knew she could stay with Elaine and Dave.

"If you'd like to pack a few things now I could take you to where you need to go."

Sylvia nodded her head again and stood up to go and pack. The detective accompanied her upstairs, but remained silent, as if sensing Sylvia's need to be alone with her thoughts.

Sylvia tried to make sense of what had happened as she packed her night clothes into a bag, tried to think who could possibly have so brutally murdered Rick. Her mind wandered as she thought about the short history she had shared with him and what her life had been like before him. She wondered if in his last moments his life had flashed before his eyes in a similar fashion.

As she went in to the en-suite bathroom she tried not to look at Rick's toiletries, didn't want to think about the fact that she'd never again see him shaving or brushing his teeth. She tried not to feel the pang in her chest triggered by the aroma of his aftershave which hung in the air.

While Sylvia's mind was wandering she had managed to push all thoughts of Rick temporarily out of her mind, but when her packing was finished she curled up in a ball on their bed and cried as she thought about Rick lying in a pool of blood downstairs. Even though she had seen with her own eyes the knife embedded in his chest, she found it hard to believe that she would never again lie beside him, share her life, hopes and dreams with him.

The detective crossed the room to sit beside Sylvia and stroke her back comfortingly until the sobs subsided. Sylvia cried about how unfair life was. Her Rick was lying dead on their sitting room floor. He had only ever thought about other people, and now he was dead while all around her selfish people continued to live their lives. She cried when she thought about the fact that he would never again hold her in his arms or comfort her. It was him she needed to put his arms around her and tell her it would be all right. Instead all she had was a detective trying to comfort her.

Accompanied by the detective, she walked down the stairs trying not to look towards the sitting room where she knew Rick lay lifeless. Stepping outside into the rain she made her way slowly towards the Garda car, lifting her face in a futile attempt to let the rain wash away her pain. It was something she and Elaine used to do when they were kids – lift their faces to the rain and laugh as their hair, faces and clothes got soaked. This time, however, there was no laughter; Sylvia doubted she would ever laugh again. She would have stood there long enough to get completely soaked as she let the rain mix with the tears running down her face, but Detective Molloy turned towards her and, with an arm around her waist, helped her to the car.

When they arrived at Elaine and Dave's house, the detective got out of the car with Sylvia to escort her to the front door, which was just as well because Sylvia felt very weak and probably couldn't have taken two steps without collapsing in a heap on the ground. When Elaine opened the door her face drained of color at the sight of Sylvia being supported by a tall, stocky woman. Detective Molloy introduced herself and explained what had happened, that she would need to talk to Sylvia about it but that she knew it would be best for her to have someone with her and be away from the scene of the crime.

Elaine put her arm around Sylvia and led her into the sitting room to the couch. She held her in her arms as Sylvia cried uncontrollably. After having some tea, sweetened with plenty of sugar to help with the shock, she eventually stopped crying long enough to answer some of the detective's questions. Elaine excused herself and said she'd be in the kitchen if she were needed.

A little later Detective Molloy left Elaine's house, none the wiser. Sylvia was in a state of shock and would need time before she could be of any help to the guards. She had answered the questions in a faltering and vague way, had left long silences where her mind seemed to be elsewhere and had been sobbing so much at times that her answers were incoherent. Detective Molloy left her with an assurance that she would be back in the next couple of days in order to ask her some more questions, leaving her phone number in the event of Sylvia thinking of something, anything at all, which may be relevant in helping with the enquiry.

CHAPTER THREE

In the waiting room Kim was lost in her own thoughts, thinking about where she'd gone wrong when being questioned, wondering what had made her mention Alex and Sylvia's relationship. If she had realized it would make him a suspect she would never have mentioned it.

At the Garda station Alex had taken charge, introducing them all and explaining their reason for being there. The guard on the desk went into the back and while they were waiting they all agreed that it felt strange and rather daunting to be there for such a sinister purpose. Up to then the only reason any of them had for being at the station was to get a form signed and stamped. A few moments later Detective Molloy arrived out to bring them into a back room.

"I'll question one of you at a time and will be recording the interviews; it shouldn't take long. It's just a formality really. There's a coffee and tea machine here while you wait. If you'll just come with me?" She motioned for Kim to follow her.

Kim followed the detective into the interview room and observed, "A very dismal room, this. It makes me feel as if I'm actually a criminal, not just helping with an investigation. It's like as if I'm going to be locked away for a very long time."

"Well that shouldn't be the case, unless of course you actually have something to do with this murder," Detective Molloy replied. Her smile was tight, her humor having a serious edge to it. As Detective Naughton arrived into the room and took a seat opposite Kim, Detective Molloy stated the time, date and people present, and asked, "What was your relationship to the deceased?"

"I've known him since he started dating Sylvia. We got on really well. He's been so good for Sylvia and so good to her. He was such a gentleman I can't imagine why anyone would want him dead," Kim said.

"How long have you and Sylvia been friends?" asked Detective Molloy.

"Since I moved to Abbeyfield when I was sixteen."

"You mentioned that Rick had been good for Sylvia. What did you mean by that?"

"Sylvia's always been a bit flighty when it comes to men. It was great to see her settling down with someone. We're all a bit concerned about how this will affect her, you know, finally committing to someone only to have this happen."

"In what way?"

"It might be hard for her to love someone again. Maybe she'll go back to her flighty ways."

"Would that be so bad? Surely there are worse things she could do?"

"Well yes, there are worse things for her but, and I don't mean this badly because I love her dearly, she has a tendency to hurt men."

"Any man in particular?"

Kim hesitated briefly, her hand moving up to brush through her short blonde hair, before replying, "I've said too much already. This is really something you should be talking to Sylvia about. I don't want her to think I'm bad-mouthing her. I wouldn't dare do that, not after all she's just been through."

Detective Molloy reached across the table and covered Kim's hand with her own. "I'm not asking you to speak ill of one of your friends. I'm merely looking for some background; it's often in the missing links of background that clues are found."

"That's all very well, but I just don't see the relevance of any of this."

"Kim, you do understand that solving this murder will give your friend closure, don't you? Surely that's something you want for her. So please, even if you don't see the relevance, I would appreciate your co-operation. So I ask again, is there any man in particular that Sylvia may have hurt, even if inadvertently?"

Reluctantly Kim replied, explaining about the relationship between Sylvia and Alex.

"So you're concerned that with Rick gone Sylvia will go back to Alex. Is he still in love with her?"

"Yeah, he's still besotted with her."

"Last Friday night you were at the house of the deceased, were you not?" Detective Molloy asked.

"Yes, it was a dinner party."

"I'd like you to take a moment to think back to that night. Were there any cross words between any of you or any tension that you can recall?"

Kim took a moment, looking over at Detective Naughton with his head bent over his notebook, pen scribbling away furiously. She then replied that she remembered the night as having been very jovial. "We all had great craic; it's so hard to believe that it was only a few days ago we were so carefree and happy. None of us would have believed that night that one of us would die the next day."

Detective Molloy thanked Kim, told her she had been very helpful and that she would be free to go after she'd had her fingerprints taken. Kim breathed a sigh of relief as she went with a guard into the next room for that purpose.

Gina sat in the waiting room thinking about her own experience in the interview room and she felt sorry for Alex that things had taken such a turn for him.

Gina was called in for questioning after Kim.

"Tell me about the relationship between yourself and the deceased."

"Must you call him the deceased? That sounds so cold," Gina said.

"Sorry," Detective Molloy said. "Tell me about the relationship between yourself and Rick."

"I met Rick after Sylvia started going out with him and warmed to him straight away. He was such a likeable guy and such a gentleman; he always treated Sylvia so well. He was just what she needed to settle her down. This is such a tragedy. I still can't believe he's dead."

"Did all of your friends feel the same way about the, I mean, Rick?"

"Yes, we all loved him."

"Were you at the dinner party of Sylvia and Rick on Friday night?"

"Yes I was. I had sprained my ankle earlier and didn't really feel up to it, but Rick convinced me that it wouldn't be the same without me. That's the type of guy he was."

"Would you say he meant that in a flirtatious capacity?"

Gina laughed. "Good God, no. He's not, em, wasn't the flirtatious one in that relationship; that was Sylvia's department. Anyway, I'm gay; Kim and I are a couple." As she noticed the look of surprise on the detective's face she said, "Kim didn't mention that?"

"No she didn't. Did the evening in question go well?"

"Yes, we had a great time. Little did we know that it would be the last we'd see of Rick."

"Were there any cross words or looks that night?"

"No, none. Like I said, it was a great night; we all had a great laugh."

"Did you ever get the feeling that Rick, or indeed any of your friends, had a problem with you and Kim being gay?"

"No, they've always been great, very supportive."

"Always? When did you first realize you were gay?"

"We were twenty-two; Kim and I were just talking over a bottle of wine one night and one thing just led to another. We haven't looked back since."

"Had Kim realized before that night that she was gay?"

"No, it came as a surprise to both of us, quite a pleasant one I might add," she said with a smile.

"It must have been some conversation that led to that realization!"

"Believe it or not we were talking about a guy we both liked. As we got drunker we talked about a threesome and it just led from there."

"A guy you both liked? Did that come between you at any stage?"

"No, because neither of us stood a chance with him."

"Why was that? You're both good looking women."

"Maybe even then he realized what we hadn't even realized ourselves yet. I know what you're thinking, that if he had thought that then he'd surely have made a move to try to get a threesome. That's not the case;

he's probably the only guy in the world who has no interest in that."

Gina looked over at Detective Naughton just then and saw that he was looking very embarrassed, the deep red edging its way up his face to fight with the grey roots of his black hair. She noticed that he didn't look up from his notebook at either her or his partner. She imagined he would have a laugh about it later with his mates but couldn't feel comfortable discussing this topic with women.

Gina continued, "It was realizing that neither of us stood a chance with him that led to us jokingly suggesting that if we wanted to get together it would have to be without him. I can't remember which of us suggested it, but then a look passed between us and all of a sudden we were kissing. The next morning there was no awkwardness at all; we both just wondered why we had never done it before."

"Does the man in question know what he's missing out on?"

"We both lost interest in him after that, and he never noticed the difference. Obviously he had never even noticed that we were besotted with him."

"Who was the guy?"

"I'd rather not say. Who wants to be reminded of their teenage crushes? It's bad enough that mine still hadn't abated by adulthood. Anyway, we've strayed from the point."

"It's interesting, that's all. Anyway, we've established that as far as you are aware there are no reasons why anyone would have wanted any harm to come to Rick. I'm very interested in the relationships between his friends; it's intriguing that you and Kim have a romantic relationship, and also there is a past between Alex and Sylvia."

"Surely none of that is relevant?" Gina asked, wondering if maybe the interviews weren't so much of a formality after all.

"We'll see," replied Detective Molloy and concluded the interview, arranging for Gina to have her fingerprints taken.

CHAPTER FOUR

Sylvia looked around at her friends as they waited for Alex and thought about how much they'd all been through together.

Sylvia and Elaine had been friends since they were four years old. Both from the estate of Redwood in a small town in Co. Galway called Abbeyfield, they latched on to each other on their first day of school, as their mothers said goodbye to them. Elaine was sitting at a table, trying to be brave, trying not to shed the tears that threatened to fall, as her mother attempted to distract her with a puzzle so that she could make her escape. Sylvia's mother brought her to the table and tried to convince her to sit beside Elaine, but Sylvia wouldn't let go of her mother's skirt as she cried into it. The smell of the flour on it from baking an apple tart with her the day before served to both soothe her and upset her even more; she wondered why she couldn't just go home with her mother and bake another apple tart. Eventually her tears dried up and she sat down beside Elaine who said that they'd share the puzzle. Her mother left as Elaine and Sylvia sat, heads bent together over the puzzle. They'd remained steadfast friends ever since, through many fights over toys and through the awkward teenage years when they watched other friends come and go.

During the lazy days of the summer holidays when they turned sixteen, Alex moved in next door to Sylvia and became friends with the two girls. Alex, a sixteen-year-old boy, was quite a romantic and over that summer fell in love with Sylvia, who had no shortage of other admirers. His infatuation started long before he saw her sitting on a rock at the beach with her feet dangling in the cool water, her profile etched against the sparkling blue of the sea, although that was an image of her that inspired many of his poems.

When the heat of the summer turned to the crisp days of autumn and Alex started at their school, the other girls became jealous of Sylvia having him serenading her with love poems and songs. Any one of them would've given their year's subscription to Just Seventeen to have that kind of attention lavished upon them. She, however, alternated her responses to him as the mood took her, depending on what other guys were showing an interest in her at the time. She either responded to the serenading by running down the stairs and out the door into his arms giving him a passionate kiss, or by shouting out the window that she would like to get some sleep.

Whenever she was dating someone else she would just be friends with Alex, and when she was single she was all over him. He was always waiting around for her to tire of her latest boyfriend. The other girls were always trying to get him interested in them when she was with someone else, the amount of make-up they wore increasing as the amount of clothes they wore decreased. However, eventually they stopped trying as they realized that he was a lost cause, doomed to a life of loving someone who didn't love him back.

Although a tall, very attractive boy with blonde hair and eyes that sparkled like the sea, he was by no means the most gorgeous guy in school or even the most popular, but he had once been voted the most sought after. When this was pointed out to him he just looked puzzled. He was completely unaware of the interest other girls had in him; that was quite possibly part of the attraction. When he played his guitar and sang he was totally focused on Sylvia and failed to notice the numerous girls simpering at his side.

Elaine, a level headed girl, was short and voluptuous with a bubbly personality that people couldn't help but be drawn to. She was one of the only girls in school who wasn't interested in Alex as more than a friend. She noticed, and felt a mixture of contempt and pity for, all the girls who went unseen by Alex. She hoped that someday Sylvia would get the other boys out of her system and have a lasting relationship with Alex.

Sylvia reflected on the close bond the three had formed that lasted through college and beyond. She was glad that like so many other people did she hadn't forsaken her friends for her boyfriend. She would need that closeness now, knew that she could rely on her friends to help her fill the gaping hole in her heart left by Rick's death. She couldn't think about that now without falling apart.

At twenty, Elaine got married to her first love, Dave. He was tall, a little on the chubby side, and full of fun. They bought a house in Redwood, a three-bedroom, semi-detached, two-story house, which had been renovated before they moved in making it quite different to the one Elaine and the others had grown up in, much to Elaine's delight.

Elaine and Dave went on to have three children, Sarah, Jody and Dillon, making their house a lively place to be. All three children had black hair like both parents, but with her brown eyes Sarah favored her father more than her mother. Jody and Dillon were very much their mother's children, in personality as well as looks, with the same hazel eyes and caring nature, while Sarah had a more complicated combination of personalities.

As the years had gone by, Sylvia's following of men increased substantially. Alex became more handsome; his blonde hair had darkened a little and his features became stronger, as did his feelings for Sylvia. The terms of their relationship remained the same, although he had grown out of serenading her, but still wrote some beautiful poems for her. As he experienced more of life his poetry became deeper and more meaningful, but still Sylvia saw him only as a friend with benefits.

After dumping a guy and while waiting for someone new she would call Alex and he would always be available for her. Their relationship had changed in so far as they had started sleeping together. Sylvia saw this as a natural progression as they went from childhood to adulthood, their passionate goodnight kisses turning to stolen moments on the couch, and eventually to sex. However, Alex viewed it as them getting closer; he saw it as making love, and started to infuse his poetry with references to tender caresses.

He was a banker who spent his evenings going to the pub with his colleagues, spending time with his friends or having a quiet night in with a book or writing poetry. He still played his guitar, often putting his words to music, and while writing or reading he tended to listen to classical music and was particularly moved by Vivaldi. His life never involved other women as more than just friends, despite the interference of his friends and family.

Sylvia was a hairdresser and her nights consisted of partying with her workmates or spending quality time with old school pals. Her current boyfriend would be fit in around her life, and whenever he became too demanding she told him it was over. She would often spend evenings with Alex when she was seeing someone else, but those evenings would be platonic. Her relationship with him was easy. For her it was uncomplicated by feelings. They could curl up on the couch together, watch a movie and finish off the evening with a chaste peck on the cheek, or when she was single end up in bed together.

Elaine spent many nights telling Sylvia to either devote herself completely to Alex or tell him that he was wasting his time and passions on her. She couldn't see why Sylvia wasn't happy to date Alex exclusively when their relationship already contained it all – romance, passion, friendship. She tried on numerous occasions to get Sylvia to dial her relationship with Alex up a notch, take him out to a candlelit dinner and give him a proper chance. However, Elaine knew full well that she was wasting her breath; Sylvia enjoyed having male attention and had always felt that if Alex didn't go after anyone else it was his loss and nothing to do with her. It was a constant source of tension between the two friends. Nevertheless they remained bosom buddies, having agreed as children that they would never let anything come between them, especially boys. It had been that time in their lives when they were going from the "boys, oh yuck!" stage to the "oh my God! What a yummy hunk!" stage.

Not long after Elaine and Dave got married, when she was pregnant with their first child, Dave had hit on Sylvia. It only happened once because Sylvia had put him in his place quick smart. She wasn't a cheater, and most certainly wouldn't break the best friend code. She was quite shocked because, until then, she'd thought Dave was a devoted husband, not to mention that she didn't think she was his type, either in looks or personality. She was reasonably good looking with warm brown eyes, long hair, slightly voluptuous hips and an ample bosom. She had more than a smattering of the freckles that so often plague redheads, which served to add a cheekiness that tied her personality and looks together and was aware that it was her personality which most attracted men, her wild nature, which she knew Dave had no interest in.

She'd informed him that under no circumstances was he ever to behave like that again, either with her or with anyone else and had told him that she would find out, and that would be the end of his marriage, not that she really believed he would ever stray. She tried to put it down to a momentary lapse of judgment, but felt she could never trust him the same way again and was fearful for her friend's heart. Elaine, who always put everyone else before herself, didn't deserve to have a cheating husband, didn't deserve to have her heart broken, especially while pregnant and feeling so fragile and vulnerable.

Since then things had been strained between her and Dave, but they were careful not to let Elaine see this. Sylvia had kept an even closer eye on him when Elaine was pregnant than at any other time, but he thought her vigilance was constant. It gave her a certain amount of power over him because he knew that even if he never strayed she still possessed the power to end his marriage. All she had to do was tell Elaine that he'd tried it on with her before. He was now wise enough to know that Elaine would believe her long-time friend over him. She would loathe being the bearer of such news, playing a part in the destruction of their marriage when all Elaine had ever done was to be there for her through everything, from the many rows she'd had with her parents to boy trouble.

Sylvia wondered where she'd be without Elaine, for it was to her she always turned in every crisis in her life, whether major or minor. She thought about how many times she had turned to her when she was having a row with Alex, how even though she mightn't like what Elaine said to her she always knew how to make everything right. Sylvia would need that now more than ever. It was Elaine she needed to pull her through, as she had done before, although it wouldn't be the same.

Nothing could ever be the same again. She thought of how it was down to Elaine that she had met Rick.

Just before meeting Rick, Sylvia was heartbroken over an ex; it was the first time she'd ever found herself reduced to a blubbering mess over a guy, unable to sleep or eat, lacking the energy to go out with her friends or contemplate life with any other guy. She would lie on her bed, listening to love songs with tears rolling down her face. Finally her appetite returned, she started sleeping again and found that her every waking moment was no longer consumed by sadness over Jerry's departure. She accepted her friends' persuasion that it was time to move on, that there was somebody else out there worthy of her love.

Elaine had worked in the bank with Alex until she decided to be a full time mother. She still socialized with the bank crew and when she heard of a party that was being thrown for someone who was leaving the bank she urged Sylvia to go along to it, knowing the time was right for her to move on. Sylvia agreed to go and while getting ready she found herself, for the first time in ages, using her hairbrush alternately as a microphone or guitar as she jumped around her room singing to her favorite songs. She knew that Alex would be there and was ready to go back to him. Elaine hadn't told Alex that Sylvia would be there in the hope that he wouldn't show up; she wanted Sylvia to bypass the Alex stage that came after every breakup and go straight for one of the other eligible bachelors that would be at the party.

However, Alex did turn up and his eyes lit up the instant he saw Sylvia. At the same instant Sylvia's eye was caught by someone else. Sylvia could imagine herself gripping that dark hair in a moment of passion, with those dark eyes looking into hers out of his deeply tanned face. She went straight over and introduced herself, leaving Elaine to inform Alex that Sylvia would be unavailable for the evening.

True to form, within minutes Sylvia had Rick on the dance floor and was swaying to a beat that had more to do with passion than with music. The only way they could've gotten closer would have been making love. They danced and talked all evening, totally oblivious to anyone else around them.

After several people passing by told them they should get a room Rick said, "Shall we go to my place?"

"I thought you'd never ask," Sylvia replied.

In the taxi on the way to Rick's place they managed to restrain themselves and kept their hands from roaming all over each other. They made small talk, although the air was rife with sexual tension. When they got to Rick's flat they found his flat mate up and crying big, gulping sobs as she clutched a glass of wine in her hand. The expression on Rick's face changed immediately to one of concern.

"Sylvia, I'm not blowing you off. I just think Mary needs a shoulder to cry on right now." He gave her a quick kiss on the lips and said, "I'm definitely looking forward to taking up from where we left off. Would you think I'm awful if I asked you to make the three of us a cup of tea?"

"Not at all. I hope she'll be okay." With a wink she added, "We have all night to enjoy each other."

Sylvia looked around the kitchen as she waited for the kettle to boil. She was impressed with the neatness; there was no way she'd be able to keep everything in its place like that. The décor was quite simple, neutral. Very nice for rented accommodation, she thought. She compared it to the house she shared and felt ashamed of the mess of the place, the décor which the landlord hadn't updated since the seventies, at least that's what it looked like to her with its strong greens and oranges and brown patterned carpets.

When Sylvia brought the tea into the sitting room she found Mary wrapped in Rick's arms. Her first impression of Mary was of a dumpy, rather plain girl with shoulder length black hair. She could see that Mary was rather short, made to look even shorter by her roundness. She realized that if Mary wasn't crying her eyes out she might actually be pretty. She felt she'd have to hold off on assessing her prettiness until she saw her in a more favorable circumstance.

Rick threw her an apologetic glance as he extricated himself from Mary's clutches with the promise of tea in his stead. As they listened to Mary's tale of woe about how her boyfriend had just dumped her in favor of some "blonde bimbo" with legs that went on forever, Sylvia's eyes wandered over the sparsely furnished sitting room and found herself once again comparing it to her own living conditions.

Sitting in a black leather recliner she felt very tempted to hit the recliner button but didn't want to be rude. It was one thing to be looking around while pretending to listen to Mary, but if she looked like she was more interested in her reclining chair than in Mary's tale of woe it would look very bad for her. Although they seem to be so absorbed in Mary's story that they probably wouldn't even notice, Sylvia reasoned. However, she resisted the temptation and just took in her very tasteful surroundings.

A glass coffee table, which lacked the clutter Sylvia was used to seeing, was placed between the two armchairs in front of the large leather couch. She was rather envious of the large wrought iron fireplace opposite the couch; a very antiquated central heating system was all her house offered. She decided then that she must move house soon. It was one thing living like that in her student days but just shameful as a working woman.

Finally, when Mary decided that she was better off without the "bastard" who had just dumped her, Rick and Sylvia went to bed but were too tired to resume their lovemaking. As Sylvia slid in between the cool sheets she wished she could have more than sleep on her mind, but her eyes were just so heavy that she longed for blissful oblivion.

"I'll make it up to you tomorrow night, I promise," Rick told her as he kissed her on the cheek.

"Morning's good for me," Sylvia said, not so tired that she couldn't muster up a bit of coquettishness.

"We'll see."

They snuggled up together, no awkwardness involved although they had only just met, and were soon in a deep sleep.

When the alarm woke them the next morning, Sylvia stretched and rolled over so that she was half lying on top of Rick. She kissed him and flicked her tongue along his lips, straddling his hips as she bit his lower lip.

"How about that promise to make it up to me?" She felt Rick's response beneath her as she slipped her tongue between his lips.

Afterwards, over breakfast, Rick expressed his desire to see her again. "Sorry it's nothing more elaborate than tea and toast. Neither Mary nor I eat cereal, so we don't have any in and we only have a fry up at the weekends. We're not used to having people here for breakfast; I'm not into one night stands and I certainly hope this wasn't one," he said.

"Tea and toast is fine, probably all I'd be having if I was at home anyway. I'd like to see you again too."

"I'll call you later."

"I look forward to it, but before you go in to work today I think there's something I should tell you."

A look of caution crossed Rick's face as he asked, "What's that?"

"I have a history with one of your colleagues, Alex." Sylvia went on to explain the nature of the relationship between her and Alex, watching Rick's face carefully to try to gauge his reaction. She hoped he wouldn't be put off by it. He listened intently and didn't seem perturbed by her admission, but she couldn't tell for sure.

"I hope that's not a problem for you," she finished. "I just thought you should know from the start since you have to work with him."

"Is he going to make it a problem for me?"

"God, no," she said. "We're just friends. We've just been more from time to time in the past, that's all. He'll be fine about you and me. I just wanted you to hear about it from me first. Not that Alex would kiss and tell of course, but I just wouldn't want any awkwardness."

CHAPTER FIVE

Sylvia tried to get more comfortable in the straight-backed chair, sighed and thought about how much she was going to need all of her friends to help her through this. She hoped Alex's feelings for her weren't going to be an issue, as she would need the comfort of being wrapped in his arms, and, although knowing it was selfish, she didn't need to worry about how he would feel while holding her. More than anything, though, she would need to draw on Elaine's strength.

She had been so lost in thought as she waited for Alex that she didn't realize she had a cup of coffee in her hands and that it was almost empty. She had been drinking it as her mind had wandered over her previous days, weeks and years, not for the first time in the last few days. She thought about her own interview with the detectives and wondered if she had said anything to inadvertently incriminate any of her friends, particularly Alex.

"How are you feeling? Are you up to this?" Detective Molloy asked, holding Sylvia's hand between her own two.

"I'm okay I guess. I'm as up to this as I'll ever be." The feeling of determination Sylvia had started the day with had been slowly ebbing away while she waited to be interviewed and she once again felt like curling up in a ball and crying until she could cry no more. Taking a deep breath she pushed her strength and determination to the fore again.

"I promise it'll be as quick and painless as I can possibly manage," Detective Molloy said as she squeezed Sylvia's hand. When she had stated the necessities for the record she asked, "Why don't you tell me a bit about Rick? How you met him, how he got on with your friends and you with his?"

"It was a few months after I had been dumped by my last boyfriend. At the time I thought it was the worst thing that had ever happened to me, but it turns out to have been the best, as I may not have met Rick otherwise. Elaine had invited me to a party her ex-colleagues were having for someone who was leaving the bank. I know it sounds corny, but our eyes met across the room. We danced and talked and I knew instantly that it was unlike anything I had ever felt before; I didn't realize it was love, though.

"We fitted so easily into one another's lives. His family and friends had great time for me. My family and friends thought he was wonderful and he got on great with all of them. Actually, I don't know of anybody who didn't get on well with him; he was just an all round great guy."

"What was your love life like before Rick?"

Sylvia gave the detective a puzzled look. "I don't see what difference that makes."

"I just want to establish the background to your relationship; it may help in establishing the background to the murder."

"I don't see how, but I don't want to stop you doing your job. I guess you know what you're doing. Well, as you may have gathered, I had never been in love before. I was just enjoying life, going out with quite a few guys, nothing serious. I was always the one to dump them, usually for someone else. I thought my ex and I really had something special, so you can imagine how I felt when he dumped me."

"Would there have been any exes, either yours or Rick's who may have had a problem with your relationship?"

"Not that I'm aware of. We had talked about our pasts. His exes have all married since he split with them and I never kept track of mine." She smiled as she said, "My friends would say that's because there were so many of them."

"There must surely be one ex, apart from Alex, that you're still in touch with."

"No. Only Alex, and that's hardly relevant." As Sylvia saw Detective

34

Molloy raise one eyebrow she objected, "You surely don't mean to say that you think Alex killed Rick because of our past flings? That's absolutely ludicrous!"

"I'm merely trying to put together the pieces of the puzzle. All of this may seem irrelevant, but when we put all the pieces together, stand back and see how they fit, how the picture looks, only then will we be able to tell what's relevant and what isn't. Why don't you tell me about your other friends? How they got on with Rick?"

"I'm sorry I over-reacted; this has been such an ordeal for me. I know you're just doing your job. We've all been friends for a long time. Like I already told you, they all thought Rick was great. Even Alex," Sylvia said.

"How long have you and Elaine been friends?"

"Since we were four."

"Have you ever fallen out with her over men?"

"We made a pact when we were sixteen that our friendship was too important to let boys come between us. It's never been a problem, as Elaine fell in love with and married her first boyfriend."

"Is she happy in her marriage?"

"What are you trying to say now, that in a fit of jealousy Elaine murdered Rick? As far as I can see you've already decided that the murderer was one of my friends, and you're just trying to establish motives so that when you discover whose fingerprints are on the murder weapon there will be a motive to tie in neatly with their prints."

Detective Molloy informed Sylvia that, as she saw it, whoever came to the house on the day Rick was killed had Rick's trust. She suspected that he or she provided him with a plausible reason for going into the kitchen and that Rick let the murderer in there alone where the knife, which was conveniently found in the dishwasher, was retrieved. Having his or her prints already on the knife meant that there was no need to bother with any gloves.

Sylvia had sat open-mouthed during that whole speech and finally closed her mouth to object. "The dishwasher is a perfectly logical place for a kitchen knife to be. Even if I went into a stranger's house, if I didn't spot a knife on a counter top, in a stand or in the sink I would immediately assume it was in the dishwasher or in a drawer. Therefore it doesn't stand to reason that one of my friends was the murderer. I may as well save you some time by telling you that the fingerprints you will find on the knife are mine, Rick's, Alex's, Kim's and Elaine's. I had help in the kitchen from them on Friday night."

"We're keeping our minds open to all possibilities."

At this point Detective Naughton interrupted, "Was there anyone else in Rick's life, perhaps at work, that may have held a grudge against him for anything. Maybe he was promoted ahead of someone else, or was up for promotion against someone who would rather not have him as competition."

"As far as I'm aware he had a great relationship with his colleagues. You'd have to talk to them about that."

"Thank you, Sylvia; you've been a great help."

Despite Detective Naughton's attempts at smoothing things over, Sylvia was seething as she was escorted to have her fingerprints taken.

CHAPTER SIX

Sylvia now felt a lot different to how she had this morning. She thought about how determined she'd been to get the investigation under way and how they'd all thought it was just a formality; it hadn't entered any of their heads that one of them would be considered a suspect.

She woke early feeling refreshed after her sleep, despite the dreams and crying that had interrupted her night. Elaine's children hadn't woken yet so there was a peaceful silence in the house. She made herself a cup of tea and took advantage of the quiet to do some thinking. The stillness of the early morning had always appealed to her. She sat in the pre-dawn dark with her hands wrapped around her cup for warmth, inhaled the steam and watched the first band of yellow and pink steal the darkness from the sky. The comfort of all the sunrises she had watched with Rick washed over her.

She decided that it was time to be level headed; there would be no more crying for now. Rick's murderer had to be found and sitting around feeling sorry for herself wasn't going to achieve anything. Yes, she had needed to cry and there'd be plenty more grieving to be done. Sure there would be other mornings she wouldn't be able to watch the sun rise without tears in her eyes, but not until she'd been of some help to the guards. They needed her to go down to the Garda station so that their investigations could proceed; she'd do that today.

The guards also needed to see her and Rick's friends who had been at the house on Friday night. She would ring them today and perhaps they could all go to the station together; at least she'd have support. She couldn't do it alone; it would be easier to remain strong for the purpose of helping in the investigation if she had her friends with her. She was forgetting that as it was Tuesday they'd all be working, except for Elaine, and she had Jody and Dillon to mind. Maybe they could meet this evening. If Elaine's mother took the children, Dave could come along too.

Having decided on a course of action she immediately started to feel better, useful again. She finished her tea and went upstairs to have a shower, trying not to think of how much Rick loved the smell of her shampoo while she massaged it into her scalp. She pushed aside the memory of him taking handfuls of her hair and inhaling deeply, tried instead to focus instead on the task that lay ahead of her.

When she came back downstairs the morning had erupted with the mayhem of excited children. She helped Elaine with the breakfasts and coaxed Sarah to get dressed for school, promising to pick her up after. With Sarah and Dave's departure the house quietened somewhat. As Elaine headed towards the shower the phone rang.

"Get that, will you?" she called to Sylvia.

Picking up the phone, Sylvia said, "Hello?"

"Hi, Sylvia," Alex said. "How are you feeling?"

"Not so bad. It's been rough, but I'm trying to be strong. Actually, I'm going to the Garda station today; they want to see all of us who were at our house on Friday night."

"I know; they rang me at work yesterday. I've taken the day off today; I thought you might want some company going to the station."

"I had actually been thinking that if as many of us as possible could go together it would be great support," Sylvia said.

"I'll ring Gina and Kim. Elaine and Dave will probably want to go together; tell them that I'll baby-sit this evening if they like."

"Thanks, Alex. Ring me back when you've spoken to Gina and Kim. I'll ring Julie, Maeve and Noel. I just want to get this over with so that the guards can get on with their investigation and find the murderer."

"Talk to you soon."

Sylvia hung up the phone as Elaine came into the room rubbing her hair with a towel. "Who was that?"

Sylvia filled Elaine in on her conversation with Alex before ringing Julie. Elaine gave Sylvia a gentle pat on the shoulder, and left her to make arrangements while she went in search of her hair dryer.

Julie sounded very cold on the phone as she informed Sylvia that she, Maeve and Noel had gone in to the station the evening before. She didn't offer Sylvia any sympathy or stay on the phone to talk about the loss of her friend. Sylvia thought this strange; she knew that Julie and Rick were very close. Maybe she resents me because she wanted to be more than just his friend, she thought as she hung up.

Just as she put the phone down it rang again.

"Probably Alex ringing back; why don't you get it?" Elaine said.

"Hi, Sylvia?"

"Hi, Alex. Did you talk to Gina and Kim?"

"Yes. They were planning on going in on their lunch break, but it didn't take much to convince them to pull a sickie. They were on their way in to work but turned their car around as soon as I suggested it. They're on their way to pick me up now and we'll be over to you soon."

"Thanks, Alex. See you later."

"That's what friends are for," Alex said as he hung up the phone.

Sylvia filled Elaine in on her conversation with Alex and also with the stilted conversation she'd had with Julie. She voiced her concerns about how strange Julie was acting.

"Everybody copes in different ways. Some people find it helps to talk but she obviously doesn't. She was Rick's best friend since they were kids. She's bound to be very upset and not herself. She's never exactly talked much to you anyway, even under the best of circumstances."

"I know, but I thought she might want to talk about Rick."

"She just mightn't be ready right now, or maybe she just didn't want to talk about him with you. I always felt that she was jealous of your relationship with Rick. It's best not to think about that now." Elaine squeezed Sylvia's hand as she said, "I'm glad you're all going to the station together. I wouldn't want you going alone."

Soon after that the doorbell rang. Sylvia went to answer it and was glad to see Alex, Gina and Kim standing there. She stood back to allow them into the house. They each gave her a warm hug, which she found consoling. Elaine informed them that she had the kettle on so they stayed for a cup of tea.

Sitting on either side of Sylvia, Gina and Kim each took one of her hands. "How are you feeling, sweetheart?" asked Kim.

"I'm not too bad today. It's good to have you all here with me," Sylvia said with tears in her eyes. She wiped at her eyes, determined to remain strong at least until she had done what needed doing today.

"We rang yesterday, but Elaine said you needed some time," Gina said.

Elaine looked at Sylvia with an apology in her eyes. Sylvia said, "She was probably right. I'm feeling more up to company today; I don't feel as if I'm going to cry every time I think of Rick."

"Has the body been released yet?" asked Gina, getting a shake of the head and a stern look from Elaine.

Catching the look, Sylvia said, "It's okay, Elaine, I can talk about it. I'll probably find out more today. There were no signs of a break-in so the guards don't think it was a burglar. He received one stab wound directly to the heart, which makes them think it was a professional who killed him. They only want to question us as a formality." As tears streamed down Sylvia's face, Kim hugged her and patted her back.

"I don't mind going in to answer some questions, but surely they need a warrant for our fingerprints," Gina remarked.

"Yes, I mentioned that yesterday to the guards, but they said that while that was true it would hold things up, and in the interest of getting the investigation underway they would appreciate our co-operation," replied Alex. Standing up, he continued, "Thanks for the tea, Elaine, but we really should get going if you're ready, Sylvia."

Sylvia withdrew from Kim's embrace, mentally berating herself for crying again. She received a reassuring pat on the arm from Elaine as they left and she told herself that maybe it was okay to cry a little as long as it didn't stop her from taking action.

CHAPTER SEVEN

The detectives re-entered the interview room, cups of steaming coffee in their hands. When Alex got the smell of it he longed even more to be away from there, sitting in a coffee shop with Sylvia, his hands covering hers as they waited for their drinks to be brought to their table, or sitting on his couch, his arms around her as she cradled a cup of tea in her hands. Things they had done together on a countless number of occasions, but now seemed as if they may never happen again if Detective Molloy had her way.

"My solicitor is on his way. I'd like to talk to the girls, let them know what's going on, that I could be a while," Alex said.

"Already done," Detective Molloy said.

"I'd like to talk to them anyway," Alex replied.

"I'd rather you waited until you've been questioned."

Alex steepled his hands in front of him and said, "I haven't been arrested; therefore I believe I have the right to speak to my friends, even to leave the premises if I wish. I am, after all, here of my own free will, although it is at your request."

"That is true. However, if indeed you have nothing to hide you will be free to do as you please after we have finished questioning you. Until then it would be in your best interest to remain where you are," Detective Molloy said.

"Fine, I'll just ring Sylvia," replied Alex. "Thank God for mobile phones."

"I don't think He had much to do with them, but go ahead," replied

Detective Molloy with a tight smile.

"May I at least have some privacy?" Upon seeing Detective Molloy's hesitation and raised eyebrow he added, "You're not going to miss me confessing to a murder I didn't commit if that's what you're thinking."

"We'll give you your privacy, but you'd be advised to watch that smart mouth of yours; it could get you into a lot of trouble."

"I think if you were in my shoes you might find yourself being uncharacteristically smart-mouthed too; it's a form of defense."

"For your defense it would be advisable to just stick to the truth, unless of course the truth offers no form of defense," the detective replied as she left the room with her partner, leaving the smell of coffee in their wake.

Tears stung Alex's eyes when he heard the sadness in Sylvia's voice as she answered the phone.

"The dragon lady won't let me come out to talk to you guys in person; this is as much as she'll let me do. I think she just wants to let me know that she's got power over me," Alex said.

"Well she would have if you were guilty, but as you're not you've got nothing to worry about. Just hang in there. It was a good idea to call your solicitor; we should all have probably done the same," Sylvia said.

"I'm afraid that now she actually thinks I am guilty," Alex sighed and raked his hands through his already unruly hair.

"Has she actually said that she thinks you're guilty?"

"No, but I'm getting that impression from her attitude."

"It doesn't really matter what she thinks; there's no way on earth she could possibly make such an allegation stick."

"Thanks for your support. You and the others don't need to stick around though; I'll probably be a while."

"Of course we're sticking around; we wouldn't think of leaving you here alone. Just chin up and tell the truth, the whole truth and nothing but the truth," Sylvia said.

"Thanks, Sylvia," Alex replied appreciating Sylvia's attempt at humor, however weak it was. "I really am grateful for the support; it's good to have friends like you in my corner. Anyway, here they are again so I'd better go."

The two detectives arrived into the interview room with Alex's solicitor, Jim, a tall, balding man with a serious face. Alex rose to shake his hand as Jim settled into a chair, lifting his briefcase on to the table.

Detective Molloy resumed the interview, recording Jim's presence before asking, "Could you please tell me about your relationship with the girlfriend of the deceased?"

"I've already told you about that."

"For the benefit of your solicitor maybe you'd like to repeat it."

Alex cast a questioning look at Jim and, at his nod, repeated his earlier statement.

"How did you feel when Rick started dating Sylvia and the relationship became serious, effectively ending things between you and Sylvia?"

"Sylvia and I will always have our friendship; it was just the end of our romantic liaison, meaning that it was time to move on with my life the way she'd moved on with hers."

"Have you moved on?" Detective Molloy asked.

"Yes."

"Do you have a current girlfriend?"

"I don't see what that has to do with anything," Alex said as he looked at Jim.

"I'm trying to establish whether or not you have indeed moved on," Detective Molloy said.

Jim nodded and Alex replied that he didn't have a current girlfriend.

"Have you dated anyone since Sylvia's been dating Rick?" Detective Molloy asked.

"No," Alex muttered, knowing it wasn't looking good for him.

"Do you intend to resume a romantic relationship with Sylvia now that Rick is dead?"

"You don't need to answer that," Jim interrupted before Alex could answer.

With a smoothness that implied she hadn't been deterred, Detective Molloy asked, "Were you at the soirée at the house of the deceased on Friday night last?"

"Yes," Alex replied.

"Were there any arguments on the night in question?"

"No, the atmosphere was very relaxed; we all had a great time."

"Was the deceased aware of the past shared by you and his girlfriend?"

"Yes he was. We worked together at the bank. There have never been any hard feelings between us."

Detective Molloy raised both eyebrows. "Not even at the very start of the relationship?"

"No."

"So, what you're telling me is that from the start you were fine about Rick moving in on Sylvia, and that he was fine about the romantic past shared by the two of you?" Detective Molloy asked.

Jim raised his hand to prevent Alex from answering. "I believe my client has been quite clear on this matter. Can we move on please? Are you trying to establish motive with this line of questioning? Just so that we're clear on the way things stand."

"I am trying to get a background to the murder, to the relationships the deceased had with his friends. If in doing so a motive becomes apparent it will be followed up on," Detective Molloy said.

"You may proceed," Jim said with a note of warning in his voice.

"The murder weapon has a number of fingerprints on it. Would there be any reason for your prints to be on it?" Detective Molloy asked.

"I was helping out in the kitchen before the party; if the knife wasn't washed from the night before it's possible that my prints would be on it," Alex said.

"Are you familiar with the kitchen layout of the house of the deceased?"

Again Jim interrupted. "I don't see the relevance of that question."

"I have surmised that the murderer was familiar with the layout of the kitchen and had occasion to be in the kitchen alone on the day of the murder," Detective Molloy said.

"I would advise my client not to answer that question at this time."

"It's okay, Jim, I have nothing to hide and I don't mind answering," Alex said.

"I would like a moment with my client please."

"Very well," Detective Molloy said and both detectives got up and left the room.

"If you're not going to take my advice why did you call me? I know what I'm doing by advising you against answering certain questions. Even if you have nothing to hide you may be incriminating yourself by answering that question. It's my job to see that you don't do that," Jim said.

"I understand that and I appreciate your being here and your advice on not answering certain questions. However, I believe it is my right to take or leave your advice as I see fit; therefore I am going to answer that question." Alex added, "It's because I have nothing to hide that I would like to answer it."

Jim asked the detectives back into the room and sighed in resignation as the question was repeated.

"I've been in their house on a number of occasions and it's not uncommon for me to make myself a cup of tea or a sandwich. As I said, I was helping out the night before the murder. So, yes, it would be fair to say that I know my way around their kitchen," Alex said.

"Are you aware of any tension at work that existed between Rick and any of your colleagues? Over a promotion or anything else?" Detective Molloy asked.

"No, Rick was one of the most popular guys at work."

"Can you account for your whereabouts on Saturday afternoon last?"

"I was at home all afternoon."

There was a pause in the interview, during which Alex heard Detective Naughton's pen scribbling across the page.

"Were you alone?" Detective Molloy asked.

"Yes."

"So you have no alibi?" Detective Molloy asked with a barely concealed smirk.

"No I don't."

"I think that would be a good place to conclude this interview. I would like to consult with my client before this goes any further." Jim was in the process of standing up as he spoke, brooking no argument.

As Alex stood to leave, Detective Molloy said, "No alibi, a motive and your prints possibly on the murder weapon. When we get a warrant for your fingerprints we'll call you. I hope you're not planning on any trips out of town, as you may be required to come in for further questioning. If your prints are found on the murder weapon we may have reason to arrest you on suspicion of murder."

As Jim left he asked Alex to ring his secretary to make an appointment. Alex then went into the waiting room to the girls, sighed and said, "I think I'm suspect number one. Thanks for waiting around for me and for your support. By the looks of things I'll need a lot more of it before this is over."

Sylvia took his hand and said, "Whatever they think they can't make it stick."

"I wouldn't be so sure; innocent people get put away all the time," Alex replied.

"Well thinking like that won't help," Kim said as they walked towards the car.

"I know a positive mental attitude moves mountains, but it really felt as if I was going down for life in there."

"If it's any consolation I felt like that the minute she started in on me too," Gina said.

"Me too," Kim said. "From the moment I walked in there."

As they drove back to Elaine's house they discussed the questions that had been asked of each of them and agreed that if any of them were unfortunate enough to have their prints on the knife and didn't have an alibi they were in trouble.

"Apart from Rick, Alex, and I the other prints are Kim's and Elaine's. Were you asked for an alibi, Kim?" Sylvia asked.

"No, but anyway I was at home in bed with Gina. She'll vouch for me. Won't you, love?"

"That depends on whether or not we're having a fight when I'm asked. If we were having a serious one I might just let them lock you up and throw away the key," Gina said as she caressed Kim's thigh.

"Gina, that's not very funny," Alex said.

"I'm sorry; I didn't mean to be insensitive. It's a shame you don't have an alibi, Alex, but you've a good solicitor; he'll work something out."

"Hey, we could always say you were in bed with us," Kim said.

"Again, not funny."

"Sorry, Alex, it's just very hard to take it seriously. I mean, the thoughts of you killing someone! You? It's just ridiculous!"

"Yeah, I just wish those detectives thought so."

As they pulled up outside Elaine's, Sylvia wondered whether Elaine had an alibi. She owed it to her friend to warn her in advance that she'd be considered a suspect. She was now very worried about the turn of events; despite Kim and Gina's joking it was beginning to look as if Alex might be in for a rough time.

CHAPTER EIGHT

While Elaine waited for her friends to get back from the Garda station she sat in her sitting room thinking back over the previous few days. She wished she could go back in time to the night they had enjoyed in Sylvia and Rick's house. The last few days were like living a nightmare. She remembered the sight of Sylvia turning up on her doorstep and how she had fretfully paced the kitchen while Detective Molloy was in the sitting room with Sylvia.

After seeing the detective out Elaine went into the sitting room to console her friend who eventually fell into an uneasy sleep. She put her lying down on the couch, knowing that even though it was a firm, comfortable couch Sylvia's sleep would be restless and she would wake up the next morning feeling as if she hadn't slept. Covering her with a warm blanket, she crept out of the room. She then rang Alex to inform him of what had happened.

"Oh my God. How awful! How is Sylvia?"

"As you can imagine, she's beside herself with grief. She's just fallen into an exhausted sleep now. I've never known her to cry so much; it's no wonder she's exhausted."

"Is there any point in me calling around tonight?"

"No, I'm off to bed now but I'll be keeping an eye on her throughout the night."

"If I came over I could sit with her and keep an eye on her; that way you wouldn't have to."

"I don't think that's such a good idea."

"I'm going to pretend I didn't hear the disapproval in your voice. I'm obviously not going to try anything on," Alex sounded hurt. "I'm just trying to help. You could get a proper night's sleep if I was there with her; that's all I meant. After all, you have the children to get up with in the morning."

"All the same, I think it would be best if you left it until tomorrow to call over."

"I'll be over first thing."

Elaine hung up, knowing that Alex's intentions were honorable but that it would be better for Sylvia to have some space to grieve before leaning on Alex. She made another few phone calls, to Kim and Gina, and to Sylvia's parents, before turning in for the night. Everyone was terribly distraught and in shock when they heard the news, which she had relayed with a calmness and strength she didn't feel. She felt like falling apart herself, but knew that she would remain the calm in everyone else's storm, as always. It was through helping her friends to cope that she would cope herself. She carried herself to bed on leaden feet, knowing that she would feel more able to deal with the tragedy the next day.

"You asleep?" she whispered to Dave as she slid in under the covers.

"No."

"Good, I need to talk to you. I can't believe what's just happened. I've just been consoling Sylvia, but I still can't believe that someone's just killed Rick."

"I know. You just never think that something like that could happen to someone you know."

"I'm worried about Sylvia. I was so delighted for her to have found Rick, to see her settling down instead of flitting from one man to another as if she might run out of time to sample every man in the world. I'm really worried that this could destroy her. I can see her being too scared to let anyone get as close to her as Rick did. I'm worried about Alex too. He wanted to come over tonight. The last thing either of them need right now is Sylvia using him as a crutch to get her over this."

"Worrying won't help matters. All you can do is be there for her. She'll need time, but eventually she will fall in love again. The best thing you can do now is get some sleep so you can be ready to deal with tomorrow. As for Alex, he's a big boy now. We really need to back off and let him do his own thing. I know you mean well, but you can't always be mother to the whole group. All we can do is to try to help Sylvia through this; we'll worry about the future some other time."

"You're right. Goodnight love." Elaine gave Dave a peck on the cheek and snuggled up with her head on his chest.

"Goodnight sweetheart," Dave replied, kissing the top of her head.

Elaine could only toss and turn fitfully. She tried to get comfortable and blank her mind, but, just as the sheets kept getting tangled around her, her head kept filling with thoughts of her friends. Although aware that Dave was right she couldn't stop herself from worrying. She thought back over the years to all the times Sylvia had turned to Alex when a relationship ended. Although this was somewhat different it didn't mean that it wouldn't happen again. Sylvia had always failed to see how selfish she was when it came to Alex despite Elaine constantly pointing it out to her. To Sylvia, Alex was her old reliable and she didn't see that she was toying with his emotions. Elaine knew Sylvia never intentionally hurt Alex, but in her grief she was likely to reach for him again and Alex wouldn't be able to help himself; he'd get his hopes up and would end up heartbroken.

The next morning the mood in the house was lifted a little by the presence of the children. They were very excited to see that Aunt Sylvia was staying but a little annoyed that they hadn't been woken when she had arrived. Well it was mostly Sarah who was annoyed. Jody, who was three, and Dillon, one and a half, just copied Sarah's annoyance with their parents.

Elaine took Sarah on to her lap, held her hand and tried to calm her. "It was better to have stayed snug up in your bed last night and have a good night's sleep. If you'd gotten up last night you'd have no energy today for spending time with Sylvia."

"I don't care. At least I'd have gotten to see her last night."

"She'll be staying with us for a few days at least so you'll have plenty of time to spend with her. When she arrived last night it was very dark and she went straight to bed herself."

Sylvia sat down beside Elaine and Sarah and said, "How about if I read you all a story after breakfast?"

A small smile started to appear as Sarah said, "You promise?"

"As long as you eat all of your breakfast first."

The three children started cheering then and Sarah decided that they'd have a race with breakfast. She said that the winner would get to choose the story. Of course she won, as Jody and Dillon didn't understand the game.

The adults were glad of the distraction provided by the children as it helped them put the tragedy of the previous night to the back of their minds, at least for the moment. However, the relief was pretty short-lived. Reality struck home when Alex, Kim and Gina arrived. Elaine's mum came over to take the children for a while because she knew Elaine would have her hands full with Sylvia. At first Sarah wanted Sylvia to go with them but she was bribed by some chocolate. Pretty soon all three children left for their Granny's with chocolate around their mouths. Sylvia's parents, Bernie and Jack, who wanted Sylvia to come home with them, arrived soon after that.

"You'd be better off in your own bed in your old room," her mum said, drawing her into a hug. "I rang your brother this morning. He's on his way from Cork now. He'll be here soon. He sends his love."

Elaine knew that Sylvia felt a deep sense of comfort in her mother's hug. She had always made everything all right with her hugs, no matter how bad things were. The large woman, with short graying hair framing her kindly face with loose curls, had warmth in her brown eyes, warmth that transferred itself into the person she was hugging. Unfortunately, she had a tendency to overdo things, never knowing when to stop fussing, leaving a person feeling smothered.

Elaine knew that the last thing Sylvia wanted was her mother fussing over her. Bernie meant well but Sylvia definitely couldn't cope with her at the moment. Having her brother there would help lessen the amount of fussing and Elaine knew she would like the opportunity to spend some time with Peter. They didn't get to see much of each other since he had moved to Cork.

"I want to stay with Elaine," Sylvia said.

"I think Elaine has enough to do with her three children. Why don't you come home and let me look after you?"

Elaine reassured Bernie that she was glad to have Sylvia stay. She knew that Bernie wasn't convinced, and later when Sylvia was being held in a big hug by her father, who looked very much like a big brown grizzly bear with his deep tan, brown facial hair and enormous size, Elaine took the opportunity to confide in Bernie that she thought it was good for Sylvia to be surrounded by the kids as they were somewhat of a distraction. Bernie just sniffed and looked put out.

Jack, who had left his daughter in Alex's care, came over to placate his wife and Elaine returned to where Gina, Kim and Dave were making tea and sandwiches. She went over to the fridge to take out an apple tart and while she was slicing it Gina asked her if the guards had anything to go on.

"I don't know. They said they'd be in touch. I hope they get the bastard who did this."

"How's Sylvia holding up?" Gina asked as she glanced over to where Alex was sitting on the couch with his arm around Sylvia.

"She's been very upset, as you can imagine. Considering they weren't that long together she had really fallen for him. She's devastated."

"I see Alex has wasted no time," Gina said with a raised eyebrow.

"I know; he wanted to come over last night and spend the night with her."

"What?!" Gina's jaw dropped in shock. "He can't possibly hope to take Rick's place, surely?"

"I don't exactly know what he's thinking. I just hope he doesn't allow himself to get too close or he could get burned yet again. He has to remember that she won't fall apart if he lets one of us console her instead of him. He was just starting to distance himself a little from her emotionally."

"I hope this doesn't make him go backwards in that regard."

"You and me both." Elaine looked over to see that Sylvia had fallen asleep on the couch with Alex's arms around her. "Maybe Alex was right; she might have had a better sleep if he had come over last night." She went over to Alex and suggested that he carry her up to the spare bedroom.

Sylvia's parents took their leave after their daughter was settled in bed. Bernie left strict instructions to ring her as soon as Sylvia woke. "No offence, Elaine, but what she needs right now is her mother."

"I think she needs to make that decision herself," Elaine said.

"Hmmpf," replied Bernie. "Besides, when Peter arrives from Cork he'll want to see her. I'm sure she'll want to see him too. So call us as soon as she wakes."

Gina and Kim left soon after that, telling Elaine that they'd be at home if Sylvia wanted them to call around later.

"Come on, Alex," Gina said.

"I think I'll stick around for a while. That is, if you don't mind," he said to Elaine and Dave.

"Alex, I know you're only trying to help, but you're not doing yourself any favors you know."

"I don't know what you're talking about," Alex insisted.

Elaine raised her eyebrow. "Don't you? The last thing either of you need is her turning to you in her grief."

"Look, I'm only trying to be a good friend to her, but I'll go if that's what you want. Tell her I'll call her later," Alex said, sounding a little annoyed.

"When she wakes I'll text you."

Later, when Sylvia woke up she went down to the kitchen. When Elaine informed her that Kim and Gina had said to ring them if she wanted their company, she just replied that she didn't want to speak to anyone.

"Alex wanted me to let him know when you woke up; he wants to call you." She paused and waited for Sylvia's response. When there was none she continued, "I'll text him that you don't want to talk to anyone right now. What about Peter?"

"Oh yeah, Mum said he was coming up from Cork today." Sylvia looked at her watch. "Will you text him for me? Tell him he can call over."

Elaine left the room, feeling relieved that Sylvia didn't want Alex's company; at least now she felt justified in telling him to give her space to grieve. She would have preferred to stay and comfort Sylvia, but she understood her need to be alone, even if it made Elaine feel helpless – and that was a feeling she hated. She closed the glass doors connecting the sitting room and dining room to give Sylvia the privacy and solace she needed. She sent a text to Alex to let him know that Sylvia just wanted some peace and quiet.

Alex rang regardless.

"I told you she just wants some time to be alone right now," Elaine told him when she answered the phone. "For both your sakes why don't you just back off a little?"

"Stop trying to make this something it's not; I'm not trying to replace Rick," Alex said.

"Glad to hear it."

"She needs her friends right now and last time I checked I was one of them."

"Yes, I'm not denying that, but right now she doesn't want to talk."

"Fine; let me know when she's talking," Alex said and hung up the phone.

Elaine texted Peter to see if he'd arrived yet and if he could call over to see Sylvia. She figured Sylvia probably did need family right now although she found her mum a bit much. She and Peter had always gotten along well and it would do her good to have him to talk to.

A little later Elaine knocked on the bedroom door to tell Sylvia that Peter was downstairs and she went down to see him. He greeted her at the bottom of the stairs with a big hug. He was a man of few words, but conveyed all he needed to convey, all Sylvia needed at that moment, with his hug. Sylvia cried in his arms and he patted her back and smoothed her hair. When she stopped crying she brought him into the kitchen and started to fill the kettle. He stayed for a while and when he left Sylvia retreated back to the solace of the bedroom.

As she got up from the couch to make herself some tea Elaine thought about the fact that Alex needed to back off and let Sylvia's other friends deal with her grief. She wished he had taken advantage, at least a little, of the fact that he was popular with the ladies. She had been witness to enough girls giving him the glad eye over the years to know that he could have any number of them if he could just cast his feelings for Sylvia aside. She couldn't help thinking about how Gina and Kim had been crazy about

Alex when they had all first met.

They were in their final year in school when Kim moved to Abbeyfield. She was one of the most beautiful girls in school. She was tall, a perfect size ten and was very interested in Alex, more so because she couldn't have him than anything else. No matter how much she batted her deep blue eyes at him, Alex just wasn't interested, even when Sylvia was dating someone else. Even when Kim was dating someone, and she had no shortage of boyfriends, her attentions were always directed at Alex and she was really annoyed that he could be so single-mindedly obsessed with Sylvia.

Gina was a pretty girl, quite petite at five foot nothing with a very slim figure and pixie like features. While she had been in school with Sylvia and Elaine all along, it was only when Kim struck up a friendship with her that she became one of the gang. She was in the same poetry group as Alex and wrote a lot about love. She, unlike Kim, was very quiet and kept her feelings to herself, only letting them out in her poetry. While it was very obvious who the object of Alex's love poetry was it was a closely kept secret who Gina was writing about. If guesses were hazarded at it a shutter would come down over her dark brown eyes as she withdrew into herself more, so after a while people grew tired of trying to find out.

It was only while in college that Gina admitted that it was Alex she had been infatuated with in school. The distance between them while she was in college in Dublin had made it possible for her to come clean. The others were all in college in Galway and while she saw them at weekends and holidays she had made a new life for herself with new friends.

Elaine wished now that Alex had moved on from Sylvia the way Kim and Gina had moved on from their infatuation of Alex, and thought of his reaction the day after Sylvia met Rick. He had rung her and read her the riot act.

He didn't even greet her with a hello, just started yelling at her about how Rick had cornered him in the canteen at lunch time and asked the meaning of the dirty looks he couldn't help throwing in the direction of

Sylvia's new man. He yelled about how he normally took it in his stride that Sylvia was with someone else, but found it impossible to deal with working alongside the new man in her life. He yelled about how humiliated he felt when Rick said that he knew all about him and Sylvia, that she had told him the whole story that morning.

"What the hell is your problem?" she responded.

"Well, for starters, why didn't you tell me that she was coming last night? What were you thinking bringing her anyway? You might have known that she'd get together with someone. Don't you think it's hard enough for me seeing her with someone else without having to work with him every day?"

That really maddened Elaine. She had been his confidante for so many years now. She had spent many tea breaks and lunch hours counseling and consoling him. Even after she left the bank he would often ring her with tales of woe over Sylvia. She would often put the phone on speaker as she went to make herself a cup of tea, knowing that she could be there for a while listening to how much he loved Sylvia and wished she felt the same way. Elaine would throw her eyes to heaven as she repeated the same advice she'd been giving him for years.

On nights out she was frequently a shoulder for Alex to cry on, metaphorically speaking. She'd have a vodka in her hand, be bouncing her knee up and down in time to the music, longing to get up and dance, but would spend the night talking to Alex about Sylvia instead. She had always tried to understand his feelings for Sylvia and always leant him a sympathetic ear, but she'd had enough of her advice falling on deaf ears. She really liked him and, although she was her best friend, she wasn't pleased with the way Sylvia treated him, but he needed to take control of the situation and stop being the victim.

"It's time you ended this infatuation; it's getting out of control. You can't say it's not taking over your whole life. Get help if that's what it takes. Sylvia will never be interested in anything long-term with you. Accept it and get over it. There's no point in holding it against Rick or I. It just isn't meant to be, so be grown up about it. It's time for you to move on. This is the last time I offer this advice. Either take it or I never want to discuss your love life with you again."

The next day Alex arrived over at Elaine's house and apologized to her. "I've been doing a lot of thinking and I know you're right; it's time to move on from Sylvia, but it's not going to be easy. She's been such a big part of my life for so long. It's going to take time, so can you be patient with me?"

Elaine gave him a hug and told him she'd help him through it.

Elaine knew that no matter what Alex said he would always love Sylvia, and she knew that adding Sylvia's grief to the equation was a recipe for disaster. Even throughout her relationship with Rick, Sylvia remained close to Alex, although her love for Rick had changed their relationship somewhat. Elaine had hoped Alex would've realized at this point that he was not the true love of Sylvia's life as he had previously imagined. However, he was still convinced that she was the woman he was going to marry; he just had to convince her of that. She thought of the pain Sylvia was facing now, how she hated seeing her like this. The previous day had been hard for her to witness; even when Sylvia was distracted with the children Elaine could tell that she was torn up inside with the agony of losing Rick.

She tried to put it all out of her mind as she started making lunch. Jody and Dillon would wake from their naps soon and would be hungry.

CHAPTER NINE

The Previous Day

It was with very red-rimmed eyes that Sylvia arrived down to the kitchen to find Sarah throwing a tantrum. She didn't want to go to school. Elaine took a moment out from trying to calm Sarah down to look at Sylvia, and noted the dark circles under her eyes from her restless night.

"Aunt Sylvia's here and I haven't seen her for the longest time, and it just isn't fair that Jody and Dillon get to stay home with her. IT'S JUST NOT FAIR!" This last statement was punctuated with much stamping of Sarah's feet.

Many rows, tantrums, promises, and bribes later, Dave managed to get Sarah into the car to bring her to school. He told her in a conspiratorial tone that he had to go in to work too and didn't think it was fair either, but at least they had each other.

With Sarah gone to school Elaine managed to get Jody and Dillon calmed down, dressed and settled in front of a DVD of The Wiggles. Elaine and Sylvia sat in the dining room where they could talk or cry in peace while still keeping an eye on the children through the open double doors between the two rooms.

"How are you feeling this morning?" Elaine asked.

"I can't believe this is happening. I feel like I'm in a soap opera. I mean, things like this don't happen in real life," Sylvia replied.

"I wish it were a soap; I wish it hadn't happened, I really do. I feel for you, Sylvia, and I'm here for you. You're to move in here for as long as you want. Not just while the guards are investigating your house, but also until you're okay to be alone again, you hear? The spare room is yours for as long as you want it."

"I don't want to be any trouble."

"Hey, no trouble at all. The girls will be delighted to have you around, and we can have some well deserved girlie nights when the kids go to bed. We'll send Dave off to bed too, or over to a friends', and we'll pamper ourselves, have girlie chats, junk food, chick flicks, face masks and make-up. Just like the old days."

Sylvia started crying. Elaine took her into her arms, rubbed her hair and crooned much like she would have comforted one of the children.

When the crying had subsided to sniffs and the odd sob Sylvia sat up and said, "I know you're only trying to cheer me up, but I can't look forward to girlie nights when I was going to spend the rest of my life with Rick."

She burst out crying again. This time Elaine left her to it and got up to make tea. When she returned with a cup of tea for each of them, Sylvia gave her a watery smile and said, "Tea mends all wounds, isn't that what your mother used to say?"

"Yeah, and Dave says 'tea kept the British army going during World War Two.'"

The two of them laughed over that.

"There, that's better now. Tea and laughter, the best medicines in the world – another motherism! You know how much he loved you; he wouldn't want you to be this upset."

"No, I know he wouldn't, but it's so hard to think about living without him. We had just bought the house and we had talked about the future. Everything was moving along so fast a proposal was on the cards, I'm sure of it, and now he's gone."

Elaine patted Sylvia on the leg and said, "Come on now, no more tears."

"I don't think I can cry any more. I've got a headache from crying so much; I need a glass of water."

Just then the doorbell rang. As Sylvia went to the kitchen to get a glass of water, Elaine went to answer the door. She recognized the detective standing there as Barbara Molloy, the one who had brought Sylvia to her door two days previously.

There was another detective with her, whom she introduced as Mick Naughton. He was a large man with a kind face. Detective Molloy asked to speak with Sylvia, and Elaine led them through to the dining room.

"Would you like a cup of tea?"

"No thanks. I'm fine," they said in unison.

Elaine retreated to the sitting room where the children were starting to get restless. No longer interested in The Wiggles, Jody was climbing on the couch and Dillon was crying and struggling to get out of his high chair. Elaine closed the connecting doors so that Sylvia and the detectives could have some privacy.

Sylvia took a seat at the kitchen table, opposite the detectives.

"How are you feeling today?" Detective Molloy asked.

"Numb. I can't cry any more, and right now I can't feel anything or even believe that this has happened. I feel that at any moment I might wake up and find that this was all a nightmare and that Rick is right beside me."

Detective Molloy reached over and put her hand over Sylvia's. "You will get through this. It will take time but you will come to terms with it. Now, I have to ask you some questions about your relationship with Rick, who his friends were and any circumstances leading up to his death that might be important to the investigation.

"The house has been dusted for fingerprints and there have been quite a number of them found. At some point we'll need you down at the station so that we can identify and eliminate your prints. We need to know who else would have cause to have their prints in your house and on your kitchen knife."

Detective Naughton sat in silence, taking notes, as his partner spoke to Sylvia.

"We had a dinner party on Friday night. Elaine and Dave were there, my friends, Alex, Gina and Kim, and Rick's friends, Julie, Maeve and Noel. I had help in the kitchen from them and the knife hadn't been washed," Sylvia said.

Detective Naughton asked for surnames and addresses and jotted them down in his notebook.

"We need all of them to come down to the station for fingerprints and questioning." At Sylvia's look of surprise Detective Molloy continued, "At the moment it's just a formality as we have to identify their prints and eliminate them. Also, we need to determine if they know anything that may help our investigation."

Detective Molloy informed her that although it was early in the investigation it was beginning to look like a professional killing. She told her that there were no signs of a struggle, indicating that Rick was taken by surprise, and there was only one stab wound directly to the heart, indicating that whoever it was knew what they were doing. She thought that perhaps it was an attempted burglary and he had been sleeping on the armchair when the assailant broke in, but there were no signs of a forced entry. She said that they would learn more when the pathology results came in. They would also be questioning neighbors to see if they saw or heard anything that may be relevant.

Sylvia thought that it didn't seem very likely that anyone had seen anything suspicious as her closest neighbors were about a half-mile away. They hadn't been thinking about the possibility of crime when they had rented and subsequently bought the house in what they thought to be a nice, peaceful, countryside area. Who would have thought that someone would travel the narrow, winding roads that led to their house, with murder on their minds?

"Now, I have to ask the nature of your relationship to Rick, how long did you know him? Are you aware of anyone who may have fallen out with him or want to cause him harm?" Detective Molloy had asked the same questions of Sylvia on Saturday evening but had received no coherent answers.

Sylvia took a deep breath to compose herself before answering. "We started seeing each other a few months ago. It might not seem like long, but it was long enough to know we loved each other and wanted to spend the rest of our lives together. We had just bought the house one month ago. I don't know of anybody who'd want to hurt him. I realize there was probably a lot we didn't know about each other, but I thought we had the rest of our lives to find out. Perhaps Noel can be of more help to you than I can. They'd been friends since primary school. Sorry I couldn't be more help."

"Thanks, you've been a great help. If you think of anything else that might help please don't hesitate to call the station. Whenever you're ready to come down to the station to let us take your fingerprints it would be great. There may be more questions we'd like to ask you at a later stage. Now, would it be possible for us to have a word with Elaine?"

"Yes of course, I'll just get her."

Sylvia went in to the sitting room to take over looking after the kids. With Jody and Dillon climbing all over her she managed to convey to Elaine that the detectives wished to see her.

When Elaine had taken a seat Detective Molloy said to her, "I understand that you and your husband were at Sylvia's house on Friday night with a number of their friends."

"Yes that's correct."

"I need you and Sylvia and all of the others who were there that night to come down to the station for questioning and to have your fingerprints taken. We need to identify the fingerprints that have cause to be at the crime-scene. I would like it if you and Sylvia could come in as soon as possible. I understand she's in a fragile state right now, but the sooner we get this investigation underway the better."

"I understand, Detective Molloy. I'll talk to her about it and ring you to let you know when we'll be in."

"Thank you; and we'll let ourselves out. Meanwhile we'll call the others in. Take care of Sylvia."

"I will."

After the detectives left, Elaine went into the sitting room to find Sylvia playing with Jody and Dillon. She realized that Sylvia was trying to keep herself occupied to stop herself from feeling depressed. Another motherism came to mind at the sight of Jody jumping around doing the flap-flaps in a state of excitement because Sylvia was going to read her a story – children are the best tonic in the world. A small smile touched her lips as she watched Jody and Dillon snuggle up on the couch together with

Sylvia reading animatedly. She crept out of the sitting room, not wanting to disturb the temporary contentment that Sylvia must be feeling at that moment.

When Elaine next went into the sitting room to put the children down for their nap she found the three of them asleep together on the couch. As she fetched a blanket that would cover all three of them she hoped that Sylvia would sleep for the duration of the children's naps.

A while later Sylvia, Jody and Dillon arrived into the dining room where Elaine was putting some lunch out on the table. As they ate soup and Elaine's own home-made brown bread, fresh from the oven, Sylvia said, "Wow, this is delicious. You have been busy."

"The only time I get a chance to bake is while they're asleep. At the weekends Sarah likes to help. She always wants to make chocolate muffins or something sweet like that so during the week is when I do the healthy baking."

"Pity; some chocolate muffins would go down nicely after this," Sylvia said. "I'd like to take Dillon and Jody with me for a walk to the school to pick Sarah up. On the way back maybe we'll stop into the shop for a treat."

"That'll make her day." Elaine smiled, knowing that it was helping her to feel useful as well as keeping the children happy because they adored Sylvia.

After lunch Sylvia put hats and coats on the two children. She put Dillon in his buggy, wrapped him in a blanket and set off with Jody skipping along beside her, chattering away. As they were waiting for Sarah to get out of class Jody started playing with Dillon and Sylvia found herself thinking that she may never get the chance to pick her own children up from school. She couldn't imagine herself ever loving anyone again or having children with anyone else. She snapped out of her melancholy as the classroom door opened and the hall was filled with children talking and laughing, running to their waiting parents or child minders.

When Sarah saw Sylvia she ran to her with a big smile. "I knew you'd pick me up, I just knew you would. Well I didn't think so at first. I was really mad all day at school. I really hated it, and then I thought about going home and I knew you'd be here to pick me up."

Sylvia laughed and picked Sarah up in a big hug. Sarah chattered and jumped up and down intermittently, as she skipped along with Jody beside Sylvia. The children were delighted with the detour to the shop. When they arrived home Elaine greeted them at the front door, laughing as she got covered in chocolate when her children hugged her.

When Dave came home from work Sylvia and the children were chatting and playing in the sitting room and didn't even notice his arrival, although the children would normally come running at him and start climbing all over him the moment he stepped inside the front door.

He went in to the kitchen with a puzzled look on his face and said to Elaine, "I was expecting no dinner to be made because you'd been busy with the kids all day as well as being a shoulder to cry on."

"The children have been a wonderful tonic. It's later when they're in bed that she'll need us," Elaine said.

Dave looked at the ground as he said, "You're better at that stuff, love. I was thinking I'd go to the pub and leave you girls to it."

"Dave, there's plenty of nights we'll want you to do that, but I think tonight she might need your support too. Besides, I'm no better at 'that stuff', as you so eloquently put it, than you are."

"I'm really rubbish at it, though, and I hate it. I mean I don't know what to say to her."

"Everybody hates it, Dave. It's not so important what you say to her as that you're there to support her. Now go and tell Sylvia and the children that dinner's ready."

He went out into the hall and called, "Dinner's ready, guys." The children raced to the kitchen, starving after spending the afternoon with Sylvia.

Dinner was a very noisy affair, each of the children vying with the other for attention. Sarah wanted to tell her father all about her day at school and the fun she'd had with Sylvia, while Dillon was banging his spoon on his high chair and Jody was doing her best to be heard over the din as she told about her day.

After dinner Dave put the children to bed, but they wanted Sylvia to read them a story. When she returned to the sitting room Dave got up and offered to make tea.

"Do you want to talk, hon?" Elaine asked, putting her hand on Sylvia's knee.

"Yes and no. I've got so many thoughts racing around in my head I feel like I'm going to go crazy, but I don't know that I can say what's going through my mind. I mean, I can't formulate it into much sense and I'm afraid to do any more talking about it because I want to forget about it for now, and I definitely don't want to cry anymore."

"I understand, but if you bottle it up you'll end up feeling worse. Maybe talking about it will help you to make sense of what's going on in your head. Is it tea you want, or would something stronger help?"

"Again – dilemma. I really want to get roaring drunk, but I'm afraid I'll fall apart. At least tea's safe."

"Well, why don't we start with a cup of tea and move on from there?"

"Sounds good to me. Anyway, if we decided to give the tea a miss Dave wouldn't be too happy after him making it."

"What was that?" asked Dave, walking into the room and hearing his name being mentioned.

"Just saying how nice it was of you to make tea for us," Sylvia replied.

They made small talk over the tea and then Elaine asked Dave to get the vodka out. In her state of grief the vodka soon hit the spot with Sylvia. She was reminiscing about her relationship with Rick, about how wonderful he was. She laughed as she retold his jokes, relived the good times they'd had together. A few more vodkas and reminiscing turned to tears, sorrow for what she had lost.

"He was my one true love. I'll never love again; I know I won't. How can I go on without him?"

"You will go on; you're a strong girl with your whole life ahead of you. Rick would want to see you making the most of your life without him. If there's a heaven you want him to be happy there don't you? And he can only be happy there if he sees you getting on with your life the best way you can. That's the way love works," Dave said.

Sylvia shrugged.

"Give it time, sweetheart. It's not going to be all right straight away, but you'll be okay eventually. Dave's right you know; part of what Rick loved about you was your strength of character. I'm sure he'll understand you falling apart for now, but I'm sure he's in heaven right now rooting for you to pick up the pieces and get on with your life."

"Thank you, both of you." Sylvia gave their hands a squeeze. "You should really be getting off to bed; I've kept you up long enough." As Elaine was about to object she said, "Stop worrying about me. I'll be okay. I reckon I'll sleep like a baby tonight I'm that tired." And she did, like an unsettled baby.

Her sleep was filled with dreams of Rick, with memories of their life together. Her subconscious created new memories, memories they hadn't had time to create themselves. She dreamed that they were older, married and had two children, a boy and a girl. Both children looked just like their father as they came running out of their classroom into Sylvia's waiting arms. When she woke from this dream she cried herself back to sleep, cried not only for having lost Rick, but for the children they would never have.

CHAPTER TEN

Tuesday the 16th of September

Elaine opened the door and when she saw the looks on the faces before her she knew that the questioning hadn't gone well. She thought that it must have been an emotional roller coaster, but was shaken to discover what happened; the last thing she expected was for one of her friends to be suspected of murder. She wondered if the week could possibly get any worse.

"I just can't believe your friends are being accused of Rick's murder. I thought us being questioned was just a formality. I didn't know how much help we could possibly be, but I figured the detectives knew what they were doing. This is ridiculous! Maybe we can talk to their superior." Elaine took Sylvia's hand. "Honey, this must be dreadful for you; it's been tough enough as it is." She gave Sylvia's hand a squeeze.

Sylvia took her hand back and said, "It gives me something to focus on, supporting my friends instead of them supporting me. I hope you have an alibi. You know, it's just occurred to me, I don't have an alibi as such. I was out shopping but I don't know if I can prove it; it depends on what time my purchases were made. I hadn't even thought of the possibility that I would be considered a suspect, but now I'm thinking that it's likely."

"Well now, that's just plain daft. I'd vouch for you there. In all the years I've known you, you've never been so in love; that speaks for itself. As for me, with my kids and Dave you'd think I'd surely have an alibi. On any other Saturday I would have, but Dave took the kids off into Galway;

they went to the Aquarium, then to Supermacs and then shopping. I had a wonderfully blissful and unusual me day. If I had gone to the spa or hairdresser I would have an alibi. However, I just had a long hot soak and gave myself a facial, manicure and pedicure, and settled down in front of a movie. So I guess we're all in it together." She sighed at the thought of spending a blissful day in a spa, relaxing in a state of slumber while having a massage, or feeling like Cleopatra as she soaked in a milk bath. She wondered if she'd ever again have that luxury, not that it was something she had done often before she had the children.

"Kim has an alibi. Luckily for her she was having a passionate day with Gina; they were in bed all day, if you can believe that," Sylvia said.

"You're all just jealous; men can't provide you with that kind of passion. It's a pity the rest of you don't have an alibi, but the detectives surely have to realize that their line of enquiry is totally way off," Kim said.

"I wouldn't bank on that," Alex said.

"Well I think it might be wise to bring my solicitor when I go in for questioning," Elaine said.

"I wouldn't be so sure; look where that got me. The others weren't seen as suspects and it's quite possible I wasn't either until I involved a solicitor, even though they were basing a lot on my feelings for Sylvia." Alex said, running his hand through his hair.

"I think I'd rather take my chances with a solicitor in my corner; it could go worse without one."

"I think that might be wise; Detective Molloy asked me if you would have any cause to be jealous of my relationship with Rick, if you were happily married. She's clutching at straws, but I don't think it would hurt to have a solicitor with you," Sylvia said.

"Well that settles it then. I'll get on the phone right away."

Elaine made arrangements for her and Dave to meet up at the Garda station with their solicitor, Joanna McDonagh that afternoon. Sylvia said that she'd watch the kids. Alex asked if Sylvia would like some company but she declined, wishing to have the children to herself for the afternoon so that she could forget all about her troubles while she looked after them.

She wasn't thinking about the fact that Alex would probably also like to have his mind occupied so that he wouldn't have to think about being a murder suspect. He could immerse himself instead in the games Jody, Dillon and Sarah would play, enjoy spending time with Sylvia.

Just as they had the afternoon organized Peter rang and asked if he could meet Sylvia for lunch. He arrived to pick her up just as the others were leaving and she promised she'd be back in time to let Elaine meet Dave at the station.

She filled Peter in on the morning and he couldn't believe what he was hearing. He had always thought Alex was a bit strange, could never understand his unwillingness to date anyone else when it was obvious Sylvia didn't feel the same way about him that he felt about her. No matter what he thought of Alex though, one thing he was sure of was that Alex wouldn't harm anyone.

When Sylvia arrived back at Elaine's she was glad she had met with Peter for lunch. She felt a lot better about things now that she'd talked them over with him. He'd assured her that once the detectives got something else to go on other than misconstruing Alex's feelings they'd end this line of enquiry.

She knew Peter couldn't know that for certain, but just hearing it made her feel better. She reflected that as usual Peter knew just what to say. Sometimes it was infuriating being his sister as she felt that compared to him she always said and did the wrong thing. At times like this though she felt very lucky to have him as a brother.

She was able to enjoy spending the afternoon with the children that little bit more after having her worries about Alex allayed somewhat by Peter.

CHAPTER ELEVEN

Dave was asked in for questioning first. As he and Joanna took their seats, Detective Molloy informed him that the interview would be recorded, stated the date, time and people present.

"How long have you known Sylvia?" she asked.

"Since Elaine and I started dating. They were always joined at the hip," Dave replied.

"Has there ever been more than just friendship between you and Sylvia?"

"I strongly advise against answering that question," Joanna said.

Detective Molloy sighed, a sigh of sheer annoyance. She hated solicitors; this particular one even more so with her smarmy self-righteousness. She looked so prim and proper and aloof and as though she hated the detective every bit as much as Molloy disliked her. Detective Molloy knew she was being petty, but the underlying reason for her dislike was that solicitors always got in the way. Joanna's presence meant that she would also have to get a warrant for Dave and Elaine's prints. Her flawless looks just made matters worse. "Were you at the house of the deceased on the night preceding the murder?"

"Yes I was." Dave put one hand on the edge of the table and lightly tapped his fingers.

"To your knowledge was there any strain on relationships that night?"

"No, we all got on mighty; there were no arguments and no lulls in conversation. It was a great night."

"How did you get on with Rick?" Detective Molloy asked.

"We got on great. Because Elaine and Sylvia spend a lot of time together it was important to them that I got on well with Rick, and it never posed a problem; he was a great guy. You couldn't help but like him and you'd be hard pressed to find a nicer guy."

"Were you aware of anyone who didn't like him?"

"No; in fact I find it hard to imagine that there could be anyone who wouldn't have liked him."

"Not even an ex boyfriend of Sylvia's, perhaps?"

Dave paused to consider this, looking over at Detective Naughton, who was writing in his notebook. "Of course I couldn't say for sure, but not to my knowledge. Sylvia tended to end relationships before they got serious so I couldn't imagine any of her exes having gotten so close as to be jealous of her relationship with Rick."

"What about Alex? He may not have been concerned for a long time with her short-term relationships, but he may have become quite irate when things got serious between Sylvia and Rick." Detective Molloy said.

"Sure Alex and Rick worked together; they were friends before Rick and Sylvia even started dating. We talked about this shortly after Rick started seeing Sylvia. He said that if she was going to get serious about someone else he was glad it was Rick and not some of the other losers she's been seeing in the past."

"You and Alex are fairly close then?"

"Yeah, I guess you could say that. He's closer to Sylvia of course and to Elaine, but we've always gotten on well. As a whole we're a pretty close bunch of friends."

"As you and Alex were the mainstay men in the group, I guess that meant that you and he spent time together away from the women on occasion, being a little over crowded with estrogen?"

"We went down to the pub sometimes; that's where we were when we spoke about how he felt about Sylvia and Rick."

"Do you think he's still in love with her?"

Again Dave paused to consider. "It's hard to say really. I think he wants to get over her, but he's finding it difficult. I think he'll always be close to her, and he'll always have feelings for her, but he's been trying his best not to let his feelings get in the way of her finding happiness with someone else."

"Had you ever discussed his feelings for her prior to that time?"

"Yes. From time to time the subject came up. I felt sorry for the guy; it's not nice to be in love with someone who doesn't feel the same way, but he never felt bitter about it. Resigned and hopeful, I suppose, is the best way to put it."

"Did you ever speak to Sylvia about his feelings for her?"

"Yes, once. She was very dismissive about it; I don't think she's ever realized the depth of his feelings for her."

"Why would you think that?"

"She said, 'Love, what is that anyway?' She laughed and said, 'I hope you know what it is since you're married, but Alex doesn't know what love is, and I certainly don't. He just thinks he's in love with me, and it seems he will think that until he actually falls in love. Maybe you know someone you could set him up with.' Then she changed the subject." Dave sat up straight in his chair and moved his hands to rest on his legs.

"Did she take any of her relationships seriously before her relationship with Rick?" Detective Molloy asked.

"Not until Jerry, the last guy she went out with before Rick. She thought she was in love with him, until she met Rick; then she knew that what she had felt for him wasn't love. I suppose she thinks the way she felt about Jerry is the same as the way Alex feels about her."

"What do you think? Is it the real thing Alex feels for Sylvia?"

"Yes I think so, but, like I said, he's trying to move on. I think that even with Rick being dead there's no possibility of any real future between them. I think he realizes that, and I believe he will find someone else he feels as strongly for as he does for Sylvia; it's just a matter of time."

"Did you ever take Sylvia's advice and try to set him up with someone else?"

"No, there was no point; he wasn't interested."

"What about since Rick and Sylvia got so serious?"

"No, he needs time to get over Sylvia. When the time is right the right woman will come along for him. I don't think it's something I should interfere with, and I know he wouldn't appreciate the interference."

"Did he ever tell you what it is that he loves so much about Sylvia?"

"It's the same thing every hot blooded male loves about her; I mean she's a knockout. She's always been very flighty though so I wouldn't have imagined anyone having a serious relationship with her before Rick came along. Love changed her. I think it's partially her unattainability that makes her so attractive to the opposite sex; I mean we always want what we can't have, and I think perhaps it's the idea of loving Sylvia more than actually loving her that Alex is suffering from."

Hmm, Detective Molloy thought. It sounds like he's had a case of the hots for the lovely Sylvia himself. She asked, "Has Sylvia ever dated or been interested in a married man?"

"No; for Sylvia being interested in someone and dating them was one and the same. If she was interested in a guy she went after him and got him, but even though she didn't believe in love she had very strong feelings about the commitment of marriage."

"So there were no wives out for revenge then."

"No; if a married man ever came on to her she was quick to put him in his place."

"I'd say she leaves a guy reeling when she wants to," the detective said.

"That's for sure; it takes a man some time to recover from that. She doesn't pull any punches; if she wants you she lets you know and if she doesn't she lets you know, and woe betide the man who makes an unwanted advance."

"Sounds like you've been at the receiving end of her refusal."

At the same time as Dave admitted, "Well, yes," Joanna objected, "Don't answer that." However, it was too late; Detective Molloy had the information she wanted.

"Thank you, Dave; you've been very helpful."

Detective Molloy watched as Dave left the room, his solicitor shaking her head as he had just provided his wife with a motive for Rick's murder.

CHAPTER TWELVE

"How would you describe your friendship with Sylvia?" Detective Molloy asked Elaine when she was seated in front of her.

"We've been friends since we were kids. We've always gotten on great. We've had our arguments, as all friends do, but nothing serious. We're very different people, like chalk and cheese really, and we don't always agree with one another's life choices, but over all we're best friends."

"Would one of those disagreements have to do with you marrying Dave?"

"No, she knew how in love I was with Dave and just said it wouldn't be for her; she enjoyed being free and single."

"What about her behavior towards Alex?"

Elaine sat up straight in her chair before replying and then she said, "Alex is one of my dearest friends. I've always felt bad for him that, of all people, he had to fall in love with the unattainable Sylvia. Sylvia and I have had some disagreements about the fact that she continually plays with his emotions, but she sees things differently; she thinks that it's up to Alex to get over her. She chooses not to believe that his feelings have run as deep as they did.

"I use the past tense about his feelings because he has moved on. I've been his confidante in matters of the heart since we were sixteen and we've had many discussions about Sylvia. The latest have been since she and Rick got together; he was very upset about the whole thing. I told him that it was time to get over her. He didn't agree at first, but after a while he said I was right and he'd do his best. A few weeks later I noticed a change in his attitude towards Sylvia. He still has strong feelings for her, but he's no longer in love with her.

"I never agreed with the way Sylvia treated him, but I never held it against her; it wasn't my place. Alex never stood up to her and put a stop to their brief flings. I could see her point that he could have laid it on the line, told her that he wasn't going to put up with brief interludes with her between other relationships. He could have, and indeed should have, but he felt that however brief their flings were they were better than nothing. I'm happy for him that he's gotten over that."

Interesting, thought Detective Molloy. Even husband and wife can't agree on how Alex took it when Sylvia and Rick got together and whether or not Alex has moved on. Trying to and succeeding are two very different things and could well be the difference between committing murder and not. "Did he ever tell you what it was about Sylvia that he loved?"

"He loved absolutely everything about her, warts and all. He was her friend as well as her lover so he knew her intimately. He knew how flighty she was and how cruel she could be, but he was very forgiving, too forgiving. He felt that it wasn't her fault, that eventually she would calm down and fall in love, and when that happened it would be with him.

"He's a romantic; whoever falls in love with him and has her feelings returned will be a very lucky woman. Much as I love her, Sylvia doesn't deserve Alex. Don't get me wrong, I was delighted for her to be with Rick, and because he was right for her she treated him right and did deserve him and to be happy." Elaine relaxed her shoulders and moved her hands to rest lightly on the table.

"How did Rick feel about the past that existed between Alex and Sylvia?"

"He was fine about it; his attitude was that they were both adults with pasts but the important thing was how they felt about each other."

"Did he object to the fact that Alex was still in her life?"

"No, but of course he stipulated that if they ever had a fight she wasn't to go running to him. He wasn't going to accept her sleeping with Alex, or anyone else, just because she might have thought their relationship was over as they'd just had a big fight. He needn't have worried about that; falling in love changed Sylvia."

"So he got on well with Alex?"

"They had been friends from work and that didn't change."

"You used to work at the bank with them, is that correct?"

"Yes; that was a few years ago now."

"Are you aware of anyone who held a grudge against Rick from work?"

"No; back then he was very popular and I believe he still is…. I mean was," Elaine said as she looked down, realizing her mistake in talking about Rick in the present as if he were still alive.

"Were you ever jealous of how men flocked to Sylvia, how she could have her pick?"

"I never had any reason to be jealous; it wasn't my style. I just wanted to meet the one, and I did."

"How would you feel if you discovered that there had been something going on between your husband and Sylvia?"

"Don't answer that," Joanna objected.

"It's okay, I'll answer this one. I'd feel the same way most women would, like killing my husband. Of course I wouldn't actually kill him, and anyway I know that Sylvia wouldn't sleep with Dave, or even kiss him. She has strong values about marriage, and always had even before falling in love."

Interesting, the detective thought. She trusts her flighty friend more than she trusts her husband. "How would she have felt if she found out Rick was having an affair? Like killing him, the way most women would?"

Elaine sat up straight again and said, "Of course she wouldn't have killed him. They weren't married; I'm sure she would just have kicked him out."

"Where were you Saturday afternoon?"

"I was at home alone; my husband had taken the kids out for the day so I could have time to myself."

"Thank you, Elaine. If we have any further questions we'll call you."

Joanna stood up, picked up her briefcase, and signaled to Elaine to walk out ahead of her.

As Joanna walked towards her car she told Dave and Elaine to call her if they had any further need of her assistance.

On the way home Elaine and Dave discussed their separate experiences.

Elaine said, "That didn't go too bad. The emphasis was mainly on Alex and Sylvia. Poor Alex; as if it wasn't bad enough that he's spent the last ten years in love with Sylvia, when he finally starts to get over her he becomes a murder suspect. Detective Molloy asked if Sylvia killed Rick because he might have been having an affair."

Dave looked over at his wife and asked, "Was he?"

"I very much doubt it. Anyway I told Detective Molloy that Sylvia would just have thrown him out if he was; that she wouldn't have killed him. I think she was trying to suss out if there were any reasons I might be jealous of Sylvia. Huh! As if I could be jealous of her lifestyle when I've got it all." She turned to Dave and put a hand on his leg as she said, "I have you and three wonderful children. How could I be jealous of her? I'd hate to have had to wait so long to find love. However, it was suggested that there was some reason I should be jealous of her, even want to cause her pain, something to do with you having a romantic interest in Sylvia?" Elaine said.

"Don't be daft; as if I'd ever be interested in Sylvia. That detective, she's a stirrer. She was just probably trying to get a reaction out of you, that's all. What did she say to you?"

"She suggested that you and Sylvia had something going on between you; those were her exact words." Elaine looked across at her husband to try to read the expression on his face. What she saw concerned her; it looked as if he was hiding something. "I want the truth, Dave. If what she said was true we can deal with it, but I don't want lies."

"I'm not lying to you. She asked me what Alex loved so much about Sylvia and she obviously misunderstood my answer. When I talked about how attractive Sylvia was she must have thought I was interested in her for myself; either that or she was just stirring shit to see if she could pin a motive on you. I mean, look what she said about Rick having an affair. She probably figures if she throws enough shit some of it is bound to stick."

Then why does he look so uncomfortable? Elaine thought. "I don't want to trouble Sylvia with this; she has enough on her plate, but I want the truth and I will ask her if I have to," she said.

"Can this wait until we get home? I need to concentrate on driving." Dave turned on the wipers as large drops of rain started to splatter the windscreen.

Which means it's true, Elaine thought with tears in her eyes. "No, I don't want to do this in front of the children," she said.

They drove in silence for a while; the only sounds were the purring of the engine, the whooshing of the wipers and the splashing of the rain against the windows.

Silent tears trickled down Elaine's face as she thought about the possibility that her perfect life might just be about to come crumbling down around her.

Dave pulled up in front of a pub and said, "Let's go in for a drink; I know I need one."

They got out of the car and walked into the pub side by side but in an uncomfortable silence. Elaine found them a seat in a dark corner of the pub where they would have some privacy while Dave went up to the bar to order the drinks, a gin and tonic for Elaine and a whiskey for himself. It was a nice pub, the type of place they could have enjoyed a relaxing lunch in, with its comfortable booths and relaxing décor. However, neither of them was in the mood to appreciate that at this time.

"Well, let's have it," Elaine said when Dave arrived with the drinks, a touch of coldness to her voice.

Dave put his head in his hands and took a deep breath. Looking up hesitantly at Elaine he began, "Look, it was a long time ago and I never meant to hurt you." Tears trickled down Elaine's face as he said, "Nothing happened, I swear to you. Please don't cry. I suggested to Sylvia that we go upstairs and even before the words came out of my mouth I regretted them. I don't know where it came from, I swear. Things have never been the same between me and her since and I swear I never regretted anything so much in my entire life. I never wanted you to find out because I love you and I would never betray you; please believe me."

"But you did betray me," Elaine said, her voice barely above a whisper. "You may not have slept with her, but only because she wouldn't do that to me, and as for not wanting me to find out, I would have sooner or later. You should have been upfront about it from the beginning. I'm surprised Sylvia never told me, but it was up to you to remain faithful to me, Dave, and to be honest with me. I really never thought this could happen to us. I did think Detective Molloy was only fishing for information; I wasn't being serious at first when I asked you about it, but when I saw your reaction I knew it was true." She put her head in her hands as she said, "I can't believe this is happening to us."

Dave reached out to take Elaine's hand, but she pulled away. "Don't touch me," she said, her face crumpling up, as she could no longer stem the outpouring of tears. Not wanting to cause a scene in public, she stood up, grabbing the car keys as she did so, and left the pub.

She got into the driver's side of the car and drove off, not caring that Dave was standing out in the rain watching her drive away. Let him be stranded, Elaine thought. He has money; he can either get a cab or get roaring drunk, I don't care. She drove to the beach where she broke down crying. She let it all out, all the hurt and the feelings of betrayal.

When she could cry no more she just sat there for a while looking out at the wild waves crashing against the rocks and felt that it was similar to the way her marriage was crashing around her right now. She got out of the car and walked along the shore, letting the rain calm and soothe her before driving home.

CHAPTER THIRTEEN

Sylvia greeted Elaine at the door. "How did it …?" The words died on her lips as she saw her friend's face and took in how drenched she was. "You've been crying, Elaine, what's wrong? You're saturated, and where's Dave?"

"Where are the kids?" Elaine asked.

"Watching T.V. Come on into the kitchen and I'll make us some tea and get you some towels, and then you can tell me all about it."

A few minutes later she joined Elaine in the dining room. "Now, tell me what's wrong."

Elaine took a shaky breath and said, "I know what happened with you and Dave."

Sylvia's eyes opened wide and her hand flew to her mouth. That's not what I was expecting, she thought. "Oh," was all she could think of to say.

Sylvia sat down at the table and folded her hands together. She said, "How did you find out?"

Elaine sat down as she raised her eyebrows. "Why did you never tell me? I thought we were friends; did you not think I should know something like that about my husband?"

"I'm sorry, Elaine, but since nothing really happened I thought it best not to say anything. If I had thought that he'd do the dirt with someone else instead I would have told you, but I could see how much he regretted it and felt that he was unlikely to ever try it on with someone again. So I thought the less said, soonest mended. I never thought you'd find out."

"Well you thought wrong, didn't you?"

"You mean he's actually cheated on you. When?"

"No, at least not that I know of. What I mean is that you were wrong about me not finding out, and if he could stoop so low as to try to sleep with my friend then he could sure as hell sleep with someone else."

"Look, I doubt it; Dave loves you. It was a mistake, him coming on to me that day. And I doubt that he'd have gone through with it anyway even if I'd been willing. He begged me not to tell you and I made him sweat it a bit before I told him that if I ever found out he'd so much as looked at another woman I'd tell you the whole story. Every time we've gotten drunk together he's had a panic attack about whether or not I'd tell you. I think that was punishment enough for him, and I think the fear of you finding out has kept him on the straight and narrow. Forgive me?" Sylvia reached out her hand, hoping Elaine would take it. She did.

"It's not you I'm annoyed with; you were in an impossible situation, but you should still have told me. If things were reversed don't you think I'd have told you that you had a lying, cheating rat of a husband? I just can't believe he'd do that to me."

Sylvia knew Elaine would have told her if Rick or any of her other boyfriends had ever come on to her. It was something her conscience had wrestled with many times. "So how did you find out?" she asked, rather than trying to justify herself to Elaine.

"In the interview, Detective Molloy seemed to gather by his reaction to a question that something had happened between you two. He's never been confronted with it before and the guilt on his face gave him away. She suggested to me that there was something going on between you two. I didn't believe her, but when I asked him about it, even when he was denying it, I knew it was true."

"So where is he now?"

"We went to a pub to talk about it and I ran out and left him there."

"Are you going to forgive him?"

"I don't know. I love him and I'm hurting like hell right now. If that's all it was and he's never betrayed me since I'll get over it, but how do I really know that he hasn't cheated on me since? It's a betrayal of trust. We need to talk about this and I need time to think about it. He'll probably come home plastered so it'll be tomorrow before I have to face him again."

A moment later Elaine realized she was wrong as she heard the key in the door. She took a deep breath and wondered how she was going to deal with this.

"I'll keep the kids occupied and leave you to it," Sylvia said, getting up and going into the sitting room to the children.

Dave walked into the kitchen and held out a bunch of flowers to Elaine. "I know right now that you must hate me; I hate myself too. If you never want to see me again I'll understand." He took a shaky breath and Elaine saw that he was fighting back tears. "I want us to get through this; if my stupidity ends our marriage I'll never forgive myself." He sat down beside her and took her hand, and this time she didn't pull away. "I know I messed up royally and I swear to you I'll do whatever it is you want me to do to make it up to you. I know I don't deserve your forgiveness, and I know I don't deserve you, but please let me try to make it up to you. I love you and I don't want to be without you, and I certainly don't want anyone else."

More than anything else it was Dave's tears that moved Elaine; in all their years together she had never seen him cry. However, she needed some time by herself so that she could think, as she was really hurting. She pulled her hand from his, took the flowers and put them in a vase.

While arranging the flowers she said, "I need some time by myself right now. This really hurts, Dave; I thought we had something special, something nobody could touch. I need time to process this and adjust to it and we'll see then where we'll go from there." She turned to face Dave, tears in her eyes. Seeing the tears streaming down his face she had to fight off the urge to run to him, pull him into her arms and tell him everything was going to be okay. Instead she asked him when it had happened, why he did it and what exactly had happened.

Dave took a deep breath before launching into the story. "You were pregnant with Sarah at the time and we were having a lot of rows and no sex. I know that's no excuse, but one day Sylvia called over when you were out and I was talking to her about how Alex felt about her. Then I just found myself putting my hand on her leg and suggesting we go upstairs. I don't know what I was thinking, it just happened."

Elaine's jaw was set as she fought her emotions. "What was Sylvia's response?" she asked.

"Need you ask?" Dave replied. "She took my hand off her thigh and said that if I valued my manhood I'd better never touch her again. I was surprised she didn't hit me. I begged her not to tell you and she said she didn't know if she could keep something like that from you. A few days later she said she had decided for your sake not to tell you but that if she ever caught me so much as looking at another woman she'd tell you everything." Dave looked over at Elaine. He walked over to her, took her hand and squeezed it. "I really am sorry about all of this; I swear to you I've never looked at another woman since and I never will. I don't even know what possessed me at the time. Sylvia's not my type; I never had designs on her before then or on any other woman since I've met you. Whatever it was that possessed me that day vanished pretty quickly."

"How can I be sure that you haven't been sleeping with other women this whole time we've been married? If you could try it on with my best friend you could sure as hell sleep with other women. I thought I could trust you, Dave. I feel as if we've been living a lie this whole time. How could you? Just how could you?" Elaine went over to sit at the table and put her head down in her arms, crying.

Dave moved over beside her and put his arms around her. Elaine felt his tears mingling with her own as he lifted her head and brushed his lips against her cheek. She pushed him away from her and said, "Go away, Dave. I can't do this now. I need to be alone."

Dave's voice caught as he said, "I'll stay with Alex until you're ready to talk about this." When she didn't respond he grabbed the car keys and said, "I'll be back to pick Sarah up for school in the morning."

Elaine could hear him upstairs pulling open drawers as he packed a bag.

In the car Dave dried his eyes and called Alex, asking if he could stay with him for a couple of days.

"What's wrong, Dave?" Alex asked.

"We'll talk when I get there. I just need to know if I can stay or should

I go to a hotel?"

"Of course you can stay; I wouldn't hear of you going to a hotel."

"Thanks." Dave hung up and drove to Alex's. He couldn't stop fresh tears from coming to his eyes every time he thought of how his marriage might be over, and all because of his own stupidity.

As he stood at Alex's door, Dave knew that Alex would be able to see that he had been crying, although he had done his best to pull himself together in the car on the way over. When Alex opened the door, he stood back to allow Dave entry into the apartment.

As Dave took a seat in the brown leather armchair in the sitting room Alex went to get him a stiff whiskey. When he returned he handed it to him saying, "You look like you need this."

Dave gave him a tight smile and thanked him. He swallowed the generous helping of whiskey in one go and, grimacing, left the glass on the table in front of him. Alex leaned over to top up the glass.

"I've been such a fool," Dave said, and he put his face in his hands. He remained like that for a long time and Alex remained silent, giving him time to collect his thoughts.

Eventually Dave took a deep breath and sat up straight, raking his fingers through his hair. He took the glass in his hand and this time he sipped it. Normally he felt relaxed in this apartment. They had enjoyed many an evening sitting like this in the cozy sitting room; the dim lighting and warm colors in the uncluttered room made it a perfect haven. However, this evening Dave was in no mood to appreciate the large wooden fireplace, the wall-to-wall bookcase filled with classics, or the classical music coming from the state of the art stereo. All he could think about was the mess he had made of his life.

"You're going to think I'm such a shit when I tell you this, and you'd be right; I am. When Elaine was pregnant with Sarah I made a pass at Sylvia." Dave paused as he heard Alex gasp. He continued, "Sylvia, of course, wouldn't have any of it. Anyway, until today it was just between the two of us. However, stupid fool that I am, when that detective started asking awkward questions I let something slip, and when Elaine went in to be interviewed that interfering detective told her what I had said. Now it's all out in the open and Elaine hates me. I don't blame her, but I wish I hadn't been so bloody stupid."

"I can't believe what you're saying, Dave. You and Elaine are an institution; I never thought anything like this would happen to you two."

"How could I have been so stupid?"

"It's called thinking with your equipment, but I thought you were smarter than that."

"So did I; I regretted it as soon as the words had left my mouth. Thank God nothing actually happened, but it could all be over for me because of that one stupid mistake."

"I'm sure Elaine will forgive you. It was a one-off - right?"

"I've felt so guilty about it that I've never even looked at another woman since."

"Elaine's a reasonable person. I'm sure she'll come round as soon as she gets over the shock."

"I hope you're right." Dave said. He then sipped his whiskey in silence, deep in thought.

Meanwhile, Elaine was lying in bed looking up at the ceiling thinking about how it had come to this. After Dave left, Sylvia had come into the room to ask how things had gone. She'd filled her in and asked if she'd mind looking after the children for the evening because she needed some time on her own.

She had come up to the room and lain on the bed crying for a long time. She had cried about the last five years of living a lie while she'd believed that she was the only woman for Dave as he was the only man for her. She had cried about the trouble their marriage was in at the time, which had inadvertently led to her husband's betrayal of her.

Mostly she had cried about what this would all mean for their future. She knew she loved Dave and he her, but was that enough? Could she trust him now? She couldn't imagine a life without him in it, but surely if he could try it on with her best friend when their marriage was on the rocks it wouldn't take much to lead him to having an affair with someone else. Could she believe him when he said that there'd been nobody else since, that there never would be again? Certainly if his tears were anything to go by, he was telling the truth. However, she had to remember all the lying of the last five years when he'd pretended that none of it had happened. Could he be lying still? Maybe the tears were because he had been found out. She knew the tears were genuine, which meant he wanted to save their marriage, but was she enough for him? Would he always feel the need for another woman?

Eventually she stopped crying and lay back looking up at the ceiling while she thought back over their relationship...

CHAPTER FOURTEEN

The girls and Alex had gone to the Canaries for two weeks to celebrate the end of the leaving cert exams. On the last night of the holiday Elaine saw him; he was playing pool with some other lads. Every time she looked in his direction he was looking at her, and eventually he came up to her and said that as she was responsible for him playing the worst game of pool in his life she'd have to buy him a drink to make up for it. She laughed and asked if that line usually worked.

He said, "Usually, but I could tell straight away that you're not like all the other girls; it would take more than that to get you to go out with me."

"And that's your follow up line to which I'm supposed to gush with pride that you realize I'm not like all the other girls, and then fall at your feet."

He laughed and said, "You sure don't make it easy on a guy, do you? First you just sit here looking gorgeous so that I can't take my eyes off you and end up losing very badly at pool. Then when I give up at pool and try to let you make it up to me you make it very difficult. Okay, I give up. It looks like I'll have to buy you a drink to get you to have a drink with me, even though you owe me one." He sighed and pretended he was put out. "Since I'm buying I get to choose your poison," he said. He went to the bar and left Elaine giggling with Sylvia over his act.

"He's cute," Sylvia said.

"Yeah, it's a pity we leave tomorrow though."

"You'll just have to make tonight count then," Sylvia said with a wink as Dave walked towards them, two lethal looking cocktails in his hands.

"What am I drinking?" Elaine asked as she took her first sip.

"Get it into you, and no complaints. It's your own fault; if you had bought the drinks like any decent girl would have you could be drinking whatever you want." He grinned at her over the rim of his glass.

They spent the evening laughing and joking and getting to know one another. Elaine discovered that he was from a little village in Mayo, not too far from Abbeyfield. They marveled at how small the world was, and how amazing it was that they had to go all the way to the Canaries to meet. Dave expressed disappointment when Elaine informed him that she was leaving the next day. He couldn't believe that as he and his friends had been there all week he hadn't met her before that night. He also expressed Sylvia's sentiment about making the night count.

When he walked Elaine back to the room she shared with Sylvia, who had graciously opted to spend the night with Alex so that Elaine could get lucky, he bent to kiss her good night. His kiss was gentle at first, then more probing. Elaine responded to his kiss but firmly removed his roaming hands when they inched their way inside her top.

"That's as far as I'm willing to go for a drink," Elaine said, smiling up at him, as he looked tortured.

"Damn, I knew I should have whisked you off to dinner," he replied. "Can I see you when I get back to Ireland?"

"You expect me to believe that you won't have forgotten all about me by tomorrow?" Elaine raised her eyebrow skeptically.

Dave looked serious for a moment as he gazed into her eyes and said, "I'll never forget you." Then he brushed her lips with his own so gently that it felt like a breath of air on her lips.

Elaine's hands trembled as she reached into her bag for a pen and piece of paper. She took a moment to steady herself before writing her phone number on the paper and handing it to Dave. Taking it off her, he folded it and put it into his shirt pocket, tapping his pocket for emphasis as he backed away from her and said, "I'll call you."

Yeah right, Elaine thought. The minute he takes off his shirt tonight my number will fall out of the pocket and I'll never hear from him again. Even if he doesn't lose my number he'll meet some other girl tomorrow night and that will be the end of that.

Therefore it was with some surprise that when she answered her phone the next night she heard Dave's voice enquiring, "Is it raining at home?"

"Of course it is. Apparently I missed summer - it happened last week, lasting four days. Don't go on about the weather over there or else I may just have to kill you. It's just so depressing to be back."

"Which do you miss more, me or the weather?"

"Tough question. We'll see if I'm less depressed when you get home. That is if you still want to see me when you come home."

"I'm hurt. I called you tonight, didn't I? Something tells me it's going to be hard to convince you that I'm serious about you."

They talked for ages that night and Dave called a few more times before he returned to Ireland. Elaine started to believe he might be serious after all, but found it hard to believe that with all the beautiful girls that must surely be splashing around in the pool outside his apartment he was taking time out to ring her instead of chatting one of them up.

When he arrived home he rang her from his parents' house and asked if he could take her out to dinner the next night. She was delighted that he was proving to be serious about her.

The next night Elaine spent ages getting ready for her date with Dave, feeling very excited. She had been out with boys before, but out for a drink or to the cinema. It felt like such a grown up date to be going out to dinner and it felt as if nothing in her wardrobe was suitable. Changing for about the tenth time she vowed that she'd go shopping soon and would have more clothes to choose from the next time Dave took her out.

When the doorbell rang Elaine ran to get it, not wanting her parents to meet Dave and start giving him the third degree. There would be plenty of time for that, she hoped, if things went well. She opened the door and called in to her parents that she was going out. Then, pulling the door shut behind her she put her hand into Dave's outstretched one. He opened the car door for her and only when she was seated and he had closed it did he go around to the driver's side.

As they drove to the restaurant conversation flowed smoothly, and when they arrived at their destination Dave told her to remain where she was as he got out of the car. He went around to her door to open it for her and then gave her his hand to help her out. He opened the restaurant door for her and when they were shown to their seats he pulled hers out for her. Elaine was very impressed with his gallantry.

As the night continued Elaine saw a different side to Dave than the one she had previously seen. Rather than joking and laughing about everything, he spoke seriously to her and spent the night gazing at her attentively, making her feel like the most special girl in the world.

When he walked her to her door that night he kissed her gently and said he looked forward to seeing her again. As she turned from him to go inside she felt elated.

Now as Elaine lay looking up at the ceiling remembering the start of the relationship her heart ached for Dave and all she wanted to do was reach for the phone to ask him to come home. She glanced over at the phone, stretched her hand out to it, but paused and forced herself instead to remember the tough times they had been through after they got married.

When they arrived back from their honeymoon they moved into the house they'd just bought. Dave was a family man and was as delighted as she to be moving into the same estate as she'd grown up in. They were both happy with the thoughts of their children growing up so close to their grandparents, and loved the changes the previous owners had made to the house. The attic had been converted, giving them a compact four-bedroom house. There were just the three bedrooms in her parents' house, Elaine and her sister having shared one room, her brother having had the box-room. In her parents' home the kitchen-dining room was separated from the sitting room and they loved the fact that the wall had been broken through and replaced with doors. The front and back gardens were quite small but had been kept well; Dave had been delighted with the way Elaine's face had lit up while talking about where their children would sleep and how lovely it would be having a garden for them to play in.

However, they weren't expecting to have a family quite so soon. They weren't long living in the house when Elaine discovered that she was pregnant and they were both ecstatic about the news. They both felt that it was the best thing ever, even though it wasn't planned. That was until Elaine started feeling very sick and the pregnancy hormones started kicking in.

Dave didn't understand Elaine's tiredness or her moodiness, and this only made her even moodier. All she wanted was a little bit of understanding. A little bit of help around the house wouldn't have gone astray either, considering she was so tired. However, all she got was demands about why the house looked such a mess and why his dinner wasn't on the table, even though she had been working all day too. She got home from work before him so he thought it was logical that she would have dinner ready for him; the insurance company he worked for didn't close until six pm whereas she was home from the bank by five-twenty. Their sex life was also suffering, partially because of Elaine's tiredness, but also because of all the rowing. The theory about the wonderful making up lovemaking remained just that, a theory.

Then one Saturday when she arrived home from shopping, she dumped her bags at the foot of the stairs, figuring Dave would surely have a go at her later, and made her way into the kitchen where she was sure she could smell her favorite dinner cooking. She wondered if her mother had come over to cook dinner for them and went through the dates in her head to see if she'd forgotten that it was her birthday or something. When she opened the kitchen door she was surprised to see Dave cooking. She found one of her pregnancy books open on the table where Dave had obviously been reading through it trying to understand the changes his wife was going through. She discovered the housework done too.

Over dinner, he apologized for his behavior and his lack of understanding. He told her he was reading her pregnancy book and wished he had read it sooner, that now that he understood more about pregnancy she could expect more help from him and more support and understanding.

She felt so proud of him that evening and they made love for the first time in weeks. Things had definitely improved after that and Dave made a permanent reversal back to his old gallant, jovial self with an extra help of understanding thrown in for good measure.

That was obviously the day he had made a move on Sylvia, Elaine realized now. Thinking logically about it made Elaine see that behaving like that had obviously set Dave to thinking about why he had done so. Wondering what the cause of the problems in their relationship was had obviously led him to reading her pregnancy book. In turn that had made him more attentive and understanding towards her, which meant that the pass he'd made at Sylvia hadn't been such a bad thing after all. With that in mind Elaine reached for the phone to tell Dave that all was forgiven.

When Alex answered the phone she asked to speak to Dave.

"I heard what happened. Are you okay?"

"Yeah, thanks for asking. It was a shock but it could have been worse. I really need to talk to Dave now, Alex. We'll talk later, okay?"

"Okay. I'll just get him for you."

While Elaine was waiting for Dave to come to the phone she felt sorry for having cut Alex short. She knew he was concerned for her, but right now it was her husband she needed to talk to. She was sure that Alex would understand under the circumstances. She'd ring him tomorrow to make sure.

She forgot all about Alex as soon as she heard Dave's voice.

"Hello, Elaine." Dave sounded nervous. "Do you forgive me?"

"I love you, I want you to come home, and yes I do forgive you. I've been doing a lot of thinking." She went on to tell him what she had realized.

"You're right, that is what made me come to my senses, made me see that our problems needed to be sorted. I figured that reading your pregnancy book to try to understand what might be going on with you would be a step in the right direction. As it turned out it made me realize what a total jerk I had been since you became pregnant. I was such an idiot back then; I had no idea pregnancy could be so tough on a woman. I just expected you to be the same Elaine you always were and had no clue that you'd be more tired and need more help with the housework and the cooking, which you were always so good at. I'm glad we're all sorted now;

I'll be home soon. I love you."

Dave hung up the phone and went back into the sitting room to tell Alex that he was going home. He filled Alex in on his conversation with Elaine.

"I'm so glad that you two sorted things out. I knew Elaine couldn't stay mad with you; she's too level headed to hold something like that against you. Especially since you two were having problems at the time."

On the way home Dave reflected that Alex had seemed strange with him and that maybe he was mad with him for having made the pass at Sylvia because of the way he felt about her. He had sensed bitterness in Alex's tone after he told him what had happened. He decided that in hindsight it would have been better to go to a hotel or B&B instead of bringing him into the whole thing. Nothing I can do about that now, he thought. I should have known he would be annoyed with me. As much for hurting Elaine as for having moved in on Sylvia while knowing how he felt about her, Dave realized.

When he arrived home he put all thoughts of Alex out of his head as he thought only of Elaine and how happy he was that she had decided to forgive him. As he parked the car he looked up at the house to see that it was in darkness except for a soft light in the bedroom he shared with his wife, the bedroom he was delighted to be welcomed back into.

When he opened the bedroom door he gasped as he took in the sight of his wife looking seductively beautiful in a sexy black negligee, the one he had bought for her the previous Christmas. He lost no time in crossing the room and relieving Elaine of the negligee, nor was there any time wasted on unnecessary words. They just fell into each other's arms as if they had been separated for months not hours. He delighted in the feel of her body under his hands, something he had very nearly lost. Well I'll never be that stupid again, he vowed to himself as he lost himself in the pleasure of making love to his wife.

That night they fell asleep wrapped in each other's arms, smiling as they relished the fact that they had not let their love escape, despite the hurdle they had faced. It was as if nearly losing each other had made them rediscover all that they loved about one another.

CHAPTER FIFTEEN

Wednesday the 17th of September

Elaine woke to hear the pitter-patter of the rain against the window. She leaned on her elbow to look at her sleeping husband, marveling that he could sleep through anything. Even if there was a gale force wind outside lashing the rain against the window, rattling the panes of glass, he would still be asleep. She remembered having to poke him in the ribs several times to remind him that it was his turn to get up with the children when they were babies and would cry during the night. She was delighted to have him home and knew in that moment that she never wanted anything like that to come between them again. No matter what he had done or could do in the future she would always forgive him because they belonged together.

It was a morning like this one that he had proposed to her in bed; it was one of the rare mornings that he woke before her and it was him leaning up on his elbow looking down at her sleeping. When she had opened her eyes he was holding a ring in his hand and she could see the diamond glistening in the dim morning light. He didn't even say the words, just "Well?" She'd been tempted to say no until such time as he proposed in what she deemed a properly romantic way. Then she had realized that no matter how he proposed she wanted to marry him and so she had said yes. However, she had then proceeded to concoct a story about how they were walking through the local park when a woman selling roses approached them and Dave had bought her a single red rose and then got down on one knee to propose.

She never told anyone the real story and had sworn Dave to secrecy about it. She knew that he had never understood her need to have people believe that she'd had such a romantic proposal. He thought he was being very romantic, proposing in bed like that. According to him there was no more intimate place to do it. He'd made a joke of it, saying that he'd been looking down at her naked body as he listened to the rain pouring down outside and decided that he wanted to spend the whole day in bed with her and that it was her naked body and no other that he wanted to spend the rest of his life with. He had said he could understand her not wanting to tell her parents how he proposed but that surely they could tell their friends the truth. She had never wanted to tell him that by accepting she felt she had sold herself short, that she should have held out for a romantic proposal. She knew that if she had said that to him he would have thought it was him and not the proposal that was the problem.

She smiled now as she realized that she'd almost had herself believing in the made up story. Now, for the first time since then, she realized that it really hadn't mattered after all how he proposed. What mattered was that they loved each other and were right for each other in every way. She could even see now how he might have thought it was romantic to lie here beside her and listen to the rain as he thought about spending the rest of his life with her. She could see that everyone else's perception of what was romantic didn't necessarily have to match hers to make them right.

As if sensing that she was watching him sleep, Dave woke up and looked up at her, his eyes groggy. "How long have you been staring at me like that?"

Elaine shrugged and said, "Not long. I was just thinking how right we are for each other."

"You're right about that," Dave said as he pulled her on top of him.

The mornings of lazy love making had disappeared with the birth of Sarah, as they rarely woke early enough to enjoy more than a quickie, if even that. This morning, however, they were able to really enjoy each other before they heard the first sounds of the children waking up.

When Dave was gone to work and Sarah to school Sylvia asked Elaine what had made her forgive Dave. Elaine explained to her that it was a mixture of the tears he had shed the night before and also her realizations of the previous evening. She said that she knew he really loved her and that making that pass at Sylvia was just a symptom of the problems in their relationship. Admitting to Sylvia the truth about Dave's proposal made her realize how silly she'd been all these years for lying about it. She'd never look at rain the same way again after this morning; even while talking to Sylvia she could feel her cheeks burn as she thought about the way Dave's tongue had danced around her skin as if in time to the plink, plink, plink of the rhythm of the rain dancing against the window. Realization dawned on her that it was rain and sunshine, making love, tears and laughter, joy and pain that made their relationship a success.

Later that morning Elaine, Dave and Alex were called back into the Garda station as the warrants for their fingerprints had been obtained. Sylvia stayed with the children while Elaine met Dave down at the station, and later met with Alex to give him support while he had his fingerprints taken and was glad when he was told he was free to go. She had feared he would be held for further questioning.

That afternoon Sylvia got a call from the Garda station informing her that Rick's body had been released. She had known it was coming, but somehow that call brought it all home to her again and she felt a dark cloud closing in on her heart, squeezing any pretence of normality out of her. Despite having immersed herself in Elaine and Dave's family lives, helping in the investigation and supporting Alex, it had only provided her with a temporary respite from dealing with the sadness of losing Rick. She knew she was going to have to get in touch with Rick's family, thought about how she had gone to see them on Sunday evening, how much they were all hurting. She was reluctant to make the call, to be instrumental in making them revisit their pain. Instead she replayed the events of Sunday evening in her head.

Sylvia called over to Rick's family to see how they were all holding up. As she had expected, she arrived to a household of Rick's distraught family members. Their family home was a large country bungalow, which seemed too big for one family, but now was bursting at the seams with people. Rick's parents and siblings were crying and there were aunts, uncles, cousins and neighbors trying to comfort them and making tea and sandwiches.

Under normal circumstances Sylvia never failed to admire the large gardens with a fountain, pond and large trees. Ordinarily she could imagine Rick's parents lounging under those trees of an evening. Now she was unable to appreciate the well cared for, bright, tidy but lived in house which Rick's mother took great pride in. Today it was all lost on her as she took in the grief around her.

Sylvia went over to Rick's mother, Janice, who with her blonde hair and blue eyes couldn't have been more different from her son. Sylvia put her arms around her, which brought a fresh wave of tears from Janice and made Sylvia well up again. Seeing the waif-like woman in such a state broke Sylvia's heart afresh.

Rick's father, Tom, came over to Sylvia and wrapped his arms around both of the women. He was trying to be brave, to hold things together for the sake of the rest of the family. For a brief moment Sylvia allowed herself to imagine that it was Rick's arms around her and not his father's; they were so alike. She imagined that it was him trying to console her, telling her not to cry. She looked up at Tom's face and saw that despite his bravery tears flowed down his cheeks as he hugged Sylvia and his wife close to his chest.

Sylvia could see Rick's sister, Maria, a replica of her mother, sitting at the kitchen table with her head down crying into her folded arms. Her brother, Damien, had his arms around her while he fought back his own tears. Sylvia's heart lurched at the sight. In a quick glance Damien could almost be mistaken for his brother.

Sylvia carefully extricated herself from Janice and Tom, leaving them in each other's arms. She moved over to sit with Maria and Damien, who had become like a brother and sister to her. Maria clung to her as a fresh wave of tears wracked her body and Damien just sat looking lost. While comforting his sister he had something to keep him occupied; now he looked deflated. Sylvia reached out to take his hand and gave it a squeeze.

Maria's sobs subsided and she sat back in her chair. "I just can't believe this is happening," she said to Sylvia. "I left the kids in to a neighbor. I don't know how I'm going to tell them that Uncle Rick isn't going to be around anymore. Life just isn't fair; they're too young to have to deal with this."

Sylvia thought of Maria's two children; Luke, who looked so like his two uncles, was five and Abby, who favored her father's side of the family more with ginger hair and blue eyes, was three. They had idolized Rick, and it was tough enough on them that their father was no longer a part of their lives as he had walked out on Maria soon after Abby was born to go to America with his new girlfriend; this was going to devastate them.

In that moment Sylvia thought about the fact that no matter how difficult it was going to be to get over Rick it would be worse if they had children. Her heart would surely mend eventually, but if they had children how would they ever get over the loss of their father in such tragic circumstances? For a brief moment she allowed herself to wonder what their children would look like, imagined herself holding their son or daughter in her arms, inhaling the new baby smell. She gave herself a mental shake and told herself not to make this any more difficult than it had to be.

Throughout the evening Sylvia was introduced to Rick's extended family, or those who would have been her extended family if the circumstances were different. She wished it were their wedding and not Rick's death that was bringing them all together. She allowed herself a small smile as she imagined all of these people in a hotel function room, all dancing and drinking, congratulating her and Rick rather than consoling her and each other.

Later that night Sylvia took her leave of the family, saying that she'd be in touch. Rick's parents were adamant that they wanted Sylvia to call over and visit with them as often as she could because she had been an important part of their son's life. Sylvia agreed, saying that it would be what Rick would have wanted. Not only what Rick would have wanted, she thought as she drove her car out of the driveway. It would be like losing him all over again if I tore myself away from his family.

That night Sylvia spent another restless night of tears, with dreams where Rick was by her side, only to be awoken as she replayed in her dreams the moment she discovered him lying dead with a knife in his chest....

Sylvia, seeing the pool of blood seeping out from under the armchair, dropped her shopping bags and slowly rounded the chair. She sank to her knees beside the lifeless body of her beloved Rick. She called his name, sobbed "No," as she saw her kitchen knife protruding from his chest right where she used to lay at night listening to the beating of his heart.

She jumped up in the bed awoken by her own screams.

When Sylvia felt able to talk again she picked up the phone to call Rick's family and discuss the funeral arrangements with them. His parents did most of the organizing but were glad of Sylvia's help.

The next few days were extremely difficult. They passed by in a blur of tears as family, friends and colleagues all gathered to say their final goodbyes to Rick, commiserated with Sylvia and commented on what a tragedy it all was. There were questions about whether or not the guards had any leads and speculations as to what had happened.

As Sylvia bent over the coffin to lay her final kiss on Rick's lips she thought her heart would surely stop beating, such was the enormity of the pain she felt. Her legs grew weak beneath her and she had to be helped away from the coffin.

The day of the burial she went through the motions of going to the church and following the hearse to the graveyard in a state of numbness. As she watched the coffin being lowered into the ground she wept, her tears mingling with the rain on her face. If Alex and Elaine hadn't been at her side supporting her she would have collapsed into the mud at her feet.

Rick's parents had invited everyone back to their house after the burial for tea and sandwiches. The afternoon was spent reminiscing about Rick; Sylvia learnt a lot about him that afternoon while listening to tales of his childhood.

"Do you remember what a climber he was as a child?"

"How could I forget all the times I was in casualty with him? And the very next day he'd be doing his best to get up into that tree house again, arm or leg in a cast. I used to call him my little monkey. There was nothing he wouldn't at least try to climb."

"Luke and Abby have followed in his footsteps. I have locks on their bedroom windows."

"Remember the time he climbed out his bedroom window?"

"Don't remind me. I got such a shock that night when I opened the front door to find him standing there in his pajamas, holding that tatty teddy by the hand. 'Teddy wanted out the window,' he said to me. We weren't long putting locks on all the windows after that."

"Still, that ability to climb stood to him when he joined the scouts. All those orienteering trips when he could climb a tree and spot what the others couldn't, all those times he played hide and seek and won because he could climb higher than anyone else."

"He always had the job of lookout when we played cowboys and Indians. He made a great sniper, too. Those rubber darts always hit us; he always found just the right spot to hide in and fire."

"Did you ever find out what happened to the shed window that time?"

"I figured one of you kicked a football through it, although none of you ever owned up."

"Rick climbed up onto the roof of the shed and he slipped and fell. He saved himself by clinging on to the edge of the roof and aiming his feet for the window sill. He was kicking wildly and broke the window."

"What was he doing up on the roof of the shed?"

"I think it was a dare, or maybe he was spying on the pretty girl next door. I can't remember. I just remember we all thought we were going to get into such trouble when you came home and found the window broken."

Sylvia wished that he was by her side, that she was learning all this about him from his own lips. She would have given anything to be sitting on the couch with him, snuggled up together drinking wine as they regaled each other with their stories of growing up. It made her sad that the life of such a great man had ended so young, that she had known and loved him for such a short time. She was amazed by the strength of her feelings for him and by how much she was grieving.

CHAPTER SIXTEEN

Sunday the 21st of September

The day after the burial Sylvia went out to lunch with Peter; it was a farewell lunch as he had to return to Cork that afternoon and to work the next day. He was concerned for her and wanted to stay longer, but she assured him that she'd be fine, that it was time for life to resume as normal, at least for everyone else. As she hugged him goodbye she knew that it would be a struggle but that she would have to make an effort to get her life back to some semblance of normality.

She decided that it was time to go back to work and to go back to living in the house that she had shared with Rick. Elaine was reluctant to let her go alone. She offered to go with her and to spend the night with her but Sylvia declined, saying that it was something she needed to do alone. Like going through the funeral, it would be upsetting, but it was necessary to walk through the doors alone into the house in order to accept her loss and gain closure.

As she brought her car to a stop outside her home she swallowed a lump in her throat. Taking a deep breath, she got out of the car and walked to the front door. As she unlocked the door tears came to her eyes; she brushed them away, took another deep breath and stepped inside. As she went into the sitting room the memory of that night came flooding back to her. She fought to push it out of her mind, to replace it instead with a happy memory, one of her and Rick snuggled up on the couch watching TV.

She went through the rest of the rooms allowing herself to think only of times when she and Rick were happy together in them, not letting the horror of that last evening spoil what the house had meant to her. She opened curtains and windows, allowing the fresh autumn breeze to blow in, circulating cool air around the house. She thought of conversations she'd had with Rick, refused to let the silence of the house close in around her.

She thought about how on many nights they had sat on the patio in the evening, sipping a glass of wine as they watched the sun set over the lake, and moved into the sitting room as it got cooler. There they closed the curtains against the black night and twinkling lights of the town. She didn't think she would ever again take pleasure in the view from her window.

She sighed deeply, pushing back the need to cry, and turned her mind back to how it had come about that she and Rick had moved in together.

After a few nights of going back to Rick's place to find Mary either in tears or whining on about how dreadful her choice in men was, Sylvia lost her patience. "Am I just catching her at a bad time in her life, or is she always like this?" she asked of Rick.

"I've only been living with her for three months. Before this she was going out with the guy who's just dumped her so she was fine."

"Is it not getting on your nerves even just a little bit that every time we come here she's so needy and we don't get to spend any time together?"

"We get to spend time together when we go to your place," Rick said, stroking her hair.

"Well my living conditions are hardly ideal either." She was living in a house full of tenants who were very loud. Every time they went up to her bedroom, which had no lock on the door, they were interrupted mid-passion by one of the girls either wanting to borrow a hairdryer or top, or to have a chat. From time to time one of them would knock on the door to tell them to keep the noise level down, like they could talk! However, at least the girls always eventually backed out of the room with an apology and a grin. With Mary, on the other hand, they rarely got as far as the bedroom until they were too tired to do much but sleep.

"Well if you're not happy about where you're living why don't you move?"

"Does this situation not frustrate you too?"

"Not really; I know this thing with Mary is bound to be only temporary, and when she's over this ex of hers we'll have all the space we want."

"I just think it would be nice to come back here and, regardless of what mood she's in, just come upstairs and do our own thing," Sylvia said.

"Try putting yourself in Mary's shoes. You'd like to think that your flat mate would put you before sex with her boyfriend, wouldn't you?"

"I suppose," she conceded. "It's just that it's every time we come back here."

"Things are bound to improve, and until they do I intend to put Mary's needs ahead of our desire for each other. It's the right thing to do."

"That's one of the things I like about you, you're such a nice guy," Sylvia said, pulling him onto the bed.

However, things didn't improve and one day, six weeks into their relationship, Rick surprised Sylvia by telling her he was thinking of looking for somewhere else to live and was hoping that she'd move in with him.

"Seriously?" Sylvia asked. "What made you want to move away from the enchanting Mary?"

"Be nice," Rick said. "I wouldn't be thinking of moving if I didn't feel ready to take the next step with you."

That silenced her for a moment as she pondered the fact that she didn't feel like running scared at the mention of taking the next step. She hadn't felt averse to the idea of moving in with Rick when she thought it was just a practical solution to their living problems. At the thought that moving in together was a progression towards something more serious she had expected to run, would have in the past. However, she surprised herself by saying, "I'd really like to move in with you."

After a few weeks of looking they found a cute little cottage to rent a few miles outside town. Sylvia thought it a pity it wasn't for sale.

"Are you saying you want to buy a house together?" Rick asked.

"Well no not exactly, not yet anyway, but this is the kind of place I could see myself living in long-term. It's so cute and dainty, and it's been renovated recently. It's got a quaint charm, but yet has a modern feel to it."

It was a thatched cottage that retained its old quaintness on the outside. It had an extension to the back of the house that was done in the old style of the rest of the house. However, inside it had wooden floors throughout, making it more modern. The old style of the windows and ceilings meant that it retained its cosines. Originally there had been two small bedrooms and a small bathroom upstairs. Downstairs there had been a kitchen cum living area. The extension had added an extra bedroom upstairs with an en-suite and a walk-in wardrobe. Downstairs the kitchen had been taken out of the living area and moved out to the extension with a utility room and a downstairs toilet with a shower. The kitchen was fully fitted with all mod cons, giving the occupants the old world charm with all the modern conveniences.

Rick put his arm around her and squeezed her. "Well you wouldn't know what might happen in a few years when we're ready to buy a house. This one might come up for sale at the right time or maybe we could convince our landlord to sell it to us eventually."

She snuggled in close to him and said, "I've really come a long way; that thought doesn't scare me at all."

"That's probably because we're meant for each other."

"You know, I think maybe you're right."

That night, as they snuggled up in each other's arms after uninterrupted lovemaking, Sylvia said, "That was wonderful. It was so nice to be able to come up to bed when we wanted without Mary stopping us with her sob stories and not to be interrupted by one of the girls. It's great to have our own place." It suddenly occurred to her that she had never gotten to see whether or not Mary was pretty. "Actually, I never got to see Mary when she wasn't blubbering. What was she really like?"

"She was a nice girl really. It's a pity you didn't meet her under better circumstances."

"Is she pretty?" When Rick looked puzzled she clarified, "Well nobody ever looks their best when they've been crying, and every time I saw her she looked pretty dreadful."

"Be nice," was all Rick said which she took to mean that Mary hadn't been pretty even when she wasn't blubbering.

Things progressed with Rick and Sylvia at quite a fast pace. Six weeks later their landlord informed them that he was putting the cottage up for sale. He said he couldn't guarantee that the buyer would be interested in keeping them on as tenants. He was very apologetic and informed them that when they had started renting from him he hadn't intended selling but there had been a change in his personal circumstances, which required him to sell. They discussed the possibility of buying the cottage together and decided to go for it.

They applied for a mortgage right away and as soon as they were approved started the purchasing process. The day the deal was sealed they went out for dinner with their friends to celebrate and splashed out on some champagne. When they all met up, Sylvia's friends couldn't get over the transformation in her. She was in love with Rick and, what's more, not only was she admitting it, but was also settling into domesticated life with him. Her family and friends were delighted for her; all, of course, except for Alex. However, he was putting up a good pretence. He raised his glass to them and wished them well, smiling as he did so. Sylvia watched him over the rim of her glass, as she enjoyed the delicate fizz the champagne left on her tongue, and suspected that he was crying on the inside as it finally registered with him that she was not going to fall in love with him as he had always imagined she would.

One evening, as she and Rick sat cuddled up together on the couch watching the evening news, a local news item caught Rick's interest. A car had gone out of control on the lake road killing the driver. There'd been no passengers in the car and no other cars involved. The brakes had failed, and when the driver tried to come to a stop the car had gone into the lake. The name of the driver was what really caught Rick's interest, Mark Lynch.

"Oh my God! That's Mary's ex."

"Maybe she tampered with the brakes."

Rick looked at Sylvia. "Mary would never do such a thing! How can you even think that?"

"I don't know her that well," Sylvia replied. "It was just a thought. She just seemed to me to be very needy and clingy, and it wouldn't surprise me to discover that she would actually kill someone for dumping her."

"Well I think that thought is best kept to yourself. I know you don't particularly like Mary, but, as you said, you don't know her that well. You only saw one side of her."

"I'm sorry. I shouldn't have said that," she said, kissing him on the cheek. "Forgive me?"

"Yes, you're forgiven. I wonder how Mary's taken the news. I might give her a call."

"We've moved away from all that. The last thing we need is to invite that neediness into our lives again."

"I can't just turn my back on her."

"Why not? You don't owe her anything. She had enough of a hold on you while you lived with her."

"If I didn't call her to see how she is I wouldn't feel right about it. It's got nothing to do with her having a hold on me. I'm concerned for her, that's all. I'd do the same for anyone else," Rick said firmly as he left the room.

A little while later Rick came back into the room. "Mary's very upset. She wants me to call around to her."

"You're surely not going." Sylvia said.

"Yes I am."

"Rick, I really don't think that's such a good idea."

"Well I do. I'll be back later."

She jumped up to stand between Rick and the door. "I really don't want her back in our lives, Rick."

"The way you're carrying on you'd swear she was my ex. Now please get out of my way and let me pass."

"The reason I'm acting as if she's an ex is because I don't think she's quite right in the head. I think she thinks you are an ex."

Rick started to lose his temper for the first time in their relationship. "You have no right to say such things about her. You don't know her. Sometimes you can be so selfish. All you can think about is how her hardship is affecting you." He pushed past her and stormed out of the house.

The whole time he was gone Sylvia alternated from being worried that Mary would turn on him to being worried that maybe she was wrong and had angered Rick for no good reason. As she was going to bed she vowed she'd apologies to him when he got home and for that purpose she put on some sexy lingerie; what better way to apologies than a little late night seduction.

Later, as Rick slipped into bed beside Sylvia he kissed her on the cheek and wrapped his arms around her. "I'm sorry, love," he whispered to her. She turned towards him. He hugged her to him and said, "You were right; Mary tried to kiss me. She didn't take it well when I told her that it wasn't going to happen." He smiled and said, "I guess I'd better check my brakes every day before I go anywhere. I wouldn't want to end up like Mark."

"Don't joke about it. It's not something I'm happy to be right about."

Even now, after all she'd been through in the previous week, Sylvia couldn't believe that a week after he'd been consoling Mary after the death of her ex, he had been killed. She stood at the open window of her bedroom and inhaled deeply, allowing the breeze to fill her with happy thoughts. She imagined Rick standing behind her, his arms wrapped around her. For the first time since he was murdered the thought of him brought a smile to her lips instead of tears to her eyes. She could almost feel his presence behind her; almost feel his breath on her cheek as he bent to whisper in her ear. She could almost hear his whisper being carried on the wind. That feeling served to calm her and she felt glad that she had made the decision to come home.

Home, that one word filled her with warmth, made her think about winter days arriving home from school to her mother's homemade soup. She was sure Rick would have made a good father; it would have been so good to have a family with him. This would have made a good family home, she thought. She had a brief moment where she considered selling it to a couple or a family but then dismissed it as she couldn't possibly let go of the memories of the short but happy time she had shared there with Rick.

That night she slept alone in the bed that she had once shared with

Rick. It was much harder to do that than coming back to the house. She tried to concentrate on remembering happy times with him, which helped to get her to sleep. However, it was in her sleep, in the silence of the night, that the sadness took hold of her once more.

She found herself awake at two in the morning after dreaming that Rick's ghost had floated in through the open window and lay beside her. She reached out to see if it had been a dream or if her fingers could touch his skin just one more time. Tears streamed down her face as the memory she had been pushing away all day forced its way in. Her body shook with sobs as she buried her face in her pillow.

When she could cry no more she fell back to sleep and dreamt of Rick's ghost again: as she had come home that fateful evening she saw his spirit leave the house through the unopened front door. She had entered the house in a state of amazement and wasn't surprised by the sight that greeted her. She didn't wake from that dream but tossed and turned.

CHAPTER SEVENTEEN

Monday the 22nd of September

Alex was called back in to the station for further questioning, as his prints had been discovered to be on the murder weapon, and he called his solicitor to meet him there. As he took a seat in the interview room beside Jim and opposite Detectives Molloy and Naughton, he felt very nervous and couldn't stop his legs from shaking. He fidgeted with his hands, alternately drumming his fingers on the table top and steepling his trembling fingers together. He remembered what Detective Molloy had said the previous week about the possibility of him being arrested under suspicion of murder if his prints were found on the weapon.

Once Detective Molloy had dispensed with the formalities she commenced the interview. She repeated the previous questions Alex had been asked. When there was no new ground covered Jim became impatient. He stated that, as there was no hard evidence, his client could be held for questioning for no more than twenty-four hours unless they managed to come up with something substantial against him.

As the day progressed everyone in the interview room became more and more frustrated and agitated. Forensics had found none of Alex's DNA on the corpse; therefore a confession or a witness who had seen Alex at the scene of the crime was needed before they could arrest him. The detective was trying to badger a confession out of Alex, or at least to get him to slip up, by repeatedly asking the same questions. Alex's answers never changed, but the more he repeated himself the more beads of sweat appeared on his forehead and trickled down his face collecting on the neck of his shirt. Two other detectives came in to relieve Molloy and Naughton at the end of their shift, meaning questioning was resumed with renewed vigor while Alex just became more worn out, frustrated and scared.

When nothing had come to light within twenty-four hours they had no choice but to let him leave, and it was with relief that he walked out of the Garda station. Feeling exhausted and with his clothes sticking to him with sweat, he looked forward to getting home, having a shower and shave and getting into bed. He was sure that it was all over the news that he had just been detained for questioning for the previous twenty four hours and knew that he'd have some explaining to do once he returned to work the following day, but for now couldn't think of anything beyond getting home, getting cleaned up and having a sleep.

Sylvia went back to work that Monday, glad to throw herself into the thick of things. Opening the door and taking a deep breath she looked around her at the familiar faces of her colleagues and the first customers of the day. Her co-workers were glad to see her back but were concerned that it might be too soon. She assured them that she was ready to return to work. Her boss, Laura, took one look at her face, pale under her make-up, and said that if at any stage she felt it was too much for her she could go home again. Sylvia thanked her but assured her that she'd be fine.

She found that being surrounded by the sights and sounds of the busy salon really helped her feel that her life could once again be full, maybe not with love, but at least with work and friendships. As she brushed a customer's hair in preparation for cutting, Sylvia looked into the mirror and took in the familiarity around her; the salon was furnished in a modern fashion, all steel and maple finishes, making it feel bright, fresh and clean. It really had the ability to lift the spirits. She remembered that when she had first started working in the salon it had looked rather drab and dreary, being an old building which had once been a very small hairdressing salon. It had been closed down temporarily a couple of years ago to allow for extra sinks and work stations to be added as well as for the décor to be changed.

Originally it had just been her, Laura and Gillian who had worked there, but since the refurbishment it had gotten so busy that Laura had found it necessary to take on two new girls, Natasha and Audrey. The salon was so busy that morning that all five girls were working. Sylvia found herself smiling as she looked around and realized that she had missed the camaraderie that existed between the girls.

Laura was a very fair boss, and her eyes were usually alight with laughter. However, this morning Sylvia noted the look of concern dulling her eyes and furrowing her brow. When Laura noticed Sylvia watching her she quickly put a smile on her face and turned towards where Gillian was regaling staff and customers with a joke. At the punch line Natasha's laugh reverberated throughout the shop, and, Sylvia was sure, could be heard outside.

What Sylvia found the hardest about being back at work was the concerned looks and comments she got from her customers, but as the day went by it got easier to put a smile on her face and make general small talk with her customers, steering the conversation away from her loss. That night she was exhausted from her first day back and found it easier to sleep and the next day it was easier to come in to work and to get on with her life as normal. Her life was still tinged with sadness but she found herself starting to enjoy living again, starting to look forward to the future.

CHAPTER EIGHTEEN

Wednesday the 24th of September

Sylvia was off on Wednesday and Thursday of that first week back to work. She rang Alex at work to see how he was after his twenty-four hours of questioning, and offered to come over to his apartment later with a bottle of wine. He said he'd rather have an early night, as he was still quite tired, despite having slept the best part of the previous day. He hadn't slept too well the night before and felt awful. Sylvia thought he sounded depressed and was worried about him. She decided she'd leave him be for that night, although convinced that a glass of wine and some company would be good for him. She knew that rather than getting an early night he was likely to sit brooding while listening to the most depressing music he could find in his collection. She would call over to him on Thursday night and wouldn't take no for an answer.

She had just started to catch up on some housework when Dave rang her and asked if she'd mind the children that night. He wanted to take Elaine out to make up for what had transpired the previous week. Sylvia was happy to oblige, glad that Elaine and Dave had put the whole episode behind them, glad too that there would no longer be tension between her and Dave.

Dave rang Elaine and told her not to cook dinner. "Sylvia's off today; I've asked her to cook dinner for her and the kids and also to mind them for the night. We're going out."

"Where to?"

"It's a surprise."

"How will I know what to wear if I don't know where I'm going?"

"Whatever you wear you'll be the most beautiful woman there."

"Thank you, but that really doesn't help."

"I have to go now; bye, love you." Dave hung up the phone quickly before his wife could wheedle out of him where he was taking her.

When Elaine hung up the phone she called Sylvia. "Do you know where Dave is taking me tonight?"

"Yes I do, and I'm sworn to secrecy."

"Come on, he'll never know; I need to know what to wear."

"I can help you with that. However, my lips are sealed as to where you're going."

"I'm really excited about tonight, but I feel bad; I feel as if I should be going over to Alex tonight after his ordeal at the station."

"Don't feel bad; you deserve tonight. Besides, I already rang him about going over there tonight and he said he just wants an early night," Sylvia said.

"That makes me feel less guilty. I'll see you soon so, bye."

Sylvia arrived over to Elaine's house soon after that and the two women went to the walk-in wardrobe, the children in tow. There they proceeded to take dress after dress out of the wardrobe and throw it on the bed after Sylvia had held the item up to Elaine and said, "That just won't do."

As each dress was thrown on to the bed Jody reached up to it, held it up to a giggling Dillon and said, "That just won't do." She then threw it to the floor and reached for another.

After a while Jody started putting one of her mother's dresses on. She then helped Dillon into a dress and went in search of some high heels. When Sylvia and Elaine had almost despaired of finding something suitable they turned towards the bed to see if they had tossed something aside that was maybe suitable after all. That was when they saw the mayhem of clothes strewn about the floor and the two children sitting among the mess with long dresses on, struggling to get their feet into their mother's high heels. The two women collapsed onto the bed in fits of laughter. At this, Jody and Dillon forgot about the task of putting the shoes on and laid back on the clothes strewn all over the floor and joined in the laughter.

"I wondered why they had gotten so quiet," Elaine said eventually, wiping the tears of laughter from her eyes. As she sat up, she said, "You can never go wrong with a little black dress so maybe I'll just go with that." Then she suddenly remembered a dress she had bought the previous year while on a shopping spree to inspire her to lose the weight she had piled on during her pregnancy with Dillon.

"What about that dress I bought last year? It's hanging in the wardrobe of the spare room. I didn't want Dave to see it until I had an opportunity to wear it."

While Elaine went to get the dress, Sylvia started putting clothes back into the wardrobe. When Elaine came back in with the new dress Sylvia dropped the one she was holding and said, "Wow! That dress is perfect for where you're going tonight." It was a long, shimmering backless turquoise dress.

Elaine had a shower as Sylvia enlisted the help of the children to tidy up the bedroom and then brought them with her to collect Sarah from school. When they arrived home Elaine had a facemask on and was doing her toenails.

"We don't go out very often so I'm making a real effort for tonight," Elaine explained through tight lips.

The children doubled over with laughter at their mother's green face. Sarah said she looked like an alien and her voice sounded funny and said that was what she'd like to wear for Halloween. The children all wanted their nails done so Sylvia became a manicurist and painted Sarah's nails pink while Jody wanted a mixture of colors on hers. Sarah then wanted to paint Sylvia's nails.

As Sylvia was painting Dillon's toenails purple Elaine said, "Don't do his fingers and don't let Dave see his toes."

Sylvia giggled and said that Dave needed to lighten up and not have such a phobia about his son turning out gay.

While Sylvia cooked dinner for her and the children, Elaine went to get into her new dress. As she was coming down the stairs she heard Sarah saying, "Look, Daddy, Sylvia painted our nails. Mummy said you're not allowed to see Dillon's toes because they're gay. How come they're gay, Daddy? Are my toenails gay too?"

Dave was so engrossed in taking in the sight of Elaine in her new dress that he didn't seem to hear Sarah's chatter. "Wow!" he exclaimed.

Elaine was chuffed; it was nice to get that reaction from her husband; it made her feel as if she was the most beautiful woman in the entire world. It was even nicer that Sylvia was in the same room at the time; it wasn't often that she got to outshine her. Not that she was jealous, just that in light of what had happened it was nice to be made to feel at least as beautiful and desirable as Sylvia, if not more so.

When Elaine entered Lana's she was glad she'd had Sylvia's help in deciding what to wear. Anything else in her wardrobe would have made her look drab in the elegance of this restaurant. Even her little black dress, suitable for almost any occasion, wouldn't have done for tonight. She'd feared that she would look overdressed, which anywhere else she probably would have. She nodded her approval in amazement as Dave sat opposite her at the candlelit table.

It felt like a first date; Dave was very attentive to her all night, from opening doors for her to gazing intently into her eyes. He made her feel like there was no one else in the restaurant. When he held her hand up to his lips and kissed each finger gently she wished they really were the only two people there. The only part of the night that wasn't like a first date was when they arrived home and made love.

When Dave shut the door behind him he pulled Elaine to him and kissed her tenderly but passionately, leaving her in no doubt what his intentions were when he got her to the bedroom. However, he took his time in getting her there, letting his hands roam slowly over her body while he kissed her with some urgency. When their need for each other was unbearable they moved to the bedroom where Dave was more attentive to her needs than he usually was, and he was usually a very attentive lover. Elaine had to bite down on her lip to keep from making too much noise.

CHAPTER NINETEEN

Thursday the 25th of September

After Sarah and Dave left for school and work, Elaine told Sylvia all about the date and the night of passion, to which Sylvia said, "What do you mean that wasn't like a first date?"

"Well, at least like no first date I've ever been on; I never put out on a first date." They giggled like teenagers at that. "I'm glad I found out about the whole thing; at least it's put a spark back in our lives."

"Was the spark missing?"

"Well it wasn't completely missing; it's just that life had taken over a bit. The magic was just hovering out of reach for a while. I mean, we were still passionately in love, but it wasn't like last night. When we woke up this morning he loved me all over again; I haven't felt that special since the kids came along."

"I suppose that's normal. I mean, it happens to everyone when they have kids, doesn't it?"

"I suppose; the kids just kind of take over; don't they? Don't get me wrong, I love them to pieces, but I just need to feel that magic sometimes too, you know?"

"Of course you do; just because you're a mum doesn't mean you're not still a woman. I'm glad everything's okay between you two again – what ye have is too special to let anything come between ye."

"Yes it is. I may have lost sight of that at first when I was so angry but I'm glad we got through it." Elaine stood up to put the kettle on. "I wonder how Alex is holding up."

"I'm going to call over to him later, give him a bit of support. Do you want to come?"

They agreed that they'd ring him at work and call over to him as soon as Dave came home from work to look after the kids. Elaine spent the remainder of the day catching up on some household chores while Sylvia kept the children occupied for her.

When Dave arrived home Elaine told him of their intentions to go over to see Alex.

"That's probably a good idea; he wasn't himself the other evening when I was over there," Dave said.

"In what way?" Elaine asked.

"He seemed really annoyed with me, bitter even, about what had happened with Sylvia." Dave shot an awkward, apologetic look towards the two women. "I got the feeling it was more to do with his feelings for Sylvia, as if I had stood on his toes, than to do with hurting you, Elaine."

"You probably imagined it," Elaine said. "I noticed all right at the funeral that he was very quiet and distant, but none of us have exactly been ourselves lately."

Sylvia considered and said, "You possibly didn't imagine it. He's never had a problem as such with any of my boyfriends, but you're a friend; he probably thought it was something friends don't do to one another, hit on each other's girls. He's right, to a certain degree, except that at the time I wasn't with him. I had just broken up with Ethan and I had planned on going over to Alex that evening but changed my mind and went out with the girls from work instead, where I met Luke. Sarah was a few months old before Alex and I got together again, so the only issue is that it was your wife's friend."

"You're being dismissive again of his feelings towards you. He's always loved you, so therefore Dave hitting on you was one friend hitting on the girl the other friend loved. So maybe you didn't imagine it after all, Dave. I just wouldn't have thought he'd react like that; it's not like him," Elaine said.

"It just made me wonder, that's all," Dave said. "How did he really feel towards Rick? I mean, they were friendly before Rick and you started going out together. Was he feeling bitter towards Rick when you two got together?"

"Not that he ever displayed, and I think we can all agree that Alex pretty much wears his heart on his sleeve," Sylvia said, as she grabbed a bottle of wine from the fridge to bring over to Alex's. She was glad that the atmosphere between her and Dave had improved since he and Elaine had sorted things out. It meant that she could enjoy hanging out with him again. She really hoped now that things wouldn't be strained between him and Alex.

In the car on the way over Elaine said, "What Alex could do with right now is a girlfriend. It would help him through all this and it might make him finally move on from you."

"I don't think he's as hung up on me as you all seem to think. He's just shy with other girls and thinks he's in love with me, but I agree; if he started seeing someone else it would be really good for him."

Dave had spoken to Elaine before about a girl in his office he thought would be perfect for Alex. She decided that she'd talk to him about it later and see if they could set something up.

Alex greeted them with hugs and kisses. As he spotted the wine that the girls had brought with them, he said, "Just what I need tonight, thanks girls, but enough about me, how are you holding up, Sylvia?"

"I'm doing okay; I think you being accused of murder is making my grief take a back seat for now. Anyway what do you mean enough about you? This is dreadful."

"They have nothing concrete to go on, and until they do I'm not going to worry about it; I have a good solicitor, and I'm innocent. They can't make it stick; they don't have enough to go on. I mean, having been in love with you and my prints being on the knife doesn't prove anything. Innocent until proven guilty, right?"

"That's the spirit," Elaine said. "I'm glad you've cheered up about the whole thing; we were a bit worried about you."

"I had a meeting with my solicitor today and he feels sure that it can't be proven beyond a reasonable doubt," Alex said as he opened a bottle of wine. "The guards have asked for my phone records to see if they can prove that I was at home that evening. They've also questioned my neighbors to see if any of them remember seeing me taking out the rubbish or anything, but they haven't come up with anything to prove that I was at home. Jim suggested that since he didn't specialize in criminal law he could recommend a colleague of his, but I have every faith in him. He recommended that I spend my time thinking of anything I may have done or anyone I may have spoken to which could prove that I was anywhere but at the scene of the crime. I can't think of anything, but he said to keep thinking about it, that I may have forgotten something that at the time might have seemed trivial.

"Anyway, Kim and Gina just rang; they're on their way over with a couple of bottles so it should be a good night."

When Gina and Kim arrived they asked Alex how he was doing. He filled them in on what his solicitor had said, to which Kim responded, "I wish I could feel that upbeat if I were in your shoes. I know what your solicitor said, but you've no alibi; if that were me I'd feel pretty snookered."

The others all threw her a look.

"What? Don't look at me like that," she said, "I'm only saying I'm glad I have an alibi; I could just as easily be in Alex's shoes and I wouldn't want it sugar-coated."

"It's called support, not sugar coating," Sylvia said.

"Well you know me; I just tell it like it is. I don't mean to be unsupportive, but I just don't see the point in pretending everything's okay when it's not."

"The way I'm looking at it is that there's plenty of time for negativity if I'm put away for something I didn't do; for now I may as well look on the positive side."

"I suggest that if we can't say something positive about it then we don't say anything about it at all and talk about something else; we're supposed to be taking people's minds off their troubles tonight," Elaine said in her stern no-nonsense voice, giving Kim a meaningful look. Kim had the grace to look contrite as the subject was changed.

Kim's blunder was soon forgotten as Elaine told them all about her dinner at Lana's. None of the others had been there yet so they were delighted to hear about how she'd had Ostrich steak. They all laughed at the look of disgust on Kim's face. While she liked cooking and eating out in fancy restaurants, to her meat consisted of beef, pork, lamb and chicken. A bit of duck or goose was okay, but that's where she drew the line. It was the most light-hearted conversation the group had had since Rick's death and they probably laughed more than it warranted, as much for stress release as for anything else.

As the night progressed the friends got quite merry and pretty much forgot all their troubles, apart from the fact that tears streamed unchecked down Sylvia's face. Throughout the night her friends wiped away her tears and gave her hugs. At one point of the night Alex wiped her tears away with his finger and kissed her eyes. Sylvia clutched his hand and leaned her head on his shoulder as he put his arm around her waist and hugged her.

Elaine looked up at the couch a little later to where Sylvia lay snuggled up asleep against Alex with him caressing her back. She stood up and said, "Come on, Sylvia, time to get a taxi."

Sylvia muttered something incoherent and snuggled up more against Alex.

"Just leave her here; she'll be fine," Alex said.

"You've got to be kidding me; you're both drunk, have zero willpower and with your pasts it doesn't take a genius to work out what would happen."

"Under the present circumstances I don't think so. Apart from the fact that she's grieving, drunk or not, how would it look if we were asked in court when the last time was that we slept together? Credit me with some sense, Elaine. I do have a spare room you know, that's all I meant."

"Hmm. I'm calling a cab and she's coming home with me."

"Alex, I think it's for the best," Kim said.

"Fine; I just thought it made sense, that's all, since she's asleep."

"Yes, but would you extend the same offer to anyone else who fell asleep?" Elaine asked.

"Of course I would."

"Hmm."

The cab arrived and they roused Sylvia with some difficulty and got her into it.

When Alex arrived back to his sitting room after seeing Sylvia and Elaine out, he discovered Kim and Gina kissing passionately. He cleared his throat to announce his presence and sat on the couch, and Kim and Gina pulled apart.

"Sorry, Alex," Gina said.

Emboldened by drink, Kim said, "We're being very rude. Would you like to join us?"

"Girls, I respect your life choice, but it's not my scene."

Kim crawled over to the couch. "Oh come now, Alex, don't be coy. Admit that it turned you on." She moved her hand slowly up Alex's thigh, but before she could do anything else she was yanked to her feet by Gina, whose face was like a dark cloud.

"Come on, we're going home."

Kim blew a kiss to Alex and said, "Oops, looks like I'm in trouble." She winked at Alex and said, "Another time perhaps."

CHAPTER TWENTY

In the cab on the way home there was silence. Kim knew she was in trouble but looked forward to getting Gina to soften up. She knew that she shouldn't have come on to Alex, even before she'd done so, but couldn't help herself. The way she saw it, it was a win-win situation. Either Alex would have been on board for a threesome, which would have been the ideal outcome, or she'd make Gina temporarily angry. She knew that Gina would come around; she could never stay angry with her for long.

Once inside their apartment Gina blew up at her. "What the hell did you think you were playing at?"

"Oh come on, Gina, it was only a bit of fun, but all the same he wanted us."

Gina softened a bit and said, "I don't deny that." She reached out and pulled Kim towards her, kissing her. After a while she said, "But that's beside the point; it was still not a good idea."

"Maybe I need a spanking," Kim said. "I do so like it when you get mad with me; the making up is so hot." She was caressing Gina's breasts as she spoke, making Gina's need for her even more urgent and making it impossible for her to stay mad.

"Just promise me it won't happen again," Gina managed to get out before Kim made it impossible for her to talk anymore by covering her lips with her own. They moved into the bedroom, discarding clothes as they went along. They both wished that Alex were with them; that fantasy made their lovemaking even wilder.

Later, Gina lay awake and thought about their relationship as Kim slept beside her. Despite the fact that they got together because neither of them stood a chance with Alex, the prospect of being with him was still uppermost in their minds and she hoped it wouldn't become a problem. She thought that the space between them, as she lay on her back on her side of the bed, Kim curled up on her own side, might well have been an ocean, they were as different from each other as two countries.

She had never been part of a couple before this whereas Kim had been in a number of relationships, and Gina hoped that Kim was more committed than she'd been in any of her previous ones. She loved Kim but hadn't said so to her, fearing that her feelings were not reciprocated. Kim had always been somewhat promiscuous and fickle, and she feared that someday Kim would just take a notion and leave her. The fear of driving Kim away by telling her how she felt was enough to keep her from doing so. She knew she was in this relationship for the long haul, but she couldn't be sure whether or not Kim was. In all other respects they were very much like a married couple; they had bought this one-bedroom apartment together and shared their lives completely. She supposed all couples, even married ones, had their fears of someone coming between them. She looked across the space that separated them and wished they were more together.

When they had agreed to buy the apartment it was just that it made sense not to be throwing money away on rented accommodation. It hadn't been a commitment of any sort; an apartment could always be sold or rented out if they decided to go their separate ways. Gina also feared that the friendship they had enjoyed since they were sixteen would come to an end if their romantic liaison ended, so therefore it was very difficult for her to tell Kim how she felt. It was hard to think of losing Kim; she feared Kim would find it as easy to discard her as to sell their apartment and throw out the stuff they had accumulated together over the years. Kim wasn't very sentimental; it was always Gina suggesting they get a memento to commemorate significant dates in their relationship. If their relationship were to end she wondered what she would do with those, knowing Kim wouldn't want any of them – the single they'd first made love to, the wine bottle from that first night that they now used as a candlestick holder, the first romantic DVD they'd ever snuggled up to. She wondered if it would be too painful to hold on to those things if they split up.

Gina had always been a very private person who kept herself to herself and so didn't confide her feelings in Elaine or Sylvia. If her mother had still been alive she would have confided in her and asked her advice. She had always had a great relationship with her; they had been more like sisters than mother and daughter and she knew her mother would have supported her decision to date Kim, despite her father's insistence to the contrary. That was his own disappointment in her talking; he was sure that because he couldn't support her decision no-one else could either. Unlike Kim, she hadn't made this choice in order to shock. Much as she loved her, she knew Kim was a sensationalist and as such could as easily turn the other way on a whim; a whim that could be brought on by Gina professing her love for her. She had said it in poetry so many times, but Kim didn't get the metaphors that implied that she wouldn't be able to live without her.

Kim took her poems at face value and didn't realize that she was saying she feared their love was as transient as the blanket of snow on the ground, already melting before the pen left the page. She didn't see that when Gina talked of a falling star, shattering as it fell to the ground, she was talking about how her own heart would break if their relationship ended. She thought Gina wrote beautiful poems about nature and never saw them as anything else. In school she could never fathom that all the great poets had deeper meanings in their poems and thought it was just something made up to torture students who would have to learn that a poet seeing a tree shedding its leaves in Autumn meant that he knew he was going to die soon.

She lay there on the edge of sleep thinking back to what life had been like before Kim and didn't like the thoughts of being back there. She had always been lonely. Sure she'd had her friends, but not that special someone. She had always envied Kim and Sylvia for their ability to just throw caution to the wind and have plenty of special someones, even if each one was quite brief. She always felt that she and Alex had been kindred spirits, loving someone who didn't love them back and there only being that one special someone. Sometimes she wished life could be simpler, that Alex could just have realized a long time ago how good they would be together and forget about Sylvia. Of course, then she wouldn't have Kim, but she and Alex would be able to communicate through poetry and that would make everything so much easier.

Now she felt somewhat akin to Elaine, if you could compare what she and Kim had to what Elaine and Dave had. If only she could bring herself to utter those three words to Kim. However, she felt that the words always remaining unsaid and always wondering was better than telling her that she loved her only to have it not said back to her. Even if Kim didn't leave her it would put her back in the same position as Alex was in, and she didn't want that; it was a lonely prospect.

She envied Kim and Sylvia their ability to say exactly what was on their minds. There were many nights like this one where Gina lay awake, thinking, and she wished she could just get it all off her chest. She had gone to a child psychiatrist once when her parents were worried about how introverted she was. Her psychiatrist said she was a deep thinker, that very often the ones who said everything that was on their minds managed to get a lot of sleep because they had no worries weighing them down. She wondered now if that was why Kim was always able to sleep so soundly.

The psychiatrist had worked with her for a while to try to make her comfortable with talking about her innermost feelings. That was when she started writing poetry; it was her way of saying what was on her mind. However, all too often people failed to understand what she was trying to say in her poetry. Alex, although himself a fellow poet, had always been too wrapped up in his love for Sylvia that he had failed to see that her poems professed her undying love for him.

She thought back to her time in college when she had no longer been quite as introverted, a fact she attributed to her new life and the anonymity of Dublin City when compared to the little town of Abbeyfield where everyone knew everyone else.

She quite enjoyed her new life in Dublin and intended staying there. However, her poetry told a different story and revealed how much she missed her old life, her friends and parents, the scenic spot where she had spent her whole life, living so close to a forest and lake, surrounded by green fields on one side, the shore on the other. Her poetry while she lived in Dublin was very grey, as she was not a city girl at heart and wasn't truly at home surrounded by buildings.

At that point she hadn't realized that she'd end up moving back home after college and become such close friends with the group again. After college she found a job in Dublin, but when her mother, Nora, became ill with cancer she moved back home. The night her mother rang to tell her she had found a lump, Gina cried all night. The next morning she left her job without giving any notice, something she would never do under normal circumstances. She took the first bus home and spent some quality time with her mother. They went for a lot of scenic drives together, had mother-daughter lunches and chats and really connected with one another.

Nora was having a routine breast check when a lump was discovered to be malignant. When she had the operation to have the lump removed the doctors discovered that the cancer had spread and was inoperable. It was a very emotional and painful time for Gina and her father, as they could do nothing for her except to be there and make her as comfortable as possible as they watched her die. When the end came Gina and her father were distraught, although there was at least the relief that Nora would no longer suffer.

After her mother died she found a job locally and somewhat reverted back to her old self as she fell back in with the old gang who had all found jobs close to home. Although grief-stricken, her poetry once again reflected the color of her surroundings. She grieved with the trees, bare of their red-gold leaves, struggled to go on as the birds struggled to find food in the ground that glistened with frost.

The whole experience had made Gina and her father very close, which is why it came as such a blow to him when at twenty-two Gina and Kim realized their feelings for each other and moved in together. Kim's parents also disapproved and thought that lesbianism was just a fad that they would grow out of when Mr. Right came along. However, at least they had the support of their friends who understood and congratulated their life choice, although it had at first come as a shock to them all.

Gina felt very bad for disappointing her father. As she was an only child she knew her father had high hopes for her. He was unable to understand why she would do this to him. She told him it wasn't so much doing it to him as doing it for herself, that being in love with Kim was the only happiness she'd known since her mother had become ill. It broke her heart to hear her father say that her mother would be turning in her grave. However, no matter how much it grieved her to disappoint her father and no matter how much she felt she was betraying her mother, her feelings couldn't be denied.

Kim, however, felt no such remorse. This was her decision and her family could like it or lump it! Her mother cried about the fact that she wouldn't produce grandchildren for her, but Kim was quick to point out the fact that her two brothers and her sister could provide their mother with all the grandchildren. Also if Kim was so inclined she could always have a child using a donor. Her mother told her not to be so crude and changed the subject, only to revert back to it every time she saw Kim or spoke to her on the phone. She told her that Gina didn't surprise her; after all, she had always looked a bit like a boy with that short brown hair, and losing her mother like that had probably sent her over the edge.

Much to her mother's horror Kim cut up her beautiful blonde hair. Her mother chided that she'd never find a man now that she looked so masculine. It was quite a feminine cut really, but when seen through the eyes of a disappointed mother the short cut also took inches off Kim's small bosom.

As she drifted off to sleep Gina vowed, not for the first time, that the next day she would just tell Kim exactly how she felt. After all, they couldn't continue on as they were without confronting certain issues - Gina had been feeling her biological clock start to tick lately. She needed to discuss with Kim where their relationship was going and if there was a possibility of them raising a child together. She hoped that pretty soon she would be able to articulate her feelings to Kim and get a favorable response.

In her more optimistic moments she saw her and Kim raising a family in a three bedroom semi-detached house similar to Elaine and Dave's. In her more pessimistic moments she saw her and Kim splitting up and selling their small, but cozy, apartment. Very rarely did she allow herself to think of the possibility of Alex, Kim and her raising children together in a three or perhaps four bedroom house.

Most of the time, however, she just saw them living like this forever without ever confronting their real feelings. Not that that would be such a bad thing, she consoled herself. After all, they were very happy together and had lovingly decorated the apartment together. Gina remembered how they had consulted each other, argued and finally compromised on subtle lavenders and yellows compared to the garish pinks and loud greens favored by Kim and the magnolia and whites she favored.

She wondered now how their parents would react if she, Kim and Alex got together. She could imagine the look of horror on Alex's mother's face, mirrored by the look on her own father's face if they were to confront them with the news that they were in a three-way relationship and were going to raise a family together. She imagined that Kim's mother would try to ignore the fact that Gina was involved and would latch on to the fact that Alex and Kim were together. She could only hope that for the sake of the children their parents could put aside their prejudices. She put her hand on her stomach and hoped that she would someday get to carry Alex's baby.

Preparing herself for the possibility that it might be the last time she would do so, knowing deep down that it would not be anytime soon she would tell Kim of her true feelings, she wrapped her arms around Kim and snuggled up to her.

CHAPTER TWENTY-ONE

Friday the 26th of September

When Alex woke up he had a sore head. He'd lain awake for some time the night before thinking about Sylvia and whether or not she would have slept in the spare room. His intentions had been pure, but if he had been put to the test he couldn't say for sure that he would have resisted the temptation.

However, with Kim it was a different story. He was glad Gina had called a halt to that whole thing; as much as it turned him on, he really wouldn't feel comfortable sleeping with Kim and Gina. Not that there would be much sleeping going on he felt sure. From the innuendoes made by Kim on a frequent basis he figured a night with them would be an all night sex marathon. They were both very attractive, but one woman at a time was enough for him, and in Kim's case he felt that she was actually too much woman for him.

As he sat looking out at the morning sky, which was heavy and grey, trying to force himself to eat something, he was sure that it had been a good idea for Sylvia to go home. It wouldn't have been good for either of them to end up in bed together again, much as he ached for her.

After a shower and drinking some coffee, he rang Dave and told him he wanted to see him for lunch. They agreed to meet at Murphy's, one of their favorite pubs. It was an old fashioned pub that was always lively at all hours of the day and night with great food and drink and a friendly atmosphere. It was one of those few pubs that still had lock-ins after hours, except of course when the guards were on the prowl, which made it a very popular spot.

When they had ordered, Alex filled Dave in on the goings on of the previous night.

"Oh, to be free and single! And you still didn't get laid! Oh, man," Dave said, tapping the edge of a beer mat off the table.

"Hey, put yourself in my shoes. I mean the whole Sylvia thing is obvious; I can't tell those detectives that I'm not in love with her any more, but that I'm still sleeping with her every opportunity I get. I know Elaine was right; if Sylvia had stayed and it was up to me we would have ended up in bed together. I can't of course say that that's what she would have wanted," Alex said, leaning his arms on the table.

"Yeah I can see all that, but man, you were being offered a threesome with two very sexy ladies. What better way of moving on than that?"

"I don't think your wife would agree with you there. If it were her sitting there she'd be saying, 'The last thing you need is to be sleeping with friends. When you move on it should be with someone new, not a friend and especially not two friends. Someone would end up getting badly hurt.'" Alex did a good imitation of Elaine's chiding, disapproving voice, poking his finger in the air for emphasis.

"Maybe, but just think how much fun it would be until then."

"Don't let your wife hear you talking like that."

"Don't worry on that score; my lips are sealed. I can only live vicariously through you. Oh, man! If I were free and single I'd never have turned that down; it's every man's dream," Dave said, and leaned back in the booth, one arm draping over the back of the seat.

"To tell you the truth, it scares me; I mean Kim seems like such a man-eater. Anyway, I don't think Gina was into the whole thing, the way she pulled her off me."

"Maybe they'll split up and Kim will go for you then."

"With no Gina there to pull her off me, that's a scary concept," Alex said and took a long drink from his glass of water.

"Man, you're weird; there are loads of men out there that'd kill for an opportunity like that and you just piss it away. Anyway, how about Sylvia? Does this mean you're not over her?"

"I'm over her; it's just that with the history and all it'd be so easy to fall back into bed with her and in love with her, but there's no future in it so I can't let that happen. There's also the fact that it could very well land me in prison; talk about giving substance to the motive."

"Well what I suggest is giving Kim a call and seeing if she's still serious now that she's sober."

"Get serious, man."

"Well I don't know how you'd feel about this, but if you're serious about moving on from Sylvia maybe you should start seeing someone. I mean if you have a girlfriend you're less likely to end up back in bed with Sylvia. It just so happens there's a girl in my office that I think would be perfect for you; I never mentioned it before because I thought maybe you weren't ready to move on. Her name's Carol. What do you reckon?"

"I'll think about it."

Later when Dave got home he recounted his conversation with Alex, leaving out the pieces where he had been so enthusiastic about a threesome. He knew he'd get an earful for that if Elaine found out he'd been trying to steer Alex in that direction. Dave was relieved that Alex seemed more like his old self again. He'd been really worried, had even contemplated the fact that Alex might indeed have killed Rick in a moment of jealous rage, just as the guards suspected. Although he'd only given that idea very brief consideration. He got up to make some tea.

Elaine followed Dave into the kitchen and said, "I'm glad he's thinking about seeing someone else; it'll be good for him. I can't believe Kim! Gina must've been livid. I knew I was right to insist on Sylvia coming home with me, and I'm glad Gina pulled Kim off him."

"From what he tells me he wouldn't have gone for it anyway," Dave said as he poured water into two mugs.

"Wouldn't he?" Elaine asked taking one of the mugs from Dave. Then when she thought about it for a moment, "Yeah, I suppose she's not his type, but still he's single and had a woman throwing herself at him. Not many men would turn that down, but maybe it was the fact that Gina wasn't into it. I'd say there was some row when they got home."

"Didn't you tell me they both had a thing for him in school?" Dave asked as he walked towards the sitting room.

"Yeah, I guess Kim's not quite over that, despite the whole lesbian thing. I wonder if it'll break them up; it'd be a pity because they're a good couple, not to mention what it'd do to their friendship if they split. It would be the end of an era; we'd be left choosing sides and choosing which one would be left out of dinner parties; it'd be awful."

"Do you think Sylvia will be annoyed with Kim?" Dave asked, sitting back on the couch and placing his mug on the coffee table.

"Why would she be? It's not as if she has any claim on Alex," Elaine said, sitting beside her husband and sipping her tea.

"Are you going to tell her?"

"No; I'd say Gina and Kim would like to work this out for themselves without their dirty linen being aired in public. I guess Alex needed to tell someone, and we're married so you told me, but there's really no need for Sylvia to know."

"It doesn't seem right that she's the only one who doesn't know."

"I'm not going to keep throwing this up at you, but how would you feel if the whole group knew about you and Sylvia? Kim and Gina are the only ones who don't know. We don't all need to know every aspect of each other's lives."

"Point taken."

The children came running into the room, putting an end to the conversation.

Despite her intentions of the previous night, Gina spent the day with Kim without expressing her feelings. They didn't bring up what had happened with Alex the night before and in the spirit of leaving things lie Gina decided it would be best not to rock the boat with revelations of love. It was better to carry on not knowing than be rejected. Besides, deep down she knew the truth of the matter; if Kim actually loved her she'd surely say it, not being one to keep quiet about things. She'd just wait until Kim said it first, even if she went her whole life without hearing those words. She was prepared to go to her grave with secrets if that's what it took.

It wasn't as if things weren't good the way they were; they were happy together in their little one-bedroom apartment. Sure, Kim was a little messy and didn't know one end of a vacuum cleaner from the other, but she was thoughtful. She was a dab hand in the kitchen and made Gina breakfast in bed every weekend. She did all the cooking, making all of Gina's favorite dishes, even if she did leave the tiny kitchen looking like the aftermath of a storm. They had a running joke that Kim should actually have been a chef instead of being a hotel receptionist and doing all of her cooking at home; at least then she would have kitchen porters to clean up after her.

While Kim seemed to have thrived on the scandal they caused when they initially started going out together it had almost killed Gina. She was glad now that it had all blown over and that for the most part they were accepted in their small town. At the time Gina had often suggested moving to Dublin together where they could be more anonymous. However, Kim wouldn't move and now Gina was glad of that; she thought it had probably made her a stronger person to withstand all that scandal. Not strong enough to withstand the fear of rejection though, she thought.

If it hadn't been for the support of her friends and wanting to be around for her father she would have left Kim in those early days and gone back to Dublin where she could hide. However, she had stuck it out, putting up with the snide remarks at work, putting in her hours and going home in the evening trying to leave it behind her. She used to visualize that in hanging up her apron at the end of her shift she was also hanging up every bit of verbal abuse she had endured that day. She liked to think of the words being written on paper and stuffed in the pocket of her apron instead of ingrained into her head to torture her. Eventually it became easier, and when her workmates saw that their treatment of her wasn't affecting her they started to accept her the way she was.

She had never felt secure. Sure, her parents had a rock steady relationship and so her family life was stable, but she'd always had a fear that it would end, and eventually it did when the cancer ate away at her mother. It gave validity to her insecurity. She was now sure that nothing would last, least of all a relationship where words of love were not uttered. Passion was great, but it didn't fill the void in her heart where she needed to feel the warmth of knowing she was loved.

She held out for the faint hope that Alex would get over Sylvia and realize that a threesome with Kim and Gina was what he really wanted. Then of course they would go to live with Alex in his larger apartment. Gina had her feet enough on the ground to know that was only a dream, that Sylvia was the only woman for Alex. Still, one could always hope, and she did. It would all work itself out in the end she was sure; patience was what was required.

CHAPTER TWENTY-TWO

Saturday the 27th of September

Sylvia was surprised to see Mary coming into the salon. Not wanting to deal with her she started to move towards the back room to take her break. However, upon hearing Mary tell Laura that she wanted Sylvia to cut her hair, she sighed and resigned herself to the job. Mary had never come into the salon before so Sylvia knew that the woman was just coming in to talk about had happened to Rick. She didn't want to talk about it, especially not with Mary. She was determined not to get dragged into such a conversation, not to have to bring the images of Rick's dead body into her mind again.

As she washed Mary's hair she struggled to make conversation; they talked about the weather and current affairs. Sylvia had no intention of bringing up either of their ex- boyfriends. She suddenly stopped in the middle of conditioning Mary's hair as she remembered Mark and what had happened to him, and then she remembered the night Rick had gone to see Mary and that she had tried to kiss him. She resumed conditioning Mary's hair in silence as her mind worked overtime.

Why didn't I think of this before? Sylvia wondered. Of course, it makes perfect sense that it was Mary who killed Rick.

"Ow!" Mary squealed.

Sylvia realized that she had been rather rough with Mary, as the possibility of her being the murderer had dawned on her. She apologized and resumed, being gentler.

As Mary was paying for her haircut she brought up the subject of Rick. "I couldn't believe what happened to Rick. He was always so nice. Who could have done such a thing to him?"

"That's what the guards are trying to find out." Sylvia hoped that her short, sharp answer would end the discussion.

"I have to admit that at first when I heard about it I thought that maybe it was you who killed him when you found out that he had slept with me the night Mark was killed." Sylvia's jaw dropped. "Of course, when I thought about it I realized that you weren't the type to murder someone in cold blood.

"I hope you don't hold it against me that I slept with him that night. At first I thought it was so sweet of him to come over to see that I was okay. Then he came on to me, and I was just so upset after losing Mark that I let him take advantage of me. Not that I minded, in fact I was flattered, quite blown away really. You shouldn't think badly of him because of it; he felt so guilty afterwards."

Mary left the salon, leaving Sylvia flabbergasted. She sat down, her mouth open in shock. Laura came over to her and asked if she was okay. Sylvia tried to talk, but no words would come out. She just sat there, her mouth opening and closing as she tried to formulate words.

Eventually Sylvia managed to answer, "I need to go out for a while." Her voice came out as a whisper.

As Sylvia made her way to the Garda station she was shaking with rage that she hadn't thought of Mary as the murderer before now. She thought of all the trouble she could have saved Alex. She was furious with Mary. How dare she try to sully Rick's memory by insinuating that he had slept with her? As if he would ever do such a thing! That girl is a psychopath, a psychopath who was clever enough not to talk about the supposed affair with Rick while I was actually cutting her hair, Sylvia thought.

She took a moment to calm down and gather her thoughts before entering the station. She went up to the desk, asked for Detective Molloy and was brought in to the interview room to wait for her. She looked around the depressing room and hoped that this was the last time she would have to be there.

Detective Molloy entered the room a few moments later with Detective Naughton and asked, "Have you thought of something that could help with the enquiry?"

Sylvia was leaning forward in her chair, both arms resting on the table. "Yes; Rick's old flat mate came into the salon just now. She was in love with him. I think she killed her ex, Mark Lynch. She's a psycho..."

Detective Molloy interrupted her. "Mark Lynch; his death was ruled an accident; there was no evidence of foul play."

There was a rustling of pages as Detective Naughton flicked through his notebook. He cleared his throat and then reiterated his partner's statement.

"His brakes failed. The night it was on the news I remember commenting to Rick that maybe Mary had tampered with them," Sylvia said.

"Why did you not report your suspicions?" Detective Molloy asked.

"Rick thought I was just being overly suspicious of her because I didn't like her, and then he went over to see if Mary was okay. I told him I didn't think it was such a good idea, but he never saw the bad in anyone. He thought she was a nice girl who was going through a rough time since Mark had dumped her. Anyway, when he came home he told me I was right to try to stop him because she had tried to kiss him. He made a joke about being careful in case his brakes were tampered with. Anyway, I never gave it any thought after that, until today when Mary came into the salon."

Sylvia recounted her conversation with Mary and noticed the detective raising her eyebrows when she told of how Mary had suspected Sylvia of killing Rick. She was quick to say that there was no way that Rick had slept with Mary; it was just the ravings of a lunatic.

"Where were you the afternoon Rick was murdered?" Detective Molloy asked.

Sylvia sat up straight. "I come to you with a possible murderer and you turn the twisted ravings of a psychopath into a possible motive for me to have murdered my boyfriend? This is insane," she said, tapping her fingernails on the table.

"Well I had thought that you and Alex might be in it together. The way

I see it you had a longstanding fling with Alex and you were free to see whomever you chose. Then you got caught up in a whirlwind romance. When you realized how serious it was getting after buying a house together you began to feel trapped, realized that you could no longer run to Alex whenever the mood took you. You thought of breaking up with Rick, but then you'd have had to sell that beautiful cottage. You decided the best way out of the relationship would be for him to die, leaving you with your mortgage paid off and Rick's life insurance in your bank account, so you killed him. I've done my homework on you; I know the mortgage is out in both your names, he's left the house to you in his will and named you as beneficiary of his life insurance."

Sylvia just sat with her mouth open in shock at what she was hearing. She had forgotten about the will. Sensible Elaine had suggested they both make a will when they decided to buy the house together. This meant that the house was now totally in her name, as opposed to half-owned by her and half by Rick's parents, unfortunately making her a murder suspect.

"Of course, the fact that he was having an affair with his old flat mate just provides you with an extra motive. So, where were you the afternoon Rick was murdered?"

Sylvia gulped down the lump in her throat before replying in a quiet voice, "Shopping in Galway, alone."

"Seems to me that you and Alex couldn't have been in it together or you'd have provided an alibi for one another." Detective Molloy paused. "So, is there anything you'd like to tell me?"

"I've told you all I came to tell you. Now I suggest you stop making up ridiculous stories and find the murderer."

"I assure you we are following up on all of our leads, of which you are one. If you're sure there's nothing you have to tell me you are free to go, but I would like a list of the shops you went into that day and the approximate times to see if any of the shop assistants remember you being there. I will be requesting a warrant for the receipts and purchases you have from that day. As soon as it comes through I will contact you." As Sylvia stood to go she finished, "If you admit you killed Rick now and save us some valuable time and resources it will look better for you in court."

Sylvia couldn't believe what she'd just heard. She left the Garda station with her mouth wide open and shaking her head. She had thought that perhaps she might be considered a suspect, but hadn't really believed it. She'd have to get her receipts together from that day and hope that she had made enough purchases at the time of the murder to place her, without any doubt, in Galway City at the time.

CHAPTER TWENTY-THREE

As Sylvia got out of her car to go back to work, she was surprised to run into Jerry, her ex-boyfriend. A few months ago, she would have been concerned that she wasn't looking her best, would have hoped that he was looking dreadful after their break-up. Now, however, she just wanted to get away from him, feeling unable to handle this situation after the morning she'd just had. He looked as cheerful as ever, his green eyes lit up and his mop of sandy colored hair slightly tousled in that devil-may-care way she'd always found endearing.

"Hey, Sylvia. How've you been? Fancy running into you like this! You're looking good." He stood back and looked at her. "What was I thinking of when I let you go?"

Sylvia shook her head. A few months ago she would have killed to hear him say that.

"I was just thinking about you earlier. Do you fancy grabbing a coffee or something?"

"I'm just heading back to work so I can't stop to chat."

As Sylvia made to push past him he turned and linked arms with her to walk her back to work just like old times.

"Well some other time then?"

"I don't think so," Sylvia said as she tried to jerk free of his arm.

"Why not? You can't deny we had some pretty good times together. It'd be good to catch up."

Standing outside the salon, Sylvia said, "Look, Jerry, I don't deny we had some good times together, but I have no interest in reliving the past with you. I have enough going on right now without you pestering me, so can you let me get back to work please?" She looked meaningfully down at their linked arms.

Instead of releasing his hold on her Jerry turned her to face him, and with his other hand cupped her chin and tilted her face up to look at him, saying, "Hey, this isn't like you. What's going on?" He wiped the tears from her eyes and hugged her. "Hey, whatever it is we can talk about it over coffee," he said.

Sylvia pulled away from him. He released her from the hug although he still kept hold of her arm. She said, "I have to get back to work."

"You need to talk to a friend and maybe cry on my shoulder. I'm sure Laura wouldn't want you to work when you're feeling like this."

At that moment Sylvia spotted Laura looking out the window at her and glancing at the clock. Laura had been really nice to her since Rick died; she didn't want to take advantage of her good nature. "I really have to go."

"Well can we meet later then?"

"No."

"I'll see you after work. I'll be right here."

Sylvia knew she should have objected more strongly, but she needed to get back to work. She opened the door as soon as Jerry let go of her arm, not responding to his statement. She berated herself for this, knowing she had just played right into his hands. There were a lot of raised eyebrows when she went into the salon.

"That was what you had to go out for?" Laura asked, disapproval apparent in her tone, as she wrote down an appointment in the book.

"No! I ran into him at the car and he insisted on walking back here with me."

"I hope you're not thinking of getting back with him."

"Of course not! What do you think I am? Rick's only just died!" Sylvia broke down crying; she had been holding back the tears since she left the Garda station and now she could hold back no longer.

Laura came over to her and put an arm around her, guiding her to a chair and motioning to one of the girls to get Sylvia a cup of tea. "I'm sorry, that was very insensitive of me. Of course you wouldn't think of getting back with Jerry, but I saw the way he looked at you out there and it made me wonder what his intentions were."

Sylvia looked up. "What do you mean, the way he looked at me?"

"That guy is in love."

"No way; he doesn't know the meaning of the word love, kind of like me before I met Rick."

"I could be wrong. Don't listen to me, sure what do I know? Every time I start seeing someone I imagine myself in love with them and think they love me and when I discover they don't I'm devastated; I hardly think I'm qualified to know anything about love," Laura said.

Sylvia couldn't help but smile at that as Natasha put a cup of tea in her hand. She couldn't count the amount of times Laura had come into work after a weekend fling and stated that she was in love, only to be in love with someone else the following week. Sylvia often thought that it was like working for a teenager instead of a grown woman.

"Maybe it's too soon for you to be back," Laura said.

"No. I'm sorry I fell apart like that, but I need to be back, to get on with my life. I'd just be sitting at home brooding. It's good for me to be busy."

"Okay, if you're sure, but just take it easy. Whenever you need to take a break and go in to the back for a cup of tea or whatever you just go ahead, and I promise not to make any more insensitive remarks." She squeezed Sylvia's hand in support as she got up to greet a customer.

Sylvia spent the rest of the day hoping that Jerry wouldn't turn up, but knew that he would. She knew that it would be the cause of more raised eyebrows, but didn't want to broach the subject again with Laura. She'd face and quell the speculation on Monday morning if he turned up this evening. She thought about their relationship and how they'd broken up, wondering why he would want to get back together with her.

Their relationship had been quite casual; they'd had a lot of fun, having so much in common with one another. They were very much two of a kind, living for the moment and enjoying spending their spare time doing bungee jumps and sky-dives. She hadn't done anything like that since they'd split up. She definitely seemed to have changed since meeting Rick;

she had different priorities, no longer desiring the thrill of seeing the ground come hurtling towards her.

Most of her other holidays had been to sunny destinations, where she would splash around in the pool to cool down, but with Jerry she'd gone skiing and sledding down the slopes and had snowball fights in Austria, warming up by a fire with a mug of hot chocolate in the evenings. She remembered how Jerry would sneak up behind her as she huddled by the fire and put a handful of snow down her back.

He was so light-hearted and she spent so much of her time with him laughing. He was very prone to acting on a whim and would often pick her up from work to whisk her off to Paris or Rome for a dirty weekend. It was never for a romantic weekend; theirs was a very physical relationship, and that suited them both.

Her friends had constantly said that it was obvious to everyone else but her that she loved him. She had always insisted that they just wanted to see her settled down, and especially with him, as they felt he was perfect for her. At the time she believed that she was meant to roam through life free and single and didn't intend to get serious about any man. She hadn't been able to imagine being in Elaine's position, having to consult a man about decisions that she would ordinarily make at the drop of a hat. Her friends, however, had thought that it was only a matter of time until she would prefer to consult Jerry about a decision rather than being without him.

Then one day, Jerry had decided that their relationship was getting too serious. He'd informed her that being tied down just wasn't for him. He uttered the words that sounded all too familiar to her: "I'm feeling trapped. I was meant to be free and single. This was just meant to be a bit of fun, but it's starting to get real heavy, babe, know what I mean? So I gotta hit the road, babe."

Usually it was her uttering some version of those words. At the time she thought that he must be seeing someone else, being unable to believe that he thought she was getting serious about him, when she hadn't even realized it herself. It was only when they broke up that she realized her feelings for him and it surprised her when she took the break-up badly.

Rather than her usual way of dealing with the end of a relationship, which was to run straight into Alex's arms until someone new came along, she had spent her nights alone, crying and not getting much sleep. Her friends had tried to help her through it but there was no consoling her. Even when Alex called around she had just cried on his shoulder, but made it clear to him that she didn't want to end up in bed with him this time. It was only when she fell in love with Rick that she realized that it wasn't love, although the closest thing to it that she ever previously felt, that she'd felt for Jerry.

At six o' clock as the girls all piled out of the salon together, just as she had feared, there was Jerry, his tall, athletic frame leaning casually against his shiny red Celica. The girls all cast an appreciative glance in his direction, aimed mostly at the car; however, Sylvia knew that he would take it for granted that the glances were aimed at him. He flashed a smile at the girls but let his gaze rest on Sylvia making it obvious, as if they didn't already know, that she was the reason he was there.

She heard Natasha sigh, and knew she was wishing it was her that his attentions were aimed at. She'd never made it a secret, even while Sylvia and Jerry were dating. Sylvia was convinced it was the fact that Jerry was loaded that attracted Natasha to him. Not that she was a gold-digger; it was just that she liked the finer things in life. Sylvia was sure that if Natasha went out with Jerry she'd be disappointed with the lack of romance in the relationship. It wasn't something Sylvia had ever been disappointed about, but now that she'd had that with Rick she wouldn't ever again want to be in a relationship without at least some romance in it.

"I'll see you on Monday," Laura said to Sylvia.

"This isn't what it looks like, Laura, I swear," Sylvia said.

"It's none of my business," Laura said with a sniff. Then she turned and walked away.

Sylvia sighed as she regretted that she hadn't told Laura that Jerry was going to be there, that she didn't want to see him; maybe then Laura would have offered to go out ahead of her to tell him to get lost.

"I wish you hadn't just turned up here like that; it doesn't look good for me," Sylvia said. "Rick's hardly cold in his grave. All the girls think that instead of mourning my boyfriend I'm taking up where I left off with you."

"What?!"

"Well you can't blame them for thinking that, with you turning up like this; just like when we went out together."

"No, I mean about Rick."

"It's a small town, Jerry; you surely know that Rick O' Hara was murdered and that he was my boyfriend."

"Yeah, I had heard, but I hadn't realized you two were dating." At Sylvia's raised eyebrow he said, "Hey, it was me who broke up with you, remember? I haven't been following you around like some lovesick teenager to find out whom you were seeing. Anyway, I wouldn't have thought he was your type; he was steady as a rock, not like you and I."

"Maybe that's why I fell in love with him."

"Ouch!"

"What do you mean, 'Ouch'? You never wanted me to love you; it would have cramped your style as a free spirit," Sylvia reminded him. She found herself relaxing back into the camaraderie she and Jerry had enjoyed during their relationship.

"I think we should go get a coffee; I'd like to catch up, and I think the side of the street isn't the best place for a heart to heart," Jerry said as he took her hand.

"That's fine, we can go for coffee just as long as you know that's where this ends," Sylvia said, "and let go of my hand."

"Surely we can be friends? And friends sometimes hold hands, do they not?"

"Well not us."

Jerry dropped her hand as he said, "Where would you like to go?"

"I'm easy." At Jerry's grin she regretted her choice of words. "You know what I mean," she said in exasperation.

They agreed on Molloy's Café, a small, cozy café across from the salon. Decorated in muted colors and specializing in coffees, herbal teas and health food, it was frequented by the local business people. After ordering their drinks Jerry asked, "So how did you manage to get bitten by the love bug? I thought we were a couple of free spirits?"

"I don't know; it just sort of happened."

"Yeah I know what you mean; I guess my timing's pretty lousy, but I've been thinking a lot about you lately and I had hoped we could start seeing each other again. I miss you and I'm not used to feeling like this. I wouldn't call it love, but I don't know what to call it. I meant it earlier when I said I didn't know why I ever let you go. It was a big mistake."

Their drinks arrived at the table just then, giving Sylvia a moment to process what Jerry had said. After taking a sip of her tea she responded, "I'll say your timing's lousy! If that's why you wanted to see me you can forget it."

"I know now's not a good time for you, but we can just hang out as friends, and in time who knows?"

"I do know; I'm not the same person I was before; being in love with Rick has changed me."

"Okay, so even if nothing romantic ever happens between us you can't say we couldn't have fun as just friends."

"It wouldn't be a good idea if you always wanted more."

"Maybe your friendship would be enough for me."

"Would it?" Sylvia was skeptical.

"It's worth a try."

"I don't think so."

"You can't say we weren't good together."

"I agree we had a good time, and if we had agreed to remain friends after we split up then that would be fine, but I'm not interested in starting up a friendship with you now."

"We could have so much fun together, you know we could, and I could help you get over Rick."

"I think I know just how you'd like to help me and I think it would be best not to."

Jerry grinned. "You know me too well." He took a sip of coffee and said, "But seriously, let's leave sex out of it for now. You're not thinking clearly at the moment. You've just been through something awful. You need some space right now, and that's fine; I'll give it to you. Meanwhile I'll be thinking about you. I'll call you every now and then to see how you're doing."

"I'd really rather you didn't."

"That's settled then, that's what we'll do, and when you're ready we can start spending some time together." The gleam came back in his eyes as he said, "And then we can get back to the sex." Getting serious again, he said, "So, do the guards know who did it then?"

"No, they're still looking into it." As Sylvia said this she realized that the guards would be interested to know that Jerry was trying to get back with her, not that she believed even for one second that it was him who killed Rick. She liked him, even if he had broken her heart; that was old news. She was over that, and she had no desire to put the guards on to him. However, it might be no harm to scare him off with the thoughts that they would be very interested in this latest turn of events.

"They're suspicious of any of my exes who still harbor feelings for me, one good reason for you not to be seen with me, don't you think?" Sylvia thought she saw a touch of fear in his eyes, but he hid it well as he finished his coffee.

"Say no more," he said, standing up. "I'll keep an ear out for the progress of the case. As soon as they have someone for it I'll call you."

Sylvia breathed a sigh of relief as he left the café. Thank God for that, she thought. I know it's only a temporary respite, but at least it buys me some time before he starts to hassle me again.

CHAPTER TWENTY-FOUR

Detective Molloy knocked on the door of Rick's old flat. When she saw the dowdy looking girl who answered the door she nearly believed that there was no way Rick would have slept with her when he had Sylvia. However, she knew that there was no real way of telling and had to remind herself again to keep an open mind. After all, if he had felt sorry for Mary, as Sylvia had suggested, and she offered herself to him, who knew?

Detective Molloy identified herself, introduced her partner and explained that they'd like Mary to accompany them to the station for questioning.

"Is this to do with Rick's murder?" Mary asked.

"Yes it is."

"I'd be glad to help; I just want to see his murderer behind bars."

At the station the detectives brought Mary into the interview room and told her they'd be recording the interview. Mary always seems too eager to be in here, Detective Molloy thought, remembering when they questioned her after Mark's death. She'd looked around her then, just as she was doing now, with a gleeful smile on her face, taking delight in the fact that she was being asked questions pertaining to a death, almost assuming that by answering she would play a role in solving the crime.

After stating the date, time and persons present Detective Molloy asked, "Could you tell me the nature of your relationship with Rick?"

Mary crossed her legs and clasped her hands on her lap as she said, "We lived together for three months, platonically of course. At the start Rick was single, but I was going out with someone. As the weeks went on I fell in love with him, and I broke up with my boyfriend for him. However, on the same day I did that Rick met Sylvia. Of course I was devastated, as I thought that maybe he didn't feel the same way about me that I felt for him. I had hoped that the relationship wouldn't last long, and I was awfully upset when he told me that they were moving in together. I have to admit that I didn't get another flat mate, as I was hoping that when they broke up he'd come running back to me. When I heard that they had bought that little cottage I thought it was all over for us.

"Anyway, one night about a week before he was so brutally murdered," she continued in a melodramatic tone, tucking a stray strand of hair behind her ears, "he came to me and admitted his feelings for me. He said he was going to leave Sylvia for me but that it would take time because the house tied them together. We made love, and then he told me he had to go back to Sylvia. I was a little upset, but he told me to be patient so I let him go.

"I was just devastated when I heard he had been killed. At first I thought it had been Sylvia who killed him when she found out that he and I had slept together and that he was planning on leaving her for me. But then I thought about how nice she is and how she could never kill anyone and I felt silly for even thinking it. I hope you do find who killed him. I loved him so much."

"Where were you the afternoon Rick was murdered? Saturday the thirteenth of September?"

Mary laughed. "You hardly think it was me, do you? Why would I do that? I loved him, and he was going to leave his girlfriend for me."

"All the same, I need you to answer the question," Detective Molloy said and glanced over at her partner who was writing notes.

"I don't remember where I was," Mary said and tucked another strand of hair behind her ear.

"You don't remember where you were and what you were doing when the man you loved was killed?" Detective Molloy asked. "Maybe you find that difficult since only a week beforehand your ex boyfriend was killed."

Mary said, "Oh, I loved him so much."

"Who, Mark?"

"Yes," Mary moaned as she shifted in her seat.

"You loved them both?" Detective Molloy asked.

"They were wonderful, so smart, so loving, gentle and sweet, and now they're both dead and I'm alone," Mary said, on the verge of tears.

Oh dear, Detective Molloy thought, maybe Sylvia was right; we might just have a psychopath on our hands.

"Where were you the afternoon Rick was murdered, the Saturday before last?"

"I think I was at home," Mary lifted her hand to rub the back of her neck.

"Do you have anyone who can verify that?"

"I don't think so," Mary said, replacing her hand on her lap.

Hmm, thought Detective Molloy. Another possibility. It's interesting that she claims both now and when we interviewed her after Mark's death that it was she who broke up with him and Sylvia claims that it was Mark who broke up with her.

Detective Molloy told Mary she would like to take her fingerprints and then she would be free to go for now. "Just one more question," the detective concluded. "Did you tamper with Mark's brakes?"

"Of course not!" Mary seemed horrified at the thought.

When Mary left the room Detective Molloy raised her eyebrows at her partner and asked, "Well, what do you think?"

Detective Molloy sat back in his chair, put an ankle on his knee and clasped his hands behind his head. He said, "I think that there's no way in hell Rick slept with her when he had Sylvia. That woman is delusional. We'd better re-open the case of the accidental death of Mark Lynch. The car will have to be examined again for evidence of tampering. I doubt that anything was overlooked; however, Mary does seem to be the type to kill. She fits the profile more than any of the other suspects, and now there's the question of whether or not it was she who broke up with Mark to consider. We'll have to search her flat, see if we can find anything there to link her to either or both deaths."

"All the same, I'm not giving up on any of the other theories." Detective Molloy said, grabbing a pen off the table and chewing it. She knew that if she kept interrogating the suspects something would surely come to light.

She rang Elaine and asked her to come down to the station at her earliest possible convenience, knowing she would bring her solicitor, which hampered her somewhat; however, it was better than not questioning her again. Perhaps she would manage to wear Elaine down, break through that calm exterior.

Detective Molloy thought back to the statements of Julie, Maeve and Noel; individually, all three were in agreement that Alex had seemed to be somewhat bitter towards Rick the Friday night before the murder. None of them knew of any reason for this, which made the detective think that Alex was possibly the most likely suspect. The people present at the party who were unaware of the past between Alex and Sylvia had picked up on how Alex felt about Rick. His friends were either protecting him or were so used to his ways and feelings that they were unaware of his bitterness towards Rick. She realized that Rick's alleged affair with Mary was a further motive for Alex.

She realized something that she had missed out on when she interviewed Julie. When the detective had mentioned Sylvia's name Julie had sniffed and looked down her nose as if Sylvia were beneath her. That, coupled with the fact that Julie had spoken very fondly of Rick, made Detective Molloy think that maybe she had designs on him and perhaps it was she who murdered him, not wanting anyone else to have him if she couldn't. It would be worth interviewing those three again, she thought.

She thought back to when they had visited Rick's family, and hoped for their sakes that she would find the murderer soon. It was always a hard part of her job, commiserating with the family of the deceased. However, when it came to the family of murder victims it was so much harder as she felt that she wasn't doing them justice no matter how hard she worked at trying to find the murderer.

She remembered how when they had called around to Rick's sister, Maria, the poor woman was struggling to try to keep it together for the sake of the children, who were mercifully oblivious to the whole thing. It was good that she had such helpful neighbors who were willing to take the children for a while in order to allow her some time to grieve.

Damien is such a blessing for the parents to have around, the detective thought now. He had moved back in with them to help them cope and he was being strong for them. She remembered how Janice had accidentally called him Rick while the detectives were there, and when she realized what she had done it had brought tears to her eyes. Tom is hurting deeply; I could see it in his eyes, Detective Molloy thought. She knew he was remaining strong for the sake of the family. Janice was the only one of them that the detective had seen openly grieving. She wondered if in private moments the others broke down and cried their eyes out. She was sure they must, as it was hard to feel that you had to be the strong one.

CHAPTER TWENTY-FIVE

Monday the 29th of September

Elaine arranged to have her mum baby-sit on Monday morning so that she could meet up with her solicitor down at the station. As Dillon was having a bad morning Elaine was feeling very frazzled by the time she left the house. After a morning of listening to him whining, the last thing she wanted was to answer the detective's questions. She would have preferred to stay at home and referee the war that was breaking out between Dillon and Jody as she made her escape. Dillon had clung to her leg the minute he saw his granny and she had just managed to coax him to go to her mother when Jody charged into him, knocking him to the ground.

When she arrived at the station Detective Molloy escorted her and Joanna once again into the interview room, where Detective Naughton already sat waiting.

Elaine sighed. I can't believe I've seen inside this room even once, never mind twice. It's not something I'd ever imagined could happen. Then again, I never would have thought that anything could happen between Dave and Sylvia either, not even him coming on to her. You just never know how your life is going to play out, she thought.

Detective Molloy took her seat and asked, "Is there anything else that has come to mind since our last chat that might help with this investigation?"

"No, not exactly. I'd just like to say that I hadn't been aware that my husband had made a play for Sylvia until you mentioned the possibility at our last meeting. When I confronted him he came clean. I will admit I was very angry and upset at first, but these things are better out in the open. Things between us are better now than they've ever been," Elaine said, sitting up straight in her chair. She didn't want the detective to have the satisfaction that she'd caused trouble in their relationship.

"Could it be that you were well aware of what had happened between Sylvia and Dave but that you are covering yourself by making out that you didn't so that suspicion is lifted from you?" Detective Molloy said with both of her eyebrows raised.

Elaine's jaw dropped; she couldn't believe what she was hearing. When she gathered herself together she said, "Is this what you do all day, sit around and make up stories? It's no wonder the murderer hasn't been caught yet if this is your idea of trying to solve it."

"I can assure you that I am doing my job. I am following all leads, and as your fingerprints have been found on the weapon you are one of the suspects. So is there anything you would like to tell me?"

Elaine sat forward in her chair, clasped her hands in front of her on the table and said, "I didn't kill Rick; the reason you've found my prints on the murder weapon is that I was helping Sylvia in the kitchen the night before and, as you know, the knife wasn't washed between the party and the murder."

"It must be tough finding out that your husband has been having an affair with your best friend," Detective Molloy continued.

"I object," interrupted Joanna, putting her finger up in the air. "There has never been any indication of an actual affair between Dave and Sylvia. You are trying to bait my client."

Elaine looked over towards Detective Naughton, wondering if he was going to step in, hoping he would as he looked much gentler than his partner, knowing his comments would surely be less waspish. However, all he did was sit there, his chin propped in his hand, his middle finger over his lip, as he looked thoughtful.

"What did Dave say when you confronted him?" Detective Molloy continued.

"That he had once suggested to Sylvia that they go upstairs while I was out, that nothing had happened and that he would never try anything like that again because he regretted it so much," Elaine said, realizing that even though she had forgiven Dave and everything was now fine between them her emotions were still very raw, making it very difficult to respond to the detective.

"However, you know that's not the full truth, don't you?" suggested Detective Molloy.

"I object to such insinuations," Joanna said.

"Were you aware of the affair Rick was having?" Detective Molloy asked.

"What affair?" Elaine asked, not believing for one minute there could be any truth in whatever allegations Detective Molloy was about to make.

"It's come to my attention that Rick was having an affair with his ex flat mate. I was just wondering if you could shed any light on that situation, but obviously not," Detective Molloy said and then concluded the interview and said she'd be in touch.

Detective Molloy rang Dave at work that afternoon and asked him to come in as soon as he could. She told him that as he was not a suspect there'd be no need for him to bring his solicitor. She hoped he'd go along with that and was delighted when he showed up an hour later with no solicitor in tow.

"So your wife knows about the affair then?" she asked, crossing her legs and propping her chin up with her hand.

"There was never any affair, but yes she knows thanks to you," Dave said as he leaned back in his chair and crossed his legs at the ankles.

"Less of the attitude please. I'm not the one who was playing away from home. I'm just doing my job."

"I wasn't playing away from home; I just came on to Sylvia. It was a one-off and it never came to anything. Why exactly are we having this conversation?"

"Did Rick know about you and Sylvia?" Detective Molloy asked, placing her hands in front of her on the table and clasping them lightly.

"To my knowledge Sylvia and I were the only ones who knew until I let it slip to you."

"However, you don't know for certain."

"No I don't."

"So isn't it possible that Elaine had an idea about it before I let the cat out of the bag?"

"No; if she had I'd have known about it."

"Not if she didn't want you to know she knew."

"What sort of rubbish is that you're talking?" Dave asked and sat more upright in his chair.

"She may not have wanted anyone to know that she knew about you and Sylvia while she plotted her revenge."

"What revenge? What on earth are you talking about?"

"Isn't it possible that your wife found out about your affair with Sylvia, kept quiet about it while secretly plotting to exact revenge on Sylvia by killing Rick – 'You mess with my man, I'll take yours away from you by killing him.'"

"My wife didn't kill Rick to get back at Sylvia for me coming on to her. She blamed me for that, not Sylvia, and rightly so since it was Sylvia who put a stop to me cheating on my wife."

"Not as far as Elaine is concerned. She's pretty convinced that it was an affair that was going on between you and Sylvia," Detective Molloy said.

"Where are you getting that information? Your imagination?"

"From your wife."

"She actually said that she thinks Sylvia and I had an affair?" Dave's voice was raised an octave or two in incredulity.

"Nothing good ever comes from having an affair. Looks like this one got totally out of control. It may all very well have been over in one day, but what's important is that your wife believed it to have been a full blown affair and exacted revenge on her best friend by killing her boyfriend."

"Even if Elaine suspected that Sylvia and I were having a full-on affair and she kept it to herself until she decided what to do about it, there is no way in hell that she would have chosen to kill Rick. It's me she would have killed, or castrated."

"That's what I'm trying to find out, so it would be better for your wife if you came clean now and told me exactly what happened between you and Sylvia. If you do so and if your wife admits to the murder she may get a lighter sentence by pleading insanity due to jealousy and betrayal."

"Sounds like I should have brought my solicitor after all. If I tell you everything that happened between Sylvia and I, will you get off Elaine's case? I know my wife and she's no murderer."

"I'm sure that before she found out about you and Sylvia she would have said 'I know my husband and he's no adulterer,' or 'I know my best friend and there's no way she'd sleep with my husband.'"

"We didn't sleep together." Dave told the detective what had transpired the day in question.

Detective Molloy told Dave that he was free to go. She thought that maybe he was telling the truth about what had actually happened between him and Sylvia. However, that didn't mean that Elaine hadn't in fact suspected an affair and that the suspicion hadn't prompted the murder of Rick. However, she still felt that Alex was the more probable suspect. Sylvia and Mary were coming in close behind, and Julie was also looking like a possibility, with Elaine being the least likely.

As she picked up the phone to ring Julie, Maeve and Noel to arrange for them to come in for further questioning, Detective Naughton turned around in his chair to face her and said, "There was no affair between Dave and Sylvia, and it wasn't Elaine who killed Rick; I'm sure of it."

Detective Molloy made her phone calls before resuming the conversation with her partner.

"I agree; even though some of the evidence points quite clearly to Elaine, I know in my gut that she isn't a murderer. It's not just the fact that she's a mother; there are plenty of those who are criminals. It's something about her personality; wholesomeness just shines out of her. However, I'm not going to let go of the possibility, just in case."

She had never been wrong before about people; even before becoming a Garda she was always good at reading people, but all the same, she could just be wrong. She had been on the force for fifteen years and in all of that time, although there had been unsolved cases, in all of the cases she had solved it had been her gut instincts that had solved them. It didn't take a huge leap of the imagination to believe that any of the suspects were capable of murder, but her gut led her to only one possibility. Detective Naughton was several years her junior and had a lot to learn, but she knew his instincts were keen, and if they were both in agreement it was probably a safe bet.

CHAPTER TWENTY-SIX

That evening after the children were in bed, Dave told Elaine about his meeting with the detectives.

When he had finished she looked up from doing the dishes and said in surprise, "Joanna let her say all this to you?"

"Joanna wasn't there; Detective Molloy had said that I didn't need my solicitor," Dave said as he made a mug of tea for them both.

"And you believed her? You idiot!" Elaine said as she took her tea and went to sit on the couch.

"Don't be like that. How was I to know that she was going to try to use everything I said against you?" Dave said as he joined her.

"Because of what happened last time, even with Joanna there," Elaine said. "I really love you, Dave, but really you have to think before you answer that detective. She has nothing to go on; she's so far away from solving this murder, and she would just love to pin it on someone whose fingerprints are on the knife. I think it would be best to bring Joanna with you the next time, but hopefully there won't be a next time. I tried to ring you today at work, as I was fuming when I came back from the station, but you were in a meeting. It's a pity I didn't get to talk to you; if I had you might have been prepared for Detective Molloy's insinuations and brought Joanna with you." She then filled him in on her own meeting with the detectives. "I really do want to let this whole business with you and Sylvia lie, but Detective Molloy keeps bringing it up," she finished.

The sound of the doorbell interrupted them. Elaine went to answer it and was delighted to see Sylvia. Dave made some tea for Sylvia, and

Elaine asked her how she had settled back at work. Sylvia filled her in on Mary having come in to the salon on Saturday and her subsequent conversation with Detective Molloy.

"Ah, that explains why she asked me if I knew about the affair Rick was having," Elaine said. She then filled Sylvia in on her and Dave's meetings with the detectives.

"That woman is unreal!" Elaine finished. "How is she ever going to find the murderer, if she keeps harping on at us?"

"She's only doing her job," Sylvia said taking a sip of her tea. "Don't get me wrong; I wish she'd let up on all of us, but if she grills the murderer the way she's been grilling us she's bound to get somewhere. Anyway, you're never going to guess who I bumped into on Saturday."

"Who?" Elaine asked, tucking into the chocolate biscuits Dave brought in with Sylvia's tea before leaving the room and leaving the girls to talk.

"Jerry; apparently he's been thinking about me a lot lately and was wondering if we could get back together."

"Just after Rick's been killed? The nerve of the man!"

"In fairness to him he hadn't realized that Rick and I had been going out together, much less been so serious about each other," Sylvia said, putting her mug down and picking up a teddy bear.

"You believe that? It's a small town; of course he knew you were seeing Rick! That means he was extremely jealous of what you and Rick had together, or else it makes him completely insensitive to what you're going through, or both, probably both. Hey, you don't think he killed Rick, do you?"

"No way; I did tell him, though, that the guards were suspicious of any exes who were still interested in me, to get him off my back. He just wouldn't take no for an answer," Sylvia said, stroking the fur of the teddy bear.

"Does that not make you think that maybe he killed Rick?" Elaine asked, tucking her feet up under her and putting a cushion at her back.

"It really gives me the creeps to think I could have been dating someone who turned out to be a murderer!"

"Which would creep you out more, to find that he was a murderer and you used to date him, or to find the next guy you date dead because he's jealous of him too? I think you should tell Detective Molloy of his interest in you."

"I hate it when you're right. I have to go to the station anyway to give in my receipts and purchases from that day of shopping to see if they can prove that I didn't kill Rick; I'll mention it to her while I'm there. By the way, what does your mother make of all of this?"

"I haven't told her I'm a murder suspect if that's what you're getting at. I don't want to give my parents heart attacks. Surely Alex hasn't told his mother?"

"He has and she's managed to make it all my fault," Sylvia said, putting the teddy bear down beside her and taking a chocolate biscuit.

"How can it be your fault?" Elaine asked taking another biscuit.

"You know what she's like; no good could ever have come out of Alex hanging out with me, it's my own fault Rick was killed, he probably killed himself just to get away from me."

"She never said that?!"

"She did. She rang me up just to have a go at me. When I answered the phone I was sure she was going to lay aside her differences with me and give me her condolences, but instead she just gave out yards to me. If it were me that had been murdered I'd be considering her as suspect number one; she'd kill me just so that Alex couldn't be with me."

"Do your parents know you're a suspect?"

"Absolutely not; could you imagine! Mum would be down there reading the detectives the riot act. Alex has only told his parents about him being a suspect, not about us, so at least our parents won't find out second hand. I still can't believe we're suspects, it all seems so unreal. I still can't help thinking that I'm going to wake up and find Rick beside me and realize this was all a nightmare. Whoever said soap operas were unrealistic? Our lives certainly seem like one right now," Sylvia said as she wiped crumbs from her jeans.

"Only if it was a soap we could hope that the writers would make it all a dream sequence."

"Like in Dallas?" Sylvia giggled.

"Talking about how soap-like it all is, you never told me Mary had tried to kiss Rick!"

"I completely forgot all about it; it happened a week before he was killed and that was a mad busy week for me. I never even gave it a second thought then, nor at the dinner party, and obviously since his murder she was the last thing on my mind until I saw her on Saturday. Can you believe she's trying to make out he slept with her? Can you imagine? Yuck!" Sylvia shuddered.

"You think it was her who did it?"

"Yeah; she's pretty psycho. I hope Detective Molloy got something on her and arrested her; I really just want this to be all over."

"Do you think she really tampered with Mark's brakes?"

"It's hard to know. It could have just been a freak accident, but it's a bit of a co-incidence don't you think? Mark dumps her, he gets killed in an accident or whatever, and then Rick, whom she thinks she was in love with and who was with me, gets killed. My suspicions are on her."

"She's definitely a more likely candidate than the rest of us. Hopefully now that the detectives have got a real suspect they'll get off our backs. So anyway, how are you getting on in the cottage?"

"Fine; I've had a few bad dreams, but that's to be expected. I think I needed to get my life back on track; I wasn't going to get over Rick staying here and staying off work; I need my mind occupied by more than Rick's murder. I thought briefly about selling the cottage but I couldn't bear to, not yet anyway. I really love it there, and it is nice having so many memories of Rick. I thought I'd be really upset if every time I went into a room I remembered him doing something there, but it hasn't made me sad at all. Quite the opposite, in fact."

"You should keep it; you don't know how your life is going to pan out. I know you can't exactly think about it right now but in a few years you could be married with kids."

"I seriously doubt that. How long has it taken me to fall in love in the first place? It's not likely to happen again is it? Not that I mind that prospect. I don't want anyone else; I only want Rick."

Sylvia changed the subject, turning the conversation to what was going on with her work mates and what the children had been up to lately. After a while she stood up to go home, saying that she had to get up for work in the morning. Elaine was about to suggest that she could stay the night when she remembered that Sylvia wanted to get on with things as normally as possible.

When Sylvia had gone home Elaine put away what was left of the chocolate biscuits and swept up the incriminating crumbs. She thought about how much her friend had changed since falling in love, how she had gone from a man-eating girl with not a care in the world to a domesticated, mortgage-paying woman in love. She thought about how much she had changed since Rick's death, not caring about whether or not she'd ever have another boyfriend again, a big leap from her pre-Rick life. She was glad her worries about Sylvia reverting back to her old self were unfounded.

Elaine found herself thinking about how drastically Alex's life would be changed if he were found guilty of the murder. Her heart ached to think of him locked up in prison. She felt sure he didn't have what it took to survive it, and if he did survive and got out in ten years or so, how would prison life have changed him? He would be harder, not the kind, considerate, caring Alex she knew and loved. For a gentle soul like him to be locked up with hardened criminals would be a tough thing for him to go through. Not seeing the sun set over the sea, the sun rise over the mountains or the seasons changing the foliage on the trees would break his heart, his spirit. She could see that despite putting a brave face on it and thinking positively about the whole thing it was taking its toll on him.

She had called over to him the night before to see how he was and found him pale and looking like he had lost weight. When she had asked him if he was eating right he just evaded her question, and he had kept changing the subject when she tried to find out how he was feeling. Not good signs, she thought; she and Alex had always spoken openly and honestly to one another. This whole thing is breaking him already. God help him if he's convicted, he'll already be going to prison a broken man. I'm afraid he might do something drastic if he were to be convicted, like doing away with himself. Elaine felt a shiver down her spine at that thought.

With any luck it wouldn't come to that. She really disliked Detective Molloy, despite her having been gentle and caring when she was first dealing with Sylvia. Questioning them all certainly seemed to be bringing out the bad cop side of her, but she did get the impression that the woman knew what she was doing and would find the person who killed Rick. She wondered what type of person could possibly do such a thing, and why. Rick was such a wonderful person; it didn't make sense for him to be killed like that. She thought about the possibility of it being Mary, and even though she had never met her she couldn't reconcile herself with a female murderer. Of course, she reasoned, there are women who are capable of murder, but surely it would take a man to wield a knife with that kind of force. After all Rick was a large, strong man.

He used to work out, not excessively, but enough to keep himself in shape. It may have been possible for a man to overpower him, Elaine thought, but a woman, surely not. Obviously he was caught by surprise, but even so surely it could only possibly be a man who had done it. Of course if Mary is indeed a psycho perhaps she has a split personality. Elaine remembered having read somewhere that sometimes when a person is taken over by their alter ego they can be possessed by an unnatural strength.

As Elaine got into bed she hoped that the case would be solved soon. She didn't know how much more of this Alex could take. Maybe this girl Dave is trying to set him up with will be a good distraction for him, she thought as she snuggled up in bed beside Dave.

CHAPTER TWENTY-SEVEN

Tuesday the 30th of September

The next morning in the interview room Detective Molloy sat questioning Maeve, a slight girl with long straight black hair who looked like she could be blown away by a puff of wind. Her features were almost childlike and she had a wide-eyed look of innocence about her. "Have you ever entertained any notions of yourself and Rick getting together?"

Maeve gave a little laugh. "Absolutely not, I only met Rick through Noel. We've been together for three years now and I've never thought of Rick as more than a friend."

"What about Julie?" Detective Molloy kept her tone light, casual. She tapped a pen on the table.

"Noel mentioned something about them going out together once, but it didn't last long; there was no spark between them apparently. I asked Julie about it once, but she didn't want to talk about it."

I knew it, thought Detective Molloy. She was careful to mask her expression. She didn't want to give her line of thought and reactions away. She cast a surreptitious glance at her partner and saw him writing away. She wondered what he was thinking. "Oh? Do you think she still carried a torch then?" she asked Maeve.

Maeve laughed that little laugh again. "Who knows? I've seen her looking at him from time to time, but who doesn't think about what might have been? I certainly do. I'm very happy with Noel, but I drift off into dreamland every now and again where George Clooney takes one look at me, falls helplessly in love with me and whisks me off my feet. I'm sure Julie has had such thoughts about Rick every now and again. Who could blame her? He was such a nice guy, and very good-looking."

"How has she been?"

Maeve sat up straight and tucked her hair behind her ear. "She's heartbroken; they'd been friends since they were twelve. Noel is devastated too, but you know what men are like; his sorrow is a lot more understated than Julie's."

"Have you remembered anything else that might be of help to our enquiry? Have you thought of any ex-girlfriends that you may have forgotten about who may have killed him?"

"No, but then, as I already told you, Noel and Julie knew Rick so much better than I did."

"I know I asked this already, but has anything come back to you about the night before the murder, any cross words or looks?"

"Only what I already told you about Alex seeming to be off with Rick. I know they worked together, so maybe something had happened that day at work to make Alex annoyed with Rick."

"Thank you, you've been very helpful. If you think of anything, no matter how trivial it may seem, be sure to let us know," Detective Molloy concluded, standing up and shaking Maeve's hand.

Later that morning Noel came in for questioning. He did not seem pleased to be there again; his large frame and cloudy grey eyes gave off very unfriendly vibes as he sat in the chair opposite the two detectives. He brushed his fingers through his balding black hair in an impatient gesture. Detective Molloy could almost hear him saying, "Can we just get on with this and get it over with?" so audible was his body language.

"You've been close to Rick all of your life. Are there any ex-girlfriends who may have been jealous of his relationship with Sylvia, who may have decided that if they couldn't have him no-one else could either?" Detective Molloy asked with her hands clasped in front of her on the table.

"We covered that the last time I was here. All his exes are now married." Noel wasn't making any attempt to hide his irritation at being there.

"All of them? Are you sure?"

"Unless he had a secret someone stashed away somewhere, and that wasn't Rick's style. I knew about all of his girlfriends." Noel tapped his fingers on the table.

"Did you know about Mary, his ex flat mate?"

"What about her?"

"So you didn't know about all of his girlfriends then."

"Mary? His girlfriend? I don't think so. You've been misinformed."

I'd imagine that his best friend would know if there had been something going on between Rick and Mary, Detective Molloy thought. "Did Julie ever go out with Rick?" she asked.

"Once back in school they had one date. He told me that when he had kissed her he felt nothing. He said it felt weird, like they were definitely supposed to be friends, nothing more."

Hmmm, thought Detective Molloy. I wonder if maybe Julie didn't feel the same way. She may have resented that all this time. "Did Julie feel the same way?" she continued, her tone conversational.

"It was like as if their date had never happened; one day she was all excited about her up-coming date with Rick, the next it was as if she had never thought of him as more than a friend."

"The date with Julie had slipped your mind. Perhaps there were others?"

"Not that I'm aware of. Rick wasn't a player; he didn't do one-night stands and casual flings."

"If you think of something you'll let me know, won't you," Detective Molloy concluded.

As Noel left the room, Detective Molloy thought about the possibilities. It would make it simpler if it were Alex, Elaine or Sylvia who was the murderer; their fingerprints were on the murder weapon. However, that didn't rule out the possibility that it could just as easily have been Mary or Julie using gloves. Lovers spurned were a definite possibility. She needed to get Julie in to ascertain an alibi and get a feel for whether or not she was bitter about the fact that she and Rick had never been more than friends. What a complicated group, she thought.

Alex is in love with Sylvia who was in love with Rick who had Mary and possibly Julie in love with him. On top of all of that there's Elaine's husband, Dave, making a pass at her best friend, Sylvia.

Later that morning Julie arrived at the Garda station and entered the interview room. She was a tall, slim girl with stylish short brown hair, who carried herself with a sophisticated grace.

"Were there any of Rick's ex-girlfriends who may have held a grudge against him?" Detective Molloy asked.

"No; they're all married," Julie answered, sitting up straight in the chair.

"Rick seems to have kept an open relationship with his friends regarding his love life, but can you be sure he didn't have any skeletons he kept hidden?" Detective Molloy asked, sitting back in her chair, her legs crossed and her hands clasped on her lap.

"Rick wasn't very secretive; he couldn't keep a secret to save his life." Suddenly aware of what she had said, Julie blushed and lowered her head.

"Did you ever have a romantic relationship with Rick?"

"No, not as such. He asked me out once; we went to the cinema and we had a good time, but there was nothing in it. It was clear to both of us that it was best to keep our relationship on a just friends basis."

"Did he kiss you?"

"Yes, but I'd rather not go into that; it was awkward. It just wasn't meant to be."

"Was it awkward the next day?"

"A little, but things got back to normal between us very quickly. It was as if that night hadn't happened, an experiment that didn't work out. We never talked about it after that."

"It can't be easy going out with someone on a first date and having all these expectations only to have it flop," Detective Molloy said.

"We were only kids. Things have moved a long way since then."

"That probably made it worse, being teenagers with all those mixed up emotions."

"It was all so long ago. I don't know about you, but I certainly don't make a habit out of reliving my teen years, especially not angst-ridden awkward moments," Julie replied. She seemed uncomfortable in her chair, moved around a little and sat up even straighter.

"Have you ever wondered what if?"

"I don't do what ifs. Life is life; whatever happens, happens."

"Everybody does a little daydreaming; there's no shame in it. So maybe you thought from time to time about how it would be if Rick and you had continued to date after that one night?"

"I've never given that a second's thought," Julie said.

Caught out in a lie, Detective Molloy thought. However, it could be Maeve's overactive, romantic imagination that had her thinking that Julie might have felt something for Rick that she actually didn't. It doesn't give me anything to go on. It would be a good idea to get Sylvia in again and see what her perceptions of Julie are.

"Where were you the afternoon Rick was murdered?"

"I was hung-over from the night before," Julie answered in a small voice. "I was in bed, sick."

"Alone?"

"Yes."

"Can anyone corroborate that?"

"I wasn't up to making any phone calls or even answering the phone."

"It must have been some night."

"It was."

Detective Molloy concluded the interview and asked Julie to let her know if anything came to mind that might be of help.

"So, what are your thoughts?" Detective Naughton asked, after Julie left the room. He sat back in his chair, crossed his arms and crossed his legs at the ankles.

"No alibis anywhere for any of the suspects. Sylvia has a possible alibi if she can prove that she was actually in Galway shopping at the time. The only one with fingerprints on the murder weapon who hasn't been asked for an alibi is Kim, and she doesn't have a motive, at least not one that I'm aware of. It might be a good idea to get her back in here, find out if she does have an alibi or motive.

"Sylvia, Alex and Elaine have motives, no alibis and fingerprints all over the weapon. Julie and Mary have motives, no alibi and no fingerprints on the weapon. I really feel as if we're getting nowhere with this. Even the searches we conducted of their houses and apartments yielded nothing."

She linked her hands behind her head and thought about the fact that the lab results came back showing no significant DNA on Rick's body. The DNA present at the scene could have been from the night before, meaning it was more likely to be Sylvia, Alex or Elaine.

"It's a pity the neighbors couldn't shed any light on the situation. I know the nearest neighbors live quite a bit away, but, in fairness, what's happened to small town nosiness? I know my neighbors know what I'm doing at every moment of every day, and they live half a mile down the road. They're always going for walks past my house and look in every time. If anything ever happened to me at home you'd have to look no further than them for some answers," she said.

"What does your gut tell you?" Detective Naughton said.

"That it was Alex. Everyone I've talked to who has seen Alex and Rick together, apart from his friends of course, has spoken of ill feeling between Alex and Rick. Some are aware of the reason and some aren't. Nobody else seems to have had any problem with Rick, apart from Mary and Julie who appear to have loved him. Their problem was that he didn't return their feelings. Mary seems quite psychotic, though. She seems more like a murderer than Alex, but appearances can be deceptive. I'm more inclined to go with my gut than the fact that Mary seems to fit the profile better. What do you think?"

"I'm thinking it was Mary. I wouldn't be surprised to find when we look into it again that Mark's brakes were tampered with, that she's guilty of both murders. I believe Sylvia about Mary trying to kiss Rick the week before he was killed; when he turned her down she killed him just like she killed Mark when he broke up with her. It's certainly more believable than him cheating on Sylvia with Mary and Sylvia killing him when she found out. Although I have to agree with you about Alex, he's my second choice for this."

CHAPTER TWENTY-EIGHT

The phone rang at the hair salon. When Sylvia answered it she was a little annoyed to find that she was being asked in for questioning yet again. She knew she was going to have to go down to the station again anyway, but had been hoping that the murder would be solved by the time the detectives had the warrant. She had brought the receipts and purchases with her to work so that they'd be at hand when needed; she couldn't bring herself to wear any of the items as they were all tainted with the memory of finding Rick lying dead, so she figured locked up in evidence was as good a place as any for them. She thought that even if she left them in to a charity shop they might bring bad luck to whoever bought them, although she did think that might just be her being silly.

This is a bloody nuisance, Sylvia thought as she hung up the phone. It had better be for something constructive and not just to insinuate again that it was me who killed my own boyfriend, she thought as she stomped off to find Laura to ask her for a longer lunch-break. Laura was reluctant at first because the afternoon was scheduled to be busy. However, when Sylvia explained what it was for, Laura agreed that of course she could have the time and added that she hoped the guards had found the murderer. Laura's reception of Sylvia had been rather cold the previous morning, but when Sylvia had explained the situation with Jerry to her she had warmed considerably.

After eating a hurried lunch Sylvia made her way to the Garda station, wondering if the detectives had discovered that it was Mary who had killed Rick. As much as she had been convinced over the previous days that it was Mary, it pained her to think of how nice Rick had been to her, how he had put his arms around her as she cried over Mark only to be repaid by her killing him. She almost hoped now that it was a total stranger, and not someone he had liked and trusted, who had killed him. As she took a seat opposite Detective Molloy she wondered if this was going to be an end to the whole thing, that they had someone for the murder, whether friend or foe.

However, she soon realized that wasn't the case when Detective Molloy asked, "Were you aware that Julie and Rick dated when they were younger?"

Sylvia's face fell; it looked like they were no closer to solving the case. She was going to have to tell the detectives about Jerry's interest in her after all. She couldn't reconcile his hands that had caressed her so lovingly with the hands of a murderer, but she knew she had to give all the relevant information she had to the detectives. She sat up straight in her chair and clasped her hands on her lap. "Rick mentioned it, yeah; apparently it was only just the one date. There was no spark between them so they decided to just go back to being friends."

"Did you ever get the impression from Julie that maybe she felt something for Rick that he didn't feel for her? That she wished they were more than friends?" Detective Molloy asked. She was sitting with her hands clasped in front of her on the table.

"Well, it's possible I suppose. Who really knows what goes on in anyone's head? I did mention to Rick once that she seemed distant towards me. He seemed to think I was imagining it, but I know I wasn't as Elaine picked up on it too. She was so warm and friendly towards Elaine but barely spoke to me, and when she did it was just to answer a question or make some scathing remark about something I had said. Rick must have said something to her because things improved after that, but I could never quite shake the feeling that she didn't particularly like me."

"Could that have been maybe because she resented you for what you had with Rick, that she wished it were her with him instead of you?"

Sylvia rubbed her neck and considered, "Quite possible," she said, "or maybe she just didn't think I was good enough for him. Who knows? But I don't think she could have murdered him if that's what you're getting at."

She knew full well that that was exactly what Detective Molloy was implying.

"I'm just trying to obtain all of the information I need. When I have acquired enough I will be able to see what's relevant and discard any unnecessary details. The relevant information should point me in the direction of the murderer."

"Well personally I think Mary fits the bill the best. I mean, yeah sure, it's a crazy mixed up situation with people being in love with those who aren't in love with them. But Mary's the only one who is psychotic enough to actually kill someone because he didn't return her feelings." Even as she said the words she hoped again that it was a stranger who murdered Rick, but of all the possible suspects at present it was easier to think of Mary as the murderer than someone who had been so close to either herself or Rick as Julie, Jerry or Alex.

"Julie may not like me, but she wouldn't kill Rick just so that I couldn't have him. She's not stupid; she knew that the best way to secure the possibility of Rick and her getting together some day would be to keep him alive. Knock me off maybe, but not him.

"Anyway, speaking of exes, I ran into an ex of mine yesterday, Jerry McCarthy. It seems he still carries a torch for me. I don't think there's anything in it, but I thought I should let you know."

"Thanks; we'll look into it," Detective Molloy said. "I believe you've moved back into your house; it must be good to know that at least the mortgage is all paid off now."

"It's a small consolation; I'd rather have Rick and the two of us struggling to pay the mortgage off together," Sylvia replied, tears coming into her eyes.

"The life insurance will come in handy too when it comes through," Detective Molloy said.

"Like I said, I'd rather have Rick. I hadn't even thought of the life insurance; it's not something that you give much thought to when you're just trying to get your life back to some semblance of normality." Sylvia was struggling to keep her voice under control as her emotions fought to come to the fore.

"I have the warrant here for those receipts we discussed," Detective

Molloy said, pointing to a document on the table.

When Sylvia regained control over her emotions she took the receipts out of her shopping bags, which had been left untouched in a corner of her sitting room since that fateful day. She hadn't had the heart to unpack them yet as they brought back too many unpleasant memories. This morning she had been in too much of a hurry to get out the door to work to let any memories surface as she had grabbed the bags. She had looked at the receipts on her break and had seen that at least some of her purchases had been made around the time of the murder.

"We'll be holding on to these as evidence. We'll need the purchases also," Detective Molloy said, holding out her hand for the bags.

"I haven't even been able to look at them yet."

Detective Molloy examined the receipts and Sylvia saw her face smoothing out when she looked at the receipt for the bottle of Chanel she'd bought in Boots.

Detective Molloy reached over and took her hand, saying, "This must all be terribly difficult for you. I assure you we are doing everything in our power to find out who did this."

The detective's sudden softening towards her took Sylvia by surprise and she couldn't stop the flow of tears. She had been doing so well holding it all together lately that she just had to let it all out now.

After Sylvia left the room Detective Molloy sat quietly for a moment and thought about how she hated the part of her job that meant she had to treat the bereaved as kindly as possible one moment, as suspects the next and back to kindly again.

She had moved to sit beside Sylvia and hold her in her arms to comfort her while she cried. She felt she owed it to her after all she had put her through as a suspect. She thought about the dreadful evening she had gone to Sylvia's house to find her in shock after the discovery of her boyfriend's body. It must have been a dreadful experience for her, Detective Molloy thought now as she remembered the sight of Rick, a beautiful man even in death, lying in a pool of blood with a knife sticking out of his chest.

It had been surmised by the trail of blood leading down from the armchair that he had been seated in the armchair when he had been stabbed, that he had slid down to the ground in front of the armchair. The state pathologist had stated in her report that death was instant, the aortic valve having been severed causing immediate unconsciousness and death within seconds. That's something, I suppose. Whoever did this deserves no less than life imprisonment, she thought. However, she was sure that whoever did this would get no more than fifteen years; with the possibility of early parole it was unlikely that they would serve more than ten years.

Detective Molloy was sure that Sylvia and Rick's family would find that terribly distressing, but she couldn't think about that now. She just had to concentrate on trying to find out who did this, and with Julie obviously lying about her feelings for Rick it meant that there was a very real possibility that it was she who had done it. She'd just have to pay her a little visit and see what that would uncover.

CHAPTER TWENTY-NINE

That evening Maeve and Noel arrived home to their spacious two-bedroom apartment. Part of a relatively recent development of apartment buildings owned by a local businessman it was a little on the pricey side, but as they both held down good jobs they weren't concerned about being able to pay the rent. They also managed to put aside money for the house they both dreamed that someday they would own. The apartment wasn't furnished as they would have chosen; it was comfortable, but a little too modern for their tastes. They had both agreed that when the time came to choose a home they would go for something a little more rustic. They liked the cottage that Rick and Sylvia had bought and were looking out for something similar.

They sat on the straight-backed red couch in the minimalist sitting room with its magnolia walls and discussed their experiences down at the station.

"I hate going over the same ground again and again," said Noel rubbing his hands over his face in exasperation.

"I suppose they have to check that our stories haven't changed and that we haven't thought of anything else that could help," Maeve said and took his hand in hers.

"We already told them that if we thought of anything else we'd let them know; that should be good enough for them. He was my friend for God's sake. Can I not grieve in peace without the guards breathing down my neck?"

"They probably get people in there all the time hiding stuff. How are they supposed to be sure that we're on the level? I got the impression that Detective Molloy thought that maybe Julie or myself had killed him because we fancied him and didn't want anyone else to have him. In fairness, if that were the case wouldn't we have killed Sylvia, not him, but I suppose they have to explore every avenue."

"She'd better not suspect that I might have killed him because I thought maybe he fancied you. Seriously, don't they have any other leads? I would have thought their time would be better spent chasing up any forensic details than who fancied who. I can't believe she could suspect you," Noel said as he drew Maeve towards him to sit on his lap on the couch.

"I remember reading somewhere that murders are usually committed by a lover or a victim of unrequited love unless of course there's some other underworld, seedy purpose for it. Detective Molloy seemed to dismiss the idea of it being me pretty quickly, but because Julie had one date with him once she thinks she could be on to something."

"I got that impression too. If it's anybody we know who did it, it's most likely that scumbag Julie used to date; he was convinced there was something going on between Julie and Rick. Some people just can't accept the idea of a platonic relationship between a man and a woman. I was glad she broke up with him when she did; I was afraid he'd start beating on her. He just seems the type, you know?"

"Did you mention that to the detectives?" Maeve asked.

"No because I don't really think it was him, just that if it was anyone we knew he'd be the most likely candidate."

"What about Alex? I mean, that Friday night if looks could kill..." Maeve left the remainder of that sentence hanging in the air.

"Yeah, I wonder what was going on there." Noel drifted off as if trying to remember something and Maeve left him to his thoughts to go and make a start on dinner.

Noel knew there was something important he was forgetting about that night but he just couldn't put his finger on it. It had something to do with Alex, he was sure of it. If only he could remember. He'd have to replay the whole scene in his head to see if it would come to him.

He remembered Sylvia opening the door to him looking radiant in a black, sparkly cocktail dress. She had greeted them with a welcoming smile and took their bottle of wine as she showed them into the sitting room, chattering the whole time. She'd left them to go into the kitchen to get them a drink and returned with a glass of wine for Maeve and a glass of whiskey for Noel.

It broke his heart now to think of the sitting room where they had all sat enjoying themselves that night, the room where Rick was murdered. He wondered how Sylvia could continue to live there. He knew if it were Maeve who had been killed in their home nothing would make him live there any longer.

Sylvia and Rick had been the perfect hostesses that night; the food was beautiful, the music was playing in the background the whole night, and the conversation and wine kept flowing.

He immersed himself in the memory of that night, recapturing the atmosphere and recalling certain conversations. He remembered that Rick had jokingly banned politics from the discussions that night, being fully aware of Noel and Julie's diametrically opposed views. They had briefly discussed such mundane topics as traffic, but the conversation remained mainly on such frivolities as T.V. shows, films, music, fashion, and sport.

They'd made an attempt at playing charades but found that they were too drunk for the game to make much sense, and the game ended in fits of giggles as the guesses became ever more ridiculous.

Noel just couldn't think of what was bugging him about that night. He blocked everything and everyone else out of his mind as he concentrated on remembering Alex to see if he could pinpoint what it was.

He remembered Alex looking at Rick on several occasions. He remembered it so distinctly because it was in complete contrast to the camaraderie of the whole night. Then suddenly it struck him that he had noticed the look in Alex's eyes as he gazed at Sylvia and how that look had changed to one of hatred when his gaze turned to Rick to see how he was looking at Sylvia and she back at him.

Noel went out to the kitchen to tell Maeve his theory that Alex was in love with Sylvia and jealous enough of Rick to kill him. He was sure of it. He was going to have to ring Detective Molloy with this new information. Hopefully he wouldn't have to go back to the station; he had seen enough of that interview room to last him a lifetime.

Noel pulled Maeve to him as a chill ran down his spine at the thought that she had been in such close proximity to a murderer. Up to now he hadn't believed that it was anybody who had been at the party that night who could have killed Rick, but just that one memory made him certain. He had always been very protective of Maeve, but right now he just wanted to cocoon her in safety until Alex was locked up. He knew she wasn't as delicate as she looked; her father, having been a martial arts instructor, had given her self-defense lessons from a very early age. However, that didn't stop Noel from wanting to protect her from anything or anyone that might hurt her.

In the three years they had been together Maeve had more than proved her ability to look after herself; they'd been out in a Galway nightclub one night when a guy had grabbed her and she'd used her self defense quite effectively to ensure that he wouldn't be bothering her or anyone else that night. Noel knew it annoyed her that he was so over protective of her, but he'd prefer her to be annoyed with him and safe than for any harm to come to her.

Maeve hadn't noticed the way Alex had looked at Sylvia but, by her own admission, she wasn't the most observant of people. She was always wary and looking out for her safety, as she'd learned from her father, but when it came to observing how people behaved towards each other she could be quite oblivious. Although she'd witnessed the dagger looks Alex had thrown in Rick's direction that had been the extent of her observations on that matter.

"Are you going to ring Detective Molloy?" she asked.

"Yeah, but I don't know how seriously she'll take me." Noel sighed as he released his hold on Maeve and went into the sitting room to make the phone call.

As he dialed the number he went over the relevant events in his head to make sure he was remembering correctly, even though he was sure he was. When he got talking to Detective Molloy he relayed his story to her and heard her taking notes on the other end of the phone. Much to his annoyance she asked him to come down to the station.

"Is that really necessary? I've been down there twice already."

"Yes I appreciate that and I appreciate you coming forward with this new information, but I'd like you to make a formal statement."

Noel resigned himself to another grueling hour at the station as he kissed Maeve on the cheek and told her he'd be back as soon as possible. She offered to go with him, but he saw no point in her waiting at the station while his statement was being taken. All the same, he was concerned about leaving her alone with Alex still on the loose. He knew he was probably being silly; Alex would have no reason to harm her, not yet anyway. After giving his statement to the guards it might be a different story. That thought was almost enough to stop him from going ahead with it, but he reasoned that if Alex was the killer and he had information that could help put him behind bars he owed it to Rick to come forward. Driving to the station with that purpose in mind he got a chill as he thought of being without Maeve if Alex were to harm her to get back at him for coming forward with the information. He fought hard not to think of being unable to put his lips to her soft cheek again as he'd just done. Images of her lying in a coffin flashed through his head. He wondered how he'd cope if the next time he got to place his lips on hers she was cold and lifeless.

Fully expecting to be grilled mercilessly as he had been the previous times Noel was surprised to find that it was simply a matter of making his statement. As he was being dismissed he asked if this new information was enough to charge Alex with the murder. He was told that his statement was greatly appreciated and that it would be considered in the process of their enquiry. Noel would have preferred a more definite reply but resigned himself to the vagueness of the detective's response.

Noel was glad to get home to Maeve and relieved to see that everything was all right. He told himself he'd have to relax and stop worrying about her safety as it could take some time before Alex was locked up for killing Rick. If indeed it truly was him, he reminded himself. Alex being in love with Sylvia and jealous of Rick didn't necessarily mean he was the murderer. It sure doesn't look good for him though, even if it's not him, Noel thought.

He didn't let on to Maeve that he was worried about her because he knew she'd be annoyed with him. He just decided to subtly ensure that they had a lot of together time so that he could keep a close eye on her for as much of the time as possible until Rick's murder was solved one way or the other.

She would be happy with that as she was always saying that they never saw enough of one another, despite the fact that compared to a lot of other couples they spent a lot of time together. As they were snuggled up on the couch he suggested that they go to the cinema the next night and she was delighted.

"To what do I owe this pleasure?"

"I just decided that in light of Rick being killed like that you just never know what's in store for any of us so we should make the most of our time together like you're always so wisely suggesting."

"I'm glad you've come around to my way of thinking; it's just a pity it's taken something so tragic for you to see things that way."

As Maeve snuggled up against him again he was glad she had accepted his explanation for him suddenly wanting to do more stuff together. Ordinarily during the week they would each come and go as they pleased, spending time together when they both happened to be home. The weekends were the only times they specifically set aside for each other. He decided it mightn't be such a bad thing after all. Maybe Maeve had been right; maybe they should be spending more time together.

CHAPTER THIRTY

Wednesday the 1st of October

Detectives Molloy and Naughton pulled up outside a semi detached two-story house the next morning. There were twenty houses in total in the estate, arranged in a semi-circle around a green play area where they could see a handful of children running around. They walked up the footpath to the front door of the cream colored house with the well tended, colorful garden.

Detective Molloy was about to knock on the front door when she paused. She could hear raised voices in the house. She heard a woman shouting, "You know I loved him. How could you possibly think I could get back with you after what you did?" followed by the sound of flesh smacking flesh.

Detective Molloy knocked on the door. Julie answered the door immediately, looking frazzled.

"Is everything okay here?" Detective Molloy asked, giving Julie a meaningful look.

"Yes thanks. Billy was just leaving." Julie opened the door wider and turned, standing back, giving the man standing in her hall a clear view of the two detectives outside the door. The man just stood there for a moment, a pulse working at his reddened jaw. Detective Molloy watched him closely and wasn't fooled by the smart clothes. She could see the roughness simmering beneath the surface and the fear in his eyes as he took in the badges held by her and Detective Naughton. He pushed passed Julie as he left, at which Julie emitted a yelp.

"Are you okay?" Detective Molloy asked.

Julie heaved a sigh of relief and sagged against the door.

"May we come in?"

"Of course." Julie seemed to pull herself together and stood up straight, motioning for the detectives to enter the house.

Detective Molloy took in her surroundings as she entered the sitting room; the house was neat and tidy, everything decorated in muted shades of creams, yellows and beiges. The only strong colours were the brown cushions on the soft beige couch, the brown curtains, and the coffee table was a sheet of round glass on a dark tree trunk shaped to look like a horse's head.

They refused the offer of tea or coffee as they sat on the armchairs and Julie sank into the couch.

"Do you want to tell me what that was about?" Detective Molloy asked, as her partner took out a pen and paper ready to take notes.

"No."

"Is he your boyfriend?"

"No."

Detective Molloy perched closer to the edge of the seat and said, "This guessing game could go on quite a while, and I don't know about you but I don't have all day. Who is Billy?"

"He's my ex," Julie answered.

"What was he doing here?"

"He wanted to get back with me."

"I take it you didn't want to."

"No."

"Was he violent towards you?"

"I don't want to talk about it," Julie said and put her hands up to her reddening cheeks.

"Look, this is important. I heard you when I was outside; you told him you loved Rick and that there was no way you could possibly get back with him after what he had done. What was that? Did he kill Rick?"

Something flickered in Julie's eyes and her jaw set. She took her hands down from her face and sat up straight. "I said I don't want to talk about it."

"Look, you can either answer my questions here or down at the station; it's your choice."

Julie took a deep breath as tears filled her eyes. She brushed them away and said, "We were together for six months and everything was great at first, and then one day when I said I wasn't in the mood for sex he hit me. I told him it was all over and he hit me again. Then he left and I never saw him again until today."

"When did all this happen?" Detective Molloy asked. She looked over at Detective Naughton and saw that his pen was digging into the paper, his face was reddening and his jaw was set. If Billy were still here she knew her partner would have a hard job restraining himself.

"Six months ago," Julie said.

"Did he hit you today?"

"No; I slapped him across the face when he tried to kiss me. If you hadn't arrived when you did he probably would have."

"I know this is hard to talk about, but did he show any violent tendencies before that day?" Detective Molloy sat further back in the armchair.

"No; well not really, at least not directly aimed at me." Julie took another deep breath before continuing, "Like a lot of people, he didn't understand how a man and woman can have a platonic relationship, and he was convinced there was something going on with Rick and me. A few times after I'd spent some time with Rick he got angry and we rowed about it. He punched the wall or kicked the door sometimes but never hit me, not until that day. Billy arrived home from the pub and saw Rick leaving. When he wanted sex and I said I wasn't in the mood he started saying things like, 'Of course you're not in the mood; you're just after having sex aren't you, with lover-boy.' Then he hit me." Julie put her hand up to rub her jaw.

"What was Rick's reaction to all this?"

"I never told him; I called in sick after the weekend and when my friends rang I didn't answer the phone; I texted to tell them that Billy and I had split up and I didn't want to talk about it. I just laid low until the bruising had gone down and then went back to normal. I never talked about Billy after that; I knew that Rick would go around to Billy and beat him up if I had said anything about his jealousy or about him hitting me, and I didn't want that."

"So, whether or not Billy's suspicions were unfounded, he had a grudge against Rick. Do you not think this is something you should have told us at the station?"

"I didn't see any need to tell you."

"This is just the sort of information we're looking for. Billy's jealousy of Rick is perhaps a motive for murder. You should have informed us when we asked you if there were any jealous exes you were aware of who might be out for revenge," Detective Molloy said.

"I don't like to talk about it; I may hate Billy and never want to see him again, but I don't think he'd kill Rick on the off chance that I might go back with him."

"Well maybe it's just a coincidence that he arrived here today looking to have you back, but, coincidence or not, we have to look into it. I heard you admitting to Billy that you loved Rick; you denied that quite vehemently at the station. Were you jealous of Sylvia?"

"Of course not; I loved Rick as a friend. We were best friends since we were twelve. When he told me he had fallen in love I was delighted for him. However, when I met Sylvia I did think he could do much better for himself than her."

Detective Molloy could tell that Julie was trying to hide the disdain in her voice when she spoke of Sylvia. "I see. Would you mind if we had a look around?" The detective was aware that Julie was within her rights to refuse to let them snoop around since they didn't have a warrant, but she hoped that Julie would co-operate, as most people with nothing to hide were willing to do. She preferred to save all the paperwork involved in warrants for more solid leads or for people who went out of their way to be awkward about helping out in an investigation.

Julie told them to feel free and they had a good look around but found nothing suspicious. As they prepared to leave, Detective Molloy said, "Well if Billy comes back don't hesitate to call the station. May I have his address please? I'll just pay him a little visit." The detective saw that the thought of that scared Julie. "Don't worry; I'll warn him off you. Even if he turns out to be not guilty of killing Rick, if he hits you again he'll be locked up so fast his feet won't touch the ground."

"This is why I never made a big deal about it the last time; I didn't want him to think I was causing trouble for him," Julie said.

"I'll make sure he doesn't think that; as far as he'll be concerned it's just a routine call in the investigation into Rick's murder. We won't let on we know about how you two split up if that's what you'd prefer. Promise me that if he comes back you won't let him in."

"I didn't let him in this time; I was hanging out the clothes and he sauntered around to the back of the house as if he owned it and went in the back door. I know I should have just run; I shouldn't have gone into the house after him. That was a stupid thing to do. I was lucky you stopped by," Julie said as she searched for a pen and paper.

"Is there someone else living here with you?" Detective Naughton asked, offering Julie his pen.

"No; a couple of years ago my father got a job in America. The company provided him with an apartment but I didn't want to go. It was too good an opportunity for him to miss out on, especially since his job here was so insecure, so my parents, brother and sister moved over there. They didn't want to sell the house in case things didn't work out for them, so it suited us all for me to stay here."

"You must miss them."

"Yeah, especially at times like this when I could do with their support. I thought they'd make it home for the funeral, but they didn't. Rick was always in this house growing up. He was almost like another son to my parents, but the company my father works for wouldn't give him time off unless it was family. They had a mass said for him in their local church over there and are lighting candles every day and praying that his murderer will be caught and sent down for life."

Detective Molloy saw the tears in Julie's eyes and felt sorry for her. She no longer believed that Julie had murdered Rick. Her heart went out to the lonely young woman who had just lost one of her best friends and whose family couldn't be there for her. She thanked Julie for her help and warned her again to look out for herself, keep her doors locked, and also to be sure to report Billy if he caused her any more trouble.

CHAPTER THIRTY-ONE

When they were back in the car Detective Molloy glanced at the address Julie had given her for Billy O' Shea and they made their way there; she wasn't surprised to find that it was in a seedier area of the town. Her partner asked if he had any prior records; he thought someone who beat on his girlfriend and came from that particular area probably had a record. However, Detective Molloy assured him that as of yet his record was clean; she had been in this town long enough to know who the troublemakers were.

When Detective Molloy rang the doorbell, a scruffy looking youth with long scraggly hair and several facial piercings answered the door. She produced her badge and introduced herself and Detective Naughton.

"Shit, Ma there's cops at the door," the youth yelled back into the hallway.

His mother arrived behind him and gave him a clip around the ear, telling him to watch his mouth. "Sorry about that," she apologized about her son as he retreated back into the house. "I hope none of my lads are in trouble." She gave an apologetic smile.

Detective Molloy introduced herself and her partner and asked to speak to Billy.

"Billy?" she asked in surprise. "What's this about?"

"We just have some routine questions to ask him. I believe he knew a Rick O' Hara."

"That's the guy who was murdered, isn't it?"

"Yes."

"I wasn't aware my Billy knew him. I'll see if he's in." She took a step into the hall and called "Billy!" at the top of her voice. A muffled response came from somewhere upstairs, to which Mrs. O' Shea shouted the response, "Get down here now." She turned to the detectives and said, "You'd better come in then."

They followed her into a small living area off the dark, narrow hall. As Detective Molloy heard someone come charging down the stairs she took in her surroundings; this room was as cluttered as Julie's was neat. Everywhere she looked she saw signs of a family's life, photographs of the children at various stages hung on the walls and stood in frames on the mantelpiece and on the top of a cabinet, which housed medals and plaques. On the coffee table there were piles of magazines on cars and motorbikes with one issue of a woman's magazine. The three-piece suite was dark brown and worn looking, and as Detective Molloy sat down in one of the armchairs she noticed that it was comfortable, but not of the variety you could sink into.

She had no sooner sat down than Billy threw open the door. When he saw the detectives sitting on the armchairs he very nearly turned on his heels and ran. Only, when he turned around he saw his mother standing in the hall with a stern look on her face that seemed to say, 'Whatever it is you've done, you'd better face up to it.'

He closed the door, turned back to face the two detectives and said, "What are you doing here? I've done nothing wrong."

Classic sign of guilt, going on the defensive immediately, Detective Molloy thought, crossing her legs and draping one arm across her lap. "I never said you had done anything wrong," she said. "We're just following a trail of people who knew Rick O' Hara to see if anyone can throw any light on his murder."

"Well I hardly knew him." Billy remained standing, looking like he was ready to bolt to the door at any second.

"You were dating his best friend, Julie, for a while, were you not?"

"Best friend, huh! That's a laugh! The bitch was two timing me with him probably the whole time I was with her."

"Is that why you and Julie broke up?"

"Yeah; of course she denied sleeping with him, but I knew she was.

One day I couldn't take any more of her lies and told her that if it was Rick she really wanted then she could have him; I was finished with all the lies and deceit. I didn't want to be where some other guy had just been, you know what I mean?" He glanced over at Detective Naughton as if to seek male empathy.

"Why were you over at her house today?"

"I heard Rick had been killed and I went over to see how she was. I may have split up with her but I still care about her, you know?"

"We heard the two of you rowing when we came to the door. What was that about?"

"I asked her if she wanted to get back with me. I miss her, you know? Only, she got all emotional and said that she had loved Rick. That hurt, you know. I mean I knew she was sleeping with him, but that she loved him was a bit of a kick in the teeth. Anyway, she said she couldn't go back with me because she had loved him and needed time and space to get over him. Well she can have all the time and space she wants because I'm finished with her. I gave her a chance and she blew it so she can go find someone else who's going to put up with her pining over lover-boy."

"When we were standing outside the door we heard her saying she wouldn't go back with you because of what you'd done. What did she mean by that?"

Billy was quick to mask his face but not before Detective Molloy noticed the look of fear, the quickening of the pulse at his neck, a nervous swallow. "Why, what did that bitch say?"

"She told me I should ask you what that meant," Detective Molloy lied.

"That I had broken up with her of course," he replied.

"Where were you on the Saturday afternoon of Rick O' Hara's murder, Saturday the thirteenth of September?"

"I was here watching T.V." His reply was defiant.

"Is there someone who could verify that?"

"Yeah, my brother, Colin."

"I'll need to speak to him. Is he home?"

Billy went to the sitting room door and yelled for Colin. A moment later the scruffy youth who had opened the door arrived in the doorway and, like his brother's reaction, turned to run. Billy caught him by the jumper and hauled him into the room.

"Thank you, Billy; you can wait outside in case I need to talk to you again," Detective Molloy said as Billy pushed Colin into the couch.

Detective Molloy asked Colin if he could account for his whereabouts on the afternoon in question.

"I didn't do nothin'. I was here all afternoon; Billy and I were watching T.V. and playing games on the play-station."

"Did either of you go out at all on that Saturday?"

"I had the flu and didn't feel like going anywhere, and Billy's been moping around since that whore dumped him for another guy."

"Who dumped him?" Detective Molloy asked, looking over at her partner and noticing that he was struggling to keep his temper in check.

"Julie; he says he dumped her, but she was banging some other guy so that means she dumped him. He's such a saddo; he needs to get a life. You wouldn't catch me letting some bitch do that to me." Colin raised his hand and motioned a back handed slap. "That's what she'd get to keep her in line." With a conspiratorial wink towards Detective Naughton he added, "Know what I mean?"

Detective Naughton continued taking notes, not acknowledging the boy's question. They left after that, knowing that at some point in the future they would be putting those two boys behind bars. However, even though both men seriously lacked respect for women, they were pretty sure neither of them had anything to do with Rick's death. It was possible that after Billy had returned from killing Rick he had coerced his brother into providing an alibi for him. He may not necessarily have admitted to Colin what it was he had done. However, even though Billy had motive, being jealous of Rick, Detective Molloy had enough experience in her career of men like Billy to know that they preferred to direct their anger and physical violence towards women. They were cowards who wouldn't raise a hand towards a man in case they'd get a beating themselves.

Still it couldn't be ruled out completely just yet, however unlikely the prospect seemed. They had to investigate all possible leads. They hoped that if Billy laid a hand on Julie again she would report it, and they agreed that it would give them great pleasure to lock that piece of shit up.

Meanwhile, they had to look into Jerry McCarthy; they had an address for him and decided they'd better pay him a visit.

When Jerry answered the door Detective Molloy introduced herself and her partner, explaining that they were investigating the murder of Rick O' Hara and in the course of that investigation his name had come up and they'd like to ask him a few questions. She noted a look of surprised fear on his face.

Reluctantly he stood back to allow them entry into a spacious bachelor pad. Everything was very masculine, from the black leather recliners to the large screen T.V. Detective Molloy noticed that it hardly looked lived in at all; his reputation had preceded him and she assumed he did most of his living in the apartment of whatever girl he was dating at the time.

Sitting on the leather couch, Detective Molloy asked, "I believe you used to date Sylvia, the girlfriend of the deceased?"

"Yeah, we had a casual thing a while back. I thought maybe it was getting too serious so I called it off," Jerry replied as he sat on the couch, facing Detective Molloy with his arm draped over the back of the couch. "I was surprised to hear that she had been dating Rick; I didn't think he was her type. You never know really, do you? I hadn't known anything about it until I bumped into her yesterday. Maybe she changed after we broke up; maybe the biological clock started ticking. It's different for women, isn't it? I mean we were kindred spirits, Sylvia and I, born free, blowing through life as wild as the wind. Men can stay living like that for life, but generally women will feel the call to pro-create. Not all women, obviously, and I certainly never thought it would happen to Sylvia, but there you go."

"Are you currently dating someone?"

"Why officer! Are you asking me out on a date?!" Jerry asked.

"Of course not. I just think Sylvia could do with all the friends she can get right now and I'm aware that if you had a current girlfriend that could pose a problem."

"Oh I am disappointed, not that I think you're my type of course. Not that I really have a type, it's just that I think cops are probably too serious for me. I don't suppose you'd care to change my mind on that score?"

Detective Naughton was trying to hide a grin as he looked up from his notes with a raised eyebrow aimed at his partner.

"Certainly not," Detective Molloy said, and then smiled in spite of herself. She crossed her legs and said, "You're probably right; I am too serious for you. So how about calling in on Sylvia, giving her a shoulder to cry on?"

"From what I know of Sylvia she has plenty of shoulders to cry on, she doesn't need another one. Besides, when I end a relationship I don't go back, not even as friends; I have enough of those; I don't need exes as friends."

Hmm, thought Detective Molloy, after what Sylvia told me that doesn't ring true. She asked him if he minded them looking around and wasn't surprised that they found nothing suspicious. She figured that if he had anything to hide they'd find it in a girlfriend's place. She asked him where he'd been the afternoon Rick was murdered. He flipped back through his diary and gave her the name and number of the girl he'd been with that day. She thanked him for his time and they left.

On the way back to the station Detective Molloy thought she'd better give Sylvia a call to warn her to keep an eye out for Jerry and to call her if he started lurking around or acting suspiciously. She would check out his alibi, but wouldn't be surprised if Jerry had charmed some girl into covering for him.

There's a distinct possibility that it was Jerry after all and not Alex, Detective Molloy thought. Indeed, if Jerry feels at all threatened by the relationship Sylvia has with Alex he could be next on his list. By the same logic, if the murderer is indeed Alex, Jerry might be next on the list if Alex were to become aware that he was hanging around again.

CHAPTER THIRTY-TWO

That evening a very drunk Billy turned up at Julie's house and started banging on the front door. Julie knew instantly who it was. She looked through the peephole to verify it. Her heart was hammering in her chest. It felt almost as loud as the hammering on the door. With shaking hands she reached for the phone. She dialed the number on the card Detective Molloy had left.

When the sound of breaking glass came from the kitchen she screamed. She hadn't been aware that the banging at the front door had stopped. The phone fell from her hands. She hadn't heard whether or not Detective Molloy answered. With fumbling hands she tried to reach for the lock on the front door. Just as the lock turned she felt hands grabbing her from behind. The scream died on her lips as Billy's hand covered her mouth.

"Stop screaming, bitch," he whispered harshly into her ear. "What did you have to go and involve the cops for? That bitch thinks I killed Rick. I could kill you for pointing them in my direction."

Julie tried to scream, but Billy's hand tightened around her mouth as he hissed, "I said stop screaming."

Julie bit back the scream, terrified for her life. Even when he had hit her before he hadn't been like this. It crossed her mind at that moment that maybe it was Billy who had killed Rick.

"I don't want to hurt you," Billy's tone softened, although his grip on her didn't. "We were so good together," he said as the hand that had been gripping her arm moved to cup her breast. He started to knead her breast roughly as he said, "We could still be good together; we could put all this behind us. I'm going to take my hand away from your mouth now. Don't scream." He waited while she nodded and then his hand moved from her mouth to gently draw the hair away from her neck. He kissed her neck and then drew in a long breath and let her go.

She staggered away from him. Terror had made her weak. She was unable to make the necessary movements to unlock the door and run. He turned her to face him.

"Look at you, trembling," he said, disgust evident in his voice. His tone changed again, softened. "Why are you so afraid of me?"

Julie cowered against the door and whimpered.

"I don't want to hurt you," he said again as his hand reached out to cup her chin. "I just want to take you in my arms and make love to you, erase the last few months from my memory, erase Rick from your memory." His tone became harsh as he mentioned Rick's name. "I know you loved that prick. I know you were sleeping with him the whole time we were together," he said. Then he smiled as he said, "Now that he's dead we can be together properly without having him between us."

Julie wanted to tell him straight that she could never again be with him. Her skin crawled at the thought of him touching her. She knew it would hurt him to know that she shuddered at the memories of them having sex. She couldn't even think of it as making love anymore. The distance the last few months had put between them gave her perspective and she now saw him for the violent brute he was. She was afraid of what he would do if she told him. She was afraid he would rape her, or kill her, or both.

Detective Molloy checked the caller ID on her phone before answering it and realized that the scream she heard was Julie. She heard a clattering sound and guessed that Julie had dropped the phone. She could hear muffled sounds and realized that the fall hadn't disconnected the call. Bringing the phone with her she beckoned to Detective Naughton and they both raced to the car. Sirens blazing, Detective Molloy sped to Julie's house with the phone connected to her hands free set. She couldn't hear much, enough to know that Billy was in the house and that Julie was alive at least. Then suddenly there was nothing. Swearing, she put her foot down more on the accelerator, willing the car to go even faster, saying a prayer that she would get there on time, hoping it wasn't already too late for Julie.

Billy took Julie's hand and led her towards the kitchen, telling her that he could do with a cup of coffee. She threw a nervous glance towards her phone lying on the hall floor, unsure if it had cut out when it had fallen. She followed his lead through to the kitchen, not wanting him to notice the phone. If he thought she had been ringing the guards he would be angry. He was scary enough as it was, conversing normally with her while on the verge of anger. She didn't want to do anything that would send him over the edge.

She entered the kitchen and stopped short. There was a gaping hole in the door where the windowpane should have been. A cold breeze chilled her and she saw glass strewn on the floor.

"Be careful not to walk on that; I'll clean it up later, but you really should wear shoes around the house anyway. It's a bit late now, but tomorrow I'll have someone come over to put in a replacement window. Don't worry; I'll stay tonight so you'll be safe," Billy said.

Julie was more scared at that prospect than that of someone else intruding through the absent windowpane. Somehow she managed a smile that she hoped was convincing. Billy was too busy rooting through her presses for some whiskey at the time to even notice her trepidation. Finding some, he turned around to her, waving the bottle in his hand. The thoughts of him with more alcohol on him made her tremble.

"I know you won't say no to my Irish coffee," he said, smiling as if this was six months ago, before their nasty break-up, and as if the break-in tonight hadn't just happened.

He started to make the coffee and then suddenly became very still. He turned towards Julie. "Tell me those sirens aren't coming for me," he said. When Julie didn't answer he lunged towards her. He put his hands around her neck and said, "Tell me you didn't call the cops on me." He started to shake her. "Tell me, bitch," he spat out at her. He suddenly let go of her and started to run.

Detectives Molloy and Naughton were nearly at Julie's when they caught sight of a figure running. Their instincts told them that it was Billy. He was running across the fields. Detective Molloy changed the course of her car to drive towards the fields. The figure was currently lifting barbed wire to make his way through a fence between two fields. She stopped the car and Detective Naughton jumped out to chase Billy on foot.

When Detective Naughton sat typing up his report later he thought that the chase had really been quite comical. It hadn't taken long for him to close the gap between him and Billy. Upon his entry into one of the fields Billy had sent sheep fleeing and as he had entered the next field he got caught momentarily in the barbed wire, making the chase very close. Half way through that field he had wobbled as his foot went into a hole. He hadn't lost much time in straightening up again, but it was enough to have Detective Naughton so close to him he could smell the fear on Billy. He had caught up to him at the next fence. Just as Billy had one leg in one field and the other in the same one as Detective Naughton he had caught up to him. He had given him the option of being dragged back through the fence and being torn to pieces on the way or coming peacefully. Billy had chosen the latter option. When he was back through the fence, Detective Naughton had read him his rights as he cuffed him and then led him back to the car.

When he was questioned he had admitted to breaking into Julie's house, but insisted it was because he was worried about her as she hadn't answered her door and he'd known she was inside. He wouldn't admit to having been rough with her or having killed Rick. He'll crack eventually, Detective Naughton thought now. He was glad Julie was going to be okay.

His partner had driven to Julie's while he was giving chase to Billy. She had arrived to find her unconscious on the floor. Julie had come around and started to scream, but calmed down when she had seen Detective Molloy leaning over her in place of Billy. She had made a complete statement, informing Detective Molloy of what had just happened and her suspicions that it might have been Billy who had killed Rick.

Detective Naughton thought that maybe they should have another go at Colin, let him know how bad it would be for him if he was covering for his brother. With Billy being held for breaking and entering it might scare Colin into an admission; perhaps Billy didn't actually have an alibi after all. They could scare Colin with the thought that if he was covering for Billy and was found out he might be joining his brother in prison.

CHAPTER THIRTY-THREE

Thursday the 2nd of October

Detectives Molloy and Naughton went back to the O'Shea house to find Mrs. O'Shea in bits as a result of what her eldest son had been up to. The whole time the two detectives were there she trembled while smoking one cigarette after another, apologizing profusely in turn for smoking in their company and for the behavior of her eldest son. She couldn't believe it; he was always the one she could count on, the one who had never given her a moment's trouble since the day he was born. Both detectives raised their eye-brows skeptically when she said that.

When Detective Molloy spoke to Colin again all she got was insistence that Billy had been with him the Saturday of Rick's murder. She noticed the fear in his eyes as she informed him that he could be charged with obstruction of justice and accessory to murder after the fact. However, he stood firm. Detective Molloy wasn't at all sure that she could believe him. When she told him that Billy was being charged with violent assault on Julie he claimed that Billy would never do such a thing, that he was too soft, didn't have the guts although it was just what Julie deserved.

Either Billy's family doesn't know him very well or they're bending over backwards trying to protect him, Detective Molloy thought. She looked over at her partner's reddened face and knew he was embarrassed at the language Colin used in her company to describe his brother's lack of the testosterone necessary to inflict such pain on Julie.

Later that morning Detective Molloy called Kim in to the station. When she arrived in and the detective had gone through the formalities, she asked where Kim had been on the Saturday afternoon of Rick's death.

"I was in bed with Gina all day."

Detective Naughton's face turned red at that and he shifted uncomfortably in his seat. Detective Molloy glanced over at him and could barely hide a smile as she thought of having to corroborate Kim's statement. She didn't think her partner would be able to stand the embarrassment of having to listen as it was confirmed that Gina and Kim had spent the day in bed together, presumably making love.

"I'm sure you'd love to have seen that," Kim said, a playful smile on her lips as she looked over at Detective Naughton.

Detective Naughton straightened up in his seat and coughed.

Detective Molloy stepped in to smooth out the situation. "That's enough of that. If you continue with those kinds of innuendoes we'll have to arrest you for obstruction of justice."

Kim immediately straightened up, her face becoming serious. "I'm sorry. I got carried away."

"It might be best to remember where you are and the seriousness of this situation. Now that we've established your whereabouts when Rick was murdered, is there anything else you've remembered that might be of help to us?"

"No. I'm sorry I can't be of more assistance to you. Can I go now?"

"Not yet." Detective Molloy glanced at her partner, knowing that this conversation was going to make him even more uncomfortable, but she had to continue. "You failed to mention the last time you were here that you and Gina were in a relationship. Why was that?"

"The subject never came up."

"Could you tell us a bit about that, about how your relationship developed?"

"We had been friends since school, and both in love with the same guy, who hardly knew we existed. We were talking one night about him. We talked about a threesome, jokingly at first, and then as we drank more wine the talk became more suggestive and we ended up in bed together. Just the two of us," she clarified. "Much as we wanted Alex there it didn't happen."

Detective Molloy kept her face a controlled mask as she took that in. She was sure Kim hadn't intended letting it slip that it was Alex she and Gina had been interested in. It was a motive for being jealous of Sylvia, but not for killing Rick. As long as Sylvia was with Rick, Alex had been available. "I'm surprised that he hasn't expressed an interest in you two. You're both very pretty ladies, and while Sylvia was seeing Rick he was a free agent." She glanced apologetically at Detective Naughton as she said, "Not too many men would pass up that opportunity."

"Yeah, well Alex isn't like most men."

Detective Molloy raised an eyebrow at that.

Kim smirked as she said, "Believe me, I've tried to seduce him but he's so taken with Sylvia that even if he's turned on by another woman he sees it as a betrayal of Sylvia. Only last week he refused the offer of going to bed with us."

Hmm, Detective Molloy thought. More proof that Alex isn't over Sylvia yet. Elaine seems to be covering for him. Perhaps she's not as pure as she seems. Maybe she's in on it with him.

Detective Molloy thanked Kim for her help and said she'd be in touch if there was a need to talk to her again. She then rang Gina to ask her to come in to the station again, throwing an apologetic glance in her partner's direction as she did so. She sometimes thought that although he was several years younger than her he acted like a man several years her senior. She could imagine her own father reacting in a similar way when faced with a lesbian relationship.

Gina arrived and took a seat, and Detective Molloy once more went through the formalities before asking her where she was the day of Rick's murder.

"In bed with Kim all day."

Again Detective Naughton's face turned as red as that of a badly teething baby.

"It's come to our attention that Alex is the guy you and Kim have been interested in for years." Detective Molloy paused to gauge Gina's reaction to that, which was one of surprise. "Why didn't you inform us of that the last time you were in?"

"Because it's not relevant."

"Yes it is. It would appear that you and Kim are still interested in Alex. Even though he's single and is aware of the feelings you and Kim have for him he's still so in love with Sylvia that he won't betray her by sleeping with the two of you. Do you deny that?"

It took Gina a moment to reply and then said that no, she couldn't deny it.

Detective Molloy thanked Gina for her help and told her she was free to go. She guessed that Gina's need to protect Alex stemmed from the fact that her feelings for him ran deeper than Kim's feelings for him, or even for her feelings for Kim. She was now even surer that Alex was the murderer.

When Gina left the station she was in a very bad mood and didn't want to go back to work. She rang her boss and told him she was taking a personal day. To say he wasn't thrilled was an understatement, but Gina felt she couldn't face smiling at customers and pretending to be happy for the rest of the day. She decided to go for a drive to the beach. It would be cold there but she wanted to think, to clear her head, to sit with pen and paper and write all of her anger in verse. She was sad and angry that Alex was being accused of a crime he didn't commit, angry with Kim for her thoughtless admissions of Alex's feelings for Sylvia and their unrequited feelings for Alex. She loved Kim, but at times like this she cursed her seeming inability to think before she spoke.

She had warned Kim before she went to the station this morning to be careful what she said. She'd figured that she would be asked in to verify Kim's whereabouts the day of the murder, but didn't think she'd have to answer questions about Alex. She would have to have a word with Kim when she got home.

Arriving at her destination, she was glad to see the black clouds rolling in over the sea, glad to see the waves being whipped into frenzy by the wind. She could immerse herself in the dark rage of sea crashing against the rocks, in the bitter cold wind that tore and lashed at the shore. She could ride the anger of the black clouds until it subsided, carried out to sea by the wind.

Having penned her verse she felt a lot better, although she knew there would have to be a conversation with Kim about it when she got home. She knew there would be a row and she hated rowing with Kim, with anyone. If only handing Kim the poem she had written would suffice, if only Kim would understand what she was trying to say and apologies for her thoughtlessness. She shook her head as she started the car, knowing that a row couldn't be avoided.

When she got in to the apartment it was to find that Kim had made her dinner and was just in the process of lighting candles. Gina almost melted, almost gave in to her inner need to let peace reign. But she didn't. She took off her jacket and went into the kitchen, knowing the mess would get her all riled up again.

Kim came up and put her arms around her. Gina put her hands over Kim's and removed them from her. Kim stood back, seeming surprised.

"Hey, what's wrong? I thought I'd make tonight special." She paused, "You do remember what tonight is, don't you?"

Gina was puzzled. "What are you talking about?"

Kim looked hurt. "You don't remember. It's the anniversary of that first night we spent together. And you always a say I'm the one who doesn't remember our special occasions."

"Do you not think it's a bit heartless to celebrate that in light of the fact that it was our feelings for Alex that were responsible for it in the first place and now you've gotten him into trouble for a crime he didn't commit, by your thoughtlessness when answering Detective Molloy's questions?"

There were tears in Kim's eyes as she said, "How can you say that? How can you blame me for that? If the detective didn't get her information from me she'd have gotten it from somewhere. Don't you think I'm as upset as you are about Alex's situation?" She put her hand up to caress Gina's face. "Do you not think that what we've got is special, that it would have happened even if we weren't both in love with Alex?"

Gina felt her heart rip in two. Kim could admit to being in love with Alex, but not to being in love with her. She turned away from Kim, tears in her eyes, and went to the table, set for a romantic meal, a bottle of red wine left open to breathe. She knew it was now or never. She turned back to face Kim, "I honestly don't know, Kim. Would it?"

Tears started to stream down Kim's face. She said, "Are you saying you don't love me, that you never loved me?"

"Well I know you don't love me. You've made it clear that you love Alex, but you've never said you love me," Gina said.

"You've never told me that you love me either, and you're always talking about Alex."

"I've told you in poetry that I love you."

"You know I don't get your poetry. I love it, but it doesn't speak to me. I need to hear it from your lips, said in plain English."

"I love you," Gina said.

Kim smiled and said, "I love you too." She went over to Gina and put her arms around her. "Now can we sit down and eat before dinner is ruined?"

Gina sat down at the chair that Kim pulled out for her. She knew that in Kim's mind this whole thing was solved now that they'd finally said that they loved each other, but Gina was annoyed with herself that she hadn't stuck to her guns and berated Kim thoroughly for her part in Alex being accused of murder. She decided to let it go for now and enjoy the delicious meal that Kim had prepared. Maybe it wasn't so inappropriate after all to celebrate the anniversary of their first night together, and she knew it would make Kim happy.

Dave arranged to meet Alex in the pub that night. He had asked his mother-in-law to babysit so that Elaine could accompany him. The plan was to set Alex up with the girl from his office that he had mentioned to him. He knew that if he didn't propel Alex into seeing Carol it would never happen. It was a perfect excuse to take Elaine out; he had made a vow to himself since taking her to Lana's that he'd make more of an effort to keep the romance alive in their relationship.

Watching her get ready for their night out he realized how much he had missed this simple, once weekly, ritual. As she sprayed herself with Chanel, the scent of it wafting over to him where he sat on the bed, he very nearly went over to remove her clothes. Instead he sighed and looked at his watch. He didn't want to keep Carol and Alex waiting. If either of them pulled out of this tonight it may never happen. Countless times he had sat with Carol over lunch or in a business meeting and thought how perfect she would be for Alex.

When Alex saw that Dave hadn't come alone he knew he had been set up. Although he had agreed to consider going out with Carol it hadn't been his plan to start that night. Seeing how pretty she was he didn't mind so much that his hand was being forced. Long auburn hair framed a square face and her smile was warm as she sat down beside him. He liked the way her smile lit up her face and the corners of her eyes crinkled ever so slightly.

After the initial introductions and conversations about work, Elaine and Dave conversed among themselves, allowing Carol and Alex to get to know each other.

As the night wore on Alex and Carol found that they had a lot in common. They laughed about the fact that that must have been why Dave thought they were perfect for each other. They discovered that they were both only children and that Carol's Dad was as over protective as Alex's Mum, both thinking no-one was good enough for their child. They discovered that they both loved reading although they were interested in different types of books. Dave had told Carol that Alex wrote poetry and she was very interested in hearing some of it. He promised her that she would someday if she was interested in seeing him again, to which she replied that she was having a great time and would love to see him again. She confided in him that she hadn't been going to come because she hated the idea of a blind date but that she was glad she had.

As the night came to an end and they were leaving the pub Alex asked Carol for her phone number, which she gave to him. When they arrived at her car she leant against it as if waiting for him to kiss her. He bent to do so but became self-conscious, being aware of Dave and Elaine's presence, so instead he took her hand to his lips and kissed it. She smiled, leaned into him and brushed his lips with her own.

Alex noticed Elaine nudging Dave, a signal that they should go and leave Carol and Alex to say their goodbyes. Alex was relieved to see them go and took the opportunity to respond to Carol's kiss. His lips touched hers and he parted her lips with his tongue. The kiss deepened and became more urgent as he wound his fingers through her hair. She moved her hands down to his firm buttocks and responded to his kiss with an urgency of her own. It was with reluctance that he disentangled himself from her and with a raspy breath said, "I think we'd better say goodnight."

"I thought that's what we were doing," Carol replied as she moved towards him again.

Alex held her at arm's length and said, "If we keep that up we'll be saying 'good-morning.' I think I'd better go. I'll call you."

He moved towards his own car, got into it and watched as Carol got into hers. He was looking forward to seeing her again, was amazed at what a good time he had actually had. Upon realizing he was being set up his initial instinct until he'd had a good look at Carol was to get up and leave, making some excuse. However, now he was glad that he had stayed. He marveled that for the first time in weeks he hadn't thought about his problems and that for the first time ever he'd enjoyed the company of another woman without feeling guilty, without thinking of Sylvia. He pushed away those thoughts for fear that they would encroach on his good feeling, and drove home happy.

CHAPTER THIRTY-FOUR

Friday the 3rd of October

When Alex rang Carol at work, conversation flowed smoothly between them, the memory of the previous night's goodbye fresh in both of their minds. Their desire to see each other again was evident in the suggestive tones and flirtatious manner in which they spoke. Alex arranged to pick her up later to take her to dinner.

He decided to take her to Luigi's, an Italian restaurant that had a friendly atmosphere; the food was beautiful and he thought it was a perfect place for a first date, not over the top and not too dowdy either. Having been there on a number of occasions with Sylvia his mouth was watering at the thought of the aromas of garlic, herbs and sauces that would assail him as he opened the door.

He arrived at Carol's apartment at quarter to eight as planned. Dinner was booked for half past eight, but arriving there at eight would allow them time for a drink at the bar. As he was driving, it would be an alcohol free night for him, but he looked forward to spending time soaking up the atmosphere while waiting for a table. It was something he had never been able to do with Sylvia, as they were always late for their dinner reservations. Much as he loved her, it had always bugged him that she was never ready when she said she would be. He was impressed to see that Carol was ready and waiting when he arrived, looking stylish yet casual in a simple black dress.

"You look nice," he said.

"Thanks. You look good too. I'm looking forward to this. I haven't been to Luigi's yet and I'm ravenous." She had a twinkle in her eye that left Alex in no doubt that she was ravenous for more than food. His face reddened as he remembered again the heat of their kiss the previous night.

He held out his hand to her and they walked to the car hand in hand, in silence. He wondered if, like him, she was imagining their hands elsewhere on each other's bodies. He held open the passenger door for her before going around to the driver's seat. Alex pushed images of her naked body out of his mind so that he could just enjoy the moment, the pleasant conversation as they drove to the restaurant.

When they arrived Carol made an appreciative sound as she took in her surroundings; Luigi's was an intimate little restaurant with murals on the walls giving it an authentic Italian feeling. While they waited to be seated they had a drink at the bar, Alex having a non-alcoholic wine and Carol having Chianti.

Alex watched as she took her first sip of Chianti, imagined the dry, slightly acidic flavor, the hint of cherry and oak that would be playing on her taste buds. Knowing exactly what he wanted to eat, his mouth watered in anticipation of the chicken in white wine sauce. It was a specialty of that establishment and Alex had delighted in it previously, the delicate flavor of the white wine enhancing the dish. He opted for chicken wings in a garlic sauce for starters, knowing that the sauce had just a hint of garlic and wouldn't be off-putting to Carol later. For desert he would have the sweet pear poached in red wine.

For starters Carol had Bruschetta with a selection of savory toppings, Tagliatellle for the main course, and a rich chocolate mousse for dessert. In true Italian style they took a long time over their food. They offered each other a taste of their dishes, each enjoying the sensuality of watching the other savor the different flavors.

They agreed that the food was excellent, the atmosphere very romantic with its dim lighting and candles at every table, and that they'd definitely have to return. Carol remarked that with the Italian waiters and waitresses she felt as if she'd been whisked off to Italy. They passed a very pleasant evening together and were sorry to see the night end. They remained at their table, talking until the restaurant was closing, in no hurry to part from one another.

On the way home they shared a companionable silence as they both relaxed in the warmth of the car. Carol closed her eyes, and Alex imagined that her head was spinning pleasantly as the wine coursed its way through her veins. As the car came to a stop outside her apartment she asked Alex if he'd like to come in for coffee, to which he replied that he'd love to.

She lived in a small estate of a combination of houses and apartment blocks. Her apartment was on the top floor of the three-story building which housed nine apartments in all. It was cozily furnished and stylish. There were family photographs framed on the cream colored walls and placed on the coffee table, and on the mantelpiece there were ornaments and more photos. Alex could see that she was a family person; she was only renting this apartment, but she had made it very homely in the time she had been living there.

They sat up and talked for hours, until eventually Alex said that he really had to go, but that he'd had a great time and wanted to see her again. Carol walked with him to the door and said she'd like that. He bent down to kiss her and found himself getting lost in passion to which she responded in kind. Pretty soon all thoughts of him going home were forgotten about as their passion moved to the bedroom.

Thoughts of Sylvia never entered his head that night and later when he awoke to find Carol by his side he commended himself on having successfully moved on.

CHAPTER THIRTY-FIVE

That Weekend

The next morning Carol buried her face in the pillow and moaned. She muttered something incoherent.

"You'll need to lift your face off the pillow for me to hear that," Alex whispered into her as he nuzzled her shoulder.

She moaned again, this time in pleasure as Alex's hands and mouth began to work erotically over her body.

After making love, as they lay wrapped up together Carol said, "What I was trying to say earlier was that I hope you don't think I'm a slut because I slept with you on the first date. I don't normally, you know."

"I don't think that. It wasn't as if you set out to seduce me, it just happened. Besides, it was more like our second date if you count Thursday night," Alex replied as he traced lazy circles around Carol's abdomen, causing her to arch her back and moan in pleasure.

"That makes it so much better then," she said.

"You really are quite insatiable aren't you?" asked Alex as he responded to her desire.

Afterwards Alex said, "We really ought to think about getting up. As I was about to leave last night I was thinking about asking you to have a picnic with me today."

"And now that I've slept with you are you still thinking about a second, or rather third, date?"

"Yes, of course I am."

"Good; I'd hate to think I'd ruined things."

"How could that have possibly ruined things? I think it was a perfect end to a perfect night," he said, giving her a kiss as he got up out of bed. He went over to the window, pulled the curtain back a little so that he could see what the day was like. "Looks like a perfect day for a picnic," he said as he noted the blue sky dotted here and there with clouds. It'll probably be a bit nippy, but I don't mind that."

"Neither do I," Carol said with a twinkle in her eye. "It gives us a perfect excuse to snuggle up close."

They managed to keep their hands off each other for long enough to get food together for a picnic. After discussing where to go they decided to drive along the coast, and would know it when they found the right place.

She really gets me, Alex thought as they drove along. Before this it had only seemed to be Sylvia who understood his connection to the outdoors. Maybe I've just never given anyone else the chance, he thought.

They found a beach a few miles away. The weather had turned bad while they were driving so there were no other people with the same idea as them. Alex had checked with Carol as the dark clouds started to roll in to see if she had changed her mind, but she still thought a picnic was a good idea. They removed their shoes and walked barefoot along the shoreline holding hands. When it started to rain Alex started to run towards the car but gave up when he saw Carol just standing there holding her arms up towards the sky and laughing.

She looks so beautiful standing there enjoying the rain, Alex thought as he returned to her to kiss her.

They walked back towards the car enjoying the feel of the rain on their faces. It was something Alex never thought he would have enjoyed; romantic and all as he was. When they arrived back at the car the rain stopped and they dried themselves off, glad of the towels that Carol had had the foresight to pack. Their clothes, however, remained quite wet, making them a little uncomfortable while sitting on a blanket to eat.

"We could just take our clothes off you know," Carol said when Alex grumbled about how uncomfortable his wet clothes were.

Alex smiled and said, "You'd like that wouldn't you? You're an insatiable minx. You know that? I think I'll pass; wet clothes won't kill me, but too much passion just might."

"You can't blame a girl for suggesting it, can you?"

"No," Alex said as he kissed her on the cheek. "I certainly can't."

After eating they wrapped themselves in the blanket and then stayed there talking and holding hands until after the sun had set. Then, with reluctance, they packed up the car for the journey home.

"Would you like to stay again tonight?" Carol asked as they pulled up outside her apartment. She slid her hand up Alex's thigh and at his reaction asked, "Is that a yes, then?"

"Yes," Alex said as he removed her hand. "Save that for inside."

The next morning Alex got up early and made breakfast in bed for Carol. He woke her up with a kiss and she started to respond with passion. He stopped her to tell her about having made breakfast. After eating they made love, joking about the mess in the bed and about the fact that they wouldn't throw each other out of bed for making crumbs.

As it was a rather cold, wet day they needed no encouragement to spend the morning in bed together. When they eventually got up it was only to light a fire in the sitting room and spend the day relaxing in front of it. They both agreed that they'd had enough of the outdoors the previous day and deserved to have a lazy day enjoying the warmth of the fire.

That night as it got late Alex made a move to go. He knew the cold air outside would seem even colder after spending the day snuggled on the couch with Carol's warm body pressed into his, but knew he had to go sometime.

"Do you want to stay the night?" Carol asked.

"I would love to, but if I don't tear myself away from you now I know I will want to spend the whole day with you tomorrow rather than going back to work."

"If you're sure," Carol said as she kissed him.

"You minx," Alex growled as he felt his desire stirring.

"Does that mean you're staying?" asked Carol in mock innocence.

"You know it does. Tonight you are guilty of seducing me."

CHAPTER THIRTY-SIX

Monday the 6th of October

The next morning, although both very reluctant, they went to work. Alex wasn't very long there when he felt the need to ring Carol. The thought of talking to her, hearing her voice, conjured up images from the weekend, which made him long to write a poem for her. He vowed that as soon as he got a quiet few minutes to himself he would put pen to paper, and looked forward to painting with words the images of her silhouetted against the sun setting over the sea, the reds and oranges reflected in the water creating a beautiful background against which to admire her.

"Hello, sexy," he said.

"Well hello. You're missing me already then?"

"You know I am. Any chance we could meet up for lunch?"

"I'm missing you too. Why don't we meet at The Lunchbox? It's halfway between us," Carol suggested.

"Sounds good to me. I can't wait."

"Me neither. Dave was asking me about our date."

"What did you tell him?"

"That it was dreadful and I never wanted to see you again," Carol said.

"Seriously, what did you tell him?"

"That I had a wonderful time and couldn't wait to see you again. He said he was trying to ring you yesterday to get the juicy details. I told him we were together all weekend, so he'll be ringing you today for a gossip. Honestly, you men are worse than women!"

"A gentleman never kisses and tells."

"That's what I told him."

"If you patch me through to him I'll talk to him now."

"You bored talking to me already then?"

"Of course not; I'll get him to put me back to you afterwards," Carol said.

She put him on to Dave, who said, "Well hello, stud. I believe you were with Carol all weekend."

"Yeah, she's pretty great. We're meeting up for lunch today."

"What did I tell you? If you'd only been more agreeable you could have been with her a long time ago. So are your friends going to take a back seat now?"

"Of course not. Anyway, a relationship with her probably wouldn't have worked before now because I wasn't ready," Alex said.

"Only kidding. Seriously though, you two can't seem to get enough of each other. She's had a huge smile plastered all over her face all morning. You've obviously made quite an impact."

"She's had a huge impact on me too. Wow! I didn't think I could like anyone else apart from Sylvia this much."

"That's good, but be careful not to take it too fast."

"Relax, man, this is just what I need. It can't hurt the whole problem with the guards either."

"Sylvia's in for a shock when she finds out."

"It shouldn't bother her. After all, how many guys have I had to suffer through her going out with? I don't mean that unkindly," Alex was quick to point out when he heard the sharp intake of breath on the other end of the line. "It's time I got on with my love life instead of waiting for her to realize what she's missing out on. I'm sorry if that sounds insensitive in light of her recent bereavement. I don't mean to be, but it's time for me to do something about the situation since I'm being accused of murder just because I allowed myself to be in love with her for so long."

"You're dead right, and I don't think anyone could ever accuse you of being insensitive. Sounds like you're really serious about Carol. We should all get together sometime soon; I'm sure the others would love to meet her."

"I'll talk to her about it and we'll arrange something."

"Maybe Friday night, if everybody can come around to ours after the kids go to sleep, just for some drinks?"

"Sounds good. Can you put me back on to her please?"

"Seriously? Didn't you just talk to her? It must be love!"

A few seconds later Carol came back on the line. "So, what did you tell him?" she asked.

"Not much; Just that I think you're great and I can't seem to get enough of you. He suggested going over to his house on Friday night for drinks to get to meet our friends. What do you think?"

"You think we're ready for that kind of commitment?" Carol asked.

"Don't joke; it'll be my parents next if you pass the test of meeting the friends," Alex said.

They agreed Friday sounded like a good idea and said that they must really get some work done.

They met in the Lunchbox, a small café in the main street. It was a popular lunchtime spot, which catered for schoolchildren and business people alike, serving a selection of meals from sausage, beans and chips to paninis and ciabattas. It was decorated in bright colors with comfortable seats. Framed photographs of the area, past and present, were mounted on the walls giving patrons something to look at and muse upon as they awaited their food.

They were tempted to play hooky for the afternoon, especially when looking out the window of the café they could see the way the sun glinted off the lake in the distance. They reluctantly agreed to go back to work and see each other that evening.

"What would you like to do this evening?" Alex asked.

With a gleam in her eye and a wink she blew him a kiss and got into her car.

"Well I know, but apart from that."

"I don't know, surprise me," Carol said.

Back at work he checked out the cinema listings and found a chick flick he was sure Carol would like. He hoped she wouldn't be disappointed after the taste of Italy on their first date. He booked the tickets for seven thirty and then had an excuse to ring her again. He didn't tell her where they were going; just that he'd pick her up at seven, hoping the element of surprise would please her.

That evening when Dave arrived home he filled Elaine in on how things were going with Carol and Alex. She was delighted, and when Sylvia called around later she informed her about the new woman in Alex's life.

Sylvia's reaction was one of shock. "What?!" she said, sitting slowly down on the couch and placing a cushion in her lap.

"Jealous, are you Sylvia?" Elaine asked, watching as Sylvia pulled at some loose threads in the cushion.

"Of course not, it's just that I'm the only girl he's ever dated; I'm surprised, that's all," Sylvia said as she put the cushion down beside her with a thump.

"I'm pretty surprised myself that it's going so well. They seem pretty serious already and they only met on Thursday night," Elaine said, putting her legs up under her on the couch.

"They spent the whole weekend together and met for lunch today and are seeing each other again tonight. I suggested they come over for drinks Friday night so that she can meet everybody," Dave said, handing Sylvia a cup of tea before sitting down in the armchair.

"Great; I'll call Kim and Gina later. I have to say, it's about bloody time; I mean he's been hung up on you, Sylvia, for far too long; it was never healthy," Elaine said.

"I agree," Sylvia said, not with much enthusiasm. "So tell us, how did they meet?"

"I set them up," Dave said.

"You did? And Alex didn't mind? I thought he'd hate that kind of thing."

"I spoke to him first about it and when he was willing I mentioned to Carol that a friend of mine was interested in seeing her. I arranged to meet him in the pub on Thursday night and arranged for her to meet us there."

"So, when you say they spent the weekend together, does that mean they slept together?" asked Sylvia.

"I don't know that much; they didn't go into detail, but I assume so."

"Sounds like a slut to me."

"Sylvia, I can't believe you of all people could say such a thing! That's jealousy talking. For starters we don't know for sure that they've slept together. For another thing I've met Carol; she's lovely, I would say perfect for Alex. And another thing, how often have you slept with a guy on the first date? Almost always, and no one's going around calling you a slut." Elaine stood up, gesticulating wildly as she blew up at Sylvia.

"I'm sorry, that was out of line; I don't know where it came from," Sylvia mumbled and promptly left the room.

"What the hell was all that?" Dave asked Elaine.

"I'd say even though she doesn't want Alex for herself she doesn't want anyone else to have him either. She's used to having him loving her and only her. She'll get over it. I'd better go see if she's all right," Elaine said, calming down once she realized Sylvia was hurting.

Elaine found Sylvia sitting on the stairs crying. She sat down beside her and put her arms around her friend. Sylvia turned to her and sobbed into her shoulder.

"That was awfully mean," Sylvia said when she'd finished crying and had separated herself from Elaine. "I didn't mean it; I don't know what came over me. I'm happy for Alex, really I am. I guess I'm not myself at the moment and I suppose I don't want things to change." At that, Sylvia laughed at herself. "I guess I'm just being selfish; Alex has always been there for me, and it'll be strange him having a girlfriend."

"Come on, Dave's poured us some wine; you'll feel better after you've got some of that into you," Elaine said, giving Sylvia a pat on the shoulder.

"Thanks, I'll just go freshen up; I'll be with you in five," Sylvia said as she turned to go up the stairs.

Elaine went back to the sitting room where Dave handed her a glass of wine.

"Is she okay?" he asked.

"Yeah, she just feels lousy for what she said. She said she didn't mean it, that she's just not herself at the moment. She's just gone to the bathroom and will be down in a few minutes."

Meanwhile Carol was getting ready for her date, unsure what to wear, as she didn't know where she was being taken. She opted for black trousers and a blue halter neck top and threw a shawl around her shoulders; that way she was ready for anything, even an outdoor evening. She was glad that the weather had taken a turn for the better since the weekend, not being ready to swap her summer wardrobe for her winter woollies just yet.

She was pleasantly surprised when they pulled up outside the cinema and Alex told her what they were going to see. She relished the opportunity for plenty of hand holding, and was sure that there would be a few stolen kisses during the soppy parts of the movie. They both agreed that part of the fun of going to the cinema was the popcorn and chocolate, that the taste of salty popcorn while the chocolate melted in their mouths was a real taste explosion. Later they went back to her apartment and made love before falling asleep wrapped in each other's arms.

They met for lunch each day of that week and spent each evening together, going for romantic walks, going to the pub for a few drinks, watching T.V and making love. Alex felt himself falling for Carol, and was glad that he had made arrangements to meet his friends on Friday night. He wanted to integrate her as much as possible into his life even though he was enjoying keeping her to himself. As Friday approached, Alex realized that he had better fill Carol in on the history between him and Sylvia. He felt nervous about it in case she would call the whole thing off, feeling a bit awkward about the fact that he and Sylvia were still friends.

CHAPTER THIRTY-SEVEN

Thursday the 9th of October

On Thursday night as they were watching T.V. Alex said, "There's something I think I should explain before you meet my friends tomorrow night." He chewed on his lip and pulled at a loose thread in his jumper.

"What is it?" Carol asked, turning towards him.

"I have a past with one of them; Sylvia and I have been dating on and off since we were sixteen and I was in love with her. It's been over for a long time now, but I thought you ought to know. Also, her boyfriend was murdered a few weeks ago."

"That's awful."

"It gets worse. I hope you'll still want to see me after I tell you this; I've been questioned in connection with the murder."

"Are you saying you're a suspect?"

"One of them, but…"

He didn't get to finish his sentence, as Carol, moving away from him on the couch, blurted out, "What! Did you not think that was something you should have told me upfront?" She grabbed his jacket and threw it at him. "You're right; I don't want to see you again."

"Can we just talk about this please? You're right; I should have told you from the beginning, but I've just been having a wonderful week and I was afraid of bursting the bubble. I'm not guilty of the murder; the suspicions of the guards are unfounded," Alex said as he reached out for her hand.

"Why are you a suspect then?" Carol asked, standing up and leaving Alex's hand hanging between them.

"Sylvia was having a party the night before the murder. I had been helping out in the kitchen before that and as a result my prints were on the murder weapon, a kitchen knife. Mine weren't the only prints on it, but the fact that I've no alibi coupled with the fact that the guards think I had a motive makes me suspect number one," Alex said, looking at his hand as he placed it on his lap.

And why exactly do they think you had a motive?"

"They think I'm still in love with Sylvia."

"Are you?"

"No; you do believe me, don't you?"

"I'm not sure. How can I be sure that you're not using me to convince the guards that you're not still in love with this Sylvia?"

"How well do you know Dave?" Alex asked.

"What's that got to do with anything?"

"Well Dave's hardly likely to set his co-worker up with a murderer, now is he? Or even with someone he believes to be in love with someone else?"

"I don't know," Carol said. "Dave obviously believes you're not guilty, but maybe he just thinks that I'll help you get over Sylvia if you are still in love with her."

"I swear to you that I'm not still in love with Sylvia. I really hope you can believe me and see past all of this because I really don't want to lose you."

"I don't know. I'm going to need some time by myself to think about this. Can you leave now? I'll call you tomorrow and we'll decide where to go from here."

When Alex arrived home he flung his jacket on the couch in frustration before flopping down onto the armchair with his head in his hands. He couldn't believe he had messed this up. His first chance at a real relationship, someone who could possibly share his feelings, and he had blown it.

Why couldn't he have been upfront about it from the start? She may have been okay about it all if he had just told her about it on that first night, or even on the second. He could have told her over dinner, but then she surely wouldn't have spent that wonderful weekend with him, and it had been a wonderful weekend. However, wouldn't it have been better to tell her about it at the start and if that was the end of it so be it? It looked so bad for him that he had left it until after all that lovemaking before telling her. He flushed with embarrassment at the thought that right now she was probably thinking he had been only after her for one thing. She must be thinking that he had chosen not to tell her at the beginning so that he could get her into bed with him.

Alex rang Dave to discuss the problem with him and see what he thought, and also to warn him that Carol might be on the warpath the next day.

"I didn't think of what sort of problems it might cause when she found out. Is she going to kill me for setting her up with you?" Dave asked.

"Well, she wasn't very pleased. Can you give me any advice here?"

"I can talk to her tomorrow for you; tell her that you're definitely not still in love with Sylvia. I'll tell her that the reason I didn't tell her about the murder was because the guards really have nothing to go on and when they've investigated it further they'll realize that you're not guilty. With any luck the actual murderer will turn up somewhere."

Alex couldn't help but laugh at the image that conjured up. "You make it sound as if the murderer is lost."

"You know what I mean," Dave said.

"I really don't want to lose Carol because of all of this. We've had a wonderful week together."

"I'll see what I can do tomorrow, okay. I'm sorry I can't be more help than that. I feel as if it's partly my fault; I should probably have waited until all this murder business had blown over before setting you two up."

"No, I should have been upfront with her about the whole thing from the very start."

"I suppose we've both done a great job of messing this one up for you," Dave said.

They ended the conversation on that note and agreed to talk the next day.

When Dave hung up the phone Elaine, who had been talking to Sylvia, asked "What was all that about?"

Dave explained to the two girls what had happened with Alex and Carol.

"It's a pity he didn't wait a bit longer to tell her about him being a suspect. I mean, if he had asked us to keep quiet about it we would have, and they're sure to unearth the real murderer soon," Elaine said, taking her legs out from under her and stretching them out on the couch.

"I don't know, maybe he was right to tell her. If she sticks by him then it shows her character. Likewise, if she doesn't it shows her true character," Sylvia argued, moving over on the couch to give Elaine room.

"Give the girl a break. If you just met a total stranger and a week into the relationship he dropped that kind of bombshell on you, how would you react?" Elaine asked.

"Well all I can say is Rick could have run a mile when I told him about Alex and me, or at least insisted that we don't hang out together any more, but he didn't. I know, before you say anything, I didn't have a murder accusation hanging over me, but Rick was the type of guy who would have stood by me. Alex deserves better than a girl who's going to run at the first hurdle."

"It's a pretty big hurdle. In fairness to Carol, how can any of us say how we'd react under the circumstances?" Dave defended her, tapping his fingers on the arm of the couch. "Don't forget I know Carol pretty well; I think she'd be terrific for Alex, and I'm not surprised this whole thing spooked her. I should have waited until he was no longer considered a suspect before setting them up."

"Look, you can't blame yourself. In fairness I would usually think of something like that, but we've all been so surprised that Alex was willing to start seeing someone else besides Sylvia," Elaine said.

"Well, whatever you do, don't say that to Carol. I think he's trying to play down how intense his feelings for Sylvia were," Dave said.

"If he's to learn anything from this it's that he needs to be completely honest with Carol. It'll come out in the end and it'll be worse than if he just came right out and said it," Sylvia said.

"I think what he needs to do is take this one step at a time. If they get past this issue, sometime in the future when they're secure in the relationship they can laugh over how much in love with you he was," Elaine said.

Sylvia yawned and said, "Well I'd better be getting home. I hope things get sorted between Alex and Carol. I'll ring him tomorrow to see how he's doing."

Sylvia headed out into the dark night and Elaine was reluctant to see her go, couldn't help feeling sorry for her going home to her empty house, no matter how much Sylvia insisted that she needed to get on with things. She felt that it was very brave of Sylvia when she knew that there was always a bed in their house for her. As she brushed her teeth she wondered how she'd cope in similar circumstances and was so glad to have Dave and the two children.

As she climbed into bed beside Dave he said, "Sylvia seems to be taking the fact that Alex has a new girlfriend very hard. Do you think she's harbored feelings for him all these years without realizing it?"

"I very much doubt it. I think it's just a case of Carol being in the way when she feels she needs Alex," Elaine said.

"Yeah, you're probably right. She has messed him around a lot over the years, hasn't she?"

"Not the way she sees it, but yes, she has. I hope that Alex and Carol go the distance. At least it'll mean that he won't be there to be used anymore. He deserves someone like Carol," Elaine said, pulling the covers up over her.

CHAPTER THIRTY-EIGHT

Friday the 10th of October

Dave knocked on Carol's office door the next morning. He was dreading this conversation with her and hoped she wouldn't be as mad with him as he probably deserved.

"Come in." When she saw it was Dave her tone changed as she said, "I have a bone to pick with you. What's all this business about Alex being a murder suspect? How could you set me up with someone who's been accused of murder?" She put her pen down on the papers she had been working on.

"I know you're mad with me and I feel really lousy about it. My timing was way off; I realize that now. I should have waited until he was no longer a suspect before setting you two up, but I honestly didn't think about it. I mean my friends and I know he's innocent so it didn't occur to me that you might have a problem with it. I can see where you're coming from, really I can. All I ask is that you give Alex a chance. When you see what a wonderful guy he is you'll wonder how he can possibly be considered a suspect. He hasn't even been arrested, so even the guards know they've nothing to go on," Dave said as he took a seat opposite her at her desk.

Her tone softened a bit as she said, "I've been troubled by that all night. I had a wonderful week with him, and I couldn't reconcile myself with the possibility that the guy I've spent all that time with is a murderer. It just doesn't add up unless he's a very good actor, or he has Multiple

Person Disorder or something. I guess if you're willing to vouch for him I'll take your word for it. That's another thing I couldn't reconcile myself with, you setting me up with someone who could be anything other than a stand up guy.

"There's just one more thing; this Sylvia person, is it really over between them? I'm not just a stop gap to help him get over her, am I?"

"No, Alex doesn't do that; he moves on when he's ready and not a minute sooner. He wouldn't play with your emotions by using you; it's not his style."

"In that case I'll give him another chance, but only because I trust your judgment, Dave."

"I'm glad; I'd hate to see you two miss out on each other over this."

When Dave left her office Carol got straight on the phone to Alex. She found herself smiling for the first time since the previous evening. She had hoped that Dave would be able to put her mind at rest about Alex and was glad that she wasn't going to end things between them.

"Hi, Alex; I think we need to talk about last night, but it'd be better to talk over lunch. How about our usual spot?"

"Yeah, sure; can I look forward to it or not?" he asked.

"I think it'll all be okay. I just want to straighten some things out."

Carol was unwilling to discuss it further over the phone so Alex had to wait until they met up in The Lunchbox at one o'clock. It was a long morning; while struggling with numbers and accounts all he could think about was Carol and how he'd like to make it up to her if she was good enough to take him back. He'd buy her a bunch of roses and take her to Lana's for dinner. When lunchtime came he couldn't get out the door fast enough and the closer he got to The Lunchbox the more nervous he became of what Carol was going to say to him, whether or not she would take him back.

Opening the door to the Lunchbox, he scanned the crowd for Carol's face, longing to see her smile at him. With an unsure smile, he sat down opposite her in the booth. She didn't look at him at first, perusing the menu until the waitress came over to take their order.

After they had placed their order Carol put down the menu and said, "Okay, let's talk. I've spoken to Dave this morning and he assures me that there's no way on earth that you're guilty, and that I'm not just a rebound girlfriend to help you get over Sylvia. That doesn't excuse the fact that you weren't upfront with me from the beginning.

"I accept the fact that we're not going to be able to disclose absolutely everything about one another from the very beginning, but that was a huge bomb you just dropped on me last night. I need for you to be honest with me, Alex. If that's something you can't do then you may as well get up and walk out that door. I deserve to be treated with respect, and if you can't be honest with me you obviously don't respect my judgment or me. So is there anything else I should know about?"

Alex took a deep breath and decided he'd better tell her about the intensity of his feelings for Sylvia. It was either that or risk losing her when she eventually found out, which he felt sure she would. "When I told you that I used to be in love with Sylvia I left out the fact that up to now she was my only girlfriend. I wasn't interested in anyone else even when she was with some other guy; I knew she'd come back to me, and she always did. She's never been serious about any other guys until Rick, and I always thought that we'd end up together, that I just needed to let her get other men out of her system first.

When she fell in love with Rick I realized that we were never meant to be together and willed myself out of love with her. Being accused of Rick's murder was the final straw; I couldn't let her hold me back from my life any longer so I decided to do something about it. I don't mean that you were an attempt to get over her. I was already over her and ready to move on, but it was the murder accusation that made me realize that I couldn't take a back seat in my own life anymore. I had to get out there and actively do something about getting a life of my own instead of being a pawn in hers. Does that make sense?"

"Yes, in a strange, sad and weird way it does," Carol said and tilted her head.

"You think I'm sad and weird then? That doesn't bode well," Alex said, twisting and untwisting a paper napkin.

"I don't think you're sad and weird; I think the situation is, but nobody's life is perfect. My first impression of you was that you're a pretty terrific guy, and that still stands despite everything. I feel sorry for Sylvia that she could have had a wonderful life with you, but her loss is my gain I guess."

"So that means that you're willing to give me another chance?"

"Yes, I am. Does our date to meet your friends still stand this evening?"

"I'll check with Dave to see if it's still all on; I'm sure it is, as I doubt they made other plans just because we had a disagreement. They're all dying to meet you."

"I'm looking forward to meeting them too."

Their food arrived and there was a gradual return to their usual camaraderie.

All that afternoon Alex felt nervous that his friends wouldn't like Carol, knowing he was being irrational because what wasn't to like? He rang Lana's to book a dinner there to surprise her, but found that they had no vacancies until the following weekend. On the way home he stopped into a florist and was almost swayed from his intention to buy roses by the array of scents and colors in the shop. As Sylvia wasn't much of a flower person there had never been much reason for him to step inside a flower shop, and on the few occasions he had he knew exactly what he wanted and just went in and out. This time though he paused and wondered what flowers would best say that he was sorry for not being upfront about being a murder suspect? A shop assistant asked him if he'd like some help and he smiled at the thoughts of voicing that question. In the end he bought the dozen red roses he had come in for, deciding that he could go for a more complicated bouquet when he knew Carol well, knew what colors and scents she liked most, what her favorite flower was, if indeed she had a favorite.

When he arrived at Carol's that evening to pick her up she was delighted with the roses and her eyes opened wide when she heard about the dinner he'd booked for the following weekend in Lana's. She told him she'd have to go shopping as there was nothing in her wardrobe worthy of such an establishment.

When they arrived at Elaine and Dave's he discovered that everyone else was already there. With some relief he relaxed as he noticed how easily the others accepted Carol into the group, not having been quite sure what to expect from Sylvia and Kim. Particularly Sylvia, but in light of the fact that Kim had recently come on to him he thought she might be a bit off with him and possibly even with Carol. He was also concerned that Carol would be disdainful of Sylvia, but they all seemed genuinely interested in getting to know each other.

When the night came to an end he was delighted to be part of a couple and leave with Carol as Gina and Kim were leaving together, while Sylvia fell asleep on the couch and ended up staying the night. They spent the night at Carol's apartment, and had a lazy day recovering from their hangovers.

CHAPTER THIRTY-NINE

Sunday the 12th of October

The shrill ringing of the phone woke Alex and Carol at nine thirty. Carol groaned as she reached out to answer it. In order to give her some privacy on the phone Alex got up and made the two of them breakfast. He decided to make them a full fry, as they hadn't eaten much the previous day; their stomachs had felt a bit dodgy after the cocktails that Dave had poured into them on Friday night. He was starving and was pretty sure Carol must be also. The smell tantalized his taste buds, making his mouth water and his stomach rumble really loudly as he brought the breakfast back to bed with him. Walking into the room he heard Carol hanging up the phone.

"That was my ex," she said. "He wants to meet me for lunch to talk about the way we left things. Mmm, that smells so good. I'm starving." She reached out and took a piece of rasher from the tray as Alex was setting it down on the bedside locker.

"Cheeky!" Alex said as he swatted her hand away. "Does he want to get back with you?"

"No, absolutely not. He just doesn't like the way things ended between us; he'd like us to be friends, or at least get some closure."

"You want to meet with him, is that it?"

Well yes, but only if you're okay with it. I mean, it's you who's important to me now not him. But we always got on very well together and I agree with him that it's a shame things ended the way they did. It's not a shame that they ended, just that they ended so badly. I explained to him that I have a new boyfriend, just so that he's under no illusions that we could be getting back together. He said that was fine; he doesn't want us to get back together, but he'd like us to be friends."

"Were you together long?"

"Childhood sweethearts, but it's been over for more than a year now; we had a huge row, he walked out and we never saw each other again after that. He came into the apartment and moved his stuff out while I was at work, and I came home to find all of his belongings gone and no note or anything. Last I heard he had gone to Australia for a year to 'find himself'. Well I guess he's found himself. Are you okay with me meeting up with him?"

"As long as he doesn't steal you away from me."

"I promise I'll call you later to let you know how things went with him and to make plans for a date tonight with you. There's no way on earth he could steal me away from you." Carol grinned at him as she popped a piece of sausage into her mouth. "Mmm, this is just what I need; you must have read my mind."

After breakfast they made love, slow and lazy, enjoying each other's bodies, each finding out more about pleasuring the other. If it hadn't been for Carol's plans to meet up with Harry they might have been tempted to stay in bed longer, but eventually they dragged themselves out of bed and into the shower.

At twelve o'clock, after helping Carol clean up after the breakfast, Alex left her apartment and went home to his own. He tried to occupy his mind and not think about Carol sitting opposite her ex for lunch; however, he couldn't help feeling a twinge of jealousy. Rather than going over to Dave and Elaine's or occupying himself he just waited for the phone to ring. He sat in his recliner and tried to read a book while listening to Tchaikovsky. He would read a paragraph and then find himself thinking of Carol, her mouth moving sensuously as she ate her lunch, and he wondered if Harry would try to seduce her, if she would resist his advances. The thought of it was making him crazy.

When the phone hadn't rung by four o'clock he got worried that Carol had been stolen away from him. He rang her apartment and her mobile and, getting no response, felt a surge of anger; he was annoyed with himself for allowing her to see her ex. Then he reasoned with himself that he could hardly stop her considering that she understood about Sylvia and him still being so close. He toyed with the idea of going to her apartment to wait outside it for her to return, but didn't want to appear jealous and possessive; that would surely drive her away from him for good. He was lucky to be getting a second chance with her and didn't want to mess that up.

So he waited, driving himself even crazier with images of Carol in the midst of passion with Harry, imagining every curve of her body as it moved to the rhythm of love's own beat, remembering how her body had responded to his touch, his tongue, his body, earlier that day. He created a rhythm of his own with pen and paper, describing her body's sensuous curves and movements like the ebb and flow of the tide, always changing, responding to the nuances of the touch of the wind and rain.

The evening passed in a blur; afterwards Alex was unaware of how he had passed it. He went out for a drive but couldn't say where he ended up. The only thing he was aware of was the jealous rage coursing through his veins, and he hated himself for it. He didn't own Carol; she was entitled to see whom she liked, but she had promised to call him, and he'd had his mobile with him at all times. Despite her assurances that she wouldn't get back with Harry he must have won her over.

He wished she would ring him to at least put him out of his misery. If she really wanted to get back with her ex, well, so be it. They hadn't been together that long so he had no right to stand in her way, but surely a phone call to tell him it was over wasn't too much to expect.

He considered trying to phone her again but wouldn't allow himself to do so for fear she would think him desperate and clingy, possessive even. He certainly felt pathetic and needy, but couldn't stop himself from hoping for a phone call and hoping he hadn't lost Carol after her giving him this second chance. He asked himself what hope he had against the history they shared together, making himself more miserable with every passing minute of waiting to hear from her.

He read over and over again the poems he had written for her, the first poems he had ever written for anyone other than Sylvia. It meant a lot to him that he had succeeded in doing that, and now he may have just lost Carol, may never have the opportunity to read this new one to her, to kiss or make love to her again. He remembered her reaction to the first poem he had written. He had read it to her in bed, after making love to her, and her response to it was passionate; she had turned out the light, creating a new image of her silhouette moving rhythmically in the moonlight.

He wondered if at that very moment she was responding to the familiar kiss and touch of Harry. Maybe she had missed him more than she realized. He put the poems on the table, smoothing out the edges of the paper they were written on and went to bed.

CHAPTER FORTY

Monday the 13th of October

Alex got up and went to work feeling a heavy weight on his shoulders and in his heart, one that wasn't just the usual accompaniment to Monday mornings. He had a horrible feeling that it was over between he and Carol.

It was a very unproductive morning at work; everything he tried to do he got wrong. It was one of those days when he wished he hadn't bothered getting up out of bed, although aware that if he had stayed in bed he would be even more tortured than he was at present, with images of Carol beside him, on top of him, under him, teasing and pleasing him. The disappointment of probably having lost her would be more palpable. He wanted to ring her but pride stopped him. If she wants me she knows where I am, he thought.

He was in the middle of sorting through a pile of papers on his desk when he got a call from Dave. "I just rang you at home because I assumed that you and Carol were pulling a sickie together, but I guess not. Only the thing is she's not picking up her phone. Have you any idea where she might be?" Dave asked.

"Last I saw of her was twelve o'clock yesterday afternoon. She was going to meet her ex-boyfriend; he wanted them to be friends. She promised she'd ring me and since she hasn't it doesn't take a genius to work out what's happened. My guess is you'll find her at his place," Alex replied, bitterness creeping into his tone, although he was trying to be pragmatic about it.

"Oh," Dave said. "I'm sorry, Alex; I never saw that one coming. She seemed to be so into you, and before she split up with Harry she hadn't been happy with him for a long time. I didn't think she'd even want to be friends with him after the way he dumped her, never mind going back with him. Are you okay?"

"I feel like shit. At least with Sylvia I always knew where I stood, but I didn't think this would happen. Makes me think better the devil you know, right?"

"I find it hard to believe Carol would treat you this way; she's no more like that than you are a murderer."

"You're wrong on that score. A person's only as good as their word; she never even rang me which means her word isn't worth jack shit."

"Don't be like that; Carol doesn't deserve to have you think like that of her, at least not until you know the full story."

"Well I can't know that until she rings me."

"It's not like her not to ring work. I hope she's all right."

"I feel like such a shit, Dave! It never even occurred to me that there might be another explanation for this."

"I'll look in the company file and see if there are any phone numbers I might be able to contact her at. She may be just upset and lying low at her parents' house or at a friends'."

"If that asshole has done something to upset her I'll kill him, I swear I will."

"I know what you mean, but that's not something you want to be heard saying."

"You're right; I don't know what's getting into me lately. Last night and this morning I was so angry with her. Now that I think he may have done something to upset or hurt her I'm angry with him, and that's not like me. I'm just so sick of getting the raw end of the deal."

"You know, everything might work out okay in the end so try not to worry about it. I'll call you as soon as I hear something. If she contacts you, you might let me know, okay?"

Alex hung up the phone and banged his hand down on the desk. He picked up the papers he had been sorting through and stared blindly at them. He wished he could turn back the clock and talk Carol out of going to see Harry.

When Dave hung up the phone he couldn't help feeling a nagging worry about his friend; Alex was acting so out of character this morning, and if the guards got wind of this side of him it wouldn't bode well. It wouldn't do for him to keep mouthing off about killing people. Dave was well aware that everybody says 'I'll kill him' from time to time, but not if they've been accused of murder and have any sense they don't. Usually Alex's temper didn't get the better of him; on the contrary, he was one of the gentlest men Dave knew. He decided to put that out of his mind for now and concentrate on trying to get hold of Carol.

He found her parents' phone number but found himself reluctant to ring them in case he worried them unnecessarily. He decided to compile a list of people he could contact before doing anything else. The company files hadn't been updated since Carol had split up with Harry, and that's where he started the search. He was hoping for Alex's sake he wouldn't find her there.

"Hello? Could I speak to Harry Nolan please?"

"Speaking."

"I'm trying to contact Carol O'Connor. She didn't arrive in to work today, isn't answering her phone and you're listed as her person to contact in case of an emergency," Dave said, flipping open and closed the file in front of him.

"Well that shouldn't be the case as we split up a long time ago."

"So you've no idea where she might be?"

"No I don't. She has a new boyfriend now; I saw her yesterday and she was planning to see him last night. Have you tried her mobile number?"

"Yes I have; she's not answering. Her new boyfriend hasn't seen her since twelve o'clock yesterday afternoon. What time did you last see her?"

"About seven o'clock. We had a long lunch followed by a few drinks; we were catching up, you know? We hadn't seen each other in a long time. Shit, she drove home; I told her I thought maybe she shouldn't. I hope she's okay."

"I haven't heard of any accidents so I'm sure it's not that. I'm sure she'll turn up somewhere. She probably has a tummy bug or something and just doesn't feel like talking to anyone."

"I don't know. You have me worried now; she was always so responsible, well when it came to ringing in sick anyway. Driving home yesterday wasn't the responsible thing to do; I wish I'd called her a cab. She seemed to be looking forward to seeing this new guy, Alec I think she called him. She'd surely have rung him if she didn't feel up to seeing him; I know she was very considerate like that when we dated. Will you ring me back if you hear anything?" Harry asked.

"Yes of course," Dave found himself answering, despite thinking very little of Harry. He does seem genuinely concerned, Dave thought.

Although Dave didn't like going through Carol's desk to find her personal phone book he wanted to ring anybody else he possibly could before worrying her parents. However much he reasoned with himself that they might be the only people who would know where she was it didn't lessen his reluctance to ring them. He thought of his own parents and how worried they'd be if they got a phone call from someone at work that was unable to contact him. He couldn't do that to someone else's parents.

He came across a couple of names he remembered Carol mentioning on a regular basis and tried ringing them. The calls brought forth no information, only succeeded in worrying her friends. Dave suggested to the friend whose name he recognized most, Melissa, that it might be best if she rang Carol's parents, as they would know her. She agreed that it would be less worrying for them if it were she rather than Dave who rang them. She guaranteed Dave that she would ring him straight back.

He had just had a very unproductive fifteen minutes when, as promised, she called him back. He pounced on the phone as if someone would beat him to it if he didn't.

"I've just rung the guards to report her missing. However, they refuse to look into it until she's been missing for twenty-four hours; that's not until seven pm this evening."

"How did her parents take it?"

"I didn't go into details. I just said I lost my mobile and couldn't find my phone book so I was just looking for her number. I told her mother I remembered their house number from all the times I rang there as a teenager. I made out I hadn't talked to her in ages and asked if they had heard from her lately. She said she had been talking to her yesterday before lunch. She told me that Carol told her about a new boyfriend, that Harry was back in Ireland and that she had been planning on meeting him for lunch yesterday. Then we just chit-chatted generally for a few minutes, and after that I rang the guards."

"Thanks for ringing me back. I'll call Alex if you'll call Harry. All we can do is sit tight and hope she turns up before too long. If you hear anything will you let me know? Otherwise we'll have to ring the guards again this evening."

"If I don't hear anything before seven this evening I'll ring you after ringing the Garda station. I just hope it doesn't come to that."

"Do you know if anyone has a spare key to the apartment?" Dave asked.

"The landlord would have one. Also Harry might if he didn't give it back to her when he moved out. I'll ask him when I ring, and I'll let you know. The landlord probably won't open the door for us anyway."

Dave called Alex and said, "I hope you've heard from her in the last hour, because Harry hasn't seen her since seven o'clock yesterday evening. Her friends haven't spoken to her since before the weekend and her mother heard from her just before lunch yesterday."

"Shit, that's not good. How did you get in touch with all those people?"

Dave filled him in on how he had managed that and on what the guards had said. "So if she gets in touch with you will you let me know?" he continued.

"Sure thing; you've got me really worried now. I wish there was something I could do to track her down."

"You could try her mobile again."

"I've rang her several times in the last hour, both her apartment and mobile; no answer," Alex said.

Dave hung up and waited for Melissa to ring back. When she did it was to say that Harry didn't have a key to the apartment. He had given her the number of the landlord, and, as she had suspected, he wouldn't open the door for her. She had explained the situation to him and he said that if the guards wanted him to open the door he'd have no problem doing it, but if they weren't treating her as a missing person until that evening neither would he.

"Another dead end then," Dave said. "Talk soon, I hope with good news." Dave hung up and tried to get some work done.

For the rest of the day work was the last place Alex wanted to be; he was completely distracted, and was only able to think of the possibility of Carol lying in a hospital somewhere so he rang Dave again.

"I have a bad feeling about this. I don't think she is going to turn up; in my gut I know something terrible has happened. I'm going to ring the hospitals; I can't believe I didn't think of that already," Alex said.

"Melissa rang me just now. Harry's already done that; he was worried that she'd had a car accident on the way home. He drove to her apartment at lunch and her car is there, so she got home safely last night but isn't there now, or at least not answering her phone or the door."

"Maybe it wasn't so wise keeping her parents in the dark; they might have a key to the apartment. If her car is there she must be there," Alex said.

"You could be right, but we can involve the guards in a few hours; let's hope we don't have to, and if we bring her parents into it at this stage and she turns up we'll have caused them a lot of heartache over nothing. I remember her telling me that her father has angina. He could end up having a heart attack, so we'd better be sure there's something for them to worry about before we ring them."

"I'm going over to her apartment now; I should have gone over there yesterday evening. Maybe she's fallen down and hurt herself and can't get to the phone. If that's the case she could have been lying there helpless since last night," Alex said.

"Harry banged on the door when he went over there at lunch, and there were no sounds from inside," Dave said.

"Shit, what's happened to her? Yesterday all I was worried about was losing her to Harry, and now anything could have happened to her." Alex hung up and put his head in his hands in despair. He had long since given up any pretence at work.

When Dave's home phone rang at half past seven that evening he had a sinking feeling that it was Melissa.

"I'm ringing from the Garda station where I've just filed a complete report. I let them know whom I've been in touch with, and who hasn't seen or heard from Carol since yesterday. All they were willing to say was that they'd look into it. I told them her car was outside her apartment and the last time she was seen was leaving a pub to go home and she hasn't been answering her door or phone since. All we can do now is sit and wait for them to get in touch."

"Thanks for all your help with this. I really hope we're jumping the gun here," Dave said.

"So do I."

Dave rang Alex to fill him in. He hated being the bearer of such bad news for his friend and wondered if Alex would ever catch a break.

"The guards are going to be thrilled to see my name on the list of people she's been with," Alex said.

"You have to try to think positively; it's not going to do any good to go around thinking like that. Let's hope we get some good news soon."

Dave got off the phone and filled Elaine in on what was going on, and Elaine took over the phone to fill Sylvia, Gina and Kim in.

When Sylvia heard what Elaine had to say she felt bad about her original reaction towards Carol now that it looked like she was missing. She didn't feel like being alone right then, as she really missed Rick, and decided to get out of the house and go over to Elaine's. She thought she might even stay the night in order to stave off the loneliness that was enveloping her.

At nine-thirty that night there was a knock on Alex's door. He hoped against fervent hope that it was Carol but knew in his heart that it was bad news. The lead weight he had been carrying around with him all day settled even more heavily on his shoulders and in his heart. He opened the door to find that he was right.

Detectives Molloy and Naughton were standing there looking very solemn. "Alexander Joseph Bermingham, you are under arrest in connection with the murder of Carol Ann O'Connor."

"She's dead?" Alex whispered in disbelief as his rights were read out to him. He couldn't believe that she was dead and that he was being arrested under suspicion of murdering her. Things were going from bad to worse. He couldn't even feel any shame when his neighbor passed by and gawked in at him as he was being placed in handcuffs. All he felt was an overwhelming sadness that Carol was dead.

CHAPTER FORTY-ONE

Tears came into Alex's eyes. He felt numb. He had found himself unable to protest his innocence as Detective Naughton clapped him in handcuffs and shoved him into the back seat of the car.

When they arrived at the Garda station Alex found himself being led into the interview room. He asked to ring his solicitor, which he was given a moment to do. He wanted to know about how Carol had been killed and where she had been found but the detectives refused to answer him. They informed him that they'd be the ones to ask the questions.

When his solicitor arrived, the questioning got underway without much preamble. He found that the detectives were approaching the interview much more seriously this time around, as if now that his girlfriend was found dead there was no longer any doubts whatsoever in their minds that he was the murderer.

"Your fingerprints have been found all over the crime-scene. How do you explain that, Mr. Bermingham?" Detective Molloy asked, tapping her fingers on the table in front of her.

"Carol and I have been dating and I've been sleeping over at her apartment a lot. I assume that's where you found her body. Can you please tell me what happened? The last time I saw her was at twelve o'clock yesterday afternoon," Alex said.

"Can you account for your whereabouts on Sunday evening?" Detective Molloy asked.

"I was at home in my apartment on Sunday evening," Alex said, slumping forward in his seat.

"All evening and all night?"

"Yes, alone. I was waiting for Carol to ring me."

"How long have you been dating the deceased?"

With tears in his eyes Alex said through gritted teeth, "Her name is Carol. Show some respect for the dead and call her Carol."

"I'm sorry, how long have you been dating Carol?"

"We've been seeing each other for a week."

"And you've been sleeping over at her apartment in that week?"

"Yes."

"How many nights would you say you slept over?"

"Seven nights."

"Seven nights. You're a fast mover, Mr. Bermingham. You were in here not so long ago in love with, who was it again, Sylvia? Now you've just started dating the, sorry, Carol and have already spent one week sleeping with her?"

"Could you please stop badgering my client? Do you or do you not have any evidence to suggest it was indeed my client who murdered, eh, Carol?" Jim said with an apologetic look towards Alex as he almost made the slip up of calling her the deceased.

"Not at this time; however, we have a team working on that right now. What we need from your client is his co-operation," Detective Naughton said, looking up from his notebook. He resumed taking notes as the interview continued.

"As you have nothing with which to detain him I demand that if he co-operates with you, you let him go unless you manage to find something on him," Jim said.

"By the time I'm finished questioning him something should have turned up. If it hasn't I promise you we will let him go." Detective Molloy turned to Alex and asked, "When exactly did you start dating Carol?"

"Last Thursday week."

"And when did you start sleeping with her?"

"The next night."

"Did you stay over at her apartment every night? Except of course for last night."

"Every night except last Thursday night."

"And why was it that you didn't stay over on Thursday night?" Detective Molloy asked.

"We had a falling out."

"What was it about?"

"You don't need to answer that," Jim said to Alex. To Detective Molloy he said, "It's hardly relevant what they fell out over."

"I disagree; it may be of no relevance if they argued over who should have control over the remote or squeezing the toothpaste from the middle of the tube, but if they argued over an ex boyfriend whom Alex was jealous of then I would say it was very relevant. Wouldn't you?" she asked of Jim.

Jim looked at Alex and said, "I'd like a moment to speak with my client, please."

"It's okay, I'll answer," Alex said. "We were due to meet up with my friends the next night and I felt that she should know about the history between Sylvia and I, and also about the fact that I was being accused of murdering Rick. Understandably she needed time to think about whether or not to continue seeing me."

"And what convinced her to see you again? Brave girl. Brave or stupid, I don't know which; there's no way in hell I'd continue dating someone who's not only in love with someone else but also suspected of murdering her boyfriend."

"There was nothing stupid about her," responded Alex. "She worked with Dave; she spoke to him about it on Friday morning. When he assured her that not only was I not a murderer but also not on the rebound she agreed to give me another chance."

"Did Dave introduce you two?"

"Yes."

"Under what circumstances did the two of you part on Sunday?"

"Her ex boyfriend rang. He had returned from Australia and felt bad about the way they had left things between them; he wanted to remain friends with her. She agreed that they had been through too much together to not try to at least remain friends. She made it clear to him though that it couldn't be more than that because I was now in her life. She arranged to meet him for lunch and she promised to ring me afterwards to arrange something for later that night," Alex said.

"Weren't you concerned about letting her off to meet her ex?"

"Not especially; I took her at her word that she had no interest in getting back together with him. They had been childhood sweethearts. Why would I want to stand in her way of a friendship with him? After all, she was very accepting of the friendship between Sylvia and me."

Detective Molloy shook her head and threw her eyes to heaven as she said, "Did she ring you after her lunch date?"

"No."

"At what point on Sunday did you start to feel that she must surely have betrayed you since she hadn't rung you?"

"Don't answer that," Jim said.

"Okay, let me rephrase. How did you feel when the phone call you had been expecting didn't arrive?"

"You don't need to answer that," Jim said.

"It's okay; I don't mind admitting that I had a mixture of emotions. I felt like a fool for having let her go to meet an ex boyfriend; I felt that I had just let him take her from me. I was mad with myself for allowing myself to be taken for a fool, and I felt betrayed, but that doesn't make me a murderer. Who wouldn't have felt the same way?"

"Feeling like that doesn't make you unique, I'll give you that. It doesn't even necessarily make you a murderer. However, when you add the fact that you're already suspected of murdering your ex girlfriend's boyfriend, that in both murders you have motive, no alibi and finger prints on a murder weapon and all over a crime scene it adds up to you being guilty," Detective Molloy said.

"It's all circumstantial, and you know it. You've got nothing that can make this stick. You may as well release my client now and go in search of some real criminals," Jim said.

At that moment there was a knock on the door. A guard stuck his head around the door. "Sorry for interrupting. Detectives, can I have a word for a moment?"

The detectives left the room to speak to the guard.

Jim turned to Alex. "I suggest coming into my office first thing tomorrow morning. I really feel that as I don't specialize in criminal law you should see one of my associates, Liam Mitchell." At Alex's reluctance he continued, "I really want you provided with the best defense and I feel I'm not the best person for the job. Ultimately the decision is yours, but that would be my advice to you at this point."

At that moment Detective Molloy burst into the room with a triumphant look on her face. Detective Naughton entered more calmly behind her.

"The murder weapon wasn't found in the first sweep of the apartment, but it's been found since; it's a kitchen knife again, and again it has your prints all over it," Detective Molloy said.

"Circumstantial. You heard my client say that he spent the night at his girlfriend's apartment on Saturday night. Surely that night, or on Sunday morning, my client had cause to use the kitchen knife," Jim said.

"I'm sure he did," Detective Molloy said, "but I'm sure you will find, Mr. O'Laughlin, that we have enough evidence on your client to charge him with murder."

"I would like a few moments to confer with my client please." Jim turned to Alex as the detectives left the room. "I hope that now you will consider taking my advice. I will do my best to get a bail hearing for you as soon as possible, but you must understand that because you're a suspect in two murder cases it's not going to be easy to get you out on bail. As soon as it is arranged please come to my office so that we can arrange for Liam Mitchell to take over the case. If bail is denied I will arrange for Liam to come and see you."

"So where do we go from here?"

"You spend some time in jail until I can arrange bail, and then we, or you and Liam, work together to prove your innocence."

There was nothing for Alex to do but settle in for an uncomfortable night.

CHAPTER FORTY-TWO

Tuesday the 14th of October

As Elaine, Dave and Sylvia sat down to breakfast they listened to the seven o'clock news on the local radio station. As the children had not yet risen they could hear the broadcaster quite clearly as she gave the news report.

"The body of a young woman reported missing early yesterday evening has been found in her apartment. Twenty-five-year-old Carol O'Connor was last seen at seven pm on Sunday evening. The Gardaí say she was murdered sometime between seven-thirty pm on Sunday evening and the early hours of Monday morning. The autopsy is due to be performed later today. A young man, twenty-six-year-old Alexander Bermingham, has been charged with her murder. He is also under suspicion of the murder of Richard O'Hara last month."

In shock and disbelief the three friends put their hands to their mouths. There were tears in the eyes of Elaine and Dave; Sylvia couldn't hold back the flow of tears. Dave's office would be shut today out of respect for Carol, but even if it weren't he wouldn't be going in. Elaine rang Gina to see if they had heard the news.

"I don't have to go in to work today. This had better be important," Gina said, sounding groggy.

"So you didn't hear the news then?" Elaine asked.

"No."

"Carol's been found murdered in her apartment."

"That's dreadful! How is Alex taking it?"

"He's being charged with her murder, and it looks like this case is strengthening the Gardaí's belief that he killed Rick." An apologetic look crossed Elaine's face as Sylvia broke into a fresh wave of tears.

"Oh shit," Gina said. "This is bad. Sylvia sounds like she's in bits over there. Is there anything we can do to help?"

"I'm going to ring Alex's solicitor now to see what's going on. Sylvia could do with some support right now as she's falling apart, understandably enough. It was hard for her to hear Rick's name on the news this morning on top of the shocking news of Carol, not to mention that it's Alex being arrested for all this. We're all finding that hard to digest, but Sylvia's emotions are very raw at the moment."

"We'll be right over."

"Thanks."

When Gina and Kim arrived, Elaine filled them in on what the solicitor had said. "He'll let us know when bail has been set. He's expecting it to be pretty high considering that it's two murders he's being accused of. I told him we'd move heaven and earth to come up with the bail money; we'll remortgage the house if we have to."

The phone rang, and Elaine answered it to find Alex's mother on the line. In between tears she managed to ask what was going on.

Eventually her tears subsided and she became irate that her son was being charged with murder. "It's come to a fine state of affairs when a boy's own mother has to hear this kind of thing about him on the radio. Who is this Carol? How did my Alex become mixed up with her? I knew he was suspected of Rick's murder, but that's just nonsense. Where do the guards come up with such rubbish?"

"Alex had been going out with Carol for just a week, Mrs. Bermingham. They only have circumstantial evidence to go on, finger prints that have a perfectly logical reason for being on the weapons, lack of an alibi, and a motive."

"Speak in plain English, dear. And call me Vera, please."

"In other words they really don't have much to go on. His fingerprints were on both murder weapons, but with good reason. They were kitchen knives, one in Sylvia's kitchen, which he had used the night before Rick's murder, and one in Carol's kitchen, which he had used earlier on the day of that murder. He was home alone when both murders took place with no one to verify that he was where he said he was. They claim that he murdered Rick because he was jealous of him and that he murdered Carol because he thought she was going to get back with her ex."

"I told him that Sylvia one would get him into trouble some day. Oh, of course I feel sorry that her boyfriend was killed, but she brings these things on herself. I always said she was trouble, that one, not like you, dear. I can't understand what he ever saw in her, and I'm sure Carol was probably not much better. Not to speak ill of the dead, mind, but if he was drawn to her she was trouble. Why he couldn't have just found himself someone like you I'll never understand. That boy is drawn to trouble; just like his father before I came along."

Wishing that Vera would keep those kinds of opinions to herself, Elaine explained to her about the bail. Vera said that she and John would take care of that.

However, when the time came and it was set so high Vera and John were glad to accept help from Elaine and Dave. Elaine thought it best not to mention to Vera that Sylvia, Gina and Kim were also contributing to the bail money. Sometimes she wondered if she were the only person in Alex's life that Vera actually approved of. She even had a problem with Dave, probably because she had always wanted Elaine as a daughter-in-law. She knew that when Vera had said that she wished Alex could have found someone like her, what she actually meant was Elaine herself.

When Alex was released on bail, he found his friends and parents waiting for him. Kim gave him a big kiss on the lips, much to his mother's disgust, and told him not to worry, that she'd fight hard in his corner to make sure he stayed out of prison. They all agreed with that sentiment.

That afternoon Alex arrived at Jim's office to meet Liam Mitchell. He looked across the desk at the tall, broad man who greeted him with a smile. Liam stood up and reached out to shake Alex's hand. He had a firm handshake that inspired confidence, and his grey hair and the fine lines on his face suggested experience, which further pleased Alex.

"Please take a seat," he said as he indicated the chair opposite his desk. When Alex was seated he said, "Now what can I do for you?"

As Alex explained his case Liam's eyes never left his and his smile never faded. His face became more serious as Alex continued but that confident smile stayed on his lips, belying the seriousness of the situation. Alex finished the story by saying, "I am aware that this doesn't look good, but I'm innocent. What are my chances of being acquitted?"

"Not to blow my own trumpet or anything, but I'm a damn good solicitor. However, I need you to work with me on this; we need to work on pinpointing your exact location at the times of these murders and finding some way of proving that you were where you say you were. Otherwise we concentrate on the fact that they only have circumstantial evidence against you and therefore will not be able to prove beyond reasonable doubt that you are guilty, and therefore must be presumed innocent." Becoming more serious he said, "However, if you could remember anything at all that would prove that you were elsewhere it would help our case."

"Unfortunately, on both occasions I was at home and received no phone calls, saw no-one and went nowhere. So nobody can corroborate my whereabouts."

"Not to worry. We can discredit the prosecution. Leave it with me."

Alex left the law offices that day feeling confident in Liam's ability to get him acquitted. Driving to one of his favorite spots, a forest where the paths were so overgrown they were practically non-existent, he contemplated his freedom. It was something he no longer took for granted. He drove with the window down, finding the cold air refreshing after having spent the night in a holding cell.

Getting out of the car he filled his lungs with the tree-scented air and set off at a brisk pace through the trees. If he didn't know this forest so well he could easily get lost, a prospect that didn't altogether faze him at the present moment. He could think of worse ways to spend his time than being surrounded by trees reaching their bare arms out to him, their crisp, golden leaves crunching under his feet.

After walking for some time he came to his favorite place to sit and write; it was a gnarled old stump of a tree. He sat down and his fingers traced the rings around the stump. He listened to the sounds of the forest, the birds singing, the wind whispering through the trees, bringing with it the occasional leaf that still clung on to the nearly bare branches. He filled his senses with the sounds, smell, feel and sight of the forest, trying not to think of grey cells and iron bars closing him off from the world.

CHAPTER FORTY-THREE

Sylvia lay awake in bed that night wondering when and how life had gotten so complicated. She had tried to ring Alex earlier but only got his voicemail. She figured he wanted to be alone and imagined that while she lay snuggled up in her bed he was out wandering in the dark somewhere, alone with his thoughts which were probably as dark as the night. She thought of happier times when life was simpler.

It was a hot afternoon in the middle of the summer holidays. The hazy sun shone out of a cloudless sky and the air was scented with freshly mown grass. Elaine and Sylvia sat on the wall of Sylvia's front garden watching the younger children in the neighborhood running around in the grass opposite Sylvia's house. The children were barefoot in shorts and tee shirts and were having water fights to cool down. Although they had long outgrown such pleasures, Sylvia and Elaine looked towards the bottles of water and imagined how deliciously cool it would feel to have one of the younger children come over and drench them.

A moving van pulled into the drive next to Sylvia's house, followed by a car, which pulled up outside the house.

"These must be my new neighbors. Let's hope there's a hunk about my age in that car," Sylvia said to Elaine.

"Bet you a fiver you'll have scored with him by the end of summer if there is," Elaine replied.

"I'm not taking that bet because I hope you're right!" Sylvia grinned.

Sylvia and Elaine hardly noticed the parents emerging from the car as they waited with their breaths held for the occupants of the back seat. All thoughts of water fights evaporated as a tall blonde boy emerged. Following his parents to his new house he stopped for a moment to watch the two girls sitting on the wall of his neighbor's house. His eyes met with Sylvia's for a moment and she took in his strong jaw and the dimple in his right cheek. The moment ended and he turned and walked down the path to his house leaving Sylvia to watch his broad shoulders and long legs.

"God, I want him," she said to Elaine.

"Odds are you'll have him. I saw the way he looked at you," Elaine replied.

As that summer wore on it became obvious that Alex wanted Sylvia as much as she wanted him, if not more. With the thrill of the chase gone Sylvia lost a lot of her interest in him and started playing hard to get.

Two weeks after Alex moved in Sylvia woke up one morning to find an envelope with her name on it on the floor inside the front door. She ripped it open and read with interest the poem that Alex had written. Seeing his signature on the bottom of the page she sighed and put her hand to her heart. Up to then poetry was just something she had to learn off by heart, but now it became romantic, something she wanted to learn off by heart. She knew that, unlike all the poems she was doing for the leaving cert, this one wasn't about death and she looked forward to getting another one from him.

She ran straight to the phone, rang Elaine and recited the poem to her.

"What are you going to do? Call in to him and tell him you feel the same. Or write to him! You could write him an answering poem!" Elaine said.

"No way; anything I wrote would be rubbish compared to this."

"Well you have to do something. You can't just sit around and not respond to him. The ball is in your court now."

"I know, I know. I just have to think about it. This poem is deep. This guy is deep; he's not like any of the guys in school."

"Ooh, he could be 'the one!'"

"Shut up! I'm sixteen, not twenty-six!" Sylvia said.

"Anyway, what are you waiting for? That poem's your invitation, not that you've ever needed one. Go get him!"

"I don't know, maybe I want to play hard to get for a change."

"Sylvia, you read the poem. They're his real feelings; you can't toy with them. That's just mean."

"No it's not. This whole love thing is a game; it's all about fun. For God's sake we're only young once. I'm not getting serious for at least another ten years. I think I'll just tease him for a while. After all, if I'm missing out on the thrill of the chase I've got to have some fun."

"Hmm," Elaine sounded disapproving.

"Look, come on over. We'll have some fun."

"If you want to tease the poor guy, fine, but leave me out of it."

"Oh come on, you know you want to see him anyway."

"Of course I do; he's gorgeous, but it's you he likes."

"You can still look and fantasise."

"Yeah, I guess," replied Elaine.

A little while later the two girls took up their favorite spot on the wall, hoping that, as they chatted, Alex would appear. When he did he walked past the two girls, briefly meeting Sylvia's eyes. After he passed by, Sylvia jumped off the wall with a wink at Elaine. She bounded after Alex and passed in front of him, turning to face him and block his way. She smiled at him and looked him in the eye.

"So, I got your poem," she said with a smile in her voice and a twinkle in her eye. "Does that mean you like me?" She put the tip of her finger in her mouth, as if she was shy.

"Do you fancy going out with me to the cinema tonight?" Alex took the direct approach.

"I might do. What's on?"

A smile crossed his face. "Why don't you choose?"

"Okay so, but you know you're in for a girlie film."

"I don't mind as long as I'm with you."

"I'll check the paper, let you know what time to pick me up," Sylvia turned to go, blowing him a kiss with a cheeky look in her eyes. As she lowered her hand he caught it, pulled her to him and kissed her long and deep.

They had a fun evening together, sharing popcorn, chocolate and the occasional kiss. As they were about to part company outside her front door he asked, "So, does this mean we're going out together?"

"I don't know. Maybe," she said.

Alex pulled her to him and said, "Can I ever expect a straight answer from you?"

"Nope."

She turned around, opened her front door, turned back to wink at him and then went inside, leaving a confused Alex outside.

The next day she found a letter inside her front door stating that Alex had had a wonderful time and was wondering if she would meet him in the Pizza Place that evening at seven o'clock. She penned him a note, stating that she too had had a great time, but that no, she couldn't meet him that night. She didn't, however, state or negate any desire to see him again, thinking she'd just keep him guessing.

That night she awoke to hear a guitar strumming outside her window. The words of Savage Garden's 'Truly, Madly, Deeply' were being sung by a very sexy voice. Upon looking out her window she couldn't believe her eyes; it was Alex outside her window singing to her. She fell back onto her bed with a sigh followed by a giggle. She couldn't wait until the next morning to get on the phone to Elaine! She just lay there taking in the words that Alex was singing.

When the song ended she heard pebbles being thrown at her window. When she pulled back her curtains the pebble throwing stopped and she flung open her window.

"I'll be right down," she called.

"You most certainly will not," her father called, standing outside her bedroom door.

Her bedroom door opened and her father stormed across the room to the window.

"Go home to bed. Does your mother know what you're up to? Trying to seduce young, innocent girls with that guitar!"

The next day Sylvia called in to Alex, mortified by her father's behavior the night before. "I'm so sorry about the way my dad talked to you last night. It was so embarrassing."

"That's okay. My mum wasn't home last night; otherwise she'd have dragged me in by my ear and told me not to embarrass her. As it is, I've been grounded. Two old biddies she's been going to art class with saw me. God! You'd swear I was seen drinking or sniffing glue. It's not even as if I was doing anything improper to you."

"Well if my dad hadn't stopped me from going out to you, you might have been seen doing something improper to me." Sylvia smiled.

"To our parents holding hands would be improper." Alex pulled her into his arms. "How long would I be grounded for if they saw me now?" Then he kissed her.

"Grounded for life I'd imagine," Sylvia eventually said.

Now as Sylvia lay awake she realized that Alex really hadn't deserved the way she'd spent the last ten years blowing hot and cold on him. At sixteen she hadn't seen any harm in the way she was treating him. There were just so many boys and there was so little time! She'd figured it wasn't her fault that he was such a sap, although a very endearing sap, always looking like a lost, soulful puppy. She could see now, for the first time ever, that she'd been heartless, although that certainly wasn't her intention at the time. As far as she'd been concerned he was just another boy who was interested in her, only, unlike the other boys, he never lost interest and was always there for her with his guitar slung over his shoulder, ready to burst into song. What was a girl to do? His poetry and serenading appealed to the romantic in her, even if at times her romantic side had been hidden deep inside the hormonal teenage side of her.

She decided that she'd go around to him to apologize the next day. All of this could maybe have been avoided if she had just stopped playing games with him and made it clear to him what her true feelings on love were.

CHAPTER FORTY-FOUR

Wednesday the 15th of October

Alex was staying with his parents, a condition of the bail. Sylvia knew she wouldn't be welcome there, as his mother had never liked her, thought she was a bad influence on her son. Maybe she's right, Sylvia thought. I led Alex on all these years and have led him into a life of trouble he otherwise wouldn't be in. She rang Alex on his mobile and asked him to meet her for breakfast in Molloy's Café. He obliged.

While they were drinking their lattés, Sylvia took a deep breath before launching into her apology. "Alex, I've been a horrible friend to you over the years, haven't I? You don't need to answer that; I know I've been mean to you. Elaine always said I was, but I never wanted to believe that I was more to you than a bit of fun.

"I should have told you this ten years ago; I know it's a little late now, and I feel so bad for that. I never believed in love before I met Rick. I always knew that I didn't love you, that I would never love you." She lowered her head and voice in shame as she said, "I've used you over the years, and I'm really sorry. It's my fault you're in this mess; if I'd been straight with you from the beginning you would have moved on from me. Maybe you'd have met Carol sooner and had longer with her, and you certainly wouldn't be being accused of murder, let alone two murders." There were tears in Sylvia's eyes as she finished her self-diatribe.

Alex reached over and wiped the tears away as they rolled down her cheeks. "Don't beat yourself up about this. It's taken you a long time to realize what you were doing to me, but it's my fault as much as yours; I knew you didn't believe in love and that you never saw yourself with me long-term. Even if I hadn't known, Elaine told me often enough. I didn't listen to her, so what makes you think I'd have listened to you? I was a fool for love, and I've only got myself to blame for that. As for this mess, well it's just life. I don't regret all the times I've spent with you, all the years I've spent loving you in vain. If this is what comes of it, it's awful, doubly awful actually because not only did I not get the girl but I've got the possibility of a life sentence hanging over me."

As the tears flowed more freely down Sylvia's cheeks Alex moved his chair closer to her and put his arms around her. "Don't cry, Sylvia; it's not your fault, it's just life. I'm to blame for how much I let my love for you hold me back.

"I do appreciate the fact that you've come here today to apologize. It means a lot to me that you've finally realized that you could have been kinder to me, and I accept the apology for that, but that's all water under the bridge. I don't accept the apology for the mess I'm in because that really isn't your fault." He kissed the top of her head. "Please don't cry, Sylvia." He put his hand under her chin and tilted her face up towards his. He looked into her eyes and said gently, "I've always hated when you cry. Please, for me, stop crying." He closed her eyes with his lips as he kissed each eye.

Sylvia pulled away from him as she realized that all too easily they could start down the dangerous road of that very familiar passion between them. She quickly pulled herself together and said, "I didn't mean to cry and I didn't mean to get your sympathy. All I intended was to apologize and to tell you that I won't ever use you again. What I've done to you is completely unforgivable and I can't understand why you're still friends with me."

"It's not unforgivable because it wasn't intentional, and I'm still your friend because I like you. No one's perfect; you've got your faults and so does everyone else, but I like you in spite of your faults. That's what friendship is all about, accepting your friends' faults and being there for them despite everything. We've both been through a pretty tough time lately, and it's far from over, but we're friends. We'll get through it and we'll still be friends no matter what. So what do you say we do something fun together today and try to forget our troubles? They'll still be waiting for us tomorrow," Alex said.

"That sounds like a good idea. What do you want to do?"

"Well we could go to the pub and get bladdered, or we could just take a drive and see where we end up."

"I think a good compromise is to take a drive and then later we can call the others and all get bladdered together."

"Sounds good."

They finished their drinks and left the café, Sylvia feeling better for having unburdened herself on Alex. She knew that he would start to forget his troubles as he drove. She couldn't understand how he always found driving relaxing. No matter how much traffic there was on the roads he never got road rage and never even stuck up his fingers at other drivers who cut him off. He just listened to music and seemed totally oblivious to the other drivers he shared the road with. Sylvia reflected that he wasn't oblivious to the point of being dangerous, just oblivious to the things other drivers, including her, became very agitated about.

They drove in a comfortable silence, both lost in their own thoughts, until Alex found a spot he felt like stopping in. Sylvia was used to this about him. She had discovered so many hidden spots in Ireland just by being with him when he went for one of his drives. He seemed to lose himself on the road and then suddenly he'd stop as if an inner voice told him that this particular spot needed to be discovered. She thought that it was probably the poet in him.

When they got out of the car it was to discover a beautiful forest. They found a small dirt path covered with colorful leaves meandering its way between the tall trees. They turned to each other and smiled. Sylvia was transported back in time to another forest not too long ago, before she had met Rick, when she and Alex had made love.

It had been two summers ago when Sylvia split up with Kenny, as he was discussing marriage. She'd said, "Marriage isn't for me. If that's what you're looking for in a relationship then you'd better look elsewhere because that's not where this relationship is headed." He'd looked dumbfounded. Poor Kenny, Sylvia thought now. He never saw it coming.

She wondered if Alex was remembering the same thing.

She went straight over to Alex after the break up to find that he was just on his way out for a drive. They ended up in a beautiful forest not unlike the one they were in now. It was a beautiful Saturday afternoon with unusually high temperatures and they were relieved to immerse themselves in the cool shade of the trees. They lay down on the grass beneath a large tree and looked up through the leaves at the clouds chasing each other across the sky. They pointed out shapes to one another in the clouds and laughed at some of the things they imagined floating by. Then their hands both reached up at the same time to point out a shape. Their hands touched and they forgot all about the clouds as they lost themselves in each other.

The smile died on Sylvia's face as she thought about the fact that it wouldn't be happening again. There was a lump in her throat as Alex took her hand to walk through the forest with her. She wished he wouldn't do that, but didn't want to stop him. She forced all thoughts of their previous encounters of the flesh out of her mind so that she could enjoy the moment for what it was – two friends enjoying some time together in a beautiful setting. She took her hand away from his because it was impossible not to think about those hands elsewhere on her body, and just the thought of it made her feel that she was betraying the memory of Rick. Alex looked down and seemed to understand why she had taken her hand away.

Later, in the pub Sylvia told Elaine that she had finally seen the light about the way she had been treating Alex and was going to stop using him for sex.

"From now on we're just friends; friends who don't sleep together."

Elaine gave Sylvia a hug and said, "I'm glad; it's taken long enough."

CHAPTER FORTY-FIVE

Thursday the 16th of October

Sylvia sat at her kitchen table nursing her first cup of coffee of the day. Her head was pounding, but she only half-regretted overdoing it the night before. They all needed it after the stress of the recent weeks. Her day at work would be torturous; as if she wasn't dehydrated enough the heat of the salon would have her practically passing out, and the noise of the dryers would whirl around inside her head. She groaned as the doorbell rang, reverberating through her skull. She made her way to the front door, hastening more than she felt able to in case the doorbell would ring again. She wasn't surprised to see Jerry at the door.

"I guess you heard, then," she said as she stood back to allow him in.

"Yeah. I can't say I'm that surprised. I always thought he was too intense."

"If you've come here to slag Alex off you can just leave. In case you've forgotten he happens to be one of my best friends."

"I'm sorry. I didn't mean to be insensitive. I know you're having a tough time at the moment and I just want to be here for you. I called over to where you used to live and the girls gave me your address. I figured since the guards would no longer be looking in my direction it would be safe to come around here to see how you're doing."

Sylvia led him in to the sitting room and they sat on the couch. Looking at her watch she figured she could spare him a few minutes of her time. "I'm doing okay. It's been rough, but right now I'm focusing on

Alex. It's helping me forget my own problems. He's going to need a lot of support now."

"Well I'm here for you. To help you to forget about all your troubles, and forget about Alex too, how about you spend some time with me?"

"I'm going to be spending a lot of time with Alex so there isn't time to strike up a new friendship with you. And you can forget about taking up from where we left off."

"Hey, can a guy not just be there for a friend without her thinking I want more than just to be her friend?" Jerry relaxed into the couch, throwing his arm over the back of it.

"You may be happy for now with just friendship, but you'd keep hoping it would turn into more. I'm not in that place anymore, Jerry. I'm not looking for a relationship, nor will I be any time soon. And I need to concentrate on Alex now and on keeping him from going to prison."

"Well maybe it'll be easier to concentrate on him the rest of the time if I take your mind off things at least some of the time. So what do you say? It can't hurt. In fact it might make you feel a bit better. We could have a bit of fun. You can't say you're not in need of a bit of fun."

Sylvia was tempted to just run out the door with him now and forget about everything for just one day. How good it would be to have a day with Jerry – he'd probably just happen to know where he could find a bit of excitement for them. In fact it wouldn't surprise her if she discovered that he had just stopped in on his way to partake in a sky-dive and was hoping she'd join him. She knew free falling from the sky would give her a feeling of such freedom that she would forget all of her problems. Even if that feeling would only give her a brief respite it was tempting. As she shook her head to deny how much she needed what Jerry had to offer, her aching head reminded her that going anywhere with him would not be a good idea today. As hard as it would be to get through work it would surely be much harder to cope with whatever head-spinning activity he had in mind. Maybe another day, she thought. However, the knowledge that it wouldn't take away her pain stopped her from contemplating it further. She was a different person now and wanted to face her problems head-on, not run away and hide from them.

"I told you before, I've changed. It's not all about me anymore, or about fun. Much as I'd love to forget my troubles and have a bit of fun, Alex is my priority now and he will be until he can be proved innocent."

Jerry leaned forward, took her hand and looked into her eyes, a serious expression on his face. He took a deep breath and said, "I know this isn't what you want to hear, but how can you be so sure Alex is innocent? He's always been in love with you." At Sylvia's look of shock, he said, "Yes, I knew he loved you the whole time we went out. It was so obvious. Every time we were in the same room with him I could tell he just wanted me out of the way. I never wanted anything more than a to have a bit of fun with you, until now, but even back then I just wanted to punch the guy's lights out for wanting my girl."

Sylvia withdrew her hand from Jerry's and said, "I know how he feels about me, how he's always felt, but there's no way he's a murderer. And there's no way I'm not going to stand by him now when he needs me."

Jerry stood up and said, "Maybe I'd better just go. If Alex sees me hanging around you I could end up dead."

Tears came to Sylvia's eyes. She brushed them away, stood up and said, "Alex didn't kill Rick, and if you really want to come back into my life you're going about it the wrong way."

Jerry reached for her hand, but she pulled away. "I'm sorry. Sylvia, I love you. There, the dreaded 'L' word. I said it. And if what it takes to be with you is just to be your friend I'll do it. I'll even help in the 'save Alex' campaign. Please, Sylvia. Give us another chance. Give me another chance."

"No, Jerry. I was falling for you before we broke up, and if you hadn't broken up with me then maybe I wouldn't have met Rick and you and I would still be together. You don't believe that Alex is innocent and he's a very important part of my life, so I think we've said all that we have to say to one another. Goodbye, Jerry."

"Maybe we wouldn't still be together. Maybe Rick would still be alive and I'd be dead. Well maybe when Alex is convicted you might think about looking me up."

"I won't, Jerry. For that matter it could just as easily have been you who murdered Rick. Maybe you set Alex up and then killed Carol to further incriminate him."

Sylvia could see the anger in Jerry's eyes. He looked like he was about to say something, but stormed out of the house instead.

Sylvia couldn't believe what had just happened. They had never rowed before. It was a shock to discover that he was in love with her and seemed to regret breaking up with her. She regretted having accused him. The last thing she wanted to do was hurt him, and she knew that he was no more a murderer than Alex was. Maybe she'd leave it a while, give them both time to cool down and then call and apologize but make it clear that that would be an end to things.

For now, though, she had to concentrate on getting through the day and then on helping Alex to get through the murder trial.

CHAPTER FORTY-SIX

When Carol's body was released Alex got through the funeral without too much difficulty. He had only known Carol for one week and, although they had become quite close, it was more like mourning an acquaintance than a lover. It was much harder on Dave, as she had been quite a close colleague of his. Alex felt quite awkward saying his final goodbyes to her, being surrounded by the red eyes and puffy, tear stained faces of the people who had obviously known her for a long time and were very upset by her death. He had thought of staying away from her funeral, thinking that it would upset her family to have him there, but Dave and Elaine convinced him to go, telling him that he had as much right to be there as anyone else. As it turned out Carol's family and friends were so distraught that they didn't notice his presence.

When the time came for only family members to remain in the funeral parlor he made as if to leave, but Melissa held him back, saying that Carol would have wanted him to stay. He remained, but felt even more awkward as he was the only person in the room who wasn't bawling his eyes out. He thought this would draw attention to him, but everyone was so intent on saying their last goodbyes to Carol that nobody noticed the face they had been looking at on the news in connection with her death.

As he watched her coffin being lowered into the ground he thought of the prison her body would be trapped in for eternity and wished the same for her murderer. As her parents each threw a rose on top of the coffin he was reminded of the roses he had bought for her, of the clothes she had never bought for Lana's, all the things he had never found out about her.

He still didn't know which flowers she liked best, which ones he should put on her grave and wished he had gone for a more exotic bouquet to apologize to her; he could put the same flowers on her grave and it would be special between them. He had bought a simple wreath, but also wanted to leave a bouquet of fresh flowers on her grave. Now if he left roses it would be the same as so many others would leave.

In the days that followed, Alex returned to work and tried to get his life back to normal. It wasn't easy; he was aware that everywhere he went all eyes were on him wondering was he, wasn't he? No matter how he spent his spare time, trying to forget his status as a murder suspect, every evening when he returned to his parents' house and every morning when he awoke in his old room the reality of it came crashing down on him. He longed for a return to those simple days, wishing each morning when he awoke to the poster clad walls of his youth that it was only thoughts of Sylvia that filled his head instead of thoughts of where he might be waking up in the future.

He just wished the trial dates would hurry up and come, although it was with the knowledge that he was looking at a wait of at least two years. Better yet would be for the guards to get off their backsides and find the real murderer. He felt sure that if these murders did go to trial his solicitor would prove his innocence in both cases. He didn't dwell too much on whether or not this was naïve, needing to believe it in order to get through each day. It was with this perhaps foolish optimism that he quelled thoughts of prison bars.

It was with trepidation that he went into the office when summoned by his boss, Mr. Lawson, to discuss the situation. He could feel the sweat rolling down his face at the thoughts of losing his job. He mopped at his face with a tissue and pulled at the neck of his shirt, feeling that it was too tight, but he didn't dare loosen it.

"This won't affect my performance at work," Alex was quick to state.

"I'm sure the quality of your work won't disintegrate. I just want to let you know that we're all behind you. Be sure to come to me if you need any character references. Just let me know if it starts to get on top of you and you find yourself needing some time off, and my door is always open if you need someone to talk to at any time."

"I appreciate you standing by me, and my work won't suffer." Alex assured him. He knew his boss must believe in his innocence. Otherwise he'd have suspended him for sure, if not come up with some plausible reason to fire him.

He scheduled meetings with his solicitor around work so as not to annoy Mr. Lawson. He knew that although he had his support it wouldn't be a good idea to take advantage of the situation, as that might change his boss's stance on matters. He arranged meetings for lunchtime and after work. He rarely ate now anyway and although he knew he was losing weight he found that he didn't have much of an appetite. Even on the evenings he made it home for dinner and found that his mother had cooked one of his favorite meals it was all he could do to force down a few mouthfuls. He knew it worried his parents; when they saw him losing weight and barely able to eat they became less able to believe that their son wouldn't end up in prison.

He tried to convince his parents that his solicitor was confident that he wouldn't go to prison, but some days he was unable to believe that himself. His solicitor revealed that the guards hadn't been able to find anyone who had seen him around his house when he professed to be there. Also he was seen in his car in the next street to Carol's the evening of her murder.

"I can't defend you properly if you're not honest with me. Being seen in the vicinity of the crime is not in itself incriminating. If, however, the witness testifies that she did indeed see you and you claim to have been at home where nobody can testify to having seen you it will look as if you are lying. So, is there something you're not telling me?"

"No. That witness must be mistaken; I was at home all evening."

"I urge you to think seriously about that statement."

"Are you saying that I should say I was out in my car? Even if I wasn't?" Alex asked, dragging his hands through his hair.

"Of course I'm not saying that. I would never suggest that clients perjure themselves. I'm only saying that maybe you've forgotten that you went somewhere that evening. If we can put you somewhere else at the time of the crime it might provide an alibi. Also, you were seen in the next street to Carol's apartment, not in the street of her apartment nor anywhere around her apartment building. So if you could remember that you had gone out that evening it might give us something we can work on."

"I was at home alone all evening."

"Are you sure?"

"Yes, I was waiting for Carol to ring me."

"Isn't it possible that as it got late you figured she wouldn't call you and you got fed up waiting and went out somewhere? Maybe to a pub or off-license?"

"I have a pretty good memory and I think I'd remember giving up on her phone call."

"You probably would under normal circumstances, but I think you'll agree that the circumstances you find yourself in are anything but normal. The mind can play funny tricks on us sometimes, particularly in times of stress."

At a later date, Liam informed him that it really didn't look good for him that there were no witnesses that could place him at home and one that definitely remembered seeing him close to Belfield Terrace. "On the stand we can try to discredit the witness, but I really would feel more comfortable if you had remembered being out driving that evening."

Alex left Liam's office that particular day feeling very despondent. He had never for one moment, until that day, truly believed that he wouldn't be acquitted. A cloud of despair suddenly took hold of him as he considered the possibility of being sent to prison. Arriving home, he rang Sylvia and explained to her how he was feeling. She told him she'd be right over and Alex felt his spirits lift a little at that prospect.

When Sylvia arrived she put her arms around Alex and said that there was no way he could be proved guilty. He instantly felt better, taking solace in the familiar warmth of her embrace.

"Thanks for your vote of confidence, but it's looking like it would be easier to convince a jury that I'm some crazed schizophrenic who has no recollection of the enraged frenzy that takes me over when I become jealous than to convince them of my innocence."

"Well now that's just crazy talk," Sylvia said. "You were convinced before today that everything would be okay. You can't let things get you down like this. Where's the optimistic attitude we were all so proud of not so long ago?"

Alex smiled a small smile despite himself and said, "He's been taken over by my other personality, the one who knows I'm guilty." Then he laughed and said, "This is utterly ridiculous. Come on, let's get out of here." A wicked grin crossed his face as he said, "That's if you still trust me." He put his hand out to take hers.

As Sylvia put her hand in his she said, "That's better. More like you. You had me worried there for a minute; I thought you had given up on your belief that you would be acquitted."

They went for a drive and ended up on the beach. It was a warm day in early spring and they walked barefoot, enjoying the feel of sand between their toes. It gave them a taste of the summer that lay ahead. Alex told Sylvia about the day he had spent with Carol on that very beach.

"You really liked her didn't you?" Sylvia asked softly.

"Yeah, she was great, so full of life and so happy. We could have been so good together," Alex said. His voice was tinged with sadness.

Sylvia looked up and saw a tear falling down his cheek. She reached up to brush it away. She had never seen Alex cry and she felt her heart lurch at the sight of the tears brimming over to spill down his cheeks. He must have felt more for her than he's letting on, she thought, leaning up to him, kissing his eyes the way he had so often done to her. "Don't cry," she said.

A small smile touched his lips as he drew away from her and wiped his eyes. "A slight role reversal; if you tell anyone I swear I'll kill you," he said, pulling her close to him.

They stayed like that in silence until the night started closing in around them and it started getting cold. When Sylvia started shivering Alex suggested that they go home. On the way home they talked about more normal everyday things and sang along to the radio.

While on the beach with Sylvia talking about his feelings for Carol, Sylvia told Alex about how Jerry had come to see her a few months beforehand and about their row. He wondered if perhaps Sylvia had been right about Jerry. He knew that she had just said that about him being the murderer in the heat of the moment, but just because she hadn't meant it didn't mean it wasn't true.

When Alex next stepped into Liam Mitchell's office it was with a much more positive attitude than the one he had previously left with. He told Liam of his suspicions about Jerry, and Liam said he'd like to talk to Sylvia about it as it could go further towards proving that his guilt couldn't be proved beyond reasonable doubt.

When Sylvia arrived into Liam's office to talk to him about the possibility of Jerry being the murderer he became more confident than ever that Alex would be acquitted. He couldn't say for sure that he thought Jerry was guilty, but his feelings for Sylvia and his jealousy of Alex, and supposedly Rick, should be enough to cast a shadow of doubt over Alex's alleged guilt.

Liam assured Alex that his guilt couldn't be proved beyond a reasonable doubt, and that his innocence didn't have to be proved; the onus was on the prosecution to prove that he had committed those heinous crimes.

The statements of his friends and family would serve to prove to a jury that Alex was a stand-up guy who was not capable of murder. Liam believed that the statement of Sylvia would surely be the jewel in the crown. If the girlfriend of the victim, whom Alex was purported to have been obsessed with to the point of murderous rage, were to take the stand and under oath deny that Alex's feelings for her were anything but wholesome and that he had accepted her new love, then the jury could no longer be sure of his guilt.

CHAPTER FORTY-SEVEN

As the court date drew closer, Alex felt less sure that he would be acquitted. His friends tried to cheer him up by taking him out to get drunk and coming over to his home with comedies and booze, but all he could muster at the funniest of lines was a hint of a smile, and the alcohol only served to take the edge off his melancholy. His parents stayed out of the way when his friends were around; they were at a loss as to what to do to take his mind off things and were glad to give others the opportunity to do so.

Sylvia was very supportive, taking him out for drives to all his favorite spots on the weekends. They had picnics and reminisced about the past, always careful to talk about the times when they weren't going out together, although all too often Alex took her by the hand and, kissing the back of her hand, looked into her eyes. Each time he did that she made light of it, referring to him as a character from one of the old movies she used to watch while growing up. She would then turn the subject to something cheerful.

She reminded him of the time the whole class had gotten together on the beach after the Leaving Cert, how they had gotten so drunk that they ended up throwing up.

"Do you remember smoking hash that night?" he smiled as he asked.

Sylvia groaned, "Don't remind me."

He laughed. "You were so funny. You told me that the stars were swimming in the ocean and that I should write a poem about it. I remember I told you not to be daft and you said that if I didn't promise to write about it you'd swim with the stars. Then you started laughing and couldn't stop."

"I remember when I got home I couldn't stop eating. When my dad went looking for biscuits after his dinner the next evening Peter got the blame for having eaten the whole packet."

"You never told me that. How did Peter react?"

"He just took the blame; it was only a packet of biscuits. He's been stoned often enough that he figured I'd had a case of the munchies. He did hold it over me that whole summer though, but once he went back to college he forgot all about it; too busy wooing all the girls to be bothered about what his kid sister was getting up to."

She continued reminiscing about silly incidents like that, keeping the conversations as light hearted as possible and kept him out really late, doing her best to fill each of his waking moments so that he wouldn't be thinking of the trial that lay ahead. Unfortunately she could do nothing about the nightmares that plagued him every time he closed his eyes. In an effort to help with that his mother did the only thing she could think of; she left the hall light on at night, just as she had when he was a little boy and afraid of the monsters he was sure were hiding under his bed. Now, however, it was the monsters he might be sharing a prison cell with that scared him and no amount of light could dispel the knife wielding crime lords with their scars and tattoos towering over him as he cowered in his cell. He didn't say so to his mother as he knew it was making her feel better to be able to do something, however small, for him.

The Friday before the trial his friends all came over to his house, each of them bringing a bottle of booze. His parents were gone away for the weekend; they had wanted to be there for him, and when a sick friend called them away Alex convinced them to go, saying that he'd be fine. Alex and his friends were pleased to have the house to themselves; it made them feel like teenagers. They joked about the only thing missing to bring back their teenage years being hash to make them totally silly, but when Kim got out the cocktail book and made very strong cocktails they decided that hash wouldn't be necessary. It wasn't long before they were all completely sozzled and had the trial very firmly pushed out of Alex's mind.

Then an unusual thing happened; an argument broke out in the kitchen between Gina and Kim. The others couldn't believe it when they heard shouting. They all shushed each other trying to hear what was going on. They only heard fragments.

"...your fault you stupid fucking bitch," Gina roared.

They heard Kim talking in hushed tones, obviously trying to calm Gina down.

"How the fuck can we fix it? You totally fucked up. One simple fucking job and you couldn't get that right."

The front door slammed and Kim came into the sitting room carrying a tray of drinks.

"Is everything okay?" Elaine asked.

"It will be; Gina's just had too much to drink, that's all. She's gone out for some fresh air and to call a cab. When she's slept it off she'll be fine."

"Aren't you going with her?" Alex asked.

"You must be joking! She'll keep tearing into me if I go with her. It's best if I just give her some space."

A little while later Elaine suggested that it was time to go. "Kim you can come home with us."

"It's okay. I have to face the music sometime," Kim replied. "I'll just have one more drink and then I'll call a cab. Hopefully by then she'll be asleep and tomorrow she might not even remember what we were arguing about. You don't mind me staying for another drink, do you, Alex?" Without waiting for a reply she got up and went to the kitchen to get herself another drink.

"Do you want us to wait with you until she's going?" Elaine asked.

"No, it's okay. You have the kids to get up with in the morning; I can deal with Kim."

Sylvia looked confused. "Sure what's the big deal? She has another drink and you pack her into a cab. He doesn't need a babysitter for that." She gave Elaine and Alex a weird look.

When the cab came for Elaine, Dave and Sylvia they left Kim settled down on the couch with a Sex on the Beach in her hand. Elaine gave Alex a meaningful look and asked him if he was sure about this.

"You make it sound like she's going to turn on him and seduce him," Sylvia said. Then her eyes opened wide as Elaine dragged her out to the cab.

As soon as Alex closed the front door Kim came up behind him and put her arms around him, one hand sliding up inside his shirt, the other sliding down to unbutton his trousers. Although Alex was immediately turned on he took a firm grip of Kim's hands and removed them.

He turned around to face her but took a step backwards to put some space between them. He was now standing with his back up against the door and Kim pressed her body up against his.

Alex put his hands on her shoulders and pushed her gently backwards. "I think it's time to call you a cab." He reached for his phone and started dialing.

Kim reached up and took the phone from his hand as her lips found his. "You know you want this," she murmured.

Alex enjoyed the kiss at first, but he quickly came to his senses again. However, at that moment Kim started to unbutton her blouse; she let it fall to the ground and quickly undid her bra, pressing her breasts up against him. He took her breasts in his hands and enjoyed the feel of them as he kissed her again, this time with more urgency and pure abandon. He was beyond thinking, so great was his desire. Kim wrapped her legs around his hips and he carried her up to the bedroom where he lowered her to the bed and undressed quickly. He got into bed beside her to find that she had fallen asleep.

He lay beside her, waiting for his erection to subside; when it did he was able to think clearly again. He realized that he'd better go and sleep in the spare room or he'd be looking for trouble. Much as he had wanted it a few moments ago, he really didn't want to have sex with Kim. He knew that if she woke up in the middle of the night or before he did in the morning and found him here she'd start coming on to him all over again, and he didn't know whether he'd acquiesce or not. It would probably depend on how much alcohol was still in his system. Or maybe not, he thought. There are worse things I could do before going to prison than having sex with Kim.

An unbidden thought suddenly entered his head; If only that had been

Sylvia and not Kim. I would give anything for just one more night of passion with Sylvia. It would almost make everything worth it. He hated the fact that Sylvia was so determined now to keep things platonic between them. He'd call over to her tomorrow and see if he could persuade her to send him to prison with a happy memory. With that thought he slipped out of his bed before Kim woke up and his resolve not to sleep with her weakened.

Gina woke up the next morning to find that Kim hadn't come home. She immediately knew where she'd find her – in bed with Alex. Well never mind, she thought. I'll just have to go over and join her; I'll just make a quick stop along the way.

CHAPTER FORTY-EIGHT

Sylvia woke up with a thumping headache and wondered who in the hell was ringing her doorbell so incessantly at that hour of the morning. She reluctantly dragged herself out of bed, giving her duvet a look and almost crawling back under it again, when the doorbell rang again long and loud. She put a hand to her head to try to still the throbbing and went downstairs to answer the door.

"Gina, hi. What are you doing here at this hour of the morning?" Her throat felt dry and she couldn't quite make the words come out any louder than a whisper. Not that she really wanted to, as, to her ears, she sounded loud enough. Then she remembered the fight of the night before and realized she would have to put her hangover aside for the moment and be hospitable to Gina. "Come in. Did you sort things out with Kim?"

"She didn't come home last night," Gina said, as they made their way to the sitting room.

"Oh. She must've crashed at Alex's. When the rest of us left she was just finishing her drink before calling a cab. She probably fell asleep before she finished it. We all had a shit load to drink. I'm certainly feeling worse for wear this morning. Thank God Laura gave me today off although it's usually all hands on deck on Saturday; there's no way I'd be able to face work after all that booze last night. How about you? That was some humdinger you and Kim had before you left. Do you want to talk about it?"

A smile crossed Gina's face. "You wouldn't believe me if I told you."

"Try me," Sylvia said, confused, knowing that Gina wouldn't be there at this hour on a Saturday morning after a heavy night unless she really wanted to talk about something serious.

"Can I get myself a drink of water?"

"Sure, help yourself. Can you get me one too, and some paracetomol please?" Sylvia asked, sinking onto the couch.

Gina came out of the kitchen carrying a glass of water in her left hand with her right hand behind her back.

"This is what Kim came over here to do the evening Rick was murdered. That's what we were fighting about last night," Gina said as she walked towards the couch. She placed the glass of water on the coffee table and walked around behind the couch, where Sylvia couldn't see her. "I see I'm confusing you. Let me clear it up." Sylvia turned to see Gina take a kitchen knife out from behind her back. She put her left arm around Sylvia's shoulders pinning her to the couch as she placed the knife in front of Sylvia's neck.

Tears came to Sylvia's eyes as she said, "Gina, I can only assume you're still drunk from last night. This isn't funny; in fact it's downright cruel. If you came here to talk, then talk. If you came here to play games then I'd appreciate it if you left and let me go back to sleep. I'm in no mood for silly games. I have a headache and still feel quite woozy from last night, so more sleep would be good if you're just here to be cruel. Did you get the paracetomol?"

Gina turned the knife around and glided the blunt edge back and forth over Sylvia's throat as she said, "Games, yes you like playing games, don't you Sylvia? You don't care who gets hurt as long as you have your fun. Well the fun's about to end, at least for you. It's someone else's turn now. It's time Alex had some fun, don't you think? And you soon won't need any paracetomol."

"Gina, I think you should just give me the knife and finish sleeping this off. We'll talk later." An edge of exasperation had crept into Sylvia's voice.

"You're not getting what I'm saying, Sylvia. There will be no later, not for you."

Sylvia started to get scared as she realized that the knife was digging into her neck and her friend seemed to have flipped out. It was only at that moment that she noticed the plastic gloves that Gina was wearing.

"You see, I'm here to complete the job Kim was supposed to do. She got one job to do and she messed it up, turned it into three jobs. Let me start from the beginning.

"You remember twelve years ago when Alex started at our school? And you remember that I was in love with him? Well do you?" Sylvia nodded her head. "It's hard to know whether or not you were aware of other people's feelings; you've always been so wrapped up in your own. Kim was also in love with Alex, remember?" Again Sylvia nodded. "Well, not so much in love with him as wanted him to notice her. If she got to sleep with him even once she'd have gotten him out of her system. Now, what I felt for him," Gina sighed. "That was real love, but the problem was he only ever had eyes for you.

"And what did you do? You used him. You never loved him. You kept him for yourself, but not happy with that, you had to have every other guy who took your fancy. You're some piece of work, you know that?" When Sylvia didn't reply, Gina dug the knife into her neck a little and through gritted teeth said, "I said, you know that?"

Trembling with fear, Sylvia nodded. She could feel warmth trickling down her neck from where the cold steel had nicked her skin.

In a more amenable tone Gina continued, "You're a bitch, you know?" Again Sylvia nodded. "But you're not completely hateful. You can be quite a good friend, but the way you treated Alex, now that just wasn't nice. All he's ever done is been nice to you. Every time you dumped him for some other guy, what did he do? He just let you go and waited for you to come back to him, and you always did.

"Even after Rick you couldn't keep your hands off him. Oh I bet you thought you were being discreet, but I saw you making a play for Alex that night on the couch when we all got drunk, and Rick not even dead a couple of weeks. That night I decided I had to do the job myself, but then Kim went and ruined things again by coming on to Alex that same night."

"What?!"

"Shut up you dumb bitch! When I want you to talk I'll tell you. Now where was I? Oh yes, I jumped ahead of myself a little. All that time that you were using Alex as if he were your own personal plaything, Kim and I were just waiting in the wings for him to tire of you. Only he never did so Kim and I turned to one another.

"It's been fun, but we both still want Alex, and that leaves us with a problem. Do you know what that is?"

Sylvia nodded.

"I want to hear you say it. What's the problem we're left with?"

"M...me," Sylvia managed to stammer in between sobs.

"You got it in one. The night before Kim killed Rick," she paused. Sylvia gasped. "Yes that's right; Kim killed your precious Rick. Only that's not what she was supposed to do. The night before, at that party you and Rick had, Kim couldn't tear her eyes away from Alex. Her need for him was reaching fever pitch and it was starting to come between us. We talked a lot about it. We both wanted him. We just needed him to get over you, and then we were going to seduce him with an offer of a threesome.

"I knew he'd never go for it until he was over you. The only problem was that it looked like it was never going to happen. You see, that night I saw the way Alex was looking at you. He still loved you. Now that was bad news for Kim and I; very bad news. So when we got home that night we hatched a plan. Well, it was my idea really.

"You had to be gotten rid of. It was supposed to be quite simple. Kim was to come over here the next evening. I had heard Alex and Rick talking about meeting up down at the pub for a few drinks to watch the match so you were supposed to be home alone. But when Kim came over you hadn't come home from Galway and Rick was here. He had called Alex to tell him that he didn't want to go to the pub after all; he didn't feel like drinking after the night before.

"So, rather than calling the whole thing off, Kim's little brain started working overtime and she decided that she'd kill Rick instead of you, cause you a little pain. It was such a stupid thing to do. She figured we'd kill you some other time anyway, but first it'd be good to make you suffer the way you've made us suffer. Oh I was glad to see you suffering, I don't deny that, but it just complicated things.

"You see, with Alex being implicated in the murder he rushed out and jumped into bed with the first slut he could find to try to prove that he wasn't still in love with you. I think that was partly because Kim scared him off by coming on to him that night after you made your little play for him. She just couldn't bide her time and wait until we had you out of the way. Obviously the slut had to die too. So instead of one murder it's now become three because pretty soon, after I've finished explaining to you how it's all your fault, you will die.

"Only, first you will write a suicide note admitting to killing Rick for the insurance money. You will write that it was your plan to go to Alex, marry him and live happily ever after with the blood money. But when he started going out with Carol you killed her, and now you can't live with the guilt and you'd rather die than see Alex going to prison for something he didn't do.

"Then I'll just go over to Alex's and join him and Kim in bed, and we'll all live happily ever after. Of course he'll mourn you a little, but we'll help make him forget all about you.

"So if you're ready to write that suicide note there's a pen and paper right there in front of you." Keeping the knife where it was, Gina hopped over the back of the couch so that she was sitting beside Sylvia. She leaned Sylvia forward so that she could write the note.

"There's just one thing I want to know first," Sylvia said.

"What's that?"

"How did Kim manage to kill Rick?"

"She just did the same thing I did this morning. She told him she wanted to get a glass of water, told him to stay where he was, that she'd help herself. She brought the knife out from the kitchen behind her back, just like I did. She walked around behind the armchair where Rick sat dozing, leaned over his shoulder, took out the knife, and before he knew what was happening she had stabbed him right through the heart. Poor Rick didn't even have time to react. It was rather stupid of her really; if she had even paused for a heartbeat Rick would have overpowered her, half asleep or not; she's strong, but not that strong. Then it would all have been over for her, but it worked out really well in the end. Our little secret dies with you.

"She ran straight into the kitchen where she had the presence of mind to use the dishcloth to turn on the tap for washing the blood off her hands, not that there was much, as she had left the knife in, stemming the blood flow. That was quite a neat trick, risky, but neat. I would be more inclined to pull the knife out, as it does more damage that way, but as it turned out she hit the heart in the right spot. She was always good at biology, said it was instinctive, hitting that spot. She wrapped the cloth up in a plastic bag, brought it home and burned it. At least she hadn't left that evidence behind.

"When she came home I was so mad with her. She hadn't even checked to see that he was dead. We only found that out later when Elaine rang us. Kim was so scared she hadn't realized that it was in the heart she had stabbed him until you told us that was how he died. I was furious with her for not wiping the prints off the knife. But when she told me that she had gotten it out of the dishwasher so that it would have loads of prints on it anyway even her own I thought it was brilliant.

"When Alex was being incriminated for the murder I started to formulate the plan about killing you and getting you to write a suicide note taking the rap for killing Rick, but then Carol came into the equation.

"Kim killed her too. I figured it was my idea so she should do her part by committing the murders. It seems she has quite a knack for it, but she didn't have faith in herself, thought it was just beginner's luck, that even though instinct led her to stab Rick in the heart, it was just luck that she got it right. She wore gloves when she killed Carol and a full-length raincoat, both of which have been dumped. She pulled the knife out that time, so that she could be sure before she left the apartment that Carol would bleed out even if she hadn't hit the heart just right. It was a stroke of luck that Alex's prints were on that knife too; it meant the guards wouldn't look any further. Not that we wanted Alex to go to prison, of course, because he'd be no good to us in prison, but I had that all worked out.

"Only it wasn't supposed to happen just yet. You were to stay alive just a little longer, until the court case was over and he was being put away. That way he'd have gotten to the stage of hating you for putting him through all of that before killing yourself. That way when Kim and I would swoop in he'd be grateful to us for taking the pain away, and, as I said, we'd live happily ever after. However, Kim has forced my hand. Since she couldn't wait any longer to bed Alex, it means that we can't wait any longer for you to die.

"Even though I love Kim so much we both need Alex to make our lives complete, and of course I'd like nothing better than to have Alex's children and the three of us could raise them together. Of course, Kim doesn't know that yet but I think she'll go for it, and even if she doesn't I'll still have Alex. I couldn't risk telling her how I really feel for fear of her leaving me; it took me long enough to work up to telling her that I love her. If she knew that I love Alex more she may not want to stick around, but with you out of the way at least I can have Alex so I won't end up alone." She held the pen out for Sylvia and said, "Now, stop stalling and write."

CHAPTER FORTY-NINE

When Alex woke up to find himself in the spare bedroom he was a little confused at first. Then in a flood of embarrassment it all came back to him, remembering with relief that Kim had fallen asleep before too much damage had been done. He wondered what Gina and Kim had been fighting about the night before and hoped that they'd manage to resolve it, hoped too that Kim wouldn't be foolish enough to disclose to Gina that she'd tried to bed him last night. He knew Kim liked to stir things up, but trying to make Gina jealous mightn't be the wisest course of action if she wanted to smooth things over with her rather than end it.

He got up and took a quick shower, being very careful to lock the bathroom door in case Kim got up and decided to join him. He knew that with no drink on him there was no way he'd let things get as far as they did the previous night. He wasn't so sure if the same were true of Kim, although she had only ever come on to him when she was drunk. However, she and Gina had just had a huge fight. Who knew what state her mind would be in? It was obvious from the last time she had tried it on with him that Gina had not been happy about it. What better way to get at Gina then, than to sleep with him?

While in the shower he thought about what he'd like to do that day. He had made no plans with Sylvia, figuring they'd wait until they saw how they felt before deciding anything. Apart from embarrassment over the end of the night he was suffering no ill effects except for maybe a bit of tiredness. He decided he'd ring Sylvia after breakfast; the hot shower was already doing a good job of waking him up and some coffee should complete the process.

As he was eating breakfast he remembered yearning for Sylvia the night before. He decided that he would talk to her about the possibility of a no strings attached night of passion to try to take his mind off the possibility of going to prison. The thoughts that this could be one of his last breakfasts as a free man produced a knot in his stomach, one that he was sure would remain with him until after the trial and perhaps beyond.

When Sylvia's phone rang out he figured she was still sleeping it off. He had no desire to remain in the house for Kim to surface and so hopped in the car, figuring he'd just drive aimlessly until he ended up somewhere and would give Sylvia a bell later and ask her to meet him. As driving was one of the only things that calmed him these days it was all he wanted to do apart from seeing Sylvia.

As if the car had a mind of its own, he ended up outside Sylvia's house. He rang her again, and when the phone rang out he got out of the car. He knew she'd be annoyed if he woke her so he went around to the back of the house and found the key she kept under the flowerpot with the dead plant in it. He'd often told her that any burglar would know to look under a flowerpot, especially one that looked like it had no other purpose than to hide a key, to which she'd replied that most burglars would think it was too obvious and would look everywhere but there. He'd often vowed to buy her a new plant, one that even she couldn't kill, and reaffirmed that vow as he let himself in quietly. He would just veg out in front of the T.V. until Sylvia woke up. She could hardly be mad with him for that; after all, he couldn't even begin to count the amount of times he had woken up to find her in his sitting room after she had just broken up with someone.

That's funny, he thought. It sounds like there's someone here, but she's not answering her phone. Strange. Sylvia never leaves her phone far from her. He moved silently through the kitchen and into the hall.

He heard Gina's voice. "Now, just let me read it before you sign it. We want to make sure you've got it right." Alex decided that it was a mistake to be here. Not wanting to interrupt, he turned around, careful to be just as silent as he had arrived. He stopped short when he heard Gina's voice again. "No, you got this bit wrong. How thick are you? I've just dictated the whole thing to you. Did you really think you'd get away with that? No, you didn't, did you? You're just playing for time, aren't you? Well it's going to do you no good you know, you're still going to die."

By the time Gina had finished that statement Alex had crept up behind her. He couldn't believe his eyes or ears, but didn't let his disbelief stop him in his tracks even for a second. He put his right hand over to where Gina was holding the knife to Sylvia's throat, pressing the inside of Gina's wrist to make her drop the knife and then brought her hand around behind her back. At the same time his left arm went around Gina's neck. Gina struggled against him in a futile effort.

Sylvia reached for her phone and rang the guards, asking to speak to Detective Molloy. With her voice trembling, she explained what had just happened. She had to pause several times to swallow the nervous lump in her throat when she thought about the fact that if Alex hadn't arrived when he did he could have discovered her later with her kitchen knife protruding from her lifeless body. When Sylvia concluded by saying that Alex had Gina pinned to the ground Detective Molloy said she'd be right over.

Not long after that Alex and Sylvia stood on the front doorstep watching as Gina was being guided, handcuffed, into the back seat of a Garda car. There was another car being sent to Alex's parents' house to pick Kim up. Alex was to meet the guards there to let them in. He didn't want to leave Sylvia alone, but she really didn't want to see Kim just then. All she wanted was a hot shower. Her neck stung from where the knife had pierced her skin, which was sticky from the trail of blood leading down to where it congealed at the neck of her pajamas. Not only did she need to clean that up, but she needed to scrub the memory of Gina holding the knife to her like that from her mind as well as the thoughts of Kim being the one who had pierced Rick's heart with a similar knife. Alex kissed the top of her head and told her he'd be right back.

When Alex arrived back at his parents' house Kim was sitting at the kitchen table. He was relieved to see that she had put her clothes back on. As he drove from Sylvia's house, visions of Kim's naked body leaping at him the minute he opened the door had bombarded him. Now she looked as if she belonged there, as if she sat there every morning to start her day by reading the paper with a cup of coffee in her hand, inhaling the scent of it as she read the headlines.

She lowered the paper, put a mischievous look on her face and said, "Now where did you disappear to?" The smile left her face as she saw both a male and female guard enter the kitchen behind Alex. "What's going on?" she asked.

The female guard cuffed her, read her rights, and told her what she was being charged with.

"There must be some mistake," Kim said.

"No mistake," Alex said. "Gina's just been arrested over at Sylvia's. She was just about to kill her, set it up as suicide and frame her for the other murders."

As soon as Kim was in the back of the Garda car Alex got in his car and went back to Sylvia's where he found her freshly showered and looking better after her ordeal. He wrapped his arms around her and kissed the top of her head, inhaling the scent of her shampoo, the one he had always loved. He thought of all the mornings he had woken up to that smell lingering on his pillow, or wafting out from his bathroom where she showered. He thought of all the times he had joined her in the shower, how close he had come this morning to never being able to do that again.

"I'm so glad I got here when I did this morning. If I had been any later I could have found you dead."

"But you didn't. So let's not think about that." Sylvia stepped out of his embrace and said, "I have to ring Elaine to tell her about this."

Alex reached for her again. He pulled her to him and said, "Not just yet. I nearly lost you for good. I just need to hold you right now."

Alex kissed the top of her head again and then placed his finger under her chin to tilt her face up to him. He groaned as he started to kiss her. She didn't resist and the kiss deepened. They pulled frantically at each other's clothes.

The trauma of the morning intensified their desire for each other, making this the most passionate lovemaking either of them had ever experienced. They made love on the sitting room floor. After they had both climaxed, Alex held Sylvia tightly in his arms, unwilling to let her go. After some time his hands started to roam her body, as if to memorize the feel of every inch of her. They made love again, slower but with no less passion. Afterwards they lay wrapped in each other's arms, relaxed and content.

"I love you."

The words surprised them both. It was the first time Sylvia had ever used those words with anyone but Rick. Alex relinquished his hold on her with reluctance as she sat up. Although they were the words he had longed most to hear and hers were the lips he had longed to hear them from, he feared that now they were out there she would want to run and hide, or take them back. He wanted to hold on to her a bit longer, let the rest of the world, their fears and insecurities wait just a while longer before intruding on their perfect moment together.

"I really do, Alex; I never realized it until this moment." Tears came into her eyes as she said, "When I thought Gina was going to kill me all I could think about was you, but even then I didn't realize why it was that you were all I thought of. Now I know that it was because I love you."

Alex gathered her to him. "It's a pity it took such an ordeal for you to realize it, but I'm glad you finally did. I love you too, I always have, but you know that already."

Later, Elaine opened the door to see Sylvia and Alex holding hands and looking nervous. She invited them in and when they were all standing in the sitting room Sylvia started to speak quickly, seeming to be in a hurry to say something unpleasant.

Elaine couldn't speak at first when Sylvia told her that she had just survived being held at knife point by Gina. Dave said they should be ashamed of themselves for playing such a sick joke in order to try to ease the tension caused by the upcoming trial.

When Sylvia showed them the cut on her neck left by the knife, Dave said, "You're serious aren't you? This actually happened." He sat down with a thud on the couch and the breath whooshed out of him in disbelief.

Tears came into Elaine's eyes and she hugged her children, as she thought of all the times Gina and Kim had babysat for them, the times they had taken Sarah and Jody off shopping or to the cinema. She couldn't believe that the two girls she had befriended in school, both of whom had stood beside her on the altar as she got married and were godmothers to her two youngest children, had committed murder.

When the enormity of it all had sunk in and Elaine and Dave had congratulated Alex on his freedom, Sylvia told them about the fact that she and Alex were now a couple. That news lightened the mood in the house and they decided that they should go out to dinner to celebrate the fact that Alex no longer had a murder trial hanging over his head and that Sylvia had finally realized she loved him.

Later that evening it was a very somber group that met up for a celebratory dinner in their local Chinese restaurant. The night was tinged with sadness as they mourned the loss of their friends, Gina and Kim. It was a place they had often met up in for dinner, a place that held many happy memories for the group. They missed the presence of Gina and Kim even though they now knew that the two girls were not who they had previously thought. There were moments during the night when one or other of them retreated inside their own heads, thinking of something Gina or Kim had said or done and wondering how much of the previous years had been a lie.

ABOUT THE AUTHOR

Yvonne McEvaddy lives and works in Headford, Co. Galway, Ireland. She was first published under her maiden name, Yvonne Gaughan, at the age of 17 when she won a Western Health Board competition to have her essay published in 100 Natural Highs.

Also as Yvonne Gaughan, in college she was a member of the Mystic Poets Society and had two poems published in their collaboration, Mystic Spirits. Yvonne McEvaddy has attended creative writing classes facilitated by Susan Millar DuMars and is a member of the Javawriters group.

Passion Killer is her first novel. Her second novel, Shadows of the Dead, will be published later this year. She is currently writing her third novel, Thief of Hearts.

Website: https://sites.google.com/site/yvonnemcevaddy/home
Blog: http://yvonnemcevaddy.wordpress.com/
Twitter: @yvonnemecevaddy